ADDED
Attraction

Pamela G. Hobbs

POOLBEG

Published 2020
by Poolbeg Press Ltd.
123 Grange Hill, Baldoyle,
Dublin 13, Ireland
Email: poolbeg@poolbeg.com

A catalogue record for this book is available from the British Library.

ISBN 978178199-399-6

www.poolbeg.com

About the Author

A native of Dalkey, Co Dublin, Pamela's childhood dream was to write and illustrate her own books, and to that end she attended the National College of Art and Design, studying Visual Communications. Although she still uses her visual side, nowadays she definitely spends more time at the laptop than the easel.

As winner in the Novel Fair 2015, Pamela gained experience from being around other writers and was subsequently selected for 'Date with an Agent' (The International Literary Festival, Dublin) in 2016, 2017 and 2018. These events gave Pamela invaluable contacts and also the impetus to write her first short story, 'Time Heals', which was shortlisted for the Colm Tóibín International Short Story Award, May (2017), a part of the Wexford Literary Festival. She is a member of the online writing group, Indulgeinwriting.ie

A day job as an Adult Education teacher in Kilkenny is challenging and fulfilling but Pamela's evenings are spent in another world altogether – that of romance and intrigue – reading and writing. "Life can be tough," she says. "Find your happy ending wherever you can."

Pamela, her husband, and two sons lived in the United States, on both coasts, for 12 years and she includes many Americans in her writing, highlighting the numerous family connections the Irish have with the US.

Acknowledgements

Considering this book was written partially during a pandemic lockdown, extra thanks go to Johnny for being my major support – not just coffee and food, but dragging me on hill climbs (within 2k limit!) and keeping me sane amidst deadlines and working from home with the day job.

Also, to the boys, their partners and the grandchild – you each bring so much joy. Having loved ones, who cheer from the sidelines, makes me grateful beyond measure.

And thanks once again to Jane for the title – you rock, sis!

Dedication

For all who have been hiding their real selves,

there is no right time to venture forth,

there is only now.

Be you.

Chapter 1

She was lying. There was no use pretending, no use putting a face on it. Not only was Molly Fitzgerald lying, by omission, she was *living* that lie. Every day. To everyone. It had to stop. It was too darn exhausting.

The realisation that it was time came when she met her sisters Ali, Caro, and Frankie who was actually a sister-in-law, for lunch in a swanky new restaurant in Sandymount. They'd been innocently chatting about something Caro had unearthed in the attic of her home in Rome when Ali had interrupted with the non-sequitur, "Hey, do you believe we all have a doppelganger?" She had asked the group in general but her gaze landed on Molly.

Caro had stopped mid-sentence. "Not sure," she said, sipping her rosé.

"I think it's a thing, but I've not witnessed it," Frankie said. "Why? Have you seen yourself somewhere?"

It was funny coming from Frankie – she was the one with a famous face and saw, or used to see, images of her own face everywhere. That was, before she had quit her acting career and concentrated on travel writing. She continued to do photographic work for various cosmetic companies because, *duh*, she was beautiful, but her image,

1

while on the odd billboard, wasn't on the front of every magazine any longer.

"No," Ali said, her forehead wrinkling. "It was the oddest thing. I could swear I saw our Molly down at the IFSC yesterday, striding across the forecourt in a navy suit, heels and carrying a briefcase!" She stared at the object of her statement, and bit on a carrot stick. "It was most bizarre."

Molly shifted uneasily on her chair. See? Lying got one nowhere. Ever. She needed to change the subject and direct the traffic, so to speak. "*Ha*," she said, "the lookalike thing must be real, so. Tell us more about the painting, Caro."

"No, seriously," Ali bloody insisted. "It was you. Except, obviously not you. I mean, it was the financial district and a good half-hour walk from the gallery, and the hair was different. This woman's hair was in a bun-type thing but, Christ, she was the cut of you. Same profile, same colouring. Uncanny."

Ali shook her head in bemusement and Molly could feel her skin heat. *Damn.* Now was not the time. But, yes, the lying had to stop. The truth did need to come out.

But not just yet. She wasn't ready. When she'd be ready – well, wasn't that the question of the ages?

Molly scooped up some potato salad and turned, with pronounced interest, to Caro. "Go on, tell me about the painting."

Caro happily continued to describe a 100-year-old landscape she'd unearthed from her new Italian family's attic and the conversation moved on.

Molly could feel Ali's gaze return to her on and off over the next hour and she studiously avoided connecting with said gaze. She wasn't a good liar, or a natural one, she was simply really practised at it. How things had got so out of control baffled even her and she was the one who'd started down this murky path, which meant she was the one who needed to fess up and 'go straight', as it were. That reality made her stomach hurt.

The women gathered their bags and left the restaurant a little later and dispersed to their various locations. Caro was visiting for a few days and was staying with their parents in the Fitzgerald family home in Dalkey. Her fourteen-year-old son Toby, also home visiting, was out with pals for the afternoon and they'd meet up later. Frankie was heading into Dublin to the loft space she shared with Dev, *their* brother, and now *her* husband. And Ali was cycling back to Rathgar to the apartment she shared with her boyfriend Gabe Mackenzie.

Molly was smiling as she took the DART train back to Dún Laoghaire, back to the flat where she now lived. It was originally Caro's and then, when she moved, supposedly temporarily, to Rome, Ali had moved in from her previous space in Temple Bar. Now? Now it was Molly's turn at living there.

And she *loved* it. Finally, a place to call her own. A place to be herself. To decorate as she wished. The pure bliss of it. It was overwhelming. No more carrying bags of clothes to change into, no more wardrobe changes in hotel bathrooms en route to work. God, the freedom this move had given her was incalculable. It had come not a moment too soon.

She'd moved in a month ago and, as the middle of February brought its usual public barrage of roses and chocolates, she could wallow in her aloneness in perfect peace. No pitying glances thrown her way by her albeit loving parents Jo and Patrick when no cards appeared, no bouquets were delivered.

No more sneaking around and hiding dry cleaning in a wardrobe in a separate bedroom to hers. Her mum wasn't a snoop. It was nothing like that. Jo was trying to be helpful and do laundry for whomever was living at the house. Molly discovered that clothes in soft plastic hanging in Frankie's old room stirred no comment as Frankie was the style queen and always had tons of clothes in various bags and coverings. Even though her main residence was in the city with Dev, she kept her 'star' clothes in the huge wardrobe in the bedroom that was still designated as hers. Molly was never so grateful for that star status as when she began her double life. But every day had been a strain. Every day an opportunity for disaster to befall her.

She turned the key, *her* key, in the door and let herself into the flat that was *hers*. Her home. Her place. Her sanctuary. Toby's old bedroom was now her office/studio and she had, at the ready, a selection of art materials to whip out as needed when a family member came calling. She'd laid down some clear rules when everyone had been in the flat delivering her things on moving day. Rule One was no one, and that meant absolutely *no one*, was to just call in. She needed notice. A phone call. A warning. A text heads-up. Her siblings were disgusted. And told her so – loudly.

"Them's the rules. You could be disturbing the Muse," she'd lied without blinking. "I'd have to stop my work and cope with you and make tea. I hate all that when I'm engrossed." That part was true. She hated interruptions and distractions when she was working. But it was still a lie.

She forgot to get groceries on her way from the train station and perused her fridge contents with a certain amount of gloom. Yogurt and cheese. *Hmm.* Some slices of ham, which on closer inspection merited the bin. Oh well. She wished she had some of Ali's kitchen-wizard skills or even a basic knowledge of cooking. *Mustn't be too hard on myself,* she muttered. *Each to her own.* She found a tin of tomato soup, heated it and toasted some sourdough bread, added cheese and was happy as anyone had a right to be with the meagre offerings. Some chopped apple and banana, added to the plain yogurt was as desserty as she'd ever get – under her own steam. The 'teach yourself the basics' cookbook on the shelf above the microwave looked as pristine as it did when her mum had handed it to her as a housewarming gift. Yeah, that was a stretch. But she had to deal with these new times – she needed to feed herself as well as enjoy the freedom of being solo.

She reached up and unenthusiastically opened the book and began leafing through it for one-pot meals and simple fare. She wrote a list. Lists were good – they accomplished a lot – just by dint of being evidence of thought and action. There, that felt better – productive even. Now all she had to do was remember the groceries tomorrow.

Molly loved her office. It was bright, clean and clinical. Her very best kind of working environment. The coffee she sipped at seven fifteen the following morning was a bright spot in her early-arrival ritual. She loved the quiet before the other workers turned up at nine. This was time for her headspace to gather itself for the day ahead. The peace and quiet of this time, the decent coffee she drank from her brew made in the communal kitchen and the two slices of toast and cheese she ate, set her up like nothing else.

She wasn't alone in the large office space. The cleaners went through every day, the sound of the vacuums an ambient noise in her background – not enough to bother her in any way. Patty was the most talkative one and usually stopped by Molly's desk for a brief exchange. Molly knew about Patty's grandchildren, her home improvements, her hernia, her astrology charts and her long-suffering husband, Herb. Patty was the real deal – Dublin born and bred and wise as any damn owl. Molly looked forward to the chats, kept a lid on the length of time when deadlines loomed, but felt the personal interaction, most often peppered with a few belly laughs at Patty's own self-deprecating stories, was a perfect way to start a day dealing with money. Lots of money. *Other* people's money.

Molly fired up her two computers and got scrolling through the various overnight notifications. She jotted down notes both physically and virtually and began a low hum as she settled in with her workload. God, this made her so happy. Scrolls of data, columns of numbers, equations, tallies. Sums. Pure mathematical bliss. She took a long draught of coffee and got stuck in.

There were several new accounts she was working on – two just boring day-to-day stuff but two others, directly from her immediate boss, were proving a tangled delight, one in the arts field, the other academia. As a junior accountant she shouldn't really have access to these types of accounts. But Molly had already made a name for herself at the firm. In fact, she came to the firm with a stupid number of awards for her accounting acumen and she was only relatively recently graduated. Three of the projects she'd done in college had received public recognition for their insightful understanding of gripping financial dilemmas and two of those projects had come first in national competitions.

While Molly was thrilled that people in the know understood how her brain worked, as opposed to, say, her family, she'd wanted everything kept on the down-low and hadn't even attended the ceremonies to receive the awards in case photographs were taken. She hated the limelight and took every opportunity to avoid it if possible. Her name on these awards was her birth name, Mary Margaret, and that's how she liked it. At work she had told them to call her Molly – her pet-name. When it became evident at a very early age that she was developing a head of curls, Ali had said she looked like her doll, Molly, and that was that.

She settled herself more comfortably in her chair as she did the normal scanning for errors or glitches – any little blip or unusual figure. She was in heaven. Her eyes flew across the rows of data, seeing them like a painting – a beautiful blend of shapes and tones, all fitting together perfectly. Or not. *Hmm …*

She peered closer at a tiny, tiny mistake. *Ah ha!* It was like an ice-cream sundae on a hot day. No, even better, a hot chocolate on a cold frosty day. Pure delight.

It took some time, but she calculated and checked and checked and calculated and realised that, yes, the bottom line was off because of this one weensy mistake – but she believed that that's all it was. Human error with not a huge or dangerous implication. She saved, printed and filed the error reports and then promptly redid them properly. Okay, not promptly. It was going to take hours. But what a lovely way to spend a Thursday.

Hunger drove Molly to the canteen about noon and she checked her options. Benson, Benson & Malone were a large hugely successful cutting-edge accounting firm. They had big-name clients and a waiting list to use their services as long as your arm. The prestige of working for BB&M wasn't lost on any of the accountants, junior or more senior. The rewards were massive. They were hugely wealthy as a company and, fortunately for their employees, very generous to staff.

Molly's own boss, Declan Twomey, a mere 28 years old, drove a frigging top-of-the-range Audi, with, he boasted, all the trimmings. Not a car person herself, Molly didn't know what trimmings that might entail and could care even less. But she was glad he was happy with his lot. A happy boss most often meant happy productive workers. And Molly was both happy and immensely productive.

The man on her mind strode into the large open space

7

and eyed the array of fresh sandwiches, wraps and soups that were delivered to the canteen daily. Yes, BB&M fed their staff. For free! Talk about a perk! The more cynical might suggest the food was laid on so no one would have to leave their office spaces and, ergo, would return to their desks sooner and continue working. Even through lunch. More goodies were delivered about three thirty for that afternoon slump, so really there was no need to venture outside at all.

"Anything good today?" Declan Twomey asked non chalantly as he pulled open the equally well-stocked fridge.

"A really tasty mulligatawny soup, by the smell of it anyway," Molly replied as she filled a bowl for herself.

"*Mulligawhat?*" Declan was clearly not au fait with the stew-like soup. And not too eager to taste it by the way he was eyeing her bowl.

"It's a traditional Indian dish and really healthy. Can you smell the ginger? And the other spices? It's got lentils, carrots, apples, onions," she rattled off. Just because she was a fairly useless cook didn't mean she was lacking in food knowledge. And she loved her facts.

But Declan held up a hand to halt her culinary progress. "Stop!" he groaned. "It sounds revolting. You lost me at lentils. Too tree-huggy for me. I'll go for a wrap. At least I might recognise what's inside."

But no. Even the falafel wraps were a step too far for his palate, so he picked a bog- standard BLT and seemed happy enough. He cracked open a can of Coke and pulled out a chair.

"Sit," he said unceremoniously to Molly, and began eating.

Since Molly had been about to sit anyway, she did. She pulled apart some soft Italian bread, spread it generously with butter and tucked in.

"God, this is delicious, you should really try some." She

glanced at her boss who was chewing earnestly as he studied his phone. *Huh.* Molly was annoyed. Why make the gesture of asking someone to sit with you over a meal, no matter how paltry, and then be rude enough to ignore them. Oh well! Manners maketh the man but in this case, no. He was a damn fine specimen of a man though, ask anyone. Most of the junior staff drooled over him on a regular basis. And she didn't blame them. Not one bit. Talk about eye candy – tall, athletic, broad-shouldered, beach-blond hair just that sexy side of tousled, sea-blue eyes and a wide engaging grin. Perfect teeth, of course, and the obligatory once-broken nose from, you guessed it, a rugby match. He was South County Dublin's ideal man. And he knew it.

He was also every junior office-admin staff's dreamboat. And he knew that too. One could even say he used his swagger to its full advantage and Molly had already heard of various escapades from the Christmas party. Not quite the ubiquitous bum-on-a-photocopier scenario but pretty raunchy nonetheless. She wondered how the head men, BB&M themselves, took to his reputation being bandied about but since Brendan, the younger of the Benson brothers, was considered a player in his day, maybe they just didn't care.

Molly chewed on that – literally and figuratively as she ate her lunch. If she ran a highly reputable accounting firm how would she want her employees to act? Only one way to find out.

"Declan," she interrupted his phone-gazing, "do your bosses not mind your reputation as a playboy in the office? Does it not, for example, besmirch *their* reputation?"

Molly had never been shy about speaking her mind. She called a spade a spade and expected people to be straight with her. She wasn't rude … not exactly. But she was often on the receiving end of open-mouthed stares as others watched her ask the unaskable.

Declan choked on his sandwich. "Christ, Molly, what a thing to ask!" He took a moment or two to recover and then said, "And what do you mean by my rep as a playboy?"

She didn't buy that innocent act at all. He was grinning now, delighted that his reputation had in fact gone before him.

"You know very well," she stated, ignoring the 'Who me?' look he was sending her. "You seem to be always getting up to mischief with the admin staff. At least, that's what I've heard. Do you ever try it on with the accountants or do you stick to a type?"

He appeared dumbfounded anew by her remarks and Molly shook her head. She was only asking, for goodness' sake. She wanted to know. Was that a crime? And then her not-very-well-thought-out question backfired.

Her boss sat back in his chair, legs splayed out all manly and muscled. He folded his arms across his chest, most likely knowing it made his shoulders look huge and important.

"Why do you want to know, Ms Fitzgerald?" he asked, a cheeky boyish grin on his face. "Would you like to be considered for the line-up?"

Molly groaned. Sometimes her stupid big mouth got her into all sorts of trouble. She rolled her eyes. "Beside the fact that I'm not remotely interested in you, in that way, it would be against company policy surely? For co-workers to have relationships?"

"That's why I pick the admin staff, hon," he said as if explaining to a child. "It's only against policy if it's boss to employee. If they don't answer directly to me, managerial-wise, it's not an issue." He leaned forward and continued. "So, if you want a piece of this," he waved his hand from the top of his head to his toes, "you are going to have to change departments. Or, we could always keep our little liaison a secret." This time his grin had lost its charm and looked downright leery.

"No, thanks – that would be a negative to any of the above. I'm happy in this department, I'm not interested in secrecy and, as I said, I've no interest in you. Romantically."

He narrowed his eyes. Wow, she thought, he really looks like a male model when he does that. What a clever trick! She vowed to practise it later, in front of the mirror. Would it make her look all mysterious?

"Who said anything about romance? I certainly didn't. I'm talking about a quickie in the closet. Or in the boardroom when everyone has gone home. Yeah, I can see you now, stretched out across the table."

Molly gave him an incredulous stare. "Seriously? Declan. Stop. You had better not say any more. I apologise for starting this conversation. I certainly didn't think it would lead to this. But now it's just … off topic. And inappropriate." She took a breath, wondering, not for the first time, how she got herself into these situations. Even though she wasn't scared of him, was well able to look after herself and didn't believe he would in fact do anything, was this sexual-harassment territory? True, she had begun it, but was it her own naivety that led her to this? If so, she really needed to watch what she said in mixed company – she wouldn't have a leg to stand on as it would be a total pot-and-kettle situation. Lesson learned. Hopefully. However, if she were a timid eighteen-year-old she might have felt threatened. But he probably knew better and only chose women who wanted his attentions. Thank God she wasn't one of them.

Molly rose from her seat, collected her dishes and scooted behind her boss who had a lazy indolent look on his face now. She stacked the dishwasher, purposefully ignoring his plate and utensils, and rounded on him.

"Take that expression off your face," she scolded him, big-sister style. "I'm not for the likes of you. Nor you for me." She wiped down the countertop with the cloth. "Now," she said as she filled her water bottle, "back to work. And that goes for you too. No loitering!"

She left as three junior staff walked in, blushing when they saw the infamous Mr Twomey. She didn't wait to see what he did – she had work to continue and he wasn't her problem.

Until he was.

Chapter 2

"Take a seat, Elliot," Bryan Benson, the elder of the two Bensons, they of the company name, said as he waved Kit into his office.

It was a large corner office, flooded with light even on the grey-chill late-February afternoon. All the surfaces in the room shone, be they mahogany – the desk, or chrome – the chair-arms. Even the floor was highly polished and the sound of Kit's shoes, as he strode to the chair, reverberated in the otherwise silent room. It was no different to the many accounting firms he had visited for this very reason, both here in Dublin for the last six months and previously in his hometown of Boston.

It was an uneasy silence, but not an unusual one where Kit Elliot was concerned. He sat and relaxed back into the seat as Mr Benson studied him. Kit was used to this too. The dawning realisation that the hopeful saviour of their failing or troubled business was, at first glance, a youngster. He wasn't, of course, but he was able to come across as young, unthreatening and 'blendable'. That's what they usually wanted for the job and that's what he gave them. Kit was thirty, had a scorchingly high IQ and, when he wasn't in a role, looked his age.

At interview, he felt it was incumbent to be the person they wanted. The mole. The sneaky bastard who would find out who was causing the many blips on their precious radar. The invisible blender. Kit knew this and played to it.

If he arrived as his normal, not-in-working-hours self, they would dismiss him as too obvious a plant. Instead, he wore his nerdy clothes, his super-nerdy glasses and let his hair flop down on his forehead in an untidy yet boyish fashion. In that guise people would just not see him. Or if they did, they would cheerfully ignore him. The point of the whole exercise.

"You, *eh*, you don't look like a financial genius, if you don't mind me saying," Bryan Benson said hesitantly. "I mean … are you? Really that clever? You come highly recommended, but …" He gestured to a pile of what Kit assumed were references as he glanced back and forth between the evidence and the supposed face of said genius.

Kit spoke for the first time. "What do you see when you look at me, Mr Benson? Be honest."

Benson hesitated, perhaps realising he had been quite rude earlier. "A young chap, nervy, a bit lost-looking. Studious, maybe – and, no offense, dorky."

Kit smiled. "None taken. Would you trust me to get on with a task handed to me or to be the office Lothario?"

Benson chuckled. "Again, no offence, but definitely the former."

"Exactly." Kit leaned forward, sharp and intense, dropping his nerd persona as easily as he had donned it. "Your staff need to ignore me and continue to do their jobs as they always have. I need to fade into the background and move within departments with ease and without comment. I'll need access to all the computers, an override password, and a title, you can manufacture one, that gives me seniority over everyone who is in your employ, should the need arise. I will also need access to the accounts of yourself, Mr Brendan Benson and Mr Edward Malone. If I can't have complete authority to search all accounts, those here in Ireland, in other locations in Europe and offshore, I won't be of any help to you. Do I make myself clear?"

Bryan Benson blinked and cleared his throat. "Well, okay then. I take it back. You are a true chameleon. My first impression was what you wanted me to see, what everyone will see. It's … off-putting. But clever. If you hadn't spoken with such authority just now, I would be seriously worried. You even looked different as you explained yourself. Have you had acting training? Anyway, you seem clear-headed enough, I suppose. But you can't let my partners know I've hired you. And I say this with a heavy heart – especially not my brother. I'm not saying he is behind the rumblings I'm hearing, but he's not been himself lately. Could be completely unrelated but …" He trailed off, obviously uneasy with this request.

"I understand," Kit said, rising to his feet. "Let me settle in for a week or two, find my way around both the physical space and the office relationships and dynamics. I'll send you written reports weekly or more frequently to that private email I've set up for you. Anything else?"

"We have two fairly recent new hires you may want to check out. I wrote their names down for you but I'm sure HR will give you a list anyway. Things have escalated since their start dates but I'm not accusing them of anything. Just a coincidence perhaps." Benson got to his feet and handed over a slip of paper which Kit pocketed without looking at it.

The two men shook hands and Kit walked to the door.

"One more thing," he said, turning back. "I work in conjunction with the CEA and the Garda Fraud Squad. I also consult with the FBI. Should the need arise, I will use their resources. I will not hide any illegal activity. But neither will I go directly to them without consulting you first unless it is imperative for the safety of your employees. Is that clear?"

Benson looked worried. "The Corporate Enforcement Agency? Do you have to? No, don't bother answering that. I knew when I asked for help I would have to go the whole way. Regardless of what it ultimately does to the firm." He sighed and sat back heavily in his chair. "The safety of my employees, the loyal ones anyway, is of utmost importance to me, so do as you must."

Kit closed the door quietly behind him and strolled down the corridor to the open reception area. BB&M took up two whole floors of this high-rise building in the financial district in Dublin. It was modern, trendy for want of a better word, and full of bright, eager, bustling accountants and wannabe accountants. Not to mention all the admin staff and interns. It was a veritable hive of activity and Kit felt his interest tingle. It wasn't his first time working in Dublin and he hoped not his last.

His was the kind of skill that got 'lent out' to those in need, by those in the know. He was a consultant, to all intents and purposes, but rather definitely attached to white-collar crime. He'd worked with the FBI most recently in his hometown of Boston but was quietly happy to be back in the city that gave him his college education – or at least a few years of it. Thanks to an Irish-born mother, he had an Irish passport, using it to visit frequently with his gran, before she'd passed away the previous year.

He made his way to the open-plan kitchen area but paused before entering. There was no going back once he set foot in this public space. He would wear his persona from now on, while in the workspace. He let his shoulders slip a little and adjusted his gait as he wandered aimlessly into the kitchen and headed towards the coffee machine.

There were three people sitting at the table chatting and digging into a tray of baked goods. As Kit poured himself a cup of black coffee several more employees entered and began chatting with those already there. He turned and faced the groupings, not making eye contact with anyone, and shuffled forwards to sit near the end of the table.

"Hi, are you new? Welcome." The cheery voice came from a woman who sat down next to him. She took a sip from her own mug and grimaced. "Bloody green tea. Don't know why I bother." She turned and looked directly into his face. "What's your poison?"

Kit blinked several times behind his dark-rimmed glasses and not all of it was for effect. She was lovely. Skin a dewy blush with peach cheeks and a mouth for sin. Her lips were soft and full, a deep berry colour with a slight dip in the centre of the bottom lip. He was mesmerised. He forced his eyes to meet hers and felt a jolt in his chest. God, her mouth may have been made for sin but her eyes were made for drowning. Dark lashes, thick and full, framed the most unusual colour of – could it be turquoise? Aquamarine? He wasn't a colour specialist but they reminded him of a summer Grecian sea. She had shaped brows that framed her features and the whole package sent a shiver through him. Then he noticed her body. And drew a suddenly shaky breath. *Get a grip*, he told himself, *she's waiting for an answer*.

He cleared his throat and aimed for puzzlement. "Poison? Is there something wrong with my beverage?" Yeah, here comes the dorkish behaviour. Sometimes his job sucked.

She let out a delighted laugh. "No, silly," she teased, not unkindly. "It's just an expression. I meant what is your drink of choice, though mine could certainly be termed poison. I don't know why I keep trying to inhale antioxidants like this but I fall for all the latest fads." She pushed her own cup aside and reached for his.

That, he was not expecting. He raised startled eyes to her face.

She picked up his mug and sniffed. "Ah," she said. "Columbian dark, if I'm not mistaken."

Kit was impressed. "How did you do that?" he asked.

She smiled. "Easy – it's one of the three blends on offer here and I've learned which ones are which by scent as I'm usually too tired to go hunting in the cupboard to find which package was used and reading the blend name. I definitely have a preference for some over others so sometimes the damn antioxidants win. Do you like it?" She eased the cup back to him.

"It's fine," he said. "Actually, that's a lie." He smiled at her, sensing an ally. "I haven't tasted it yet so I really don't know."

She beamed back at him, waiting as he raised the cup to his mouth and sipped.

Nodding, he tilted his head to one side. "It's not awful."

"Damned with faint praise. I like your honesty. The regular espresso roast is better and the Guatemalan is good if you need a serious boost."

"Good to know, thanks for the tip. I'm Kit by the way." He offered his hand.

"Molly," she answered, shaking with a firm grip. She pulled back instantly. "*Ha*, you must have been standing on cheap carpet – you gave me a slight electric shock." She shook her hand, staring at it in puzzlement.

She raised her eyes to his, apparently baffled, and despite his intention to always stay below the radar, it was hard to look away. Too hard.

There was no carpet involved, cheap or otherwise. He'd felt the crackle too. Impossible, but real – they'd hit sparks off each other.

"What department are you joining, Kit?" Molly asked after a moment or two.

"I'm, *eh*, a bit of a 'jack of all trades'," he said. "My job is to be available to all areas as you face down the forthcoming audit."

Molly groaned. "Oh, poor you! That'll be tough. It's hard enough getting ready for the audit in one place with one boss and a specific number of accounts. It'll be so hard to get up to speed on a variety of them. Let me know if you need help finding your way."

She got up from her seat. "Hi, Jen!" she called to a newcomer. She turned to look down at Kit. "Best of luck, Kit, hope you settle in well."

And she sauntered off, her body swaying with a grace and ease of movement that had blood pooling in Kit's nether regions.

Oh, come on, you've seen curvy bodies before, in well-fitted jackets and hip-skimming skirts, with shapely calves and sexy heels. Get. Over. Yourself.

He watched her go till she was out of sight, turning a corner down the hallway. Well, now, she was a chatty one but not, he felt, indiscreet. And she was the only one who had spoken to him, made an effort to make him feel welcome.

Jen, the newcomer, was tall, a willowy blonde and a stunner. She gave him a cursory once-over glance and finding him obviously wanting, sat next to an expensively suited man about ten years her senior, at the opposite end of the table. She flipped her long hair behind her shoulders and began what Kit thought was a cringe-worthy flirtation. The suit didn't seem to mind, and the two bantered back and forth as Kit sipped on his now cooling coffee. Columbian, huh? Identifying coffee by scent was not a skill he had ever acquired or needed but he was surprisingly charmed that Molly had. He was, also surprisingly, charmed by the entire encounter with her.

Rising from his seat he reached into his pocket and pulled out the folded paper he'd got from Benson. And wouldn't you know it? Two names appeared in a dark scrawl of black ink.

Seán Donnelly and Molly Fitzgerald.

Yeah, sometimes his job just sucked.

Rows of data stared back at her. No, of course they didn't. Data doesn't stare. But for all the work that was happening in Molly's office, it might as well have been a stalemate of some sort. For the first time in a long time, she couldn't settle into her work. It wasn't that she was faced with anything new. They were very similar accounts to those she'd tackled for several days now. She'd heard on the grapevine that there was a new hire called Elliot who was supposedly a whizz kid and a real stickler for i-dotting and t-crossing. She was all on board with that, nothing made her happier than a 'clean' sheet. All totals perfect, all matching all in line. Her kind of bliss. She hadn't met Elliot yet but a couple of the younger interns said he was gruff, nerdy and rude. Molly was pretty good at making her own judgements of people. Ever since she could remember she could get a 'hit' from someone, whether they could be trusted or not. Whether they were kind or not. She could sense a dodgy atmosphere a mile away and it had given her the confidence to speak her mind.

Not at first, mind you. When she was quite small it freaked her out, this ability to just know things about people. To sense their feelings, both good and bad. Granny Flynn, her mother's mother, had sat her down and told her she was so lucky to have inherited the gift and she must treasure it always. Granny had made it feel like Molly had something special, and not in a freaky way. That lasted till secondary school when some classic mean girls had tried to bully her and cut her off from other potential friends. It had hurt. It hurts when you are thirteen or fourteen and being made to feel like an oddity. It hadn't lasted long. Molly had discovered she had a deep well of inner confidence and her talent at art gave her a place to fit in at her school. Creative types stuck together and if by the age of sixteen she'd also realised she had a talent for numbers, she kept that on the down-low. Super-odd *and* geeky? Nah, that was too much for any teen and Molly learned to pick her battles.

She got up from her desk and stretched. Her jacket hung over the back of the chair as the heating in the building was kept at a comfortable 20 degrees. She always put it back on when she left her office space as it was bad enough having roundy hips, but roundy boobs too? That was an invite to ogle too far. Molly knew that if she didn't cover her chest area, at least partially, an unhealthy amount of men spoke to her breasts and not her face. It was infuriating, ignorant, and at this stage in her almost twenty-five years of life, a good twelve of them with said breasts, boring. She wondered if she should just speak to men's crotches? Maybe she'd give that a try the next time a man neglected to make eye contact as opposed to boob contact.

Speaking of eye contact, or lack thereof, but not in a boob way, Molly hadn't seen Kit in the last couple of days. And she'd surprised herself by watching out for him. No reason she could put her finger on ... just ... he seemed nice. Odd, yeah, but hey, take a look in the mirror, Moll. He had struggled with eye contact but at least it wasn't because his eyes were glued lower. They had just not quite met hers. Except that one time when they shook hands and he'd appeared as shocked as she was. He'd literally taken a jolt backwards. She'd been surprised at the colour of his eyes. A pale steely grey with a darker rim around the outside of the iris. Most unusual. Frankie, her sister-in-law, had lovely grey eyes but they were darker than Kit's and the colour made his appear different. Rare, to her anyway.

He had quickly looked away and they'd continued with the conversation which she had, truthfully, forced on him. But, hey! When she'd started at BB&M it had meant a lot when someone made an effort to make her feel welcome. She always liked to pay it forwards.

I need caffeine, she thought, *not* antioxidants, and she reached for her jacket.

"Hello again," a voice spoke from behind her.

Molly whirled and almost bumped into the person she'd been thinking of moments before. She had skills, powers even. But not superpowers – she couldn't make people appear. But she could, and frequently did, open her mouth and insert her foot.

"Oh, I was just thinking of you," she said and groaned silently. What a bloody idiot! No one admitted they were thinking of a person. That was just dumb.

"And I was thinking of you," Kit said.

Oh. Well, maybe some other people were as gauche as she was.

"I was heading to get a coffee and thought you might like a tea?" he continued. He took the jacket from her hands and held it so she could turn and slip her arms through.

"Thanks," she said as she did.

She eyed him carefully as they left the office. He wore a turtleneck under a knitted waistcoat, and brown slacks. His clothes could not be uglier if he tried. He needed an intervention in the worst way.

They walked to the canteen.

"Tell you what," Molly said, "you get me a regular cup of tea, not green nonsense, and I'll return the favour by giving you some fashion advice."

Kit blinked at her from behind his glasses. "Fashion advice?" He glanced down at his ensemble, frowning. "Do you think I need it?"

"Hell, yes. In fact, I would be doing you a disservice if I didn't burn eighty per cent of what you are wearing."

He grimaced. "That bad?"

"Worse," she said.

When they were seated with their drinks, Kit sighed in resignation.

"All right," he said, "what has to go?"

Molly eyed him thoughtfully. He could barely keep the smile from his face as he watched her appraise him with a thoroughness he found rather endearing. And strangely compelling.

She sipped some Barry's tea and groaned with apparent pleasure. "Do you want me to be honest? I have to say," she continued before he could answer, "I usually am – and even to a fault, so think carefully before you say. It may be hard to hear." She cupped her hands around the mug and studied him gravely.

"Do your worst," he said.

"The slacks have to go. They are hideous. They're hideous *because* they're slacks. They look like they belonged to a travelling salesman from fifty years ago and even that is an insult to travelling salespersons everywhere. The turtleneck?" She shuddered. "Very few, and I mean *very* few, men can carry that off. You, Kit, are sadly not one of them. Or maybe you could be but not with the knitted contraption you are sporting. It looks like your elderly granny knit it."

Kit could feel the corner of his mouth twitch. He couldn't smile. He wouldn't. She had to believe him to be as clueless as he was behaving. He looked down at the offending vest.

"She did. Gran did knit it for me. On her deathbed." Was that laying it on a bit thick?

"Oh please! She did not! I was joking! No self-respecting grandmother would make her beloved grandson walk out in

23

the real world in that, even if she did knit it herself. It's got frigging owls all over it."

She folded her arms as she sat back in her chair, satisfied she'd made her point.

"Okay, so she wasn't on her deathbed, but she did knit it. For me. And I couldn't refuse. She knit me some garment every year for my birthday since I was a kid, and since she has passed I feel closer to her when I wear them."

"Yeah, I'm not buying that malarkey either. And where did she pass to? I mean, I can hear the Yank in your voice – you're New England maybe? But I don't understand why no one can say if a person has died. It's all, passed or passed on. The person died, for goodness' sake. Say the words, why don't you?"

Molly had been gesticulating as she spoke and Kit was mesmerised.

"Good point," he agreed. "I guess it has become unusual to say died, nowadays – certainly where I come from. But you're correct, my gran died. Last year. I miss her." He had *no* idea where that came from and was instantly mortified. This woman, with her natural candour, was making him forget himself.

Molly reached over and rested a hand on his arm. "Well, I'm sorry for your loss," she said, sincere and direct. "It sucks big time to lose a grandparent. I know. I really miss mine. I shouldn't have been so flippant. I sometimes speak first and think later. I apologise for sounding callous or uncaring, it's not what I meant. We say 'passed away' here ourselves, so that rant was uncalled for. How did she die?"

Yes, direct. And honest. No one ever asked, it was such a personal topic, but Molly Fitzgerald went straight to it.

"She got hit by a car, broke her hip and it didn't mend properly. She spent weeks in hospital before going into a care home but she just kind of faded away." Kit swallowed as the guilt gnawed away at him. All that time living with virtual strangers. His mother had been busy so rarely got home but the neighbours had visited regularly. Essentially, however, the elderly woman had died as a result of a stupid accident and that still made him so angry. His own part, or lack of it, was a burden he was unable to release, nor did he feel he should. Work commitments had allowed only two brief trips last year and at least the last one had coincided with her death. He had been there at the end and that was something to cling to in the dark days that followed. Sure, he was an adult and had faced death before, but Gran had been such a huge part of his childhood and then his college days when he stayed with her, in that tiny two-roomed house in Stoneybatter. He'd loved it there. Dripping in local history, every neighbour had a story to tell, a life to be heard. Endless long evenings listening to scandals and gossip, some so embellished that no one believed the heart of them, and no one cared either.

Long summer evenings as the exams drew ever closer, Kit had studied, laptop on his knees, sitting on a blanket in the Phoenix Park, a short stroll from the house. Families, lovers, joggers, power-walkers and the odd deer had taken up space there, not to mention the low but enthusiastic applause from the twilight cricket games. It was a golden time for Kit and he'd savoured it.

"What hospital was she in?" Molly asked the prosaic question, though what difference it made he wasn't sure.

He looked at her earnest expression and realised she did want to know.

"Why? Does it matter?"

"I suppose not, but some are better than others. Same as anywhere. Any city. Any county. And, unfortunately, price and/or health care play a role. Just saying." Molly sipped her tea.

"St James'," Kit supplied. This woman was a sorcerer,

prying information from him like a pro. "Fortunately she had an excellent health-care plan, so the bills were paid for and the home she was in was covered. It was sheer bad luck she didn't mend well. Mum said Gran was always a poor healer, even with things like the flu. Still not sure how true that was."

"Does your mum live in Boston? What does she do?"

Kit straightened. This had to stop. "*Eh*, why don't you go back to the fashion help? It seems of more immediate import than my life story."

"*Oops.* Sorry. I get caught up sometimes and forget where I am or what track I was taking. Right!" She put her cup down and stepped back. "If, and it's a *big* if, you have to keep wearing owls on your torso, may I suggest you pair them with a white shirt, no tie, and navy chinos? We have dress-down Fridays here so you could change to jeans on those days, but do not ever, and I mean *ever*, wear those atrocious trouser things you have on again. Relegate to the bin, please, as not even a person in dire need of clothing would choose them. They could do serious harm to the unsuspecting."

"Got it," Kit said with a nod. "You'll not see these offensive weapons any more. And I want to compromise with the tie situation. I will wear one four days of the week, with a proper shirt and never a turtleneck. Promise!" He did a swipe at the centre of his chest in the time-honoured fashion of promise-giving.

"Excellent," Molly declared. "We have progress. We can discuss hair and glasses another day. I have to get back to my accounts. They won't reconcile themselves."

And off she went, those legs drawing his gaze and holding it as she sauntered down the hall.

Hair and glasses? No. That was a step too far. He'd let her think she was having her way in the clothing department and meanwhile he would find out exactly what accounts she was reconciling.

Chapter 3

February slipped into March and the wind grew bitter. Molly wrapped a scarf around her head and neck as she walked briskly from her train station to the office. She'd adapted that American custom of walking in runners and keeping her proper shoes under her desk or, depending on the situation, a pair got tucked into her shoulder bag. She knew it was not a good look for her – runners, nylon tights and a below-the-knee skirt. Very few people, in fairness, could get away with it, but Molly congratulated herself on her total lack of ego as she tucked her chin beneath the lambswool scarf. Shit, it was cold.

By the time she reached the office, discarded her outer layers, slipped on her three-inch heels and inhaled a cup of coffee, she was back on track. She expected that her nose would take some time to be not quite so pink but, as she was here as early as usual, very few individuals would notice. Patty might tease her, but the cleaner would make it a gentle ribbing, not an ugly comment. Molly fired up her computers and, as she waited for them to 'waken' she strolled down the hall, cup in hand, and out into the open office area.

Twelve desks sat in rows of three and all were presently unoccupied. She didn't blame the admin staff for clocking in and out right on time but she hoped one of the owners, or whoever was in charge of payroll, would sanction some overtime as with the audit now under way, paperwork and correspondence was at a high.

Molly liked to do her own emails and check-ins with her specific clients, making appointments as needed, but several of her co-workers used the admin staff for that purpose. It was encouraged, in fact, as it meant the accountants had more time for number-crunching. But since number-crunching was her bliss, she mostly got through her work quickly and had the time for admin herself. Glancing along the wall of offices that faced the open space, she realised there were lights on in two. That was unusual. This was normally her alone time. In fact, it was barely seven, so even more unusual. She walked over, staying on the carpet runner that was centred on the wooden flooring so as not to alert anyone.

Declan's office door was slightly ajar and she peeped in, giving a light tap on the jamb so as not to freak him out. Declan Twomey was not seated at his desk. He wasn't in the room at all. Another man sat in his seat, another man was staring intently at the computer and writing in a notebook at his side. Not Declan Twomey.

Kit.

Or a version of Kit. Maybe she'd been too good at the fashion advice or maybe he was a really attentive student, but this Kit didn't look anything like slacks-wearing, owl-covered Kit.

Hell, no.

Granted she hadn't seen him in days, things had been crazy with audit fever going on, but still. This kind of change was huge.

"Give me a minute," new Kit said, never lifting his eyes from the screen, his hand still writing, apparently unerringly, as his eyes focused on the information on the computer.

"Sure," Molly agreed, keeping her voice low as the tension in his body was almost palpable.

His glasses sat next to him and his hair was brushed back from his forehead. He wore a once-crisp white shirt, tie dragged down and top button open. The sleeves were rolled up, neatly in folds, and the dusting of dark hair on his rather fine forearms kept Molly mesmerised for too many seconds. He had muscles, this dorky former fashion-disaster man. She let her eyes trail up and over his torso. *Hmmm* ... where did those shoulders come from? He was a sloucher. A huncher. She'd seen it herself. All bumbly and uncertain. With a very deliberate yet almost bouncy walk. Her senses on alert, she breathed deeply and watched. And waited.

A few moments later, Kit closed the notebook, reached for his glasses, put them on and, dragging a hand through his hair, had the usual floppy, innocent lock of hair fall forward. He pulled down the sleeves of his shirt and straightened up the tie. He pulled out a memory stick from the computer and switched off the machine.

He stood up and, before her eyes, Other Kit was back. Former Kit. Poorly dressed nerdy Kit. Molly shook her head slightly. Had she just imagined the whole few minutes before when it looked like a different person was seated at Declan's desk?

Which reminded her.

"Are you working for Declan too?" she asked, her tone neutral as she saw him pocket the memory stick.

"*Hmm?*" His query was as absentminded as his stance. "Oh, this!" He gestured to the work area as if he'd just remembered why he was there. "Like I told you, I'm just helping out where I can. Mr Twomey needed some figures checked so I was getting that done before he came in today."

"Declan is out of the office till tomorrow," Molly said.

"He is?" The question came across as bafflement. "Oh. Well, I needn't have rushed this so," he said as he walked towards her.

Before she realised it, they were out in the hallway, the light was switched off and the door pulled shut behind them.

Kit shoved his hands in his pockets and, tilting his head to one side, he indicated they walk on. His gait was awkward and uneven as he led them to the canteen. He walked over to the coffee pot she had brewed on arrival and waved a mug in her direction.

"Sure, why not?" Molly answered his unspoken question, a million of her own flooding her brain. She handed him the mug she'd forgotten was still in her hand from earlier and he filled it up.

"Do you recognise the blend?" he asked, handing it back.

"Guatemalan."

"Impressive, Molly. You *are* good."

"No," she admitted, her innate honesty not letting her take the compliment. "I made the coffee earlier and chose the blend."

"Ah. Well, thank you." He sipped his own brew and peered over his glasses at her, deepening the nerd Kit look. "Are you always in this early?"

She walked around the table and took a seat, crossing her legs and leaning back, aiming for relaxed, for natural. She didn't feel either of those states. She felt confused. As if she were watching a movie. Specifically, *Superman*. The Christopher Reeve one. Clark Kent was definitely here in the room with her – but back in Declan's office? She had absolutely seen a completely different version of Mr Kent. The Superman version. Just a hint, admittedly, and gone before she could really process it, but Molly was nothing if not discerning. She knew she couldn't ask exactly what he'd been doing in Declan's office. It was none of her business. She was a junior accountant and he'd been brought in as a – well, whatever he was.

"I'm usually in first," Molly said, answering his question. And then asked one of her own. "I thought the other new guy, Elliot, was supposed to be the one helping with the audit? I suppose I'm just surprised you're working with Declan and I didn't know it even though he's my direct boss."

"Elliot?" Kit asked.

"Yeah. I haven't met him but the admin staff said he was gruff and rude. And a bit peculiar." The second the words were out of her mouth she knew. God, she was an idiot.

Open mouth, insert foot. She was spectacularly good at that and had just done it again.

She studied his raised eyebrow as he waited her out. *Damn.* Back to honesty, she thought. Clear up your own mess and speak the truth. It was her maxim. Except the living-a-lie part. But she'd get to that.

"You're Elliot, aren't you? I thought it was a first name but, I gather from the look you're giving me, it's not."

"Correct. Kit Elliot, Accountant at Large, at your service." He swept a mock bow.

Molly wished, not for the first time in her life, that the ground would simply open and swallow her up. But alas, no ground-swallowing was taking place this morning. She groaned.

"I'm sorry, Kit," she said. "I need to think before I speak. I didn't mean any offence. And I should know by now never to listen to gossip. You may be a total nerd but you have never been either gruff or rude to me."

His lips quirked. "Total nerd?"

"Hey, it takes one to know one. I'm including myself in all things nerd-related."

His gaze caught hers, holding steady, silver-grey eyes so beautiful even in the early-morning canteen light.

31

"You are not exactly the typical nerd, Molly. I mean, look at you."

She rolled her eyes. "I'd rather not, thanks all the same. And I guess nerds come in all shapes and sizes. Anyway," she stood briskly and straightened her skirt, "I've work to do. Catch you later."

And without a backward glance, she strode purposefully out the door and back to her office.

Kit sighed. Close. Too damn close. He shut his eyes briefly and drew in a deep breath. All he could see was the sway of Molly's hips as she exited the canteen. He shook his head, banishing the image. Way more important was that she had found him scrolling through Twomey's work. Kit wasn't yet sure what he was looking for but he was making a deep search on everyone's computer and seeing the way things stood. An audit could take up to three months and they were halfway into it. Even the admin staff were on edge. Kit got that – when one's work was being scrutinised by others there was bound to be a certain amount of anxiety, even amongst those whose work was completely above board. He had gone through all the senior directors, their admin staff, the next-level managers and was now on the assistant-manager level. Declan Twomey was just one of many, but every time Kit encountered him he left with a feeling of unease. Not anything specific. Not the way his police colleague, Flynn Fitzgerald, got 'feelings' – they were just creepy. No, Kit's were just the plain old 'I'm not sure I like the look of you' kind. Nothing otherworldly. Just a gut reaction. It could, of course, be put down to the image he himself was portraying. His method of presenting his fake self so people would chat around him, without including or even noticing him, worked spectacularly well with Declan Twomey for several reasons. Twomey mostly saw only himself and those in his entourage. Anyone who didn't fall into his idea of what an up-and-coming highflyer should be, didn't make it into his posse. If you weren't part of the 'bright and beautiful', forget it. Declan saw the Kit he was expected to see. Geeky, gawky, nervous and introverted. A non-entity. Zero threat to Declan in any way, shape or form.

However, the plan had almost been blown when Molly had appeared at the door earlier. Her sharp, observant eyes had studied him intently. He'd felt them bore into his body even though he refused to make eye contact. He hadn't been *in* his role and needed a moment to re-cast himself. She was too damn smart and he almost blew it. He had to keep his shit together where she was concerned because she and Seán Donnelly, the other recent hire, were next on his list. Maybe he should have started with the last-in crew but Kit liked to get a feel for the big picture and, for that, he liked to go from the top down. He believed that managers' style permeated the rest of the staff and if the powers that be were clean and above board, their staff might well be too.

So far, Bryan, the senior Benson, Kit's immediate, if temporary, boss, appeared squeaky clean. His accounts and all his business dealings were in order. Edward Malone, the third partner, and the older man by two years, came across as weary and overdue for retirement. His grey hair was stylish, his clothing impeccable – bespoke suits every day – French cuffs with monogrammed cufflinks, handmade shoes. The whole package and yet … Kit felt he just wanted out. The bags under his eyes betrayed a distinct lack of sleep and, maybe, some underlying health problems. But like his partner, Benson Senior, his accounts and business dealings all appeared in order.

Brendan Benson, on the other hand, was a slippery customer. The youngest of the three business owners, he was suave and sophisticated. Late fifties, he was sporting all the trendier styles and often wore a cravat to the office. He drove a Ferrari, red naturally, and had what looked like a permanent tan. A diamond ring winked on his pinkie finger and the latest Rolex encircled his wrist. But looks and style aside – Kit knew how deceiving that could be – he never seemed to do any actual work. He went to the races and played golf during the day. He visited the theatre and art-gallery openings in the evenings. And yet, his many accounts all tallied, were all present and correct. There were a couple of locked-out folders on his computer that Kit wanted to access but was biding his time. Kit liked to play the long game. He liked to make his presence as non-threatening as possible while slowly infiltrating the tightknit group of those who held all the key accounts. The younger Benson was the holder of the accounts from some seriously large, publicly known, firms. All those accounts were pristine.

And Kit didn't believe a single piece of the data.

Molly glanced at her watch as her internal phone rang. Damn, almost six thirty and she had been just about to leave. But duty called and she was a junior.

"Molly Fitzgerald," she said into the handset.

"Mr Benson would like to see you in his office," a starched voice intoned.

Molly gulped. *Flip*. Had she done something wrong? "Of course, Miss Cassidy, I'll come right up."

Oh Lord. She placed a hand on her suddenly jumpy stomach and slipped her heels back on. When she got on a roll and was lost in the numbers, she often tucked one leg beneath her on the chair, her shoes kicked off under the desk. She straightened her skirt, smoothing out the wrinkles, and shrugged on her jacket. Tucking a long errant curl back into the heavy bun, she quickly left her office and headed to the centre staircase.

Benson Senior had a corner office – as did Brendan Benson, who everyone called Benson Junior even though they were brothers not father and son, and Mr Malone. The fourth corner office was the boardroom and all four aspects had a fine view of the city.

Miss Cassidy was a woman of indeterminate years, maybe mid-sixties, Molly suspected, but the attire was straight from office manager of the bygone era brigade. A neat, well-ironed, buttoned-to-the-neck blouse in a pastel colour topped with a cardigan, also buttoned to the neck, in a shade darker than the blouse. The woman's hair was chin-length and cut razor-sharp, and she wore a tortoiseshell plastic hairband every day, holding the dull grey hair back from her face. She had few lines and skin like alabaster. Her lipstick, her only nod to glamour, was a soft pink and, without it, Miss Cassidy would simply fade into the background. But the visual was only half the picture. Miss C, as the juniors called her, was a whiz. In all ways. She had an excellent telephone manner, still used shorthand when it was required, could type a silly amount of words per minute, was an awesome gatekeeper for Benson Senior and, this shocked many of the youngsters in the office, knew her way around computers like a boss.

When Molly arrived at the desk situated a few steps from Senior's door, Miss C was speaking in that clear but crisp voice she employed with those she felt needed a certain amount of behavioural training. She saw Molly, indicated with one raised finger and a slight glance in her direction that she should wait a moment.

Molly did, her nerves drumming steadily, as a cinema reel of possible issues ran through her brain. She really hoped she hadn't screwed up. She wanted to keep this job. She *loved* this job.

"You may go in, Ms Fitzgerald," the secretary said coolly. "Mr Benson is waiting for you."

Molly straightened her spine and, tapping lightly on the door, opened it and went inside.

Chapter 4

Kit closed down his laptop, finished up his notes and flopped back onto the couch. He rubbed his eyes, the heels of his hands digging deep, as he let out a long breath. It had been some day. Every day was different in Kit's world. It was how he liked it. It might look, to an onlooker, that he was dragging his dreary self from one boring computer to another but, to Kit, each time he opened up another machine and trawled through the data, it was all his shiny birthday gifts in one fell swoop. All he had to do was unwrap each particular item, align and realign them in ways that made sense to his forensic brain and, *voilà*, the truth would set him free. Sometimes it was hard to maintain an air of apparent disinterest, especially when he came across a titbit of information that tied things together or led him down a different path. These were all moments of joy to him and, yes, he did know he was odd in all ways that word implied.

Did he care? Usually not. But now the image of a curvy, chatty yet sharp-eyed brunette tended to slip into his downtime reverie way more than he liked. He didn't in fact know what colour her hair was. He knew it was brownish. Though earlier, when the sun had caught a fallen curl in a certain way, he could have sworn it turned bronze. Those damn falling curls were a distraction. They looked silken and soft. So touchable. He wondered how long her hair was if let loose from its clip. Was it curly all over? Should it matter? No. Did it? Strangely, yes. And then there were her curves. He was as clued-in as the next twenty-first century man about sexual harassment and the #MeToo movement and was totally, one hundred per cent on board. His way of thinking about it was to constantly refer back to how it would feel if some random man took liberties with his mum, or gran, or his sister – if he had one – or his daughter, also hypothetical. But he did, always, try to think things through and not make assumptions.

With Molly Fitzgerald he was failing spectacularly.

All proper, well-figured-out thoughts went away when he brought her lovely person to mind. Or worse, when she was standing, sitting, leaning, walking, drinking coffee for God's sake, in front of him. Only his years of 'smoke and mirrors' when it came to his roleplay at work prevented him from actually drooling. It wasn't that she was particularly beautiful, like a film star or model. It was maybe that her eyes were a stunning aqua colour that drew him inexorably in. Or that her mouth was full and deep pink, her nose very slightly tilted or that her eyebrows were perfectly arched and so expressive. Or even that the creamy column of her throat tantalised him when he tried not to look at all her other features but absolutely refused to let his eyes wander south to those luscious curves and generous hips.

No. He knew he couldn't let himself study her any more intently and certainly not in view of anyone else. It was becoming harder and harder to ignore what he suspected was a sizable crush on his co-worker who was, inconceivable though it seemed, a possible suspect in the case he was trying to solve. None of this made him happy in the work sense. But in every other sense – the touching-feeling-sense part of him, those thoughts made him very happy indeed. He barely knew her. Had hardly spoken with her and, although the few conversations they'd shared had been for the most part fun and flirty, he really couldn't say he 'got her' yet.

To make matters worse, he had asked that she be put on a special project. One that he would be able to monitor remotely and follow her every move. He was doing the same for the other recent hire, Donnelly, but no bells were ringing there yet. The way Kit had set things up, any searching, changing, deleting or adding of information on this new account would set off a signal on his laptop. The new firm's account was sent to Declan Twomey as leading consultant and, with Molly as junior accountant, the one doing the work, Kit was hoping to kill two birds with one stone. He had a feeling about Twomey, but, he acknowledged, that could be bias. And he also had a feeling about Molly. This was complicated by those other pesky feelings, but Kit was nothing if not professional and knew when to back off.

Which was why he was determined to get to know Molly Fitzgerald a little better. Purely in the interests of the case, of course. Leaning forward he drummed his fingers on the table. He could ask her on a date – they weren't answerable to each other at work – or at least not officially. He thumbed open his phone screen and glanced at the calendar. Two possible events that might not need an actual date were highlighted. The first, BB&M-related, was a charity event in a couple of weeks. Black tie and in a swanky hotel, it might be just the place to get Ms Fitzgerald to let her hair down – maybe even literally. It wouldn't be weird that they went together as it was for the firm and he could sell it as such rather than perhaps get a flat no for a *date* date. That might work. Benson Senior could get him an invite as it would also give Kit a better overview of the managers' interaction and group dynamics.

Pleased with his decision and plan, he tossed his phone aside, stood up and went back into the small hall to continue scraping at ancient wallpaper before he allowed himself a trip to the takeaway.

Molly was in her element. A new firm, an up-and-coming sports agency, had landed on her desk. It was Declan's 'officially', according to Benson Senior during the chat they'd had in his office, but she was to take the lead and only read Twomey in if necessary. It was such a thrill. In the case of most of the firms she had handled up to now she'd been the assisting accountant and, although she got to liaise with the clients, everything was still Twomey's responsibility. The way Bryan Benson sold her this one, it was *hers* regardless of Twomey's name on the top. The thrill of it. She felt giddy inside and, although that feeling was tempered with some anxiety, she was on her way. She could *feel* it.

The fact the agency was a sports one and she wasn't the sports aficionado of the year, neither fazed nor lowered her delight in the slightest. One of the great things about accountancy, about numbers and how they worked, how they did their magic, was it didn't matter one jot what the company was. The accountant didn't have to have season tickets or name every court or field position to know if the business was running smoothly and, more importantly, was legally and fiscally compliant.

Metaphorically shoving up her sleeves, Molly got to work. Sports Star Services was relatively new and she wondered even as she opened up the accounts' history why they were auditing themselves so soon. Most businesses needed a few years to build a pattern and get a flow going but she wasn't going to complain. If she did this right, they might ask for her again and she'd have her very, very *own*, actual own client. *Yay.*

Several hours later, she was, unusually for her, almost bored. Everything was perfect. Everything clean. Even every bloody cent rounded correctly and adding beautifully. *Damn.* She wanted a challenge. And now, she also wanted a coffee. And a big old slice of chocolate cake. Heaving a sigh, she closed down her open tabs and pushed back from her screen. Her navy suit skirt was wrinkled again, and she swore she would shop for both a new suit in a better-quality fabric and a few old-fashioned nylon slips to help with the creasing. What she would do if the summer brought a heatwave was a problem for another day.

The break area was empty, and she set about brewing a pot of coffee. It was the dreaded three o'clock slump and several employees would wander in shortly. Sure enough, she was just laying out mugs and plates, because why wouldn't she, she was there, when footsteps echoed down the hall. Jen and the newest hire, Seán, wandered in, chatting brightly. Seán looked like a mini-Twomey, as he was bred from the same cloth. They could well have gone to the same school and university, which was not uncommon here in BB&M, and Molly determined to find out. She greeted the new arrivals with a smile and, even though she wouldn't be considered one of the cool ones, she knew she was pretty good at fitting in.

She offered coffee and indicated the tray of baked goods delivered earlier that afternoon. She sat with them, sipping her own drink and chatting about the day so far. Then she angled the conversation to schools and, sure enough, Seán had attended school in the south of the city – not Twomey's but the sister-school a few minutes down the road. Both having attended fee-paying schools, these young men were among the privileged few. They talked about people they knew in common – this was Dublin after all and it was hard not to find at least one familial or a-few-degrees-of-separation connection once the year of leaving school was established.

Molly's siblings had all initially attended private schools as they too were privileged, but had, one by one, opted for a co-ed state school instead. By the time it was Molly's turn for secondary education her parents had just enrolled her in the co-ed, bypassing the all-girls institution a few minutes' walk from their home. Molly had enjoyed it – to a point. Bitching and bullying were common social discourse amongst teenagers the world over, and Molly had weathered it with as much grace as she could.

Seán had played rugby for his school, naturally, and had the build and confidence to go with it. He had a braying laugh but was undeniably handsome and only a couple of years younger than Molly. He was an intern and still in the throes of exams. Many of the new hires were studying when they were first employed. It was a known fact that accountancy exams were the *worst* and everyone repeated them all or some of them, at least once. There was no shame, even a certain amount of bravado in the quantity of repeats.

"Yeah, I'm on my third repeats," Seán was saying with zero embarrassment. "Like, I just don't have the time for studying. I'm on the squad for my club so, like, priorities and all."

"How many times did you sit the exams, Molly?" A voice had joined in the conversation.

Molly was startled when she turned to see Kit standing behind her.

"Oh, hi, Kit!"

Molly looked about and saw the room was quite full, the noise level rising.

Kit stood awkwardly, turning a cup around in his long fingers, so she scooted her chair over to make room.

"Sit, why don't you?" she offered.

Kit took the seat, nodding briefly to the others, and turned his attention back to her. "How many times?" he repeated.

Now these were the kinds of questions Molly usually avoided. They were just too … personal. "Oh, you know, the usual," she said airily, throwing him a glare. How could she get him to shut up? Fortunately, Seán and Jen were talking together and seemed to have lost interest so she turned fully to face Kit. "That's not the type of question you should ask in front of people."

Kit looked puzzled. "Why not? That's what you were talking about, wasn't it? Results? Exams? Repeats? All I was doing was joining in."

Damn. He had a point. The reality of course was she didn't like *answering* that question. It always led to misery.

"I know. You're right. I just think it's no one's business how many rounds anyone else takes to get the exam! If they offer the info, fine, but one shouldn't ask. Some people are super-smart on the day to day, but exams don't suit the way their brain works. And they have to do it several times. It's not remotely indicative of how good an accountant they might be."

Kit smirked. Actually smirked. "How many times, Molly? You can whisper – I won't tell." He leaned forward rather dramatically, hand cupped to his ear.

What a goofball! She laughed, she had to. It seemed so in character with his normal quirky demeanour. But then again, maybe not. He was just the type of person to be unaware of how others saw him. He didn't seem to be conscious that the women in the office didn't flatter and flirt with him the way they did with Declan and Seán and several of the other male employees.

"I'll tell if you will," she said, getting into the mood of it. "But first, did you do your accountancy exams here in Ireland? The playing field must be level."

"I did my primary degree here, in business. And I did an accounting degree at night at the same time. It was a lot, but I like to study. Sue me." He shrugged, attempting a nonchalance that didn't quite match the wariness in his eyes.

"And then?" she prodded. "Did you study in America too?"

"I did. I did my Master's there and then some follow-up courses that don't really matter as they weren't necessarily accounts-related. Now, you." He sat back and folded his arms, waiting.

Molly considered him, narrowing her eyes. "*Ha!*" she declared. "You didn't say if you had to do a bazillion repeats. *Truth.*" She jabbed a finger at him, poking him in the upper arm. *Huh*. Muscle there too. Not just wide shoulders that now looked *narrower* than the morning in Declan's office but that must be a clothing or posture scenario. One's shoulders didn't change within the space of a few days, surely?

Kit heaved a sigh, dropping his head forward to his chest. "I passed mine first time, every time," he mumbled. He flicked his eyes to hers. "But that's just me. I'm a nerd, remember?"

"Put it there, kiddo." Molly stuck out her hand to shake his. "Me too."

Kit blinked. Took his glasses off, rubbed them with a paper napkin, and replaced them. "What, all of them?"

"Yup," she sighed. "Nerd partner here. And, like you, I was also doing a different degree by day." It felt strangely liberating admitting that. She'd never, she realised, said that out loud to anyone before. Those who knew her from the art world had no clue about her maths brain and those in her night classes and now her job didn't know she had an artistic bone in her body. And now Kit Elliot was about to know. And she didn't mind. Go figure. What would he say if he knew she was still studying? Still taking more exams when she could, in order to be as broadly accomplished as possible?

"So, what degree did you do?" he asked. "Was it in finance or maths?"

Molly took a long drink of her now cooling coffee. In for a penny.

"I did a fine arts degree," she admitted.

She thought of it as an admission, she realised – as something to be whispered about, or brushed over. In her home, in her family, and amongst her parents' peers, a fine arts degree was the pinnacle. The Holy Grail. The proof of one's artistic and creative worth. Yes, her father was a history professor and not especially creative, but it was in the arts *field*. Not science or chemistry or one of those "dreadful rote-learning subjects where no one used the art of discourse". She was mentally quoting her father. She almost but not quite followed her declaration with an apology. She really needed to stop doing that. She needed to own both sides of her. She would. In time. She hoped.

"Fine arts?" Kit was full of incredulity. His eyebrows headed due north in his forehead. "Wow, I didn't see that coming."

"Yeah, I know. I keep it hush-hush here in BB&M or I'd be laughed out of the place."

Kit had the grace to look abashed. "I'm sorry." He rested a hand on her arm. "That came out wrong. I meant *wow* in an amazed and truly impressed way. Honest."

He grinned at her and she couldn't help it – she grinned right back. She hadn't noticed Kit's grin before. And she really should have. It was both charming and bashful. It was also slightly crooked, and damn, there were dimples.

Dimples! She filed that titbit away along with the broad shoulders, tight muscles and very non-Clark-Kent persona she had glimpsed so briefly the other morning.

"It's okay," she said. "I get it. Trust me, I do." She scooted her chair a little closer, ensuring no one could hear. "My family would be horrified to know they had a traitorous 'left brainer' in the crew."

Kit studied her for a moment, puzzlement in his eyes. "Wait. Do you mean to tell me your family don't know you're an accountant? How can they not know?"

"And that's my cue to head back to my office. Enough personal info for one day. Duty calls."

Molly scraped her chair back, stood and took her cup to the dishwasher. When she headed back past Kit he was standing by the table, shoulders hunched, hands shoved deep into the pockets of his trousers.

"Sorry." His voice was hesitant. Regretful. "I didn't mean to pry." Before Molly could dismiss his apology, he turned and said, "So, back to work. What's on your plate at the moment? Anything interesting?"

As they walked back along the walkway, sidestepping other employees hurrying late to the canteen, Molly told him very briefly about Sports Stars Services and how deadly dull their accounts were. "I know I shouldn't complain," she said, "but they are crystal clear and so easy. I want a challenge! And I was so happy to be given this particular set to work on. Oh well, I'm probably moaning where others would be thrilled." She threw him a half smile, well aware that she sounded like a whiney complaining brat. I mean, who wanted their accounts to be difficult? That was crazy. Alas, it was also her.

"Have you gone through everything?" Kit asked.

She tilted her head at him. "I think I've one set left and then I'll put them to bed."

"*Hmm …*" Kit said nonchalantly.

"What do you mean, *hmmm*? Do you know something about them? Have you an inside track?" In sudden excitement, Molly grabbed his arm, pulling him to a halt. She faced him, eyes wide with enthusiasm. "*Spill!*" she demanded.

Kit looked uncomfortable. "It could be nothing," he began, "but I heard one of the owners is in a bit of financial difficulty. But it could be nothing."

Or it could be something, Molly thought. She grinned at Kit. "Thanks for the heads-up. I'll go a layer deeper, once I've finished the next set."

She rubbed her hands together in anticipation, Kit completely forgotten as she turned into her office, her energy revitalised and not because of the break.

Closing down his computer, Kit reached for his shoulder bag and put his laptop inside. The work he'd been doing that afternoon had warranted the use of his own laptop and no trace left on the office desktop computer. Slipping the USB stick into his pocket, he switched off the lights and headed out. It was Thursday and he needed to get to the club. He glanced at his watch, grimacing as he realised he'd have to cycle very fast through the Dublin traffic back to his small home in Stoneybatter on the north side of the city, if he wanted to be on time. Those lads would give him hell if he was late, especially considering timekeeping was a skill he was doing his best to impart to them. Plus, this Thursday-night practice was an extra he'd insisted upon. Not much good if he screwed it up himself.

He hurried past Molly's door, glancing through the glass panels, and saw her staring at her screen, fingers tapping away. He smiled. He wondered what she would make of the secret file he had embedded into Sports Star Services accounts. Would she find it? He bet she would. But the real question was, what would she do then?

Chapter 5

What to do? What to do, indeed. Molly tossed and turned, kicking her duvet away and flopping her pyjama-clad legs flat down on the bed. *Damn*. She could not get comfortable and her brain wouldn't settle. Had she only discovered the juiciest of nuggets of information because Kit had suggested it, or would she have found it anyway? She'd never know the answer to that, but now she had the insight, her next step was to decide a plan of action.

There was a chain of command, of course. And protocols. Steps to be taken, and she would take them. She would just double and triple-check her work in the morning, with fresh eyes. Yes, that was a good first step. A plan. Always good to have a plan.

Sleep still eluding her, she threw back the covers and got up. Switching on the bedside lamp she found her slippers, shoved her feet into their cosy covers and headed to her spare room. Her studio. Her *office*. But this time, at two thirty in the morning, she was using it as a studio. She reached for her large sketchpad, opened to a fresh page and propped it against her easel board. She rummaged among her Conté sticks and finding a shortish piece in terracotta, began to draw.

The issue had never been that she couldn't draw. She

could. And extremely well. She was streets better than Caro who was considered to have a 'good eye'. Not only was Molly's eye excellent, she was a really talented interpretive artist. When she was finished with a drawing it not only looked like the object, person or view, it looked *better*. Although Molly loved her art and still did the occasional commission, it no longer gave her a buzz, if indeed it ever had. She drew all the time as a child, mainly because she could. And because she earned loads of attention. In her reckoning, most young people liked praise, especially from their parents. The Fitzgerald parents were no different. They were thrilled she had such talent. Finally, one of their brood was going to excel in the arts.

When Molly was little the senior Fitzgeralds hadn't yet known that Dev would also show great talent and skill through photography. They were excited when Caro showed promise with a pencil, dismayed when Ali showed none and over the moon when Molly appeared to never *not* have a pencil and pad in hand. Flynn, the eldest, had never shown aptitude for any of the arts. He had been a deeply thoughtful boy, head in a book or solving puzzles. No surprise then with his choice of career or his academic achievements. That brainiac had left school at sixteen, for goodness' sake, with top marks in everything, finished his Law and Political Science degree from Trinity College with a first, and joined the Gardaí by age 20. The rest, as they say, was history. Her big brother was one of the most sought-after investigators when it came to tough criminal cases. Not just in Ireland but also via the FBI and Interpol. Smarty Pants.

Molly could paint too, though she preferred dry media as, being as messy as she was when creating, the clean-up was huge when water or oil was involved. As she let her arm and hand loosen from weeks of lack of use, she began to breathe deeply and relax. It was odd that nowadays her

49

relaxation, for the most part, came from a spreadsheet. But every so often she felt the pull of the chalk. She changed the page and began again – not disgruntled or upset with her first piece – just ready to put down what was, apparently, on her mind.

An hour later she heaved a sigh and, standing and stretching, dusted off her hands. She was smudged all over and needed proper soap and water. She stepped back and appraised her work. There he was, Kit Elliot, masquerading as Superman. Her first discarded page showed him in his bumbling Clark Kent persona. This more detailed study was of Kit sitting at the computer, intently focused on his screen, and she realised now, looking at him with fresh eyes, smoking hot. *Huh*. She'd only seen him that way for a few minutes yet that was what her brain had focused in on – Kit Superman Elliot. Go figure. Molly knew she didn't fancy him. He was impossibly gauche and awkward ninety per cent of the time and his total demeanour was geeky tech nerd. And yet, where had her subconscious gone? *Yup*. There.

She washed her hands in warm soapy water, drank some warmed-up milk and shuffled exhaustedly back to bed. The second her head hit the pillow, she was out.

The following morning, she glanced at the large drawing propped against the easel board and smiled. It was an excellent likeness.

And probably one she'd never see again. She shut the door of her office and went to work.

Yes! Her little nuggets of incorrect calculations were still there. She went over everything again, detailing in a notebook which file led the searcher to the next and so on. It was a bit like a maze, though not that complicated. She wouldn't get lost and could easily backtrack. Molly wasn't a hacker and in no way a computer whiz. She just knew numbers and patterns. The fact that she also had what some people referred to as a sixth sense was less needed in this profession, thankfully. She could rely on facts, not *feelings*.

A psychologist would have a field day with her, Molly thought, as she walked briskly to Declan's office to show him her findings. There she was, living a lie, pretending to her family to be one thing, to be gainfully employed in that one thing, and here she was, inhabiting a space that was nowhere near that life. And yet it was the life that brought her joy. God, she was a screw-up.

She tapped lightly on Declan's door and entered at his grunt of acknowledgment. He was sitting at his desk, looking all D4 handsome and rugger-bugger-like, his hair tousled and sharp shirt all crisp and fresh. Just like him. She knew she should be swooning, even just a little, but – she paused to test her heart rate, her stomach nerves, her *anything* and … nope. Nothing. Not a flicker of attraction to this good-looking man.

"What do you need?" he asked, glancing up from his phone.

She turned her head slightly and saw his computer wasn't even on. And it was well past nine in the morning. Maybe he was working on his phone. She did that sometimes. Calculations and stuff. He glanced back down at the implement and, with a quick grin, thumbed out some response and put the phone down. Not work then.

"I have something I'd like you to look over with me," she said, choosing her words carefully. She didn't want him to look over the work *for* her but instead picked the word *with* to show how in charge she felt in this situation.

Declan frowned. "Now?"

"Yes. Now." She sat down. "I think I've found some anomalies in the Sports Stars Services accounts that could, if left unattended, get them in trouble down the line. As senior accountant on this, I'd like your input." She handed him her USB. "It's all there, in their named folder."

51

He put the USB down on the desk.

"I'll wait," she added as he made no attempt to switch on his machine.

"Can't it wait?" he complained. "I'm busy."

She couldn't hold back a sarcastic glance at his non-active computer and then back at him. "Really?"

Picking up the memory stick with a sigh he switched on his workstation and, flipping open the button on his jacket, leaned forward and inserted the stick.

Moments later he was scrolling through the columns of data, flipping from one file to the next. It wasn't like he had to find the information as she had already highlighted it for him.

"What seems to be the problem?" he asked, confused.

Molly gaped – but inwardly. She knew her jaw was hitting the floor metaphorically but couldn't let her consternation show.

She rose and went around his desk. Clicking open another file, she pointed to various highlighted sections on the spreadsheet. "Look there," she said. "Every fifth client is charged double, and the extra amounts get filed in a personal account, not one attached to the company. They were stupid to leave the file there and I did have to dig for it, but it's all there in black and white. Those extra charges do not get run through the official books."

She took a step back and rounded the desk again to sit in the chair opposite him. She leaned her arms on the cool glass surface. "I know it's not much now, not huge gains, but if they continue to do this long-term, well, they will make a lot of money that won't ever see a tax return."

Declan eased back in his chair, steepling his fingers in a manner suited to one contemplating a very serious matter.

"Well caught, Molly," he said at last. "Leave this with me. I'll look into it."

Molly's shoulders drooped. This wasn't what she wanted. She didn't need him running interference. She knew she couldn't go over his head with it, but she didn't want him taking over either.

"No. Please don't. I can handle it. I'll arrange a meeting with the directors of Sport Stars Services and give them a chance to explain. If we nip this now, show good faith with them, they may stick with us. They are an up-and-coming group, I gather, and it would be irresponsible to lose the potential business."

Declan didn't seem convinced. "I don't think so, Molly –"

"Let me try. If I find myself floundering, I'll ask for help. Maybe. This may be just a test – they may have done it just to see if we are thorough. I've heard that's a thing." She hadn't in fact heard any such notion, but it was *possible*, she reasoned.

"I'll copy this and keep it in my files but, okay, go ahead and sort this. I'm not sure I want to have that conversation, basically accusing the company of fraud. But give it a go and see what shakes out."

Molly danced for joy – on the inside – as he copied the file to his desktop.

She held out her hand for the memory stick. "Thanks, Declan. You won't regret it. I'll sort this and keep their business."

She walked quickly to the door, eager to get back to her desk. She had a plan to make, and people to phone. It was going to be an exciting day.

Kit knocked lightly on her open door sometime after noon and took a moment to watch Molly Fitzgerald in action. She was entirely oblivious to him as her fingers flew over the keys in front of her while she scrutinised something on her second screen. That was impressive. She was most likely rearranging data from one account into a set of personalised spreadsheets in another. It was what he did all the time. Sure, copy and paste was a thing – via a stick – but it felt good to make your own way of sorting data.

She had a tiny indentation between her eyebrows as she worked, and a tantalising curl hung from her messy bun. How he wanted to slide his finger in through that ringlet, just to see how it would feel. And then to let it bounce back. He was fascinated with her hair, and his gaze was continually drawn to that sumptuous lower lip . . . and this was getting ridiculous.

"Hey," he said instead of woolgathering, "would you like to join me in the canteen for lunch?"

Molly's head flew up, startled, her eyes finding his, hers still glazed over. The aqua colour so unusual. Startling, clear, pure. Welcoming. He blinked to banish his thoughts even as she blinked, coming back to the reality that it was time to eat.

"Sure," she agreed after a moment. She closed programs and rose from her seat, reaching for the blazer hung over the back.

"There are coat-hangers for that, I believe," Kit said as she shrugged it on.

Molly smiled but ignored his comment.

"Kit," she said as she left the office, her voice going to a persuasive singsong, "do you mind if we go offsite for lunch today? I wouldn't mind brainstorming a few things with you and don't really want an audience."

"Sure," he agreed, and they veered towards the lift. "Anywhere in mind?"

"How do noodles and sushi sound?"

"Show me the way," he said enthusiastically.

A few minutes later they were settling into their booth and beginning to browse the menus. Kit liked fresh sushi, having spent a considerable part of his life in Boston where some amazing sushi restaurants were located. He wasn't the biggest fish-eater but he knew he could get all kinds of freshly made, non-pescatarian, delicious food here.

They chose, both ordering a selection of the vegetarian sushi complete with tangy and sweet dips, and handed back the menus.

Molly leaned forward and rested her forearms on the table.

"Can I pick your brain?" she said. "I know you have a role to play with BB&M and I don't want to step on toes, but I think I found something in the Sports Star Service account that I mentioned to you yesterday. And I'm not totally sure I'm doing the right thing."

Kit pushed his glasses up his nose and thought quickly. He hoped his plan wouldn't backfire and send Molly off on a tack that might not have a good ending for her. He had, it now seemed, assumed she would just do her due diligence and be happy with that. Note to self, never assume, especially with Ms Molly Fitzgerald. He needed to find out what she *now* knew and what she intended to do with that knowledge. But he also had to take a back seat and, unfortunately, let her hang herself if that was to be the case.

It wasn't. Quite the contrary. In a way.

She began with "I want to meet with them."

"You want to *what*?" Kit tried to keep the panic from his voice. Christ, maybe she *was* going to hang herself. So much for his smarts – he had totally fucked this up – not thinking through what she would do – assuming, yes, that again, that she would simply do the figures and hand it back. He was a complete idiot.

"I'm going to meet and ask them about it," she said calmly. "Why wouldn't I? I mean, maybe it's a test."

A test? What the ever-loving ...?

He listened to her explain what she had discovered and how it had transpired. They made way for the plates of food when they arrived, and he listened intently as they divvied up the tantalising dishes. She was smart, he knew, and clever in the way her brain moved laterally as well as directly. She had shown insight and tenacity to find what he had planted and now he was the one up shit creek. Sports Stars Service were a fake company – they didn't exist, for God's sake, and she was going to try to contact them? Why the hell had he not figured that in? She would probably google them, for fuck's sake.

This was a veritable train wreck.

He was going to have to stop her. Now. *Think, think.*

"Have you discussed it with Twomey? Or one of the Bensons? What do they think?" he asked, hoping to stall the runaway vehicle that was Molly.

"I mentioned it to Declan but made it clear this was *my* account – Mr B Senior said so. If I don't take some initiative at this level, they will never give me the big names. I *want* the big names, Kit. My dream is to work with large corporations, not just doing their books, but showing them financial strategies and work practices that could help them invest and make more of their collateral." She paused to drink some water, her eyes shining over the rim of the glass. She popped a sticky rice roll into her mouth, dabbed the edges with a napkin and smiled.

She looked starry-eyed and excited. He hated to be the one to burst her bubble – but burst it he must.

But before he could open his mouth, she continued, "I know I'll have to take more classes and get more qualifications, but I can do it. I've already set that in motion. And, yeah, I know I'm odd. I've been told that for years, for different reasons, but now I know it's true. I would rather stay in and work on an account than go clubbing with my art-college pals. Even my sisters have to drag me with them when shopping or going out on the town. It's just not me. And I don't care."

Well, that was interesting. She sounded defiant and proud and he couldn't help smiling back at her. He needed to save this situation and send her on a different track.

"I think you talking to the Sports Stars Services reps is a good idea in theory. However," he held up his hand to stop her speaking, "maybe give it a day or two? Let the information settle. Rest. Mull it over." He focused on his plate and ate, hoping she would just agree and leave it at that.

"But why? If it was my business and I'd laid a trap for my accountant, I'd want to know how quickly they picked up on the errors and what they intended to do about it."

"Yes, but you don't know that it *is* a trap. Maybe they're a load of shysters and are intentionally breaking the law. Maybe they're dangerous." He was clutching at straws, he knew it but, God, she needed *not* to try to contact a non-existent company.

"Oh please, you've been watching too much TV!" Molly declared as she wiped her fingers dry on her napkin, pushing away the fingerbowl. "I'm not sure what series, but it sounds fun." She dipped one of the seaweed-wrapped bundles of finely diced vegetables into a sweet sauce and continued to eat.

Kit covered a smile with his hand and shook his head. "No TV," he said. "Just concern that you might get yourself involved in something a little, let's say, out of your depth."

Molly straightened and glared at him. "Think I can't handle a little mystery and sleuthing? Ha! I'm the youngest of five – I know my way around subterfuge, let me assure you. Potential crooked businesspeople don't scare me."

"Well, they should."

"Nah," she said. "I'm good. I believe most people are straight in their dealings and if I deal up front with them, tell them what I've discovered, they'll either be delighted I found their ruse so quickly and be happy with our company or be horrified that mistakes have been made."

"Or," Kit interjected grimly, even though he knew this wasn't a possibility, "they'll know *you* know they are crooks and either accuse you of being in the wrong or try to stop you taking it further." The trouble was, in Kit's real life that was exactly the scenario that could play out. People could get hurt. In his line of business, while not always the physical kind of hurt, people did get damaged. Long term. With a prison sentence. But, of course, Molly Fitzgerald knew none of this.

"You're being overdramatic," she said, adding some food from her selection to his plate. "Anyone would think you watch that show *White Collar* too much – the one where the FBI get involved."

Shit, if she only knew. Changing the subject, Kit brought up various co-workers and the kind of work they did and soon the conversation slid into safer territory as they finished lunch. It was easy, their chit-chat, their back and forth. It was enjoyable – possibly the most relaxed meal he'd had in ages – other than the 'I'm going to call the Sports firm' part. That, not so much.

Crumpling their napkins on the table, they rose to leave, realising they might well have overshot their lunch break.

Kit angled himself forwards and took charge of the bill, despite her instant protest.

"I've got this," he said. "I appreciate your suggestion to leave the premises – I'd still be stuck in the canteen, so it's the least I can do."

"Thank you so much, Kit, I'll get you back another time," she said as they turned in the direction of the office.

She nudged his shoulder in a friendly manner and then froze. Stopped dead beside him. "*Nooooooo*, not now, not bloody *now!*" she exclaimed in a groan. Spinning into him, she sent him an imploring glance. "Just play along with me, please," she begged. "I'll explain later."

With that she buried her face in his shoulder, wrapping her arms about his body. Instincts took over and Kit, bemusedly but quickly, did the same to her, enveloping her in a bear hug and resting his head on the top of her curls. "I gather you are either a) hiding from someone or b) showing someone what you think they should see," he whispered in the direction of her ear.

There was a muffled response, indistinct in any language, but it sounded like "*Oh God!*".

"There is, of course a third possibility," he chuckled, amazed to find he was enjoying himself. He liked the gutsiness of her being so impromptu. He liked the fact that, for whatever reason, she trusted him to play along. And he really liked the way she felt snuggled in his arms. Her body fit to his, her curves to his flat planes. He could feel all her softness and, damn, but it felt *fine*.

"What?"

Her voice was muffled, and he realised he hadn't finished his train of thought.

"Ah, yes. Point three. You were overcome with lust and simply couldn't hold out any longer."

At this, she murmured, "Alas, Mr Kent though you are, I have to go with Point One. I'm hiding."

"Mr Who?" Kit was baffled. Who on earth was Mr Kent?

"Never mind," she said and pulled back, looking about her from a slightly ducked head. Seemingly satisfied that whoever she was hiding from wasn't there any more, she stepped away, shook out her shoulders and started walking briskly in the direction of the office. "I don't have time to go into this subterfuge now but, if you like, you can come to dinner in my flat and I'll explain. Maybe tomorrow night?" Then her hand flew to her mouth. "Oh, I don't mean a date. Not at all. I mean as friends. I'm embarrassing myself now, amn't I?" She groaned and then just blundered on. "Let me know later. Drop a yea or nay into my inbox and we'll go from there."

Kit paused as they reached the security entrance for the building and placed a hand on her elbow, slowing her as they walked through the doorway.

"Relax, Molly. I had a fun lunch. There is no need to be embarrassed. I'll check my calendar and get back to you."

He sauntered ahead of her towards the stairs, a grin on his face and his hands shoved into his pockets.

She was a treat and he'd really enjoy a meal with her in her home. Time to check his calendar.

Chapter 6

It was a yes. Kit had popped his head around the door the previous evening and said, yes, tonight was free. And she had promptly put it out of her head. Hey, she was busy! But it was tonight now and what the heck was she supposed to do? She didn't entertain. She could barely cook for herself for God's sake – how was she expected to produce food for another human being? When her family had helped move her in, it had been pizza all around. Take-away pizza, not even frozen, cook-at-home stuff. She was frigging doomed. Should she phone Ali and ask advice? Hell, no. It was her own bloody fault she'd made the offer in the first place. She'd felt obliged as he'd been such a sport, hiding her as she ducked her head into him, cooperating in her subterfuge without any warning. He must have thought her a right idiot, but he'd played along. He definitely deserved a thank-you dinner, at the very least.

Molly figured she'd better let Kit know what he was in for – or *not* in for in this case. She emailed him before leaving her office, thinking she might be able to grab something that could be reheated.

To: numbersman@gmail.com
From: mmfitz@gmail.com

Subject: food or lack thereof

I should've made it clear before asking you over for dinner that I'm less than adequate at cooking. I mean I can cook potatoes and steak but I don't have food in the house and I don't even know if you are a steak-eater. So, new plan. I'll get takeaway on my way home. I know you like sushi but there are none near me – ergo, fish and chips or Indian? Or if that's all too pedestrian I could hunt for Thai? Even for a non-date-friend meal I suck at this. Sorry! M

She packed up her things, put on her runners and listened for a reply. A few moments later a *bing* signalled on her phone.

To: mmfitz@gmail.com

From: numbersman@gmail.com

Subject: re: food or lack thereof

No worries. I cook. I'll bring the ingredients for something simple and make it at yours. That work?

Crikey. He could and would cook? What a dreamboat! There could only be one reply.

To: numbersman@gmail.com

From: mmfitz@gmail.com

Subject: re: food or lack thereof.

Yay! Bring it!!! I'll get a couple of bottles of wine. I'll text you my address and see you about 7pm.

Oh my GOD, the relief! He wasn't pissed off nor had changed his mind because of her lack of proper skills. She might even enjoy this evening if she could just remember to forget it was the first time she would have ever entertained a man in her own space. *Ever*. Okay, need to put that fact out if my head, she thought, or I'll begin to freak out and that isn't acceptable. She needed her head straight and her mind clear. She was about to tell an almost stranger about her big lie. Her living-a-lie life. But oddly, Kit didn't feel like a stranger; he felt like a friend.

Her phone buzzed in her pocket. A text from Kit.

Do you have tins of tomatoes? It's usually a kitchen staple but just wanted to check.

Did she? She closed her eyes for a moment as she visualised her cabinets in the small kitchen. *Yup.* Saved from looking like a total idiot. She texted back in the affirmative and as she walked up the road from the train station to her home, she smiled.

Another text arrived.

Never mind the tomatoes. Do you eat salmon?

She replied, again in the affirmative – it was one of the few fish she would actually choose. This could be fun. She'd get to see Kit Elliot in a new light. Maybe get to know him a little. She lowered her work bag as she dug for keys and, if she'd been in a different mood, could have bemoaned the fact that her first male non-family guest wasn't even a boyfriend. Oh well.

Molly hurried through the small apartment plumping cushions, whisking old magazines into the recycling bin and cleaning down the counters. She put the bottle of white wine in the freezer and placed the red next to the fireplace. She had a habit, a damn good one she acknowledged, of leaving the fire set in the morning before she left for work on a Monday, just in case she would arrive home exhausted and chilly during the week and there it would be, all ready for her. As it turned out, she rarely lit it during the week as most of her time was spent at her computer in her home office/spare room and she had a space heater there if needed.

She had put a match to the fire first thing upon arriving home and a bright blaze danced merrily in the grate.

She set the table in the kitchen, using old bone-handled cutlery purloined from her grandmother's house, and a set of place mats and napkins bought on a holiday in Brittany.

The French knew how to do table-dressing that was for sure. She picked a few tulips from the large terracotta pots in the tiny back yard and plonked them unceremoniously into a jam jar. Yes, she needed to purchase a couple of vases, but it was far down her list of 'must buys'. A jam jar could suffice just fine. Now the age-old question – *what the hell to wear*?

Deciding to let her other self be on display this evening, Molly chose a well-worn flowy skirt in royal-blue velvet. She added a loose cotton long-sleeved T-shirt in a lighter blue and several strings of beads in a variety of colours, shapes and sizes, including both the blues she was already wearing. Happy with her look, she slipped into her old comfy Doc Marten Mary Janes matched with stripy cotton tights. Kit was going to get a shock, that was for damn sure. Before she could decide what to do with her hair, the doorbell rang and, glancing crossly at the alarm clock on her bedside table, she groaned. It was bloody five past seven already. Pulling the clip from her hair, she ran her fingers through her curls and went to open the door.

When she opened the door wide and smiled straight into Kit's eyes, he lost his breath. Just for a second or two but there it was, gone. Static. No breathing. His lungs simply stopped working. Molly was a vision in shades of blue, her eyes the bluest of all. And her hair, *holy fuck*, her hair. Masses of it. All around. All over. Curls spiralling off in all directions. Absolutely outrageously gorgeous. He didn't know if his mouth actually fell open but Molly tilted her head to one side – making those waves ripple and sway – in a questioning gesture.

"Right," he said, clearing his throat. "Hey. I'm here." God, he was a frigging disaster. Talk about stating the obvious but, since it was imperative he stay in character, he supposed he should act like the dork he was portraying so perfectly.

"Come in," Molly said, her smile widening. She stepped back and reached to take one of the bags he was carrying as he crossed the threshold. She peeped out behind him and noticed his bike. "You cycled here? With all this?" She hefted the bag. "Are you mad? That must have been crazy difficult. Let's put these in the kitchen and you can wheel the bike into the shared hall – it'll be safer."

With that she turned and strode in what he assumed was the direction of the kitchen. He followed, still slightly dazed, put his other shopping bag down and returned to the front entrance where he collected his bike and left it leaning against the hall dado rail. He shut the front door and, inhaling deeply, headed back into the fray.

Molly had begun emptying the bags and was holding each item up for inspection.

He joined her in taking out the shopping. "Do you really not cook much? What do you do for food?"

"Well, now. That's a question." Molly appeared to give it some thought. "I eat out quite a lot. And, in fairness to myself, I lived at home till just a couple of months ago – early February in fact, so I mostly ate at home. And I am mortified to admit, my mum still sends casseroles home with me." She raised her hands in the universal gesture of defeat. "I know, I'm a walking disaster. But I was given loads of cookery books so I know I will get around to that project. At some stage."

Kit chuckled. "I can't believe you consider learning to cook for yourself a project."

He began unwrapping the salmon and, without invite, pulled open drawers and cupboard doors as he looked for the utensils he required. He gathered the tin foil, black pepper and butter he had brought from his own home and started to make his parcels.

"White wine?" he asked as he turned on the oven, "but

no worries if you don't. Water will do." He retrieved a small baking dish from his bag as Molly stared, fascinated by his forethought.

"I have both," she said, answering his wine question and took a Sauvignon Blanc from the freezer.

He nodded approvingly and splashed some in around the pieces of salmon.

She took the bottle back and poured some into two glasses.

"Can you talk me through what you're doing so I can repeat it another time if it's tasty?" she asked.

"*If* it's tasty?" Kit tried to sound offended but Molly was so natural he knew she was asking because she sincerely wanted to know. He held up the packet of microwaveable brown and wild basmati rice. "I realise I should have checked before I came but I assume you have a microwave? This is a really quick, tasty and healthy way to get grains and fibre."

She stared at him while pointing to the microwave on the counter next to the toaster.

He could feel a blush rising in his cheeks. "Okay, I know I sound like a granddad, but when you live alone it's very easy to get into bad habits. Trust me, I've been there."

She raised an eyebrow. "I sense a story here. Do tell," she said, taking a seat and leaning her elbows on the table. "I'm all ears."

Kit handed her a packet of green beans and a scissors. "Maybe later, after you've told me your secrets, I'll divulge some of mine. In the meantime, make yourself useful and trim these."

He reached for a saucepan and filled it with water, putting it on the stove to boil. Checking the temperature of the oven he slid in the dish with the tinfoil parcels of salmon.

Then he began prepping a salad. Quickly he sliced tomatoes, cucumbers, radishes and peppers. He washed some torn lettuce – a mix of arugula, butter, romaine, iceberg and a handful of rocket. Fishing under the sink he found a salad spinner and took care of the leaves.

He was conscious of Molly happily snipping away at the table and when he glanced at her and saw the tip of her tongue peeping out between those luscious lips, he did his best to discourage an unwanted surge of lust. Now was not the time. It was never the time to get involved with a co-worker on a case. Especially one he wasn't a hundred-per-cent sure of. His gut told him she was solid, but he knew he had to have hard cold facts to keep his boss happy. He'd get those. In time. This evening was for fact-finding of a different kind. And maybe even some fun and relaxation. He glanced at Molly again and realised he was really looking forward to the next few hours.

The man could cook. Yes, it was simple fare – perhaps she could indeed manage it herself – but that didn't stop it being delicious and tasty. She was well impressed and finished writing down the entire step-by-step process. She'd make it for the girls next week, she decided, and completely blow them away.

They cleared the plates and Molly pulled two Magnum ice-cream bars from the freezer. "These are part of my staples," she said, tearing open the packet. "The ones with the almonds are my faves. And almonds are healthy, right?"

Standing, his back to the counter, Kit took his, discarded the rapper in the bin and bit in. The crackle of chocolate snapping as he did drew Molly's attention to his mouth. It was a fine mouth. Firm lips, not too pink, not too full. She disliked a wet lip on a man. It was distracting and not in a good way. And since she didn't fancy women, or if she did it was only in the abstract of beauty and form, she didn't notice female lips. But Kit's mouth had a way of pulling her attention. As for his teeth, he definitely had those done Stateside. They had that straight white look that used be seen only on Americans but the Irish, in fairness, had caught up and had good orthodontic practices. Still, there was something about an American smile. Kit's, anyway, was … sexy, she supposed. Molly was not known for wooing men, for swiping right on Tinder or whatever app was the choice de jour. She rarely dated. She'd had a few boyfriends over the years but nothing serious and none who made her think in terms of sexy when considering the man's mouth.

They opened a bottle of red to have with their ice-cream dessert and found seats in the living room, the fire giving off a warm glow. She took the couch, shoes kicked off, feet tucked up underneath her skirt and Kit sat in the old but oh-so-comfy armchair. Molly considered him from beneath lowered lashes. He really shouldn't be handsome. He was, though, in that understated way, the Clark Kent bumbly awkward way. His hair fell over his forehead as usual, his glasses needed shoving up his nose and then she noticed his hands. *Oh. My.* He held the ice cream in one hand, the other propped open beneath to catch drips. Even as she studied the long fingers and broad palm, he shoved up from his seat, strode to the kitchen and returned with paper towels. He handed a sheet to her.

"Don't want to mess your carpet or my trousers. But this was a great idea. The perfect amount of sweetness."

He sat back down for all the world like he belonged there. In that chair, in her living room, her kitchen, her home. Molly tested that feeling internally, listening to her senses, waiting for alarm bells, but none sounded. *Huh.* She relaxed back, wrapping the wooden stick from her treat in the paper and putting it on a side table.

Kit collected her rubbish and with his own in hand

went to the fire, tossed them in and added more fuel. Sitting back down, he took his glass of red wine, crossed his long legs at the ankles and studied her quizzically.

"What? Do I have ice cream on my face?"

His mouth twitched. "No, but I'm waiting. I want to hear the story of why you, hiding from a person, had to bury yourself into my torso rather than face them. Spill. You owe me."

Molly groaned. *Grrr*. She did owe him. She had used him and now instead of her feeding him as a thank-you, she'd been fed, and rather deliciously, by him.

"Okay," she said, "I know when I'm beaten. But I warn you, it's nothing spectacular or anything. But it is my secret. Hang on a sec." She got up from the couch, grabbed the bottle of red from the table and topped up their glasses. "You may need this and, even if you don't, I do."

She got herself comfortable and, glass in one hand and the end of her necklace clutched in the other, she began her story.

Even as she recounted her childhood – briefly – who needed a year-by-year? – she knew she must sound like a total spoiled brat. There was no trauma, no drama, no awful siblings pulling her hair – no, wait, that part did happen – no uncaring parents. She described how her family gelled. How they connected. She knew she was lucky, privileged.

But it had never been enough. She told Kit about her talent in art. She explained that her grandparents on both sides were cultured, artistic and indeed patrons of the arts in many ways. One set had a wing endowed in their name in an art gallery in Dublin. The other side had names inscribed on plaques on doorways around the city, mentioning their literary contribution to not just Ireland but the world. Every Fitzgerald sibling had grown up with visits to the theatre, the concert hall, art galleries, literary talks and recitals. They had all been offered, encouraged, to play an instrument. They'd been given acting lessons and dance lessons.

Privileged indeed.

When she had shown signs of artistic talent, her parents had been thrilled. Sure, her older sister Caro could draw well – she went on to study art history, and her other sister Ali was an amazing chef and master baker with her own TV show, for God's sake. But Molly could *really* draw. Extremely well. She had an amazing eye and could replicate anything put in front of her. But, even better than that, she imbued everything she drew or painted with *life*. Her work shone. It dazzled. People *wanted* it. She knew from as early as ten years old that she would go to Art College and become a painter. Everyone knew it. It was assumed. A given.

Except, as her teens progressed, Molly began to doubt herself. Not her talent, but her desires.

"So, wait," Kit interrupted. "You really are that talented in something completely unrelated to numbers, to accounting, to finance?" He took a sip of wine, waiting for her answer.

"Yes," she said. "I really am. That's no boasting. I can draw and paint, in pretty much any medium. I even like watercolours as it takes patience and I've discovered I have a lot of patience when it comes to getting an end result. I suppose that's where the numbers come in."

"So, you went to college to do accounting? Despite what your family wanted?"

"Ah, no. Not exactly. And herein lies the problem." She stretched her legs out, readjusted her position on the couch and held a cushion to her belly. "Basically, I went to art college. It was fine. I did fine. Okay, I did very well. But I was bored. *Sooooo* bored. There was nothing new. Nothing fresh. Not even my own brain, and that was the worst of it." She looked straight at Kit before continuing. "My lying began in fifth year in school. I took extra classes in economics and accounting and dropped art. I didn't need to study art, for God's sake. We were surrounded by art history books at home, I knew the curriculum from my pals taking it so I just slid into the other classes instead. I sat art for my Leaving Cert, aced it. But I also got As in higher maths, accountancy and economics. I didn't let my parents see my results sheet as all they were interested in was if I got the A in art. I'd already been accepted into college based on my portfolio so that just cemented it." She sighed. "I should have told them about my other subjects but the prevailing thought process in my house was people who had 'maths brains' had zero imagination, couldn't think for themselves – as least not laterally or universally – and were boring as – well, as anything that you can think of that doesn't include the arts. It put me in a difficult position."

Kit leaned forward in his seat. "I don't really understand why. Could you not have just shown them your results? They would have seen that your brain works in several ways and maybe they would have been proud of you."

"I was afraid to take the chance."

"What happened next?"

"I went to college as I said. But by second year I was also doing accounting at night. Twice a week I'd pretend I was staying late for project work but instead attended classes that would ultimately bring me my other degree. I used an accelerated programme as I found the early stuff easy."

"Impressive. You did two degrees at the same time."

"You did too, I think you said. So, no biggie. All I know is the night-time degree did not bore me. Not at all. I *loved* Tuesday and Thursday nights. I'd come out of the class buzzing with new knowledge, new awareness of how things clicked. Worked together. Made sense."

"When did you eventually tell your parents?" Kit put down his wineglass and braced his elbows on his knees, his face full of interest and, it had to be said, some amusement.

Or maybe it was bemusement, Molly couldn't be sure.

"Tell them? Are you mad? That's the whole point. They haven't a clue. They think I work in an art gallery in town."

Chapter 7

She must be kidding. She had to be. No one could live their life pretending to be doing one thing but actually doing another. Right. *Pot and kettle*, thought Kit, wincing even as his thoughts formed the conundrum. That was *exactly* what he was doing but he wasn't admitting it to anyone, not anytime soon. There was no way he could call her on her deception – he was deception personified. But he was being paid for it. It was his job. Hers was a choice.

"Don't any of your family ever visit you at the gallery? And see you aren't there? This makes no sense."

Molly sighed. "I know it's bonkers. I worked in the gallery on Saturdays through my college years and worked the odd opening night – usually Thursdays. Those evenings I skipped my accountancy lectures and some family member, usually Caro or Dev, would swing by to avail of the free wine. Then, when I pretended to continue working there, I made it very clear that my work time was fluid and that I often had to do errands during the day so dropping in wasn't an option. To be honest, they were mostly busy in their own day jobs and I was no more likely to drop in on one of Caro's lectures than she was to swing by the gallery."

Molly shifted on the couch, her thoughts elsewhere

momentarily. He let the silence lie.

She continued. "The real worry was my parents. Dad teaches in Trinity, only down the road, but fortunately his workload this year is heavy and, to be fair, he'd give me a heads-up if he was dropping in. Mum, on the other hand, showed up unannounced a few times but Melanie, the owner, was a real star. She covered for me because I still do help out at the special openings, if it's a big one, a particularly well-known artist, and she needs to keep me on side as I do enjoy the banter with the potential buyers. For someone who likes their own company, it's the one time I enjoy social occasions. And I know my stuff. Mum still comes to the ones I'm working and so lives on in blissful ignorance. Neither Ali nor Flynn have any interest in the art world so have never been a threat. But … I know this state of play can't last much longer."

"So what has you keeping a secret career from your parents got to do with hiding from someone the other day? Was it your mum?"

Molly squirmed in her seat. The soft blue of the T-shirt pulled against her breasts and he didn't even notice that. Nope. Not at all.

"*Nooo!*" she groaned out the word. "Worse. It was actually my sister Ali."

"Why is Ali seeing you worse than your mum?" It seemed a fair question, he figured, since her angst seemed to derive from her parents not knowing her secret.

"Because I think she already suspects. Several weeks ago, she accused me of having a doppelganger. But, of course, it wasn't a lookalike – it was *me*. She went on and on about how this person looked so like me but she knew it couldn't be because this person was dressed smartly, in business attire. And we all know I would *never* look smart."

Molly took a long drink and closed her eyes on a sigh.

Kit considered all she was telling him and, importantly, what she was keeping back. He wasn't a fool. He could read between the lines as much as the next person. And he also knew what it was like to be pigeonholed. Labelled as one thing, knowing it wasn't the *whole* thing.

"Where do you come in the family?" he asked.

"The baby."

"Ah, it starts to make sense. How many siblings do you have?"

"What do you mean '*Ah*'? And I'm the youngest of five."

She sounded curious now which was better than disheartened which was definitely how she'd been beginning to sound.

"Your family cares about you, obviously. You fit the role they've made for you. If you do something different, it throws them off. Makes them feel unstable or off-centre. You, in their eyes, must remain as they have moulded you."

"Where did you come up with that mumbo-jumbo psychobabble? How many brothers and sisters do you have?"

"I'll have you know I've studied family dynamics and the laws of sibling relationships. In psychology. At college."

She gave him a long assessing look – and snorted. "Crap. You did not. You're making that up. And how many do you have?"

"None. I'm an only. And how did you know I was fudging the truth?"

Molly grinned. A smile so wide and perfect his heart stuttered. He wasn't sure he'd ever seen a smile quite that beautiful. Full of fun and delight. Natural and unreserved. She had dimples on each side and she looked so young, so damn innocent, that Kit's heart, when it fell back into rhythm from the shock of the smile, felt warmed. He didn't know how that happened and he certainly wasn't about to analyse why but he was aware of it.

"*Gotcha!*" she cooed, delighted. "There is something else I suppose I should tell you if we're going to be sharing secrets but I'm not sure you're ready to hear it. Most people aren't."

"Now I'm intrigued," Kit said.

And he was. But he also felt he needed to go. This was getting out of his control. He felt it slipping away. His aim was to get to know her subtly, understand her. See if she was on the level when it came to BB&M. He wasn't supposed to be enjoying a meal, chatting, studying dimples. That wasn't the plan.

He stood, albeit reluctantly.

"But it will have to be another time. It's getting late and we both have an early start tomorrow. I really should go."

Molly jumped up. "Of course. I'm sorry. I didn't mean to ramble on." She collected the glasses and hurried to the kitchen.

Then she grabbed his jacket and, before he could think of backtracking, she had the front door open and was edging his bike backwards towards it.

Kit felt like shit. He'd made her uncomfortable. He followed her quickly and rested a hand on her arm.

"Wait. Stop. Listen to me." He waited till she met his gaze, her blue eyes strangely luminous in the darker light of the hallway. "I've had a lovely time. Next meal is at my house, though it's not nearly as comfortable as yours. You'll know why when you see it." He dropped his hand from her arm and took hold of the bike. "But I really have to go. I'll see you in the office in the morning. We have to finish our discussion on your secret and figure out how to tell your family."

She opened her mouth to protest – he could *feel* it coming.

"No. I mean it. We'll strategise. You *are* going to tell

your family and if we can't put our clever brains together and find a way, our careers and all our planning and dissecting of information are a waste of time."

He backed the bike out onto the doorstep and carried it down the few steps. Flinging one leg over the crossbar, he readied himself for the cycle home.

"Sleep well!" he called and propelled himself forward, alternatively glad to leave and wishing he could stay.

We will strategise, he'd said. *We*. Molly rinsed the wineglasses and wiped the counters. She might not be a great or even decent cook, but she liked a clean and orderly home. She went about her flat, turning off lights, making sure the fire was low, plumping cushions and straightening throw rugs so they all lay symmetrically against the back of the couch.

We. She had a partner in crime, or in this case, secrets. She hadn't really had a *we* before. Her few friends from school and later, college, were fine but not one of them in either college knew of the others. She was so damn tired of keeping her life compartmentalised that until Kit had suggested they could look at her problem together she hadn't realised how lonely it had all made her feel. Maybe that could change now.

Kit was almost as peculiar as she was. That was kind of comforting. If he was a regular guy, all naturally handsome and suave, she wouldn't be telling him a thing. Guys like that never came on to her anyway. Her list of boyfriends, short though it was, comprised two artists, one activist and one environmentalist. Not your standard Dublin 4 selection of the Declan Twomey squad of men. She didn't mind. Maybe one day, when she was in her thirties or forties, an older man would see her worth and choose her as a companion.

And that was okay. Mostly.

She was the heroine in her own life and she would save her own day. She turned out the lights in the living areas and, following her bathroom ablutions, hung up her clothes and tugged on the long flannel nightdress she preferred. Could this be part of the problem? Her night attire? She laughed aloud as she pulled her duvet up and close about her body. Did she wear clothes for others? Absolutely not, she decided. *God*, she thought a few moments later, that was so untrue. Before she stopped lying to her family maybe she should stop lying to herself.

Molly turned over and shifted on her mattress to get more comfortable. She did wear clothes for others. She had spent the last six years wearing flowing skirts and ancient colourful cardigans and funky scarves all to play the role of art student, art-gallery assistant. Nowadays, as she had her own place and her new job, she wore smart suits and dress-up, grown-up shoes, with her hair tidied away in a clip. Thank God those days of changing en route were over – and there, that was the truth. They *were* over. She had to remind herself that she never needed to apologise for her choices again.

She wasn't there yet. She had to, no, she *and Kit*, had to come up with a way to gently break her real life to her family. As for this evening? Busted. She had totally dressed for Kit. To show him the other side of herself. The side she was used to. Since she was letting him in to her alternative dimension, it had seemed only fair. No one would believe the Molly that went to work each morning in navy and grey suits was an artist too. He'd seemed surprised, but not, thankfully, too shocked.

Usually clued in to how other people were feeling, oftentimes too much, Molly had found Kit a bit of a stone wall. She hadn't, admittedly, tried hard – it had felt intrusive somehow – but she found it hard to get a read on him. Her previous boyfriends had been easy. They had wanted one thing. Yes, sex. Obviously. But when that was unforthcoming, they, in fairness, accepted her offer of companionship. *Friendship*. If Molly could have earned a euro for every time she had friend-zoned a man, she'd be buying her smart suits in boutiques, not regular department stores. She'd have sex one day, she thought, *she hoped*, but that day was not today. Or tonight. Obviously. She wasn't even in the mood to try the few toys her sisters had made her buy.

Tonight was all about the numbers. As she closed her eyes, she let herself go over column upon column of data. Beautiful numbers that did exactly what she requested of them: they added up.

Yet when Molly woke early the next day, her nightdress was twisted around her legs and her heart was hammering. It wasn't numbers she had spent the night dreaming of. It was a tall, dark, dorky nerd named Kit Elliot. She definitely needed to take antacids before bed as *that* dream was way too complicated to decipher, even for her smart brain.

The morning following the dinner with Molly saw Kit organising some work for a couple of undercover cops. He had an 'in' with the police force already and these two owed him a favour. He briefed them thoroughly, gave them a mobile phone to use and told them to wait for a call from Molly. They would then come to her office, play their parts, and leave. Then they would dispense with her services. At that stage Kit knew he would be sure just how far Molly would go for a client and in which direction – on *or* off the books. He hated tricking her like this and wished he could do it another way. But some deep digging on his part had turned up some irregularities on the senior-management accounts – ones that Declan Twomey worked on – and since Molly reported to Twomey, he needed to eliminate that thread.

He sauntered into the canteen for lunch and spied Molly seated by herself, eating a sandwich with one hand and scribbling in a notebook with the other. He chose his own fare from the selection left by the company and plonked himself unceremoniously next to her.

"Hey," he said, full of scintillating conversation.

Startled, she swung her head in his direction, blinking those aqua pools slowly as if she had just woken up. He decided that startling Molly Fitzgerald was a thing he should do as regularly as possible because when she looked at him like that, all wide-eyed and lovely, he was entranced. Who didn't need a little entrancement in their lives? It was now a thing he definitely needed.

"Hey, yourself," she replied. And smiled.

"You know the rules are that you leave work in the actual office and use this canteen for *break* time – that means no work, right?" Kit angled his head to catch a glimpse of her notes but, seeing only a scrawl, he opted for directness. "What are you working on?"

Molly put down her sandwich and pulled the notebook closer. "You'll laugh at me," she said. "It's not work, so I'm not breaking any rules."

God, she was adorable. So honest – *he hoped* – and beguiling.

"What then?"

"I'm compiling a list of things to say to my parents that won't sound hurtful or ungrateful. I'm afraid when I do tell them I'll forget everything I want to say and so I thought a list would be a good start."

Kit adopted an affronted stance. "I thought we were going to strategise together? You can't start without me!"

"I wasn't sure you meant it," she said, her voice low as a few other employees had turned to look in their direction at his tone.

"Of course I meant it. Put it away for now and we'll work on it later. Can you come by my office after five? I'll order in food and we can take an hour after the official workday is done, to help gather your thoughts. We can get a head start on the strategy. Does that suit?"

Molly smiled again, straight at him. "Perfect," she said and closed the notebook.

Now, he thought, would be a good time to ask her to come to the swanky dinner dance he was supposed to attend. Could he use it as a swap-a-favour kind of deal with her? He'd help with telling her parents and she could be his plus-one. Yeah, he reckoned, that'd work. He'd bring it up this evening and wait till their strategising was done to guilt her into being his 'date'. It puzzled him that he believed he'd have to entreat her into attending. Getting dates, hell, getting laid was not ever a problem for him. When he wasn't playing a dorky accountant, he cleaned up okay and his lady friends had never complained. But Molly was a challenge in a different way. She was such a mixture of sass, smarts and innocence. He wasn't yet sure which of those traits attracted him the most, but he was pretty damn sure they were neck and neck.

He ordered Indian, having checked for any allergies and/or preferences and was laying out the containers on his office table when Molly walked in, a bounce in her step.

"You look pleased with yourself," he commented, setting knives and forks to one side on top of a bunch of paper napkins.

"I had a very good day." She all but glowed as she spoke.

Without waiting for him to serve, she angled her way around his desk and snagged a piece of Peshwari naan,

81

tearing it in two and handing him half. "*Mmm*, delicious!" she said around the fragrant flatbread. "That group account that was bothering me got in touch!"

Oblivious to Kit's sudden stillness, she prattled on happily. "They were great. I met with a really nice guy from the firm called Dave Larkin, for coffee and a brief chat. He does the books for them and he told me they had put in a trigger to see if the person managing their account would catch it. I knew it! I can't wait to tell Declan I called that one. They seemed very nice in general, as a company, and I just hope they pay on time and ask for me again." She turned from dishing out food on her plate and grinned at him.

Shit. He felt like a rat. He had played her, arranged for all this to fall into her lap and now it was going to be taken away. Should he warn her there would be no payment, no repeat business? That there hadn't, in fact, been any real business to start with? That the Dave Larkin meeting was just a set-up?

No. He couldn't betray the people paying him, though it sure felt like he was betraying her. It wasn't a feeling or situation he relished. The situation was not new to him. Many times in the past he'd had to dissemble, use subterfuge, even con people outright, but it hadn't ever bothered him before. Lying to Molly, intentional and necessary as it was, felt like he was doing something really wrong.

"Good for you," he said instead of owning to the truth. "I'm glad you got that sorted." He took his own plate and began loading it with a lamb saag dish and some rice. They took seats on the far side of his desk. He'd already pushed back various items to create space and pulled in two chairs from the canteen.

Molly paused in lifting a fork of food to her mouth and said, "Not that I'm complaining, but didn't you say the next time we ate it would be at your home? You've seen mine – isn't it time to show me yours?"

Kit stared at her in bewilderment. Didn't she know she had just made all manner of suggestions with that last sentence? Her face was calm, innocent and not remotely flirty so maybe not. God, she really was naïve. He swallowed and took a sip of water.

"Yes. I did say that but I'm reneging on that suggestion. For good reason."

"What reason? Is your home a disaster? I wouldn't mind. I know I'm a neat freak but I'm okay with mess as long as it's not mine."

Kit quirked his eyebrow at her in disbelief.

"Oh alright, I hate mess, no matter whose it is," she agreed and laughed. "But I won't judge. I promise."

"It's not the mess or lack of it. It's … it's just not ready." Kit didn't know how to explain.

"Explain."

He groaned. "Did you just read my mind?"

"Not exactly," Molly replied with sincerity.

Kit noted her suddenly serious expression.

"What do you mean '*not exactly*'. Are you psychic?" And wouldn't that just put the damn cat among the pigeons? All he would need on this job was someone second-guessing him and figuring out his game plan.

Molly shifted on her seat. She wiped her mouth with her napkin, drawing his attention to her lips and if that wasn't a classic distraction technique, he didn't know what was. Unfortunately, he knew by now that wasn't Molly's style. He was being distracted. Him. She wasn't doing anything on purpose. But, God, that *mouth*.

"That's for another day," Molly said politely. Firmly. "I want to know about your house and what its collection of issues are. I assume there must be some or we wouldn't be here in the office."

That was another thing that intrigued Kit about her.

Another woman would not bring up the not-going-to-his-house scenario because they would think he was stalling them due to lack of interest. With Molly, what you saw was what you got. Okay, other than the whole 'hiding her real self from her family' part. Maybe she just didn't hide with him. She was guileless and open. It was utterly charming. Refreshing. Addictive.

It was time he shared a part of himself. The part that wasn't also living a lie. Christ, they were a pair.

"I live in my gran's house. Well, technically, it's mine. She left it to me when she passed last year."

"She died, Kit, remember. She didn't pass anything or anywhere, she died. You need to say the words. I accept the term 'passed away', or even for those for whom religion is a thing 'passed on', like to heaven, but passed, on its own, just drives me crazy. Was she religious? Are you? God, never mind, that's too personal. What age was she?"

Molly spoke in a simple direct way that he couldn't take offence at, even though his gut hurt to hear it. But she was right. People rarely said die or death or dead anymore for fear of upsetting others. Were they all too precious to deal with the facts? Not Molly Fitzgerald anyway. And she didn't shy away from the religion card either.

"Right, she died." He cleared his throat. "She was eighty-two and until months before her death had been sprightly and active. Then that damn car hit her, she broke her hip and never really recovered." He paused. Took a breath, then another. "And she *was* religious, or I remember her being so. Not a daily communicant, but a weekly Mass-goer. I made sure she had the Last Rites, and a Catholic burial, as she wished, but she didn't pray the Rosary every night or anything. I went to Mass with her as a kid but I'm not exactly a staunch believer now. Time and circumstances can change a person."

He glanced up and caught Molly watching him, chewing thoughtfully, her eyes sombre.

"Anyway," he continued, "the house is now mine but I haven't had time to make it mine, if you know what I mean. The few months before she pass ... died, my mother and I took it in turns coming over to stay here so we could visit with her in the home, but neither of us focused on the house or its state. So, it's in a bit of a mess. I've been trying to sort through her things – all her furniture, her stuff, was also left to me so it's ... a lot."

"What did she leave your mum?"

Kit stared at Molly. Did she just ask that incredibly personal question? No one had asked that. They wouldn't dare. It was kind of rude. *Wasn't it*? But this was Molly. Guileless, remember? Not a hurtful bone in her body.

So, he told her. "Half of her savings. Gran worked in Guinness's all her adult life and had been given sound investment advice to help her save, both while she was working and with her retirement pay-out."

"What position did she hold?" Molly wiped her hands on her napkin and reached over to place the closed container in the brown-paper carrier bag. "No, let me guess," she said. Tapping a finger against her lip in a thoughtful manner she narrowed her eyes. "She did their books. Their ledgers back in the day and eventually their accounts proper."

Kit was stunned. *What the hell?* How on earth could she have guessed that? Maybe it wasn't a stretch based on his own abilities but, come on! "Did you google her?"

Now it was Molly's turn to be stunned. "Your granny can be googled? Like with actual results? *Hah!* That's a hoot. No, I didn't google her – I don't even know her name."

"Do it," he said, smug now, knowing what she would find. "Hannah Elliot."

She whipped out her phone and began typing. "*Oh! My*

ffffing God! Your granny is a legend!" she gasped as she unearthed the facts concerning a very special woman.

Hannah had begun as a clerk, worked hard doing ledgers and bookkeeping. Before long, her boss noticed she was coming up with new, better ways of basic accounting and he gave her more and more responsibility. By the time she was in her early forties she was head of her department and had legions of trainees following her every word. In her mid-fifties she took all the accountancy exams, never having had a chance to go to college, and she got top of her class in every one. Not only was that a really cool accomplishment but add in that she'd never finished school and was a considerably more mature student than even the mature students. She won several prizes in the accounting field.

As Molly squealed, Kit knew she must be reading the part about his gran winning the same prize Molly herself had won. She looked up from her phone, her mouth open in what he could only assume was surprise and he hoped, with a measure of pride, awe.

"A legend," she repeated, her voice hushed. "*Wow!* You must be the proudest grandson *ever*. And she was beautiful too – brains and beauty. Just *wow*."

Kit found himself grinning back at Molly, relief and delight at her reaction flooding him. Warming him. Tightening his throat. He rarely told anyone about his gran's achievements but he'd known, felt, that Molly would get it.

"Yeah. She was the best. I'm ridiculously proud of her. And, more importantly, she knew it. She and Mum didn't always have the best of relationships and they were estranged for a while. But when I came into the picture, all that changed."

Kit put down his own fork, stood and wandered his office space, hands shoved into his pockets. He could feel Molly watching him but she stayed silent, letting him reminisce.

"A baby, especially a fatherless one, can really bring two mothers together. I was born in the US – Mum had gone over illegally to look for work, but my natural dad was of Irish descent. He scarpered when he heard I was on the way. We never talked about him. And my mother brought me home, when I was tiny, to Stoneybatter and Gran."

Kit turned to gauge her reaction. She was chewing thoughtfully on a piece of naan.

"Those kinds of dads are better off absent," she said. "Though, I know from personal, or rather family experience, the absent father can rear his ugly head when least expected."

He raised a curious brow. "I sense a story."

She waved it away. "Another time. This is about you. So, no dad growing up then? Uncles? Strong male role models?"

Kit winced. That was also definitely a story for another time. "Too complicated and convoluted to go into now. It's a short and unpleasant tale. Let's clean up, get a coffee and start strategising. This is supposed to be your planning time."

Molly appeared to take the hint and, without another word, she packed the half-empty containers away and they took the bag down to the kitchen area. She put the bag in the fridge and brewed some coffee.

"What dessert would you like?" she asked as she opened the treat cupboard. "We have chocolate digestives, fig rolls, some weird brownie thing – definitely a no – and, *hmmm*, jersey creams. Not the greatest selection. Pick your poison."

"Milk or dark chocolate for the digestives?"

"An excellent question. And your answer may determine our friendship, so be careful."

"No pressure, then. Dark all the way."

A grin split Molly's face. "Definitely going to be best mates with you. Correct answer." She reached for the pack as he poured two coffees and they headed back to his office where they could relax.

Kit could not keep the smile from his face as they settled down and dipped their biscuits into the warm liquid. "Now," he began, "how do you want to play the big reveal?"

Chapter 8

She texted everyone. Sunday lunch was a normal get-together in the Fitzgerald household. Her mum usually put on a big pot of something – not the usual roast as it might not stretch – but a stew or casserole or meat pie. The siblings had been known to bring a plus-one on occasion and there were times, though rare, that no one could go. It wasn't a dictate but, if you were about, it was expected you'd turn up. Molly let her parents know she'd be bringing a friend but didn't specify who. She then texted all the siblings and their significant others and asked that, if possible, they attend on Sunday. As a carrot, she said she had something to tell them. And when the barrage of replies came asking for details, she deflected.

They, she and Kit, had decided she would use him as a buffer. He was willing, poor guy, and she purposefully didn't alert him to the madness that was her family. As an only child, he wouldn't be used to the ribbing and the teasing. Or the insults, friendly though they might be. He'd see it in the flesh, soon enough.

Then they had argued over what she should wear. As Molly got ready for the lunch, she mused over the fact that Kit got it. He understood that armour of clothing. But they disagreed. She wanted to wear her own arty clothes so she'd be comfortable. Kit said that was a cop-out. A pretty stormy argument ensued. He won.

"You wear the clothes for the job you want," he'd insisted. "And in this case, you need to wear the clothes for the career you now have. This is also who you are. Part of who you are as much as the creative arty side. Own it. Embrace it. But maybe add a little colour."

She'd thrown a biscuit at him for that remark. Coming from the most boringly/drably dressed man ever, he had some nerve.

She took his advice. Staying with charcoal grey in the suit itself, she changed the style a little. Bought one with a jacket that had a waist.

As Molly stood before the mirror now, her nerves edging up, even she had to admit the aqua blouse underneath, the string of beads – a nod to the old her – and more fitted jacket really looked well. She slipped into her heels and twirled her curls up into a messy bun. Soft but away from her neck, giving her a more business-like look. And then she brought out the big guns. Blue eyeliner and brown shadowing. Crikey! Even she knew that was a good look for her. She made a note to wear it more often. A dash of mascara and swipe of pink lippy and she was set.

She heard the beep of the taxi and, stomach churning, straightened her shoulders, picked up her shoulder bag and headed out the door.

The taxi stopped in the village of Dalkey where Kit was waiting outside a landmark pub. He had taken the DART there. When he opened the taxi door and got inside, she gulped. He was wearing his glasses, his hair still flopped forward, he had the Clark Kent vibe for sure but, wow, gone was the goofy waistcoat and slacks, his normal office attire. Instead he wore a white button-down, a navy sweater, and navy trousers. Proper man trousers. With a belt. She glanced down at his footwear. Converse. And no socks. That shouldn't work. But, it so did.

She swallowed, her throat suddenly dry. "You look great," she said, sticking with honesty. Though if she was totally honest, she would throw in a few superlatives. She didn't want to even imagine those words – that could lead to a very dangerous path indeed.

"I must return the compliment," Kit said, staring at her intently. "What have you done that's different?" His eyes searched hers but, being a man, he failed miserably.

"It's called make-up," she said with a twist to her lips. "And, yeah, I know it does wonders and all, but it's a hassle in the morning."

"Have you ever worn it to the office?"

"God, no. It's bad enough being a curvy woman without drawing attention to the face as well. I want to be taken seriously."

He studied her face and then let his eyes drop to her blouse, and the beads, the fitted jacket, her heels. "You look pretty badass to me. Both serious and sexy."

She frowned. "See? I don't want to look sexy. Not ever." She knew she sounded defiant but she'd seen what sexy could do. No one took you seriously. They only wanted the sex part. And your brain was completely discarded as unnecessary.

"Never?" Kit sounded incredulous. "Why not? It can come in handy at times – I'm reliably informed."

"Well, it's not on my radar. Can't imagine a time when it might be." She turned from his intent gaze, feeling herself flush and wondering at the fluttering in her belly. She glanced out the window. "We're here. Game on."

Standing outside her family home, she paused and took a deep breath. Kit squeezed her arm gently.

"It will be fine. They'll be proud of you. You'll see. It

may take a bit of getting used to, but it will be worth it. No more hiding."

Christ, what a hypocrite he was. No more hiding. How's that working out for you, Elliot, he asked himself. He was the worst. Hiding in plain sight and keeping secrets was his modus operandi. And Molly hadn't a clue. She trusted him, he could tell, and the mere fact that he couldn't tell her a real thing about himself sucked.

That wasn't strictly true. She knew about his gran and a little about his mum, and the fact he didn't know who his birth father was. That was a lot right there. More than he told most. Certainly, more than he ever told a co-worker. But therein lay the rub. To him, Molly didn't feel like a co-worker. She felt like a friend. And one should never lie to a friend.

That was not working out well for him.

He took notice of his surroundings as they walked across the gravel driveway. A beautiful home from the Georgian era, it was double-fronted and three storeys high. A creeper, not yet fully in bloom covered the front walls and the door, with its elegant fan light above, stood open. Flowerpots and beds were arranged beneath the windows and the grass areas to the left and right were neat and well kept. This was a loved home, he thought as they approached the door. Voices could be heard inside and, as they sidestepped the various vehicles, Molly named the people he was to meet. It was then he realised he didn't know anything about her siblings other than she was youngest of five. And she had the one sister who she'd hidden from before, Ali. He didn't even know the others' names. That was about to change.

"Dev and Frankie's jeep," she touched the older vehicle, "Gabe's SUV, and the boring grey sedan belongs to my eldest brother Flynn. He has zero style when it comes to cars. But there's a reason."

Kit stilled. *Flynn. Fitzgerald.* That couldn't be a

coincidence, could it? He never gave a thought to her last name. It was common enough. But this, if it was the Flynn he knew and worked with, this was a whole different matter.

No time to figure it out now. Molly was calling "*Hello!*" as she entered the hallway.

It was a lot. As the family were milling around the kitchen and what seemed like dozens of people busied themselves going back and forth between counters and the large table in the centre which was already set, he noted how colourful everything looked. How charming. Like a set for a *Home Style* magazine.

He glanced around the room as Molly paused when one by one the collective stopped talking, silence descended and *everyone* stared at her. She threw him a 'See? I told you' look and straightened her shoulders.

Before the comments could start, Kit took charge. He stepped forward, reaching a hand out to greet the older woman who was staring open-mouthed at Molly.

"Hi, you must be Mrs Fitzgerald. Molly has told me a lot about you." Okay, that was a minor lie, but hey, anything to cover the awkward silence.

The woman took his hand, swinging her head back and forth between her daughter and Kit.

"Pleased to meet you," he said. "and thank you so much for including me in this Sunday get-together."

They shook hands and she insisted he call her Jo, then he turned to shake the hand of the older man who had moved from where he was filling a decanter on the sideboard.

"Sir, a pleasure to meet you," Kit said in his best 'I'm a decent bloke, no need to worry' voice.

Molly found her own voice and, clearing her throat, said, "Hey, everyone, this is a friend of mine from work, Kit Elliot! Kit, this is my family. I'll let them introduce themselves so you can remember their names better but, despite the looks they are all sending your way, they don't bite. Much. Jesus, Flynn, stop glaring, you'll scare him off!"

Kit caught Flynn's narrowed eyes and shook his head very slightly, indicating, he hoped, that they shouldn't reveal their acquaintance. Of all the Fitzgeralds in the country, Kit had to rock up to this family, the one that had nurtured Flynn Fitzgerald, the badass police operative who had ties to world security departments in several countries in Europe not to mention the CIA and the FBI. It was a mystery to Kit how such a young man, late thirties only, could be such a high-ranking official and so sought after, but he'd heard the stories, he'd researched the legend, he'd listened to the chat about Fitzgerald, he knew the respect the man held. And having worked with him since last summer, on and off on several financially driven cases, he gladly gave him his own respect. He certainly didn't want to lose credence by his involvement with Flynn's sister. Interesting that Flynn himself didn't know about Molly's other life. It would be very interesting indeed to see how this afternoon would play out.

Flynn narrowed his eyes, the exact same colour as Molly's, and gave an almost imperceptible nod. Kit released the breath he'd been holding. His cover was safe. For now. But he'd bet he was going to get an earful later.

Introductions followed as each sibling shook his hand. They did so while flipping their heads to Molly and back to him with varying degrees of astonishment, shock, disbelief and downright incredulity. Kit found himself getting defensive on her behalf. I mean, *come on*, he thought. She was wearing a smart suit, not a *swim*suit or anything outrageous. He was just about to speak on her behalf when he gave himself an internal kick. He hadn't the right. They weren't a couple. He was here as support, moral support, nothing else.

And then a stunning woman clasped his hand and said, "Hi, so nice to meet you. I'm Frankie. I voluntarily married into this madhouse so not sure what that makes me!"

Before Kit could stutter out a response, a man, darkhaired and blue-eyed, wrapped an arm about her shoulders and hauled her close. "Happy," he said, "And smart, that's what it makes you. Hi, I'm Dev, the handsome talented brother. Nice to meet you."

They shook hands and, noticing Kit's starstruck look, Dev took pity on him.

"Yeah, this is Francesca Jones, famous movie star and now famous travel writer. Keep your hands to yourself. She's mine." He grinned as he said it because by the glow on Frankie's face it was patently obvious that no matter what man drooled at her feet, she had eyes for only one.

Kit blinked in total disbelief. Molly was *related* to Frankie Jones? What the ever-loving hell? His world view had just changed – he'd shaken the hand of stardom.

"Don't mind him!" Another Fitzgerald took his hand. "I'm Ali and the silent dude behind me is MacScot. Gabe Mackenzie, actually, but whatever."

The blonde with the short spikey hair had an impish grin and showed no reverence for anything, Kit could tell. He realised that he'd met Gabe before, briefly last summer when he and Fitzgerald had been discussing a case. He seemed like a solid guy and they acknowledged each other with a nod, but no overt recognition on either part. Weren't they the professionals?

"Let's eat!" Jo Fitzgerald called.

Amidst the scramble for seats, Flynn approached him and muttered, "We'll be talking about this. Later."

Kit knew the voice was supposed to intimidate, and normally it would but in this instance Kit felt vindicated. He'd had zero knowledge of the relationship between

Molly and Flynn when he began investigating her and if anyone should be feeling pretty shit about this scenario, it should be big brother.

Molly indicated Kit should sit opposite her, and he sat and spread his napkin on his lap, wondering how this was all going to go down.

The food was delicious. Some kind of beef stew with vegetables, lentils and barley. And a mound of buttery mashed potato that would gladden anyone's taste buds. There was a large bowl of green salad and crusty French bread, courtesy of Ali, it turned out.

"Yeah," she said as he complimented her. "I'm trying my hand at baguettes. Not quite there yet, but if I have to take a trip to France to prefect the art, well, so be it. I'm happy to suffer for my art."

A few chuckles and jibes followed this comment but it was Patrick Fitzgerald who brought the conversation, in a roundabout way, to the issue at hand. The reason they were all there. Molly's text.

"Do you work in the art field also, Kit? In one of the galleries? Or are you a buyer, perhaps?" The last was said with a certain amount of scepticism because, neatly dressed though Kit was today, no one would mistake him for a man with cash for art.

Kit shook his head. "No, Mr Fitzgerald. I'm an accountant."

As puzzled glances went around the table, Kit noticed Gabe had reached behind Molly and appeared to be rubbing her back in a circular motion. She didn't seem at all perturbed and even leaned back into his touch. Kit flicked his eyes to Ali. Was she aware what her boyfriend was doing? They had come across as being in sync when Kit had been surreptitiously watching them earlier, but this seemed like rather blatant behaviour. Her partner was rubbing her sister's back in what could only be described as a moment of intimacy. Molly turned her head slightly and smiled at Gabe, mouthing, *Thanks, I'm okay*. Did he already know about her deception? This was getting confusing.

"But I thought you said you worked with Molly?" said her father. "Do you do the books for her gallery?"

Kit caught Molly's eye and nodded. This was it. This was her time. She needed to come clean. To tell her truth. To trust her family would understand. She stared back at him and he held her gaze unwaveringly. He tried to send her all the good vibes. To show his support. His belief in her.

One by one, the voices around them stopped as all realised that Kit hadn't answered the question and that he and Molly were unnaturally still.

It was time.

Chapter 9

She'd known this time would come. Had wanted it. Yearned for the courage to face it. To be free of the lie she'd been living. The deceit she'd perpetrated on her family. Okay, overly dramatic there, Moll, she told herself. This secret wasn't bad, as such. It wasn't an Ali-sized secret like the one that had rocked the family when it had finally emerged last year. That had been a whopper. This was . . . a more acceptable, whitewashed bland type of secret. Yes, that. It was harmless. No one was injured in the keeping of this secret.

But they might feel hurt. Left out. Bewildered.

Molly knew she was stalling and took a deep breath as she heard the silence in the room. Everyone was waiting for her to speak. Kit nodded again, slightly, urging her on. Another breath.

"I'm an accountant too," she announced. And waited.

No one moved. No one spoke.

Finally, Ali said, "Are you dressed like an accountant because you and Kit are on the way to a fancy-dress party? We could have guessed accountant. Or businesswoman. Advertising exec at a pinch." She looked at the others for confirmation.

They nodded in agreement.

Yes, it seemed her suit was definitely playing its role.

Before she could continue, Frankie spoke. "Wait, should we WhatsApp Caro and let her hear whatever you want to tell us about your party?"

Molly sighed. "There is no party. I'm a qualified accountant. I have been for over a year now." She met her parents' perplexed looks with her chin slightly tilted. "I don't work in an art gallery. I work for an accountancy firm."

More silence.

Then from Frankie again, "I'm calling Caro. This is getting weird." She pulled her phone from her pocket, dialled and waited. Still no one spoke.

Their lack of questions and chatter was freaking Molly out – her family were *never* quiet.

"*Hey, sweets!*" Caro's voice came out loud and clear from Frankie's phone and when she switched to video Frankie turned her phone about to encompass everyone.

Caro waved cheerily at them all and, as she took in Molly's attire, her face was a picture. "Moll! What on God's earth are you wearing? You look like you're heading to an office!" At the complete lack of response from her parents and siblings, Caro's expression changed. "Okay. What's up?"

Molly sighed once more. And then a fierce wave of determination flooded her body. *This was ridiculous.* It was a suit, for goodness sake, not a see-through catsuit! Enough was enough.

"See?" She spread out her hands in an exasperated manner. "This is why I never said anything! I knew the lot of you would slag me and make me feel stupid. But that stops here. I refuse to pretend anymore. I am a qualified accountant. And I'm very smart. I took accounting classes at night from second year in Art College, graduated from both courses with a first in each. I'm numerically gifted as well as artistic and you'll all just have to deal with it." She let out her breath in a whoosh as her family stared back at her.

"So, you *don't* work in the art gallery?" her mother asked tentatively.

"No, Mum, I haven't worked in the gallery since last June. Except for the openings that are extra-important, the ones I make sure you are invited to. So, yes, but only very, *very* part time. I got my last set of accountancy exams the previous September and interned at one of the big firms in Dublin during the following nine months."

"But you went to the gallery every day." Her mum sounded confused. "I saw you head out."

"And did you also see me carry a large tote bag? I changed in the ladies' at the firm every morning. This," Molly indicated her suit, "this is how I dress every day now. And I like it. It's *me*. Or at least, *also* me."

Then the talk broke out, loud and Fitzgerald-style all the way. Everyone speaking at once, with all the questions flying in her direction. The most obvious one they needed an answer to was "Why? Why hadn't she said anything?"

With Caro still on the line and the phone angled in Molly's direction, Molly tried to explain. She turned to see Kit leaning back in his chair, slightly removed from the family group. But she felt him. She needed his silent strength. His presence.

Straightening her shoulders, she said, "This is why. You're all shocked. You can't believe I'm that intelligent. Or that driven. All you've ever seen is what you want to see. Your little sister, your daughter, who fitted nicely into the artistic mould. Slightly funky, arty, odd. We all know I'm odd, that hasn't changed, but I find a peace in my numbers that I've never found in painting."

"But you are so good at art!" her mother practically wailed.

"And in fairness you didn't give us the opportunity to support you, keeping all this a secret," Ali accused her.

"Pot, kettle, Ali," Dev supplied and no one could disagree. "You kept the biggest secret of all, and didn't let any of us in. We could've been there for you. That was your choice, remember, so you can't really blame Moll. And no offence," he grimaced at Molly, "yours isn't quite as harrowing or dramatic."

Ali flushed slightly and Molly saw Gabe rest his hand on Ali's lower back.

Molly turned to her parents. "Look, I get this isn't a big deal, not in the grand scheme, but I felt I'd be letting you both down. You've always been so proud of my talent. Delighted that your family's artistic gifts, from both sides, were passed on. And I do still love to paint. I hope I always will, but it doesn't light me up. Not the way solving a mathematical problem does. I like the way my brain is working."

Molly paused to take stock. Sure, her heart was beating faster than normal, her skin felt slightly clammy, but she hadn't been struck down by lightning. The world was still turning on its axis. She relaxed her shoulders and allowed a small twitch of triumph reach her lips. She would survive and, catching Ali lean back against Gabe, she felt chagrined at how insensitive she must have appeared. How up herself she must have come across! She needed to have a quiet word with Ali.

Caro spoke into the void that is a person waiting on the line. "Go you, Molly, and the clothing looks great! I'll look for some nice blouses for you here in Rome and send them on. Maths whiz! Who knew? See ya!"

To a chorus of goodbyes, Caro signed off and then Molly's dad spoke for the first time since the 'reveal', as she was calling it internally.

"Your great-grandfather, the black sheep of the family

101

on my own father's side, was a mathematician of some note, I believe."

"Now you tell me?" Molly groaned. "Seriously, Dad? I could have used that knowledge as I studied my ass off, night after night. It would have been nice to think some of my ability was inherited."

Kit cleared his throat and spoke for the first time since she'd begun her tale. "Show them your clippings, the awards," he suggested. "It will help them to see your credentials. How valid they are."

As Molly dug beneath the table for her bag, Dev asked, "What awards? Did you win something?" He was so competitive and had won many photography prizes over the years.

"Don't want to be outshone, brother dear?" Molly's voice was muffled as she searched in her tote. She settled back in her seat and, clearing a space, opened a folder out on the table. It was a selection of her certificates as well as newspaper articles lauding her merits and achievements.

Ali snatched it up, flipping each plastic-covered page. "Holy shit! You *are* famous. Here!" She handed the folio to their parents. "Sorry, Moll, I'd no idea. You're fricking awesome!"

Gabe reached over and kissed the top of her head. "You are feeling a lot lighter, aren't you?"

Molly smiled at him. He was an unusual man. So different from your run-of-the-mill police detective, whatever that looked like. Between himself and Flynn, she supposed there *was* no standard. But Gabe was another level different. Molly had sensed it the moment she'd met him and they'd shared a connection ever since. Gabe's talents, for want of a better word, came to him via both sides of his family. His mother was a member of the Osage Nation from Oklahoma and had passed many of her spiritual and sensitive gifts to him. He could sense and read people with

102

uncanny accuracy. He could also trace people using some kind of dream methodology. Molly didn't really understand it all but she believed in him completely. And then there was his granny on the Scottish side. Granny Fiona was a 'seer' and a highly respected member of clan Mackenzie, called upon regularly to help make sense of sundry matters.

Gabe rarely talked about his abilities and he used them as infrequently as possible, while on the job. Ali, not at all an empath, loved to tease him unmercifully about his *awareness* and his absolute lack of it when it came to all things social-media-related. Yet, anyone with half an eye and zero sensibilities could see that those two were a match made in nirvana.

The *oohing* and *aahing* over Molly's awards and written pieces, the praising of her work continued as the selection made the rounds of her family.

"And you used Mary Margaret instead of Molly? Why, love?" Jo was puzzled but unable to prevent a sense of pride entering her voice.

Molly smiled. "I figured none of you would be reading those pages but if you did happen upon them, if I'd used Molly, the name would pop out at you."

Patrick sat back, a glass of red wine in his hand. "It says there you won the highest prize a new accountant can get. When *were* you going to let your family know of your accolades?"

Molly winced at his mild but definitely accusatory tone. More honesty was needed. "I wasn't going to. I didn't see the need. It doesn't make any difference, or at least not to me. I just want to do my job. And I want to continue to study, when I can." She turned towards her new friend to include him in the conversation. "Kit thought you should all see these. It was his idea."

Her father hauled himself up from his chair and reached over to shake Kit's hand. "Thank you, young man – we, the family, appreciate your urging her to do so."

"I felt it was important. You should know just how smart your youngest child is. She's making a real difference at BB&M."

"And what exactly is *your* role in the firm?" It was Flynn who spoke and directed his question not at Molly but at Kit.

Well, shit, what a sly bastard Flynn Fitzgerald was turning out to be! Kit knew he couldn't really blame him, but this was underhand. They both had to continue to pretend not to know each other, fiscal integrity of the firm being at stake, so Flynn was playing the concerned brother. Kit got that. Or thought he did. He didn't have sisters – he didn't know how protective he might be if he had. But two could play at that game.

"I've been hired in a temporary measure to help out during a company-wide audit," he said coolly.

"What are your qualifications? And where did you get them? You sound like you're from Boston or at least spent time there."

Molly interjected, punching Flynn lightly on the arm. "Leave him alone. You're not the boss of me. And it's none of your business what Kit does, how he does it and how good he is. He's my friend and that's all you need to know."

Kit felt a glow somewhere in the region of his chest. She was defending him. Standing up for him. Championing him. They hadn't known each other long but she referred to him as a friend. It was how he was starting to feel about her.

And, yeah, he could go on fooling himself that that was *all* he was feeling. He wasn't about to analyse the tingle along his skin when she was near, the heat in his blood as she walked towards him, her particular smile lighting that beautiful face, the buzz he got when they chatted. The weird thing was, it didn't matter if it was work-related or general chat, her mind and the way she thought, scrutinised and disseminated information fascinated him. No, he wasn't about to go down that road.

He turned to Flynn and reeled off his own degrees.

Then he smiled at Molly. "It's fine. You're lucky to have such a devoted big brother. Though if he's a detective it's surprising to me he didn't figure out your ruse. Maybe he isn't as highly ranked as you said. Or maybe his guard was down."

Flynn narrowed his eyes, threatening retribution, but in fairness what could he say? *Gotcha!* thought Kit, inwardly smirking.

Flynn grunted, turned to his little sister and said, "You've done good, Mary Margaret. We're really proud of you." He kissed her cheek, gave her a small squeeze and, with another glare in Kit's direction, stood up from the table and sauntered out of the room.

Heading back in the taxi later, Kit let Molly process out loud all that had happened. She was on a high and he couldn't blame her. Her revelations could not have gone better. He was thrilled for her and told her so.

"It's thanks to you," she said on a happy sigh. "I don't know how much longer I would have procrastinated. I'm a big baby, I know it. So, seriously, thanks a mill." She leaned into his shoulder, nudging him with her own in an affectionate gesture. "You are *the best!*"

The best. God, if she knew his own secret. If she knew that he was using her to get his own job done, he was pretty fucking sure she would not think him the best at anything. Except lying. He was pretty excellent at that. Amazing what years of practice could do.

The taxi pulled up outside Molly's flat and she turned

to him again. "I owe you, Kit Elliot, big time. We're official friends now so you can call on me to help you, support you or whatever. Even with your gran's place. I can wield a duster with the best of them. I'll help. And be happy to do it. Just let me know."

She climbed out of the taxi which was to continue to the DART station so Kit could get back into town. He waved and closed the door.

He was a coward. He pulled out his phone to ask the question he wished he'd been brave enough to ask in person. He told himself he was allowing her space to think it through. Not to put her on the spot. But, ultimately, he was a coward.

He texted:

Totally forgot to ask earlier but could you come as a plus 1 friend to the BB&M spring gala next Saturday night? I've been asked to attend and now that you are 'out and proud' maybe you could rock a party frock and come along? Let me know within the next few days. It's black tie.

He hit send and then slapped his forehead. He shouldn't have made reference to being out. That was stupid and insensitive. Maybe she was gay. Maybe she had good friends who were and she'd be insulted he was comparing a person's potential vulnerability in coming out to her revealing a secret of her own. God, he was an idiot. Should he apologise? He groaned as he paid the taxi and headed down the steps to get the train.

His phone pinged and he glanced down, half dread, half hope stirring.

A gala! Yay! Send me the deets and I'll be there. I get to dress up – and not in an arty way …

Kit heaved a sigh of relief. She'd come with him.

It'd be okay. And, *phew*, not insulted.

Chapter 10

Molly went shopping.

But not alone. Ali and Frankie would never forgive her if she went solo to outfit herself for a special occasion. And since she had never asked their advice before, this was a big deal all around. She hated dressing up and they knew it and forgave her anyway. And cheerfully signed up for the 'Buy Molly a Dress' expedition.

They met up the afternoon following the big secret reveal and started with a late but light lunch. Molly had taken some personal time from work, a rarity for her. She was getting anxious and could barely eat, but Frankie and Ali were starving so they ate their weight in grilled cheeses. Yes, Ali was eating, actually eating – not pushing her food around her plate as normal – and she was glad. Happiness led to a full tummy, if what she was witnessing was any proof.

"Come on, girls," Molly urged as they lingered over coffee. "Can we just do this?"

Even though Frankie was not a native Dubliner, it was she the women turned to for shopping advice and best stores to hunt down. She was, after all, a former model, world-famous actress and all-around clothes horse. She knew her designers – both national and international – and yet still, damn her, managed to look divine in jeans and T-shirt.

They gathered their belongings and sauntered out onto Grafton Street to hit the boutiques and top-end departments. Molly was partly dreading the venture and partly looking forward to it. Over lunch Ali and Frankie had been so complimentary on her suit attire, exclaiming that they had never even known she, Molly, had such a lovely figure. A waistline had been on display in that suit– never before seen due to her usual flowing garments. Frankie was excited to open up a whole new world for Molly and they had prepped Caro to be available for a WhatsApp call from various dressing rooms – she wanted to be in on the choices.

Two hours later Molly regretted opening her mouth about the gala. She regretted recruiting two women who had endless energy for selection after selection. And she really regretted ever showing her shape. The consensus was she needed a figure-hugging dress with some *va-va-voom* to showcase her curves. Kit needed to see her curves, they said – they meant her boobs – and now Molly *really* regretted ever bringing Kit to their home.

So here she was, sitting on the train clutching several stylish bags in beautiful hues and sporting ribbons as ties. No regular paper bags for these garments. But, wow, she was still feeling stunned with the dress they had all agreed was *the* one.

The comments had almost been funny. Frankie, and Ali who was not known for her fashion senses unless you counted combat trousers, threw around styles like 'fit and flare' and 'fishtail'.

Molly had been insistent. "No fish. None. I'm not pouring myself into something that makes my bum look more ginormous than it already does. I've seen *Say Yes to the Dress* and I know the dangers to be found in all the clever names that really mean tacky satin and loads of bling. I'm having none of that."

But then Frankie suggested 'mermaid'.

Again, Molly was aghast. "No marine creatures of *any* variety," she groaned but Frankie calmed her down.

"I mean I want the theme or vision of a mermaid – not the actual skin-tight look. Trust me."

When Molly hung up the dress a little while later, she couldn't restrain the dreamy sigh that escaped. It was beautiful. A deep sea-foam taffeta, with a ruched bodice and fitted to below the waist, extolling that asset big time. Then it flowed to the ground – not all poofy – it was a stiff taffeta after all, but with an elegance and style that amazed the viewer. And it was strapless. *Almost* strapless, Molly amended. She had balked at no straps and refused to even try it on – she had boobs, for God's sake, and couldn't anyone see that waving those puppies around would be a disaster without support? The stylist, of whom Frankie was, naturally, a client, saved the day. She had produced a chiffon scarf in the exact colour, intending it to be used as a wrap with the dress, but magically affixed it as a halter-neck coming from the outer sides of the corseted bodice and encircling the back of her neck. Frankie had suggested that the corset and structure would be enough, but Molly was adamant. There was no way she was walking into a ballroom, full frontage on show, without at least the minimum of support. And the fact that the addition of the attached chiffon created a unique gown made Molly extra happy.

They had gone for a coffee while the stylist made the adjustments as a favour to Frankie and, when they returned, the woman had included an extra wrap as an accessory, and some aquamarine diamanté hairpins to nestle in her curls. There were still shoes to buy, but Molly wasn't worried about that. Frankie knew someone who knew someone who could get her fitted by the weekend. Of course she did.

Molly was set.

Chapter 11

Kit adjusted his bow tie, shoved his hands in his pockets and leaned against a pillar. Molly had refused to come to the event *with* him, citing all manner of excuses regarding hair and footwear, but promised to appear before nine o'clock and the beginning of the meal which was to be followed by speeches, a charity auction and finally dancing. The hotel ballroom was splendidly decorated in spring flowers and the grandeur of the dresses and the tuxedos made the whole room look like something from the nineteenth century.

Sensing something, a stir in the crowd, a hush or a pause, Kit turned and felt the breath leave his body. She was *radiant*. Glowing. And, like in the movies, the crowd parted to let her walk right up to him. Her lips curved in a small smile but her eyes were hesitant. Pulling his hands from his pockets he reached for her, taking her hands in his as he simply stared.

Realising the silence was becoming awkward, he cleared his throat and catching his wayward breath spoke in a reverent tone.

"You are beautiful. The colour, the dress, shit, your *hair*, it's . . . incredible. You look incredible." God, he was a tongue-tied idiot. But *Christ*, she was a vision. The curls were partially attached to the sides of her head but more spiralled down about her almost bare shoulders. He didn't know shoulders could make his groin tighten and his stomach clench. Her skin glowed, sparkled. Could skin do that? The neckline of her gown arched over her breasts but dipped in the centre cleverly but elegantly showcasing her stunning cleavage. Kit had to swallow again as his throat had dried up.

"Thank you," Molly said, her smile widening. "What a perfect reaction! And you look very handsome yourself."

Kit found his voice and, releasing one of her hands, tucked the other in the crook of his arm as he led her to their table. They had been seated at one of the head tables and Kit hoped Molly wouldn't wonder at that choice. Hopefully she'd assume it was because she worked for Twomey. The younger Benson and his wife were at their table, along with two other senior accountants and Declan and his date, Lisa from HR.

Greetings were exchanged and Kit felt a surge of pride as the gentlemen in particular eyed Molly with obvious envy. *Yes, guys, she's with me. The nerd. The geek. Tonight, I get the dream woman. Suckers.* He knew he was both petty and childish and let those feelings roll right off him. The women at the table were complimenting each other on their outfits, the way women do, and eventually they all sat. Molly sat to his left, Lisa to his right with Declan on her right.

As the wine was poured by discreet waiting staff, Kit edged his chair closer to Molly's.

"Okay?" he asked. "Would you prefer an aperitif rather than wine? I'm happy to get you something from the bar."

She leaned towards him while keeping her eyes front and centre, taking it all in. "I'm good. This white wine is really good. It's all good. Oh God, I sound like a compete nincompoop. How many times can I say good? No, don't

111

answer that. I'm now adding rambling to all my goods. Just shoot me."

Kit chuckled. His job was to put her at ease. *Ha!* Kind of hard to do when her fragrance was wafting his way, filling his senses with hints of exotic pleasure and his eyes were constantly drawn to the dip in her bodice, the slant of her shoulders, the dewy sheen on her skin.

He needed to focus and remember his role for the evening. Study the head honchos in the firm as they relaxed amongst their peers. Watch for any tell-tale angst or anxiety from all the players *and* not draw attention to himself. That last part was going to be difficult because, with Molly on his arm, all eyes would be on them.

He remembered very clearly Flynn's terse words to him earlier that day. They'd been playing phone-tag for several days – on purpose from Kit's side. Nothing Flynn had to say to him did he want to hear, or so he thought. Turned out he was wrong.

"Don't mess with my sister, Elliot. She's not like you. She may have a brilliant brain for numbers and data but she is also an empath. She can see and feel things out of the normal. Her sensitivity to atmosphere and especially stress and danger is uncanny. Mess with her and you are a dead man."

Kit was in no doubt Flynn meant every word. He was strangely happy to know Flynn was looking out for his baby sister, the way a good brother should. He wondered how many other 'dates' of hers had been given that same warning. Kit doubted Flynn actually meant what he said. It was a turn of phrase, surely. Hopefully. What Flynn didn't realise was that he'd just unintentionally given Kit another way to use Molly for his own ends.

Unfortunately for Molly, Kit was just selfish enough to use it.

* * *

It really was stunning. Molly sat back and let her gaze wander. Chandeliers – electric, of course, but on dim, threw out a lovely glow but what made the atmosphere special were the candelabras on each table. They made the light twinkle and dance. And speaking of dancing . . .

"Hey, handsome, you want to tread the boards with me?"

Kit looked at her over the rim of his glass and raised a brow. "You'd take a chance on me actually knowing how to move to music? That's pretty daring of you."

"I happen to know that people who are good at mathematics are also often really good at music. I can't remember the actual reason, but I assume it has to do with measurements and logic or something."

Kit grinned and lowered his glass. "Okay then, on your own head, et cetera."

He stood and held out his hand to catch one of hers. She rose too and together they walked out onto the central dance floor. The orchestra were playing a waltz. Not all the guests knew how to perform a real waltz but that didn't matter. The ambiance created by the swirling skirts, interspersed with the standard black-and-white of the male attire, more than made up for technique.

Molly rested one palm in his hand and the other on his shoulder. As they moved, surprisingly well, she noted, she entered into an almost dreamlike state. This was a perfect evening. Kit had thrown her off balance when she'd arrived. So snazzy and smart in his tux. He'd worn the old-fashioned winged collar instead of a standard shirt and leather braces instead of a belt. She'd wondered if he'd wear his Converse – it would have been just like him – but, no – black shiny lace-ups did the job just fine. He wore his glasses and his hair still flopped forward but, my God, Clark Kent was definitely on the wane and Superman was emerging. He took effortless control both in manoeuvring her around the dancefloor and earlier too, during the meal, with the many conversations going on about them. He'd ensured she was included in them all, asking her opinion and listening when she and, to be fair, others spoke. It was almost like he was acting the part of a grown-up as opposed to his normal more relaxed boyish displays.

She liked it.

The only fly in the ointment was Chloe Benson, the younger Benson's wife. She was everything a society wife was expected to be – if you bought into that kind of thing. And Chloe obviously did. Tall, blonde, reed-thin and dripping in diamonds, her expression remained aloof and snooty. That could be the Botox and fillers and not her natural demeanour, Molly acknowledged silently, but she doubted it. Molly knew several people who used enhancements both chemical and natural, and it didn't stop them from being lovely people or good friends. You couldn't keep the snootiness out of the eyes though, could you?

As she and Kit twirled, she was conscious, too conscious, of the strong hand resting at her waist. She hoped her corset was doing the job and her flesh was not moving independently of the dress. Oh well, she was what she was. Normally her curvaceous figure didn't bother her. She ate and enjoyed her food. Only indulged in so-called bad treats on occasion and walked a lot. There were times she yearned for Caro's figure – the one all the women in her family wanted – but hey, this was what she had. But now, feeling the heat of long fingers pressing her flesh through the sensuous fabric she wished she'd done extra side-bends at her last Zumba class. Silly really, since it would have made no difference. The last class she'd attended was weeks ago. She sighed.

"That sounded rather weary – everything okay in that

brain of yours?" Kit asked, dipping his head slightly to catch her eye.

As usual Molly answered with no filter. "Just bemoaning my lack of Zumba classes," she said. "Maybe I wouldn't have so many rolls if I just was more consistent."

Kit looked puzzled. "Rolls? Bread rolls?"

"Oh, aren't you sweet! And innocent. And blind, thankfully." Molly reached up and patted his cheek. "Never mind, I was really thinking out loud, and I need to remember not to do that."

"I like that you speak your mind. You say what you're thinking. So many people only say what they believe others want to hear. You're not like that."

"I'm not that different. Just lack a filter. Oh look!" She tipped her head in the direction of Lisa and Declan, who were dancing close by. "Looks like trouble in Paradise."

Kit angled their bodies so he could get a glimpse of the pair. "Why do you say that? They appear very poised and elegant."

"Yeah, I'm not buying it. Look closely at Lisa's face. There is tightness around the mouth and her eyes are unfocused. I can feel the disappointment rolling in waves from her. And Declan's attention is definitely elsewhere."

Kit turned his eyes back to hers. "Feel her disappointment? How can you do that? We aren't even that close to them."

Molly gave herself an internal kick. *Idiot. Keep your stupid touchy-feely stuff to yourself.* Aloud she said, "I can sometimes pick up on strong emotions nearby. Doesn't always work. Sometimes I'm wrong. Forget I said anything." Except she was never wrong. She wondered why she was picking up on Lisa. She barely knew her. They had exchanged words in the office, in passing, and when Molly had gone to HR for all her paperwork when she was hired, Lisa had been very helpful. Molly hadn't 'felt' anything then. Maybe it was Lisa's connection to Declan? There had been times Molly had felt waves of . . . frustration, or maybe dissatisfaction emanating from Declan and she'd put it down to work pressure. He was under a lot of pressure. He answered directly to Brendan Benson, who could, it was rumoured, be a real badass. Maybe she should pay more attention the next time she was with Declan. Or maybe … *hmm*, that was an idea …

The music ended and they sat back down. Molly asked Kit for a brandy from the bar and when he went to do her bidding, she moved seats to sit next to her boss. Declan and Lisa had also taken their seats and were sipping their own drinks.

Yup, the atmosphere between them was definitely on the chilly side. Declan turned his back on Lisa and let his eyes wander up and down Molly's body. She held herself still, determined not to squirm.

"Hey, beautiful, want to dance?" He lurched from his seat and took Molly by the upper arm.

If she hadn't wanted this encounter, hadn't wanted to check him out, she would have easily twisted away from him. But something was telling her to go with him, to *listen* to him, as only she knew how – with her gut, not just her ears.

The contrast with Kit was startling. Declan was a smooth mover, no doubt about it, but instead of making eye contact and chatting about nice inconsequential things, Declan had two modes: stare at Molly's cleavage or stare at Chloe Benson.

Intriguing. His gaze never went back to settle on Lisa but each turn they did about the dance floor, if Chloe was out of his line of sight, Molly's boobs got the attention – another few degrees of a turn and it was Chloe who was pinned with his bold stare. Molly decided not to be insulted but went for amused. That was until she allowed herself to open her mind.

And *wham! Gosh, he had the hots for Mrs Benson – big time. That was interesting for sure. And, yes, he liked a woman with larger breasts – go, me!*

Molly ended the dance by excusing herself to the ladies' room. She'd spotted both Lisa and Chloe making their way there and figured a little reconnoitre was in order. She waved a hand at Kit, indicating to give her a few minutes, as she saw him return to their table with drinks. Nipping quickly around some tables, she got to the ladies' first and closed one of the stall doors for privacy. She might as well make use of the place so she gathered all the bunches of dress fabric up so she could use the loo. What a pain it was! How on earth did females back in the day manage? So much material was both cumbersome and dangerous. Someone like her, not used to this level of finery, could easily damage the cloth – she could stand on it or get it dirty. She needed a lady's maid for sure. But, with her luck, if she'd lived back then, *she'd* be the lady's maid.

The outer door opened and the click of high heels could be heard tap-tapping on the marble flooring. It was Chloe who spoke first.

"Is it serious between you and Twomey?" Her voice was as sharp and brittle as Molly had expected. Around the dinner table, she'd barely uttered a word.

"Excuse me?" Lisa replied. "I'm not sure that's any of your business."

"You are incorrect. I know the protocol in the company. No fraternising with your colleagues."

"Declan and I don't work together – we are not even in the same department – there is no conflict. And anyway," Lisa sighed rather dramatically, "it appears he has more interest in one of his own kind – I mean Molly Fitzgerald –

an up-and-coming accountant – a rising star, so the rumour-mill has it."

Molly held her breath. She had not been expecting to hear her own name mentioned in dispatches. The sound of a handbag clip being used and rummaging. She could imagine one or both of the women reapplying lipstick and, yes, the pop of lips pressing and parting was soon audible.

"Well, whatever about you and Twomey being a mismatch from the company's perspective, that Fitzgerald girl is definitely breaking rules. And I won't tolerate it."

"They only had one dance," Lisa said. "It's manners to ask those at one's table to dance – I'm sure Mr Benson would agree with that. Besides, Declan likes women. *All* women."

Chloe harrumphed. "He's only as bad as the next man. Put breasts on display in that vulgar common way and even a saint would be ogling. It's disgusting. I'm going to lodge a complaint with HR."

"In fairness to Molly Fitzgerald, there is nothing about her or her dress that is vulgar. And *I'm* in HR and I can tell you that your complaint wouldn't hold water. No offense, Mrs Benson, but your own dress is actually way more revealing."

Molly almost snickered out loud. Clamping her hand to her mouth, she silently cheered on Lisa. Go, the HR department! She made a mental note to do something nice for Lisa as soon as she could. It was true. Chloe Benson's dress was open practically to her navel. The only thing was, there was nothing to fill the garment. It also had a slit up one side, displaying an expanse of well-toned thigh. She wouldn't, pardon the pun, have a leg to stand on.

Chloe wasn't done. "Everything about Molly Fitzgerald is vulgar. She's fleshy and loud. Her hair is a disaster and she hangs out with all those techie people. Or so I've heard. People like her have to rely on their brains because their looks and figure are an embarrassment. And if her attire isn't enough to bring the HR department down on her shoulders, I'll let it be known she and Declan Twomey are an item. I saw the way he looked at her. I'm not stupid. I know how these office girls are, after the main chance at the least opportunity. Well, she'd barking up the wrong tree there, let me tell you."

On that untrue statement and bitchy delivery, she marched out of the room.

Molly heard Lisa run some water, and a few minutes later the sound of a towel being tossed into a basket. Then Lisa too click-clacked out of the women's lounge.

Molly took a moment. She could feel the heat in her cheeks. Could feel the dampness in the palms that held yards of taffeta off the floor. Slowly, she finished up and opened the stall door. She washed her hands with deliciously scented pump-soap, dried them with a downy soft towel and, finally, as she lathered on a matching hand cream, she raised her eyes to the mirror.

She could see the unshed tears. She could feel every pinprick of hurt those unkind words had thrown. She wasn't immune to pain. She knew what she looked like. She knew how she came across. Big, blowsy, know it all, direct on the one hand yet deeply introverted on the other. A complete mix-up. Not everyone's cup of tea, for sure. But to be summarily dismissed because she didn't look or behave like others? Unkind. Back to mean girls at school, all over again.

Wiping a stray tear that had sneakily escaped, Molly straightened her shoulders. Kit thought she looked incredible. He'd said so. Granted he was a nerd and didn't get out much, so maybe it didn't really count, but Declan had liked what he saw too, right? The girls thought she looked lovely in her dress. They thought *she* was lovely. That would have to do. Those that counted, cared. Liked her. Supported her. She could, *would*, be okay with that.

Her evening spoiled, her secret detective caper a washout, Molly wanted to go home.

Kit wasn't psychic but even he could see something wasn't right. Molly walked towards him at only half sparkle.

While she'd been gone, he'd done his sleight-of-hand investigating, using his unobtrusive looks and geeky demeanour to work to his advantage, looking vacant and bored. He'd taken out his phone and pretended a concentration on the apps that was pure mirage. His ears were open for business. He wondered, now that Molly had shown her hand with regard to reading others, if they could compare notes. If he told her what he'd overheard maybe she'd share some of her intel too.

She approached the table and, still standing, took the brandy snifter from his hand and downed it in one. He was impressed she didn't fall into a fit of coughing and was about to tell her so when he caught her eyes. Yes, she was definitely troubled. It wasn't his imagination. What the hell had happened in the bathroom?

Before he could ask, she spoke.

"Can we go home now?"

Kit didn't hesitate. "Absolutely," he said.

He took the empty glass from her unsteady fingers and felt a sudden fury with whoever had hurt her. Because she was definitely hurting. He draped her light wrap round her shoulders and guided her, his hand to her lower back, from the room. Maybe it was rude to leave without saying an official goodbye to the hosts, but this was not a time for niceties. Molly needed to be gone, so that trumped manners.

He hailed a taxi and gave the address of Dún Laoghaire Pier. It was an unseasonably warm evening and he felt a stroll down the pier would be just the ticket. They could just go as far as the bandstand if her shoes were paining her. Women's shoes were a mystery to most men other than the fact a pair of high heels could look very sexy. Especially when teamed with very little else.

Molly stayed quiet in the taxi and Kit chatted lightly about the auction items from earlier in the evening, keeping up a light easy patter so she wouldn't have to participate. When they arrived, he paid the driver and helped her out.

"Oh," she said. "Why are we here? I wasn't paying attention."

"Thought a little fresh air might help blow the cobwebs away. And if you feel like talking about what upset you, I'm here to listen."

Molly angled her head at him. "I'm crap at hiding things. I do try, usually, but with you, I don't know, I seem to feel able to let my guard down."

"I'm glad." Kit took her arm in his and they began a slow meander down the lower level of the pier. The unwritten rule was you walked down one way, either the lower level next to the boats or the upper level with a view over the wall towards Sandycove and Dalkey, and you walked back along the other level. The moon was almost full and the light clinking of ropes against masts was a charming background hum. It was early in the season for sailboats to be launched so the noise wasn't as obvious as it would be on a full summer evening, but it soothed nonetheless.

They were silent at first, both lost in their thoughts.

"I learned some things," Molly spoke into the darkness, her head tilted away from Kit. "Some interesting things and some … personal things. Declan Twomey has the serious hots for Chloe Benson. Did you know that?"

Kit whistled low through his teeth. Well, now. That was news indeed. "Did he tell you?"

Molly laughed, the sound dry and not in actual amusement. "No. Not in so many words. But he couldn't take his eyes off her. When they weren't directed down my bodice, that is."

"What on earth does he see in Mrs Benson? She comes across as bitter and unhappy."

Molly chuckled, her tone lighter. "Yeah, she's a piece of work alright. She warned Lisa away from Declan, and then she warned me away from him."

Kit halted. "What? She said that? To you?"

"Oh no. Not to my face. I was in the loo stall and she didn't know I was there. But she referred to me in all sorts of charming ways and told Lisa she would report me and Declan to HR if we became or indeed were an item." Molly looked directly into Kit's face. "It could be pure jealousy. She seems very uptight."

Kit shook his head. "I can't see it personally, but no accounting for taste. She's considerably older than him, though that shouldn't matter, but she *is* married to one of the owners and *that* should make a difference."

"You're so sweet – thinking married people shouldn't have the hots for someone else."

"That's not what I said. Or maybe it is, but what I meant was, it's one thing to have a crush on someone other than your spouse – I imagine that happens in a long-term relationship of any kind, but the point is not to act on it. You make vows for a reason. It doesn't mean you are blind and can't appreciate another person or even, I suppose, have that crush, but that should be the end of it."

"Like a free pass kind of thing?" Molly laughed. "I think that's healthy. Each partner gets to have a free-pass crush – someone you can admit to really fancying without the other person freaking out. Like a celebrity crush."

"As long as it's just a fantasy or a celebrity, which is

never going to happen anyway! Imagine if your partner said they really fancied your best friend or neighbour? That could be awkward."

Molly snorted. "Crikey, that would put a strain on things alright. So, who's your free pass? Who would you tell your wife or girlfriend was the one you could, theoretically, cheat with?" She leaned against the bandstand railing and looked out over the water, waiting for him to answer.

"It's a tough one. I might have said Francesca Jones, but now that I've met her and she's a member of your family, that'd be just weird. Maybe Kacey Musgraves? She's a crossover country singer and I like her music as well as her looks. Or J Lo."

"*What? J Lo?* Are you kidding? She's way older than you!"

Kit folded his arms, propping a shoulder on the tall iron bandstand post. "You asked. I told. Who's yours?"

There was a long pause during which Kit studied Molly's profile. She was so pretty. The moonlight highlighted the curve of her cheek and slightly pert nose. Those curls, somewhat tumbled now and out of their pins, teased him. Lured him. Begged him to touch and twist one silky strand around his finger. He could feel his heartrate quicken as his gaze fell on her shoulders, the line of her collarbone and the swell of creamy breast visible under the arch of her dress. He swallowed, his mouth dry. He wrenched his eyes away and stared hard at the mast of a sleek sailing boat. That was better. He could look at these lovely smooth lines and not get all hot and bothered beneath his clothes.

"*Hmmm*, maybe Sam Heughan, the guy who plays Jamie in *Outlander*. Or James McEvoy who was in *Atonement*. They are both appealing to me."

Kit groaned. "Seriously? Don't they both have Scottish accents?"

"Because they *are* Scottish," she explained patiently.

"Is that why you and your sister's boyfriend get on so well? Because you fancy him and his accent?" God, where did that come from? He sounded like a jealous lover. *Idiot!*

She gaped at him, her mouth open. "Do you think that's why? That I secretly fancy Gabe Mackenzie? Wow, why didn't I think of that?" she deadpanned. And then shoved him in the shoulder. "You mad yoke! Of course not. Though I can see your reasoning – Gabe is rather yummy in both the looks and the personality department. And you're right, we do get on. We connect. In a *sibling* way." She paused, thinking it over. "I don't know why I've never fancied him. I should, given my choices a moment ago, but no. He's not my free pass." She pushed away from the cold concrete and shivered. "And, of course, there is Ali to contend with. She'd bury my body where no one would ever find it."

Kit laughed as he shrugged out of his jacket and, despite her protests, draped it over her shoulders.

They began walking back along the pier towards the town. Their pace was slow, measured, comfortable. Molly didn't complain about her feet or the chill and Kit steered them in the direction of the hotel that faced the seafront.

"Let's get a hot port in the bar and then I'll walk you home," he said. He wondered if she'd ever tell him what else Chloe Benson had said. Because a word to HR about a non-relationship was not what upset her. Molly was made of sterner stuff than that.

He also realised, as they settled on bar stools and sipped their drinks, that he hadn't told her what he'd learned about Declan.

That Declan Twomey was up to his eyes in debt.

Chapter 12

It took a few days. More than Molly expected, in truth, for her to feel back to her old self. Despite the kindness and support of Kit after her bathroom 'encounter' with Chloe Benson, she still felt . . . less. Less than her usual confident, capable, and driven self.

And that totally pissed her off. She was letting Chloe in, letting her *win*, and that simply wouldn't do.

Maybe it didn't help that she hadn't seen Kit since he'd walked her home after the drink at the hotel the night of the gala. He'd been conspicuous by his absence and he'd left no word. That alone had made her realise how close they'd become over the previous few weeks. Their breaks always seemed to coincide, they had done some work together on several occasions and had stayed late eating pizza – and working of course – on a few other nights. She had, she thought, come to rely on his presence. It was oddly comforting.

Despite the flash of Superman when spied in his tux, he was, in her head, Clark Kent. Her gentle, funny, smart and kind nerd. He didn't hang out with the others in the office; he was hers. They got each other. They were friends. And now he was gone without a trace.

Surely he wouldn't just *leave* without telling her? That would kind of belie what she'd just been telling herself about their friendship. She knew he was on a timeline – she wasn't sure exactly what that was, but the audit was almost done, so might he be reassigned? She needed to ask him, or at least find out somehow. The thought of BB&M without Kit was a thought she did *not* like. A trip to see Lisa in HR was on today's agenda. But, first, some flowers.

Molly swung by a roadside flower seller on her lunch break and, as she walked back briskly to the office, marvelled at how free she felt. No more dodging behind cars if she saw someone she thought she recognised. No more avoidance of places in the centre of the city where she might encounter one of her siblings.

She'd been such a fool.

What kind of moron thinks her world will fall apart because she's an accountant and not an artist? Her kind, that's who. But of course, it wasn't that which had worried her as much as the lie – the keeping it secret. And why, she mentally head-slapped herself, had she ever thought *that* was a good plan? Thinking back to the first time she'd enrolled in accountancy night classes she tried to recall why she hadn't just gone home and said "Hey, I'm doing night classes in accountancy. Turns out I'm not only loving it, I'm really damn good at it." How hard would that have been?

Tucking the bouquet of flowers under her arm, she pulled her phone from her pocket to check her messages. None. Nothing from Kit. She sighed and opened the main door of the firm's building.

Lisa was charmed. And grateful – and a little embarrassed when Molly explained her presence in the cubicle

"You didn't need to bring flowers – but I'm so pleased you did – these are gorgeous. Honestly, there was no need."

Molly smiled at her. "Hey, there is always a need to

support other women. And you stood up for me even when you didn't know I was there – so that definitely deserves flowers. And in case you wanted an in with Twomey yourself, I'm not interested in him in that way. Not at all."

"Oh," Lisa was flustered, "I thought I was. At first. He can be very charming. And he's got a great reputation with the ladies. I was coming down from a bad relationship and thought a fling with him would be a way 'back on the horse' so to speak, you know?"

Molly didn't know. Not really, but she got the gist. "Sure," she said with as much aplomb as she dared. "Ride that horse!" Oh no, that was the wrong thing to say – next *yee haw!* would be likely to make an appearance. She needed to shut up.

Lisa, kindly, just smiled again. "Anyway," she said, "a few dates with Declan were enough. And he did seem rather distracted by you, so feel free to tread those waters if you want. I'm done with him." She sniffed her bouquet and stood to locate a vase. "I'll keep these here in the office – keep any other potential admirers guessing."

She winked at Molly who sighed at the woman's confidence. She wished she was as confident as that with men. Maybe she needed a plan. A strategy. She was good with those. She could plot out how best to get good 'form' with the males of the species. She had work to do, serious research if that was the case. There was lovely Lisa happily 'riding' Declan Twomey just as an excuse to not get out of practice and there was Molly, completely surrounded by no experience whatsoever. Not only did she need a plan, she needed a partner in crime. She knew the women in her life would give her all sorts of advice should she dare to tell them of her lack of . . . anything. Perhaps they already knew?

But no. She needed a man's brain, a man's insight into what they were looking for.

She needed a Kit-style of brain. One that was both logical *and* male.

But first, she needed to delete the weird email she'd received that morning. As Molly got ready for work, at her flat, she always glanced at her work mail to see if anything urgent came up overnight. This morning had been as normal except one that read 'urgent' and had a BB&M address. She clicked on it, and within seconds figured it must be a joke. The wording suggested that she, Molly, switch some numbers around on a specific account, giving the client a heftier invoice. If that was done successfully, Molly would be well rewarded.

It was obviously a joke. Someone messing with her like one of those 'caught on camera' shows. Best way to deal with it? Delete and ignore. She should have done that immediately.

Done.

Kit's brain was about to burst. Could you have data overload? Yes, you could, he decided as he took the reheated pasta bake from the oven. Thank God he'd had enough foresight to cook earlier in the week as once he'd got stuck into the reports, all brain cells were totally occupied. It was after seven now and the noise emanating from the area of his belly, the insistent growling, told him it was time. He pulled a baguette from the counter, not so fresh now, but beggars and choosers et cetera, so he tore it apart and took the lid off the butter. Yeah, it was a carb overload but, difficult times, difficult measures.

He dished up a bowl of the sausage-and-tomato-filled macaroni cheese and thanked his gran and the gods for making him learn to cook his first year in college. He'd stayed with his gran in this very house and at least two nights a week she'd insisted he try out a new dish. And she was an appreciative audience. She'd learned herself out of necessity rather than desire. She needed to eat, she needed to feed her daughter and she needed to save money. Takeaways and fast food had not been an option – way too costly – so from scratch it was. Gran had taught him to get to the markets at the end of the day, not the beginning, and pick up the vegetables that wouldn't be used the following day, still fine, but half the price. She'd instructed him on what meats to ask for at the butcher's and how to get the cuts that were right for the menu. She'd done all that herself, on her way home from work a couple of times a week and on a Saturday. But Gran had had his mother to feed. He had only himself.

The Mac and Cheese was tasty and filling but somehow, unsatisfying. Perhaps that wasn't the pasta's fault but his own company. He had found it hard these last few days, working from home, imagining a continuing work life without the bright star that was Molly Fitzgerald. How could he feel so connected to her when they, in truth, barely knew each other? Not true. They did know each other. On a basic and natural level, they gelled. She was smart and funny, and innovative in her work. Not to mention beautiful. Really beautiful. The sound of her laugh kicked his gut, every time. And if *he* was the one who made her laugh? The prize.

He put his bowl in the sink and returned to his reports. One more day at home, in peace and with no interruptions, and he could hand in his first set of findings. He was in a conundrum of sorts. He could trace where the funds were depleting, he could track the accounts used, he had found a number of completely fake accounts, but, and this was the biggie, although he had two suspects in mind, they had, very cleverly, covered their tracks.

The official audit was over and he needed to stay on

longer to come to conclusions and make recommendations that would satisfy the senior director of the company. Unfortunately, it was looking more and more likely that the answers wouldn't, in fact, satisfy that director at all. Far more likely to create a bigger problem than the solved one that would be put in front of him.

That part wasn't Kit's problem. Not ultimately. He was grateful for his superior hacking skills, his understanding of the dark web along with his ability to fly under the radar as he did his digging. But he knew his results would cause hurt. They usually did. That was his job: to weed out the 'bad guys' and move on. White-collar crime was as alive and well and flourishing in Dublin as it was anywhere else.

He sighed now, wishing that Molly and her direct straight talk was here with him. She'd have a quirky way of looking at things and make him smile with her very personal and very individual notions. He really liked that about her. He'd kept her in the dark about these last few days because she'd probably offer to help, and this was something that had to be kept from everyone until he was certain. But he could finish up by mid-afternoon and invite her over for dinner tomorrow night. He could show her his house, ask her opinion. Get a different perspective on what needed doing and how to decorate. He had the money. Gran had left not just the house but the other half of her considerable savings which enabled him do a serious renovation. Some bits were already done, but he was basically living in a building site. At least he wouldn't be tempted to do something stupid.

He looked around at the drop cloths and stepladder in his living area. He'd cleared a desk space for himself but there was no way these surroundings would encourage romantic or even lustful leanings in anyone. He'd be safe. Or more to the point, she'd be safe. From him.

He got his phone and opened his texts.

Hey, any chance you'd like to come for dinner tomorrow evening? I've been working from home and now I'm going stir crazy with my own company. You'd help me not go over the edge ... K

As soon as he hit send, he wondered did that sound like a backhanded invite? He was bored so she'd do? Christ, he was overthinking things again. Worrying unnecessarily. If she felt used, she'd say so.

His phone pinged.

Ha! Was wondering where you'd escaped to! Are you asking me cos you're bored out of your mind?? Are you expecting me to entertain you? Because I'm actually okay with that ... text me the address and let me know time and what I can bring.

Kit laughed. Excellent. She was on board and not insulted.

Come after work. I'll text you the quickest way. Use the red line Luas and walk from Museum. No need to bring anything. I'll cook and get in some ice cream for dessert. See you at 7.

As he stacked papers and sorted them into folders, he realised he was grinning. Happy. Expectant. It had been a while since those emotions had reared their heads. Maybe his luck was going to change.

Molly swung her arms as she sauntered up towards Stoneybatter, the area where Kit lived. It was old Dublin, north of the River Liffey and oozing charm. So much of it had been gentrified but she understood that Kit's gran had been in the house her whole life so she would be considered local. There were cafés, restaurants, bookshops, small grocers and of course, a bazillion pubs – some old, some new. It had a lovely vibe and, as she neared his small terraced house, she noted the freshly painted doors, the brass accessories of letterboxes, knobs and door knockers all shiny and proud. This was a street where people cared. They probably had a residents' association. And she'd bet Kit's gran had been a part of it.

She rapped on the navy-blue door and waited for the sounds of movement within the small home to come closer.

The door opened and a flustered Kit waved her in with an oven mitt in his hand. "Sorry – popping the pie in the oven. I mean, shit. Welcome. So glad you could make it. Come in." He stepped back, allowing her into the very small entrance hall.

She grinned at him as she shrugged out of her coat and hung it on the rack on the wall.

"This is cosy," she said, knowing she couldn't keep the smile off her face.

"Is that code for miniscule?"

"Compact, maybe," she agreed as she followed him into the main room.

It was in a state of organised chaos. Or so it seemed. There was a two-seater couch along one wall and an armchair at an angle next to it. There was what looked like a folded drop cloth for painting – stains oddly visible in an abstract way – lying next to the armchair and a folded stepladder against the dado rail. The walls had that pale pink colour of the newly plastered not-ready-for-paint vibe. The floor, wide planks, was half sanded and that half was a warm and soft mellow golden colour. The left side remained dark and stained. There was serious work to be done here, that was for damn sure.

Molly followed Kit – open plan all the way through, an arch with about a metre of wall on either side dividing the two small spaces, the front from the back. The living room was facing the street and a dining area was to the rear. He walked ahead of her as she paused to survey her surroundings. A stairway, leading upwards from the living space, had treads the same soft gold as the newly sanded part of the floor. They'd be noisy, for now, but with a nice runner they'd look great. The banister was a modern addition. The balustrade beams were stainless steel, the handrail painted wood. Very cool.

The scents wafting from up ahead were tempting and Molly kept walking. She heard Kit cursing but it didn't bother her. When Ali was baking – at home as opposed to on TV – she had a potty mouth so the use of swearwords never bothered her. Plus, she had a brother named Devlin who was a champion curser, so there was that. The kitchen was narrow but really well laid out and was obviously an addition. A recent one. It looked like an IKEA build so was fresh and funky.

Kit closed the eye-level oven door and dropped the mitt onto the counter.

"Apologies, I got caught off guard on my timings. Started reading a report and lost track of time."

"No need to apologise," she said. "I totally get that. And I'm not in a rush, so there's no need for panic. But I may I ask where your fridge is – this needs chilling." She held up the bottle of Viognier and waggled it at him.

"Thank you, that's a lovely one. But didn't I tell you not to bring anything?"

He took the bottle and pulled open the door of an integrated fridge. All the panels were painted in the same pale blue – almost duck-egg – and looked streamlined and fresh. The stove was one of those fancy induction types and she was impressed.

"Something smells great," she said, sniffing the air just as a loud gurgle came from her tummy. Her eyes flew to Kit's and they burst out laughing.

"No hurry? Really? That's not what your stomach is saying. Luckily for you I have some antipasti all laid out. And I'm starving too so we can dig into that."

He opened the fridge behind him again and took out a bottle of Prosecco. He poured two flutes, handed one to Molly and led the way back into the dining space.

"Cheers!" he said as they clinked glasses.

He pulled out a chair next to the small dining table. It was already set and had a large oval plate stacked with cold meats, cheese, olives and diced and sliced veggies. A plate of crackers was beside it and each place setting had a small china plate between the knives and forks.

Molly sat and helped herself. "This is a great idea and, the best bit is, if we leave some of the cheese, we can have it again after dinner!"

Kit chuckled. "Christ, you read my mind! I do have ice cream, a really good one, but usually about half an hour after dessert I crave salt, so yeah, I thought of the twofer too."

Grinning at each other they clinked glasses again and, as they selected various offerings for their plates, Molly chatted about her impressions of the neighbourhood as she'd walked through.

"I don't know this area at all but from the map it looks like the Phoenix Park is just a few minutes away. How cool is that? The whole park for your back garden!"

"I know. I run there most mornings before work."

The fork, en route to Molly's mouth, paused. "You *run*? Like, every day? Who are you and where is my geek-slash-nerd friend?"

Kit looked slightly embarrassed. "Yeah, it's not something I usually tell people," he said, pushing his glasses up his nose. "But I sit a lot. A *whole* lot and when I was in college I was on the cross-country team and it got me into running, just for the love of it. And according to research, see, geek

134

part, the adrenalin rush and endorphin release is good for the brain so I just keep doing it. Kinda scared to stop now, to be honest. Imagine if I stopped my daily run and all my brain power just went *poof*!"

He used his hands to make the sign of a world blowing apart and Molly laughed.

She'd noticed his wide shoulders the morning when he'd been at Declan's desk and she'd definitely noticed his strong arms and shoulders when they'd danced. But the clincher was when they walked on the pier and he'd gallantly removed his jacket to drape on her shoulders. The way his shirt had stretched across that chest? *Whoa*, that had been a bit of an eye-opener. Now, knowing his body was built because he sweated for it ... well, that just made her toes curl in all kinds of delight. It shouldn't, but damn, it did.

"I doubt your brain would lose its power if you walked instead of ran, weirdo, but you keep running if it floats your boat. Now," she said before he might ask her what she did to keep her brain alive and kicking, "what are your plans for in here? The kitchen is fab but even I, in my decorating ignorance, can see *this* room needs work."

That, it turned out, was a bit of a mind-teaser. There had originally been two small rooms which were now one space, albeit with an arch between. He was keeping that, he said, as he liked the visual divide. But he was stuck on colour and wall-coverage choices. Should he paint? Wallpaper? Both? They discussed it as they sipped their bubbly and nibbled on the antipasti, and he begged for her input.

"Your flat is so cosy and stylish," he said, unintentionally complimenting Caro and Ali who had both had a hand in making their respective marks on the place.

"Truthfully, I think you should go relatively neutral

here, keep the flow in warm grey and cream. You can add changeable colour with cushions and floor rugs seasonally."

He raised his eyebrows. "What, like Christmas themes and summer themes? That sounds way too time-consuming. And way too much shopping."

"It doesn't have to be – and you need to purchase only once and keep them in storage. Arnotts' home and bedlinen section has a sale at the moment. I can look for you after work on Thursday – it's late-night opening. Plus, you should definitely go back to IKEA – they have great selections and the way they lay out the examples is great for ideas."

Kit got up from the table and removed the antipasti plate to a sideboard. He reached for a decanter of red wine, placed it on the table and headed back to the kitchen.

"Can I help?" Molly asked as she moved glasses and plates about, making more space.

"Nope, thanks, I've got it. Oh actually, yeah, can you bring in this bowl of salad?"

"Sure." She got up and joined him in the small space.

She took the wooden salad bowl full of mixed greens, the wooden serving spoons and the bottle of dressing and returned to the dining table. Moments later Kit carried in a steaming casserole dish and put it on a mat in the centre of the table. He disappeared back to the kitchen and came back with a bowl holding several baked potatoes, their skins crisp and brown. Everything smelled so appetising that, despite the earlier starter, Molly's mouth was watering. Picking up a carving knife and slice, Kit cut into the food, produced a portion of lasagne and slid it onto her plate.

"Hope you're okay with no meat in this part of the meal but I figured this would be a good balance."

"I love veggie food," Molly said, adding a potato and some salad to her plate. "A previous boyfriend of mine was a vegan and I tried it to be supportive. It was fine. But I missed eggs and cheese. And I really missed steak. But I love mixing things up. Sometimes I'll do veg only for one week out of each month. When I lived at home, Mum varied it a bit too."

He served himself, then sat and cut up his food in that American way before putting aside his knife.

Molly took a bite of lasagne and moaned in sheer ecstasy. "*OhmygodKit*," she mumbled around a mouthful of food. "This is scrumptious."

A hint of colour glowed on his cheeks as he thanked her and dug into his own food. The taste of mixed aubergine, courgette, tomato, carrot and celery along with creamy cheese sauce, the crispness of the grilled mozzarella on top, the buttered open baked potato and fresh zingy salad was perfect.

Kit looked at her over the rim of his glasses. "You really think it's okay?"

She groaned in appreciative response and held out her glass for some Rioja. "*Yummmmm*," was the only answer he was going to get till her appetite was sated.

He seemed fine with that.

Which was just as well, because, damn, this food needed serious attention. Molly became aware of music in the background and was surprised to hear Moving Hearts on low. That brought about a discussion, between mouthfuls, of the best of Irish music, which of course led to other music. And, lo and behold, Kit Elliot played the fiddle!

She gaped at him, dumbstruck. "Seriously? You really play? When did you learn? That's awesome."

"I started learning aged about seven and kept it up. I really like it – it's great for concentration. In college," he paused to tear some bread apart and mop the sauce from his plate, "I played in a few different bands – mostly Irish stuff but a bit of classical too."

Molly lowered her knife and fork and studied him. "You are a man of many talents, that's for sure," she said and, as he grinned lopsidedly at her and her stomach took that opportunity to flip over, she wondered what other talents he might have and if, maybe, they'd be of some use to her. Definitely food for thought.

They took coffee and ice cream in the living-room space through the arch and it was indeed gorgeous ice cream. Pistachio and choc-chip with a drizzle of some unpronounceable liqueur dribbled over the top. Whatever it was, it tasted delicious. Molly licked a dribble of chocolate from the top of her lip and became aware that Kit's spoon had paused halfway to his own mouth.

He was staring at her. Or rather at her mouth.

"What?" She flicked her tongue across her bottom lip and thought she heard an odd, strangled sound coming from him. "It's just chocolate – no need to be the Good Manners Police."

"That's not . . . it's not . . . never mind." He stood abruptly, left the room and returned with a damp piece of paper towel. "Use this," he said and handed it to her. "Or no, let me."

He crouched in front of her and as she held her hands wide, spoon in one, bowl in the other, he gently wiped away the offending chocolate. He didn't meet her eyes, not at first, just focused on the ice-cream remains.

I must be a really messy eater, she thought, *or he's being very thorough.*

A moment later she realised that while he was breathing rather heavily, she was holding her breath. At that instant their eyes met. And held. Steel-grey to aqua-blue, the seconds spun away as they stared at each other. Everything froze. Sound. Movement. Thought. Kit's eyes flicked to her partially open mouth and back to her gaze, a question now in his. Her lips tingled and buzzed in anticipation. *He's going to kiss me, he's going to kiss me . . .* they moved, together, in the slowest of motions, infinitesimal fractions of space as their mouths grew ever closer. Her heart was hammering so loudly in her chest that she felt the whole of Stoneybatter must hear it. *He's going to kiss me, he's going to kiss . . .*

A loud thud from above had them jerking apart as if hit by falling debris.

"What the fu . . .?" Kit stood, stepped back and took a breath.

Molly stayed seated, her heart having changed its thumping to one of fright as opposed to – well, she didn't know what.

"Did something fall?" she asked, her voice coming out as a squeak. She cleared her throat and tried again. "What *was* that? The noise, I mean . . ."

Kit shook his head, clearing his own throat. "Sorry about the fright. I, *ah*, I may have forgotten to tell you I don't live here alone." At her puzzled look he jerked his head in the direction of the ceiling. "My roommate," he explained as if that was any explanation at all.

Molly rose from her seat, placed the bowl and spoon on the side table and folded her arms.

"I think there are many things you haven't told me," she said accusingly. "Are you going to introduce me?"

He shrugged. "I guess now is as good a time as any. Come on."

He headed towards the stairs and she followed shakily. She climbed the stairs, studiously avoiding letting her brain return to the moments before the loud noise had interrupted whatever was happening. *Stop thinking*, she ordered her brain. *Just stop.*

The wooden treads felt smooth under her feet as they

mounted the stairs, the banister cool and firm. And if her eyes strayed to Kit's ass, snug in well-worn jeans, well, that was merely proximity. And she was grateful it wasn't her substantial rear before him. Small mercies and all.

Kit turned left at the narrow landing and pushed open the sanded but as yet unpainted door in front of him. It was a small house and it seemed that there were only two rooms upstairs. Evening light spilled across golden floorboards, bare except for a small rug next to a large bed. The space was not roomy and Molly peeped around Kit's shoulder to discover the mystery occupant.

A marmalade cat sat on the rug, washing its face, not a care in the world, and certainly paying zero attention to the new arrivals.

"Sometimes this cat stays so quiet I forget it's here and other times its presence is more than felt," Kit said with a certain amount of strain.

Molly pushed past him and knelt down in front of the furball. She reached out a hand to rub over the feline face and was instantly rewarded with a purr.

"Hey, kitty," she said, "aren't you pretty!"

The cat angled its face into the petting hand and the purring grew louder. Molly looked up at Kit who seemed mesmerised by the sight.

"How long have you had him?" she asked, stroking the soft back which arched beneath her touch.

Kit hunkered down beside her and rubbed the cat under its chin. "Scout was my gran's cat so came with the house."

"Oh," said Molly surprised, "a female? How unusual. Most marmalades are male, I believe."

Kit gathered the cat into his arms and stood. "How did you know Scout was female?" He walked back out into the small landing area and began heading downstairs.

Molly followed. "*To Kill a Mockingbird*, right?"

"Impressive." Kit grinned back at her over his shoulder. "Most people don't get the reference. They think she's a he. That the name is like a Boy Scout."

"It was my favourite book for years. I wanted to be called Scout – she's so badass."

Kit let Scout down onto the floor. She immediately wound her body about his legs, the purring even louder.

"Wow, she really loves you," said Molly. "Look at all that snuggling."

"Cupboard love, alas." Kit walked through to the kitchen. Opening a press, he took out some dry cat food and put it into a dish placed against the wall. "She knows where her next meal is coming from. Fortunately, I have three neighbours who are happy to feed her when I'm not about, so I don't have to worry about her fading away."

Molly smiled. He was such a lost cause. He might try to sound a tad irritated with the gorgeous cat but every gesture, every stroke of his hand over the cat's body, the way he had cradled her in his arms on the stairs, belied him. He loved that cat. Maybe it had started out because she was his gran's – but now? Molly would wager Scout held a very warm place in Kit's heart.

She glanced at her watch and decided to take her leave. She had lots to think about. Lots to dwell on and some decisions to make. That almost-kiss earlier had complicated her decision-making in a big way but she'd still look at all the angles. She was a maths person after all and she was all about the logic.

She wandered back into the living-room area and picked up her bag. "I'm going to head out, Kit," she said, aiming for nonchalance.

"Sure," he said. "I'll just grab my jacket and walk you to the Luas."

She was about to protest but one look at his 'don't

argue' face had her closing her mouth again. Fair enough. She really should have expected that, but it was still sweet.

And thoughtful. Definitely messing with her decision-making. Oh well.

They closed the front door behind them and started walking.

Chapter 13

At least she didn't ask me to play the damned violin for her, Kit thought as he tidied away the dishes. What an evening it had been. Fun, interesting and, yeah, flirty. He had so nearly kissed her. So very nearly. That mouth of hers – that bottom lip – soft, inviting. Plump and luscious.

Christ!

He shook his head, switched off the downstairs lights and rechecked the door locks. Scooping up the cat, he went upstairs. He dropped her none too gracefully in her cat bed next to his own. She stayed there during the night but when she had a chance took her daytime naps on his bed covers. He didn't mind. She shed a bit in the spring but nothing a shake-out couldn't fix. The sound of her rhythmic purring was a balm to his often overly busy brain and, he knew, at the ripe old age of fifteen, she wouldn't be with him forever. As his last link with Gran, that was pretty damn sad, but he was a realist above all else. Had to be.

He undressed and lay down, restless in body and mind. The walk to the Luas hadn't been awkward though it should have been. But then, this was Molly. She chatted about the neighbourhood, the history and the cat. She barely let him get a word in and he kept wondering if he should apologise. But what would he be apologising for? Nothing had happened. It had been a moment, sure. But that was all. And maybe she hadn't felt the stirring of blood, the beat of his pulse, the awareness that flooded his body as he ached to touch her.

Maybe she thought he was that exact geek she wanted to be friends with. Probably for the best. Definitely for the best. She was a complication, albeit a super-sexy one, his life didn't need right now. He had to finish with BB&M and then decide where to go next. Maybe, if more work came up in Dublin, he could ask Molly out on an actual date at some stage.

Maybe she'd laugh in his face. He'd been friend-zoned, very obviously. He had to live with that even if he couldn't convince himself to like it.

When the alarm went off on Saturday morning Kit groaned, as he did most Saturdays at this time. Why he had ever begun this stupid stint, he didn't know any more. He was lying, of course. He knew exactly why.

He pulled on his athletic gear, grabbed his bag, put Scout out the back door into the yard and hopped on his bike. It was one of those beautiful late-spring mornings and the city hadn't yet woken up. He loved it this early. Not even eight o clock, late for some, but for a weekender it was practically the dawn. He cycled through the streets, wending his way easily and smoothly to the park and the open green spaces and trees. It wasn't the biggest city park in Europe, the one he remembered from attending college in Dublin City University, but Mount Bernard Park, a smaller less glamorous one, a nice nine-minute cycle from his house, suited his needs perfectly. It had a court.

This morning he cycled past the more popular spots and headed to the fenced courts a bit farther in. Practice started at eight thirty and he always tried to be early. He needed to send a message to the boys and that meant he couldn't say, and not do. Biggest rookie mistake of all sports coaches. He parked his bike in the designated area and noticed a few lads were already on the court shooting hoops. Excellent. That's what he liked to see early on a Saturday. Enthusiasm. Dedication. Hope.

"*Lads!*" he called, and they turned as one, a collective grin across a number of their faces. Of course, that quickly turned to grumbling and moaning as they couldn't possibly be seen to be happy to be there. Not cool. "Get in formation."

"*Ah, sir!*" a boy of fifteen who was continually in the growth-spurt phase and seemed to inch up week by week, yelled out. "*Do we have to?*"

Or at least that's what Kit thought he said. The accent was strong and most likely embellished for the 'blow-in'.

"Connors, you know the drill. It's warm up or don't play. And it's *coach*, not *sir*." Kit threw his backpack down on the ground next to the bench and reached for his notebook and whistle.

"We were," Connors complained. "We were exercising just now." He tossed his curly mop in the direction of the hoop.

Kit raised an eyebrow at him, staring him down. Grumbling, but compliant, the lad joined the others in the centre of the court and they began their stretches.

It had taken time. And patience. And a *lot* of resilience, on his part, to get the boys to this point. They hated the discipline or at least they pretended to.

In the beginning, several months earlier when Kit had been asked to coach the boys, he'd been eager and delighted to help.

Then he met them.

A more motley crew he could not have envisaged. They hated him on sight. Week after week, Kit had almost given up. Thrown in the towel. They were disrespectful, rude, cheeky, irreverent and angry. So angry. He finally realised that more than anything they needed to vent that anger in a safe place. He could give them that. He could give them a court to play on. To run, jump, manoeuvre. To let off steam. So much damn steam Kit could open a sauna. But Saturday by awful, frustrating, heart-breaking Saturday, he kept at them. And they kept returning, reluctant and griping, but returning.

At some point Kit realised they needed his discipline, his rules, his no-bullshit straight talk and, more than anything, his routine. He turned up. Every week. They began to count on him and, in an unexpected and satisfying way, he began to count on them. He pushed them physically and, as he got to know them better, emotionally.

And they returned for more.

"Jason, *faster!* You can do better. *Come on!*" He always drove them extra hard at the beginning of practice, only easing off when he knew they were giving their all, so that by the time they were done and he could genuinely congratulate them on a great couple of hours' work, they lapped it up.

They finished their obligatory stretches and warm-ups just as Pieces, a seriously tough nut, arrived. He sauntered over to Kit, all bravado and swagger, and jerked his head in bare acknowledgement.

Kit sighed. "Pieces, so glad you could join us. Do your stretches and an extra five minutes of push-ups because you're late."

"*Fuck that,*" Pieces ground out, shoving his hands in his pockets. "I walked here, didn't I? That's warm-up enough."

"No, it isn't. You know the deal – if you want to be a part of this team, you act like a team member. That means you warm up properly because if you don't and you get a cramp on court, you let others down, not just yourself. That is *not* being a team player."

Pieces was so named because when he was about eight, he broke his leg in several places and his little brother kept saying it was "in bits and pieces". He was called Bits and Pieces for a while but his pals eventually shortened it, and it stuck. Now he glared at Kit like he wanted to kick something, hard.

Kit waited, breathing evenly, casually holding the team rota on a clipboard and inwardly crossed his fingers. Pieces could be very unpredictable. He could just turn and leave and that would be a damn shame. Instead, this time, he swore fluently and turning his back to Kit began his leg stretches. But not before Kit noticed some nasty bruising around his upper arm and neck. Shit. *Not again.*

Saying nothing, Kit turned back to the other youths and called out the team places and handed them their tabards to suit up. He sometimes had a few subs to wait their turn but none today. That meant ten boys in total were here. Still, it was a good turn-out from such a diverse crew. He was proud of them, beyond proud.

The game started, five against four, but within a few minutes Kit glanced back and noticed Pieces doing the required push-ups. Now that was progress, in a big way. There was a local mini-tournament coming up in late June and he didn't want to bench any one of these lads, as the subs weren't always reliable, but these boys put their hearts into the training as well as the games. They all deserved a chance. No, they wouldn't win the prize, wouldn't probably even get close, but by God they *would* go a few rounds come hell or high water.

Some of the guys needed this competitive drive more than others and some just needed to get out of the house or, in some cases, off the street corner. Kit had known many of their back stories before he'd even agreed to this venture, but the more he learned from the boys themselves, the more he was able to help. Even in small ways. He knew when to push one and be lenient on another. When to praise and when to rail. When a hand on a shoulder was needed and when a phone call was necessary. Kit loved it all. He was invested and that was something he hadn't expected and it was turning into something good.

He blew the whistle for half time and let them collapse around the bench, glugging from the water bottles he insisted they brought. He tried to instil hydration into everything they did and for some it worked. For others, not so much.

He gave some pointers, changed positions, and offered specific advice. He put Pieces into the centre, wanting to see if the boy had worked on his shooting since last week. He had serious potential and all he needed was practice. Granted, a lot of practice, but he lived close to some public courts and could play when he wanted to. *If* he wanted.

"Okay, lads, Pieces is shooting guard on the blues – get him the ball, let him score. Jase, you are same position on the reds." He clapped his hands together once. "Get to it," he said, grabbed his stopwatch and blew his whistle.

They worked hard. Sweat poured over their skin, and lanky hair became saturated as the sun made its appearance. They ran and jumped. They pushed and shoved. They swore at each other and swore some more. And they scored.

Pieces didn't let him down – he *had* been practising. "*Great twist, Pieces!*" he shouted as a beautiful three-pointer sailed cleanly through the hoop and they high-fived each other.

As the game went on Kit became aware of someone standing near the entranceway to the wire-enclosed court, observing. He hoped it wasn't one of the boys' dads – that had become problematic in the past. He didn't want to ban anyone from watching their kid play – but a rowdy, mouthy parent could be a real issue. He purposely didn't turn to see who was there, focusing on the boys themselves. Congratulating them, ribbing them and generally trying to let them know he cared.

"O'Leary, a word." The voice wasn't overloud – it just carried.

Kit sighed but was also relieved. Flynn Fitzgerald often showed up at the Saturday workouts, mainly because it was he who originally set them up, and he liked, he said, to check in and make sure everyone was behaving. See for himself if his brainchild was benefiting the intended. Flynn, Molly's brother and Kit's sometimes work colleague, had seen for himself how lacking in facilities and structure parts of Dublin city were, especially for the young male population. Instead of just bemoaning the situation, he did something about it. Organised this group of lads into a type of boys' club with rotating, and occasional, volunteers to help out in both sports and after-school academic assistance.

Pieces took one look in Flynn's direction and, like most lads of his ilk, must have assumed he was in trouble and tried to scarper through the only exit from the court. It was pointless. Without seeming to move, Flynn was there, right in front of the boy, casually but thoroughly blocking his path.

"This won't take long, Pieces," Flynn said, his tone even and unconcerned. "I want to ask you a few questions."

The boy made as if to dart off but was given the Flynn Special – a look that forbade any flight. Flynn looked at Kit as he eased the youngster away from prying ears. "We won't be long," he said and took a few leisurely steps away from the court, Pieces along with him.

As Kit gathered the others about him and doled out sliced oranges, he gave details of the upcoming games –

times, venues et cetera. The boys chattered and slagged each other, eventually picking up scattered hoodies and bags and heading off in groups of three and four.

Kit sat on the bench and studied the body language playing out between Flynn and his young charge. It looked like Flynn was the bearer of tough news and Pieces was not taking it well or certainly not wanting to hear it. But Kit bet on Flynn and, sure enough, after a bit more posturing from Pieces his shoulders suddenly slumped and, defeated, his head fell forward. Not moving an inch, Flynn waited and within a few moments the boy looked up, straight into Flynn's face, and spoke quietly.

Kit couldn't hear the words – he wasn't meant to – but he saw. The kid was hurt and yet resigned. Another moment and Flynn rested his hand on the boy's shoulder, holding him steady as one of Pieces' hands scrubbed at his eyes. *Shit*. Actual bad news then, not just a lecture. Kit waited some more and they both walked back to where he now stood, bag in hand, ready to go. He held out a bottle of water to Pieces without a word and the boy drank as if parched.

"Can I help?" Kit asked Pieces, catching his eyes, noting the bleak look.

"Nah, you're grand. I'll be alright. Fitz will tell you. I gotta go. Me ma needs me." With a jerked nod towards the detective, he left.

Kit looked expectantly at the other man. Flynn let his head fall back in what looked like defeat but Kit knew was probably exhaustion. Nothing defeated Flynn Fitzgerald.

"It's a shitstorm," he said quietly. "I'm telling you because it may affect O'Leary's attendance at your practice." He sighed and met Kit's enquiring gaze. "O'Leary Senior was brought by ambulance to hospital during the night. He died this morning." At Kit's gasp, he nodded once and continued. "Yes, there was an altercation between father and son last night – according to both Mrs O'Leary and Pieces himself, the boy was defending himself. Not at first, mind you. Initially, Senior beat up on his wife and when Pieces tried to intervene the Father of the Year beat the crap out of his son too. According to both injured parties, Senior left about twelve thirty and wasn't seen since. The hospital say they got a call around four thirty, following a fracas in the street, and severe damage had been done. He died from internal bleeding a few hours ago. His blood-alcohol level was off the charts." Flynn rubbed wearily at the back of his neck and rolled his shoulders. "No one can place Pieces at the scene but I had to ask."

Kit started. "You think the kid killed his father? Are you nuts?"

"It's been done. Many times. But in this case, no. I think O'Leary Senior was a nasty piece of work and most likely pissed off any number of people. My job is to find out which of the many did the deed. I believe Pieces didn't know about his father. He appeared shocked when I told him. He cares about his mother and wouldn't intentionally add to her burdens by getting thrown in Juvie. How did he seem to you?"

Kit pondered for a moment. "He was late to practice, and I got on his case but, although he was stiff and I had noticed the bruising on his arm and neck, I didn't think he was acting guilty or scared. Just, I don't know, dejected. Which makes sense if he'd had a rough night with his parents. How's his mum?"

"She has broken ribs, a black eye and a split lip. She was, dare I say, almost relieved when I turned up on their doorstep with the news earlier. The neighbours in the flats beside and below them all heard the incident and could verify, by the shouting, pretty much what both mother and son said." Flynn looked down at his shoes, sighing. "Pieces has potential. He has a clever brain if he would allow himself the luxury of school. Ah, well. We shall see."

"It's a shame," said Kit.

They exchanged a few more words on the topic and then abruptly Flynn said, "About Molly, what's going on between you two? Aren't you nearly done with BB&M? I read your latest report and gather things are close."

That threw Kit off balance. Typical Flynn. Make his prey feel secure, lull them into complacency and then, *wham!* Not this time, not this guy.

"Good segue, Fitzgerald, but no cigar. Molly is doing great at work – she is so damn smart she will make her way up the accountancy ladder in double-quick time. As to anything else? Mind your own."

"So, there is something else going on? Between you two?"

"*Not. Your. Business.* She's a grown woman and I'm fairly adult myself, despite appearances. If she, or I, have anything to tell you, ever, we will. Until then, butt out."

Kit smirked at Flynn's intractable expression. He hated being thwarted but, in this case, there was literally nothing he could do. Kit didn't work *for* him, he worked with him, in a bi-lateral sense. Several agencies working together, all on the same page. If there had been hierarchy involved, maybe he would have had some chance but, no, not this time.

"See you around," he said to Flynn as they parted ways. "And let me know if I can help with Pieces or his family, okay?"

Flynn nodded, lifted a hand in salute and sauntered off to a parked nondescript grey car.

Kit loved getting one up on one of the smartest men he knew and cycled back to his home with a smile on his face.

The smile broke into a grin when he realised he had a visitor. He registered that his heartrate had kicked up and determinedly put it down to peddling faster – though he knew he was lying to himself.

Molly Fitzgerald was sitting on his windowsill, chatting

to his next-door neighbour, Mrs McCabe. They were both holding mugs, a packet of biscuits between them.

His morning was about to get even better.

She watched him come towards her. Studied, with interest, the solid form of him as he came closer. What on earth was he wearing? Not a helmet, anyway, the chancer. Dublin city streets could play havoc with a cyclist, her sister Ali told her so.

Kit pulled his bike to a stop and swung a leg over the bar. Shorts. And a tank top. That's what he was wearing. It was only mid-April, not exactly summer, but he appeared all dishevelled and, yes, sweaty. Why did that make her heart kick up a beat? Sweaty man, who would have thought?

"Hey," she greeted him with awesome manners. "Hope you don't mind that I came by? Mrs McCabe was kind enough to tell me you are usually out on a Saturday morning but to wait as you'd be back around ten-thirty, and look," she lifted her wristwatch to him, "she was bang on!"

Mrs McCabe snorted. "He does get delayed, betimes, but usually it's in or around now," she said and drained her mug. "No, love, hang on to the biscuits, himself might need some energy after chasing a ball around." She gave a hearty wink to Kit and, taking Molly's mug, went back inside her own door, leaving the two of them alone.

Kit handed Molly his house keys. "Would you do the honours? I'll wheel the bike through to the back. Thanks."

Molly opened the door and stepped back, allowing Kit through. He brushed by her and she inhaled all the scents. Shampoo, manly sweat, and oranges. Oranges? *Huh.* She wasn't blind, so couldn't help noticing a catalogue of specific things. Really. Couldn't help it. Not at all. Broad shoulders, muscled arms, a sprinkling of chest hair beneath his vest top, amazing thighs and calves. Did she mention the arms? The thighs? Well, definitely worth a second go around. God, what that man hid behind some very ugly clothes! It was a sin. Should be outlawed, in fact.

Molly closed the door in his wake and followed him to the kitchen. She shivered as he dragged one hand through his damp hair and left it all mussed. He really, really should have looked ridiculous in those baggy shorts and sleeveless nylon vest.

He did not.

She paused at the kitchen counter, waiting till he returned to the kitchen from the small back yard. Scout came in meowing and winding her body around Molly's legs, so she bent to stroke the soft fur.

"She's a big baby, needs all the attention, don't you, Scout?" Kit angled around her, dumped his bag on the countertop and reached for the cat food. He replenished Scout's bowl and poured a glass of water, offering one to Molly too. She refused. She was finding it hard to swallow and didn't think practising in front of Kit would be a great plan. She was sure to choke. Instead, she watched him drink. Watched his throat move, the droplets of sweat trickling along his collarbone and down his chest beneath the fabric. He dragged a hand across his mouth and grinned.

"So, to what do I owe the pleasure?"

What, indeed. She'd tell him or ask him rather. But first, she would use her direct personality to discover a few things.

"When you said you run, it's not all you do, right? This," she waved her hand up and down in front of his body, "this does not look like running gear. I'm no expert but I know stuff. Plus Mrs McCabe did mention a ball. Soccer? Tennis? She didn't mention what type or size of ball."

"I coach basketball on a Saturday morning. And I usually play a bit with the lads too. Hence the outfit." Kit folded his arms across his chest and waited. He knew more was coming – he knew that much about her already. One question was never enough with her.

"And those arm muscles. Biceps or whatever? Are they from weights? Cos they look like something from a magazine or a movie poster and you're supposed to be my geek pal, not Captain Fantastic. You're not playing fair." She smiled as she spoke because he looked so bashful and self-conscious.

"I told you I need to burn off energy to create mental energy – and sometimes I go to the gym and lift weights too," he admitted.

"*Hah! I knew it.* Sneaky bugger, aren't you? Pretending to be all nerdy and awkward but really not. I've found you out. And, you aren't wearing your glasses!" She pointed to his thick-lashed eyes.

His hand flew to his face, clearly having forgotten he was glasses-free.

"Contacts?" he said but it came out as a question.

"Not buying it. Go take a shower, you're distracting me. I'll put on the kettle if that's okay and make coffee."

"Knock yourself out," he said and headed to the bathroom.

The trouble was, Molly discovered, that since the bathroom was in the new annex, she could hear the shower running. That was very, *very* bad for her imagination, especially having seen a goodly portion of his delectable non-nerdy, not remotely geeky body. She focused on the coffeemaking task at hand and blocked all muscle and shape and sinew and firm smooth skin . . . *Block. It. Out.*

When Kit came back into the kitchen, in actual clothes that covered skin, Molly breathed a sigh of relief. Yes, she had a mission, and yes, that mission was now a slight bit more challenging than she had anticipated, but *hey ho*, on we go! He was towelling dry his hair as he reached for his mug and he groaned when he took a sip.

"God, Molly, you make a seriously decent brew. Thanks."

"We are a family of coffee-drinkers. Actually, we are a family of everything drinkers, come to think of it. Lots of tea, water both still and sparkling, copious amounts of wine, brandy and other sundry spirits. *Yikes!* We really are quite the liquid-inhalers."

She smiled at him because she couldn't not. He looked freaking adorable. All messed and fresh. Clean and shiny. Eminently touchable. But not yet. First, she had to lay out her plan. It wasn't that it was devious, more like crafty. And if it meant she had to use feminine wiles and manipulation, so be it. She wasn't proud.

He looked at her expectantly over the rim of his mug, one brow raised.

Yup. Batter up, as they said in all the baseball films. Maybe she should be thinking of basketball analogies instead.

Maybe she should stop stalling.

"So, the thing is, I need your help," she began.

"Sure, with what?"

"Sex," she said.

Kit choked on a mouthful of coffee and had to take a moment to breathe.

"Oh, don't worry," Molly chipped in, crossing her fingers behind her back, "I don't mean you. Gosh, no. I mean, you're probably a bit like me in that department. No, I need you to help me strategise a way to get Declan Twomey to have sex with me." She smiled. And waited.

His face was priceless. Complete shock and yet total blankness. He put his mug on the counter, very carefully. Moved it in from the edge and turned the handle around. Classic displacement activity, Molly mused. Excellent.

"Let me get this straight, you want to have sex with Twomey? I thought you didn't like him in that particular way? You said so, I'm pretty sure you did." He raked a hand through his hair.

"Correct. I'm not a huge fan, in that particular way, as you so gracefully put it, but needs must."

Kit gaped at her. "Needs must? What does that even mean?"

"Well, he's an expert, isn't he? Or so he announces to all who will listen," she said, as if explaining to a child. "So, who better to show me the ropes? They say one should always go to the best, when you want the best, right?"

"Show you the *ropes*, Molly? What the hell? This sounds like a shitty idea. Why would you even want that?"

Molly smiled, playing her trump card. Or at least she hoped it would turn out to be her dealmaker.

"Because I'm a virgin."

Chapter 14

She was kidding. She had to be. There was no way the smart, gorgeous, sensuous and sexy woman standing before him had never had sex. Was *everyone* blind?

"That's a joke, right?" His voice came out on a croak. He cleared his throat. "I don't mean to be disrespectful, but have you *met* you?"

Molly dimpled at him. "Aren't you adorable? But no, it's not a joke. I'm the joke. Me. Almost a quarter of a century and still no cherry-popping going on here." She sighed and looked forlorn.

Kit tried to get his head around this new information. "But you've had boyfriends, haven't you? And surely, they weren't all daft as well as idiotic? Oh," he hesitated, "is it a religious thing? Again, no disrespect meant."

"And none taken. Relax, Kit. It's not like I don't know what we're talking about! No, it's not religion dictating my virgin state, though I do like a good Mass. I just never felt like sex. Never thought any guy I was with deserved me, the internal me, that is. I've been left in no doubt that I'm fancied, but that just hasn't been enough. I want someone who knows what they are doing and I've gone out with some dweebs. Of course, I didn't know that when first dating them. They just turned out that way." She sighed, wandered back into his living space and flopped into an armchair.

He found he really liked the way she had felt comfortable enough to make the coffee and use his space. It felt . . . good. Natural. Yet, new.

"I presume you've, you know, fooled around?" Oh shit, he could feel himself blush. He was a grown man, for God's sake. Everyone fooled around before the deed, so to speak, she'd know that. Wouldn't she?

Molly snorted. "Fooled around? Yes, I've fooled around. I'm not chaste in the purest sense of the word. I've done stuff." Now she was blushing and, God, it was adorable. A delicate pink on her lovely cheeks, her eyes lowered as the flush deepened. She twisted the hem of her cardigan in her fingers and refused to meet his gaze. She was wearing what he supposed she called her arty clothes, and they looked pretty damn good on her.

Except her curves were hidden almost entirely by a loose flowing dress and the oversized cardigan. The colours were spectacular on her which is probably why he hadn't noticed the lack of curvature. The turquoise cardigan was the exact shade as her unusual eyes, making them sparkle and shine in her freshy scrubbed face. She didn't appear to be wearing any make-up – but what did he know? Her dress was a soft rose, the perfect tone of her full lips and, again, that was what he'd noticed when seeing her on his windowsill, sipping tea, like she belonged there.

And now she was sharing all manner of personal, *private* information with him. Did he want to know this about her? Surprisingly, it turned out the answer was yes.

Kit sat down in the chair opposite, elbows on his knees, hands dropped between them. He needed to come across as casually interested as opposed to full-on focused or he'd scare the shit out of her. But focused he was. There was no way Twomey was getting his grubby hands on this amazing woman. Over Kit's dead body.

"So," he said, casual as you please, "you want Declan Twomey, sexpert extraordinaire, according to himself . . ."

"And half the women at BB &M," she interjected.

"*Noted*," he ground out. "But seriously, why him? If he's that smarmy and, okay, experienced, wouldn't that make you just another notch on his belt? And where do I come into this plan?" Christ, he was glad he remembered to ask that question.

"*Ha*, you're my biggest plus in this endeavour!" she cooed delightedly, all embarrassment gone. "I figure you, with your super-smart analytical brain, could help me draft a list of things to do to get me properly noticed by him. So he'd be entranced by me. What do you think?"

Entranced by her? What idiot wouldn't be entranced by Molly Fitzgerald? But then Twomey was also a very self-centred and greedy individual, as Kit had reason to know. And the jerk had already at least noticed, *ogled*, some of Molly's attributes at the gala.

But he said, "You're just as smart and analytical as I am, Molly. You don't need me."

"Oh, but I do," she insisted, leaning forwards herself, matching his pose. Unfortunately, the neckline of her dress gaped and showed a delicious hint of cleavage and Kit found it very hard to drag his gaze to her face. *Eyes up*, he reminded himself, *she trusts you*.

She continued, "I need a man's perspective. An insight, if you will, of what you, as a man with a penis, might want in a woman."

Kit choked. She didn't pull her punches, this one. A man with a penis. Yup. That was him alright. One that was rapidly changing shape beneath his grey sweatpants.

"Couldn't you ask your brothers, or your sisters? They either have a penis or have become acquainted with one. Ask them."

"No, silly," Molly said patiently. "I don't want them to know I'm so pathetic. That I'm a failure in the sex department. They already think I'm odd as two left feet, so I am not adding to their assumptions, thank you very much." She clasped her hands together in entreaty. "It has to be you, you're my only hope!"

Kit was halfway between feeling chuffed she asked him for help and horrified that she expected he would. And also pissed because she hadn't asked him for the sex part, just the aiding and abetting. But he owed her the courtesy of giving it some thought.

He sat back and crossed one ankle over his knee and folded his arms. He stared at her for a moment and then said abruptly, "Just so we are clear, you want *me* to come up with ways for *you* to entice Twomey into your bed, correct?"

She nodded.

"And you actually want to have sex with him? For your first time?" He knew his voice was sounding incredulous, but seriously?

She nodded again. "Well, I suppose it doesn't have to be Declan. I could pick someone else. But I don't know that many people at work that I could ask."

"You trust me enough to ask me the impossible," he countered, mildly curious as to why he was getting angrier at her ludicrous suggestion by the minute.

"Of course, I trust you," she said. "Just not for . . . you know, teaching me about sex."

"I'm good enough to show you how to get another guy to teach you though, that's what you're saying." Yes, the ire was certainly rising the more he thought about her request. "Why didn't you ask me to teach you?" The second the

161

words were out, it was too late to retract them. They were there, out there. Waiting for her response.

And it came. "You?" she laughed. *Laughed.* "But you're as geeky as me, surely. I mean you've probably had sex, because, you know, you're a man. But, experienced? Like Declan? I, well, *huh* . . . now that you mention it, I had just assumed you were a bit of a newbie, like myself." She paused, studying him as if seeing him for the first time. She let her gaze roam, from his head to his feet, and back.

He sat straighter in the chair, arms still folded, and tried not to preen. To flex his muscles. Wait, she had already commented on his physique – he couldn't be that abhorrent to her then.

"Maybe you assumed incorrectly. Maybe I have way more experience than you think. Maybe I've got lots of valuable experience and could teach you all manner of things. Things you hadn't even thought about." Okay, now he was turning himself on, imagining all the things he could do to her, with her, on her, *in* her. *Dammit. Bad, bad idea.*

"Do you?" Her question was breathy, a little flustered.

"Yes," he said, firmly, letting his eyes lock on to hers. "I have more than enough experience to initiate you into the art of sex. I know I could do a better job than Twomey, that's for damn sure. At least I would take care of you. Were you even going to tell him you were a virgin?" Kit could feel himself getting angry and frustrated all over again.

It was the stupidest idea and now he was running with it. Him. He was offering to have sex with Molly Fitzgerald, virgin. He gave himself a virtual head-slap.

He was going to hell.

She looked back at him, holding the moment, as if trying to read him. Believe him. Trust him.

"I hadn't thought that far ahead. But you're probably right. You and your smarts. Okay," she said firmly. "You can be my first."

The relief. It hit him like a thunderclap.

Before he could think better of it, he stood and, reaching forwards, took hold of her hands and pulled her up to stand in front of him.

"Lesson number one," he said.

And he kissed her.

She didn't really remember the Luas ride into the city centre or crossing to get the DART back to the flat. She didn't remember walking through the streets to get to her home. She did, however, remember the feel of him. The taste of him. His touch. His scent. His strength.

Christ on a bike. Her plan had worked. Maybe a little too well. But, she'd take it. She'd take it as she relived the feel of his lips, the pressure, the power, the *command* of him. He just upped and took control. Like a fecking boss.

She closed the front door behind her, dropped her keys on the hallstand and floated to her living room where the couch looked extremely inviting. She collapsed on a sea of cushions and let out a long breath. Holy God, had her plan ever worked!

Now what? They'd devise a series of lessons, he'd said. Oh, would they, she'd asked. It had been a simple enough kiss in the kissing scheme of things. No mouths were opened, no tongues were used but, the feel of his on hers, the pressure and easing, over and over, changing position ever so slightly each time he lifted his lips a fraction – like he was *learning* her. Like he was mapping her mouth to fit exactly to his. He held her hands against his chest and didn't touch her anywhere but her mouth. And it had felt so fluttery in her belly. Like jitters before an exam but in a much nicer way. It had been a wonderful first kiss. She had, it seemed, maligned him. He did know what he was doing. But then, she was no fool.

163

Ever since she'd seen him behind Declan's desk that time, acting all Commander in Chief, she'd begun to notice other things. Little things. And she'd paid attention in that way of hers. Listening to what was *inside* as well as on view.

She'd noticed the way he paid attention when others were speaking, how his head would tilt *just so* before he made some particularly relevant comment about the topic at hand. How he never ever spoke down to anyone. Never. Not the secretaries, not the cleaning staff and not his junior staff. In fact, he treated everyone the same. She'd been privy to a conversation with a couple of senior accountants including Benson Senior himself and had noted how Kit had been the same. Articulate, respectful and unfailingly knowledgeable.

It was impressive.

It shouldn't have been, but Molly had been at many meetings where serious dick-waving had been the order of the day. With Kit, while you couldn't say what you see is what you get – because it wasn't – she could see he was *real*. Once you looked beyond the goofy clothes, the hunched shoulders, the overlarge glasses and the almost bumbling demeanour, the real Kit was there – front and centre. And she liked him. She'd realised as they became more friends than co-workers that a lot of that affectation, as she was calling it, disappeared. Whether it was because he was comfortable with her or he forgot to act that way, well, the jury was still deliberating. All she knew was she liked all the Kits. Each version she saw, each version she knew. And now the version that kissed so simply and yet so perfectly. She liked that one a lot.

He wanted to do a lesson plan. What on earth could that entail?

When she'd suggested Twomey as her deflowering partner she had been lying through her teeth. There was no way she would let that egomaniac, smarm-laden excuse for a gentleman near her vagina. No way no how. She had decided on Kit without even realising the exact moment. Lying in bed at night, imagining sexy times with a blurred-faced lover, had changed lately. The face wasn't blurred at all. It had dark floppy hair, dark-rimmed glasses over stunning grey eyes. A quirky smile that could both smoulder and grin and beautiful fine-boned hands that could move over a computer keyboard like a freaking king. The morning she woke, breathing fast and furious with the image of those hands on her body – that was when she definitely knew who was going to be her chosen man. The man for the job.

Was she expecting him to fall for her, to be her actual boyfriend? Of course not. He was temporary. He'd move on to the next accounting gig. He might even leave the country. So, no, she was not relying on his staying power, or at least not that kind! Plus, look at her. Molly was well aware that most men of a certain age, strike that, every age viewed porn. What they saw there, skimpily dressed if dressed at all, gyrating across a bed, with any number of hard bodies, was not what a man would see if he peeped beneath Molly's clothes.

She'd watched some porn. She'd been horrified, terrified, frightened, fascinated, mesmerised and yes, a tiny bit turned on. But her takeaway message? Men might fancy her. Crave her, even lust after her. But porn star she was not. Nor did she want to be. She wanted . . . well, a partner. Someone to love and care for. To be loved and cared for, in return. Was that too much to ask? So far, the answer appeared to be a resounding yes.

You only had to look at the women in her life to see why it was different for her. Frankie, film star and sister-in-law extraordinaire, beauty personified – yes, even with her recent scar, she was a genuinely beautiful female. Her face, both before and after her nasty encounters a couple of years back, still graced billboards and the odd fashion magazine. Not as much now, by her choice, but she was just that gorgeous. Molly's sister Caro had that timeless, effortless beauty that radiated confidence and intelligence. She certainly had both, but what captured and captivated people was her smile. It lit up every space about her. Seeing how her husband's eyes followed her about a room? That should have been sickening but, damn it, was just bloody romantic. And as for Ali, the baker and master secret-keeper? She had her own special kind of attraction. Fine-boned and whippet-thin, she resembled a French street urchin but one with style. Hard to describe her appeal but, Christ, she had it in spades. The camera *loved* her and the reviews for her shows where she taught the uninitiated how to make scones – okay, that was being super-simplistic – well, those reviews were phenomenal and she was fast becoming a star. Molly was so glad for her. So unbelievably relieved that the darkness that had hovered over Ali's head for most of her life was now lifted. Not gone, it would never be gone, but lightness had replaced all the sorrow and pain. That was a very good thing.

Molly was under no illusions about her own attractions. She had cool hair – if you liked crazy curls in dark auburn veering towards chestnut. She had good eyebrows, all the Fitzgeralds did, and the same freaky eye colour as her oldest brother Flynn. They weren't quite aqua. Nor were they turquoise. Just a very odd pale, yet intense, icy blue, but she liked them well enough. Then there was her body, all those roundy curves – in all the right places, sure, if you *liked* a lot of round. She did not. Exercise was not her bag, leaping and running were too much for her ample breasts so walking kept her fit. She walked a lot. Every day. Back and forth from home to DART and on to the office. On dry days she always stopped a station before her own and walked the extra, hence the delectable runners she carried in her large tote. Walking suited her. It allowed her overly busy mind to settle to one thing. Or at least that was the aim. Not always successful but many a thorny maths problem got solved on a good long walk.

So why had she really chosen Kit? She knew the innate gentleman in him would balk at her asking Declan to have sex with her. Molly knew if she'd asked Declan or even put herself in his way on an office night out, she would have ended up in his bed. He didn't have a discriminating bone in his body. For him, any woman would do. For all she knew, any man either. But Kit? Kit was different. She knew that as well as she knew herself. One thing she always acknowledged about herself was her ability to read people. Sometimes it was a feeling. It could be a wave of cold air or the equivalent of an aura that warned her off walking down the same side of the street as a stranger. Equally it could be a roll of warmth that made her feel safe, secure. Welcome. Kit was in the latter department but there was also something else she felt around him. The fact that she couldn't *see* all of him at all. He was holding something back. Not in a dangerous way. She felt no fear from him, but he did have secrets, that she knew one hundred per cent. But then, so did she. And after that one kiss, she wasn't entirely sure *safe* was a word she would be using in relation to him ever again.

Molly looked down at her legs, stretched out before her on the couch. Shapely, from all the walking, but not by any means what she called summer legs. You couldn't just whip these out and show them off. They would need a lot of attention. And that brought her to the other problem. Shaving. Would she have to shave her legs every day in case one of those days turned out to be *the* day? *Gah!* That sounded like a lot of work. And her bikini line? And her underarms? Okay, that last bit wasn't a problem. Daily in the shower and all that, but the rest? *Ugh.* She'd better invest in some decent products. She remembered Caro complaining about these very things when she first decided to put herself out there after years of being a mum, and only a mum. Molly had laughed at her. Told her she was falling into male ideals of womanhood et cetera.

Karma was indeed a bitch.

Molly hauled herself off the couch. It was only early afternoon and there was studying to be done. Accountancy was like that. There was always studying for yet another exam. Yes, she was that person.

Remembering a text she'd received earlier, like the email from before, asking her to fudge some bottom line, with the temptation of a big pay-off, made her cross. What idiot could possibly think she'd be bought? For any sum of money? Whoever it was needed to get real and stop contacting her or she'd have to do some digging and find out who it was. Probably another joke, but she didn't have the headspace for it. Not today. Today, as she made a sandwich to take to her little office, she knew thoughts of *that* kiss and Kit's lesson plan and when she might get to hear what that entailed would keep her occupied. Thinking those happy thoughts would make studying so much more challenging, and therefore fun, than figuring out some joker's attempt at humour.

Kit switched off the sander, tugged his mask down and wiped the sweat from his forehead. Manual labour sucked. It wasn't that he was afraid of sweating – he ran and played basketball to get that done. It was the hard graft for a specific job that entailed concentration and skill, two things severely lacking within him right now. Granted the lack of skill was a no-brainer – he'd been learning how to sand floors on the fly for only a few weeks. But his trusty concentration? His one amazing never-let-him-down talent? *Gone. Kaput.* Moving the damned heavy machine in one direction or another was, or should have been, child's play. He'd already completed all the upstairs and half the downstairs floors and they looked great, So, he *could* sand. That wasn't in fact the issue at all.

The issue was Molly.

Everything Molly-related was crowding his head. Her plan to seduce Declan with his help? Crazytown. Her belief that he would do it? Would help her? Complete nonsense. No man in his right mind would encourage any woman to sleep with Declan-bloody-Twomey. Twomey was an ass. Anyone could see it. He'd thought Molly smarter than that. She was bright and clever and sharp and could have any man she chose. Couldn't she see her own attributes? To throw herself and her *virginity* away on a jerk like Twomey? That was the most ridiculous thing she'd ever said. Granted he'd not known her that long, but any fool could see her thought process was clear and intelligent, any fool . . .

Yup, shit, he'd been played. *He* was the fool.

A grin split his face as he realised Molly wanted *him* to take her to bed. That's what she'd wanted all along! There was no way she would have had sex with an ass. No way! She'd saved herself all these years for the right man so he should have seen right away that she would never sell herself short. God, she was good! And he'd almost fallen for it. Okay, he *had* fallen for it, but he'd also put her straight. She needed to do this mission of hers properly. And he was exactly the man to help.

He'd told the truth about his experience. He knew what he was doing. Any woman he'd slept with in the past had been a pleasure and an education. Every woman was different. Unique. What worked for one did not work for another. The man who made the assumption that it did was a fool. The trick was to listen. To pay attention. To analyse. And if being a maths genius helped, well, wasn't he lucky? No, it wasn't a numbers game, it wasn't a game at all. But it was all in the details – and that, *that* he could do.

Shit, though. She was a virgin. He'd never slept with a virgin before and had kind of assumed at this stage he would have dodged that bullet. Some men might think that it was a privilege to be a woman's first. They were right. It was. But those same men often also assumed that they would be her only. Or their possession.

Kit was under no such illusion.

No matter that he might have started thinking about Molly way too often, way too intently, long before her offer – he knew that anything he had with her would only be short-term. Could only be. Who knew where he'd be sent next? Just because he was doing up his gran's house, okay, *his* house, didn't mean roots were being planted. He'd been shunted from one place to another most of his life – roots were not a thing. He wanted the house to look well, to feel like a home, his home, but one he could still leave, because that was what he did. He took a job, did the job and left. There was no room for relationships, of any real kind. His only proper longish-term one was in college. It had been good but she wanted a life in California, as she had every right to, and he didn't. He'd needed to be in Boston at the time, ugly though that situation had been, and so he'd stayed. For the trial. Which reminded him, *phone Mom.* Check in. Be a good son, no matter what. He checked the time and calculated the zone difference. Another hour and he'd phone.

Kit loved his mother, he knew he did, but as a duty now. Not the same way he'd loved Gran, but that was fine.

Gran hadn't dragged him about, expected all kinds of loyalty and shit. Gran had just been there. Always. No questions, no demands, no recriminations. But what did he know? Being a parent versus a grandparent had to be different. Maybe Gran hadn't been a great mother. A rather distant one according to her daughter. But, reasoned Kit, Gran had been working full time. And, yeah, so had his mom, at least until his early teens.

He shook his head. Gran was gone. He had to move on. His mother was alive and well if not exactly living the dream. And she expected him to check in on her fairly regularly. He could do that much. He might not always like what she had to say, but those were the breaks. She didn't particularly like all his conversational contributions either, so a bit of the pot and kettle there.

He reached over to the photograph on the sideboard, remembering how grateful he was that Molly hadn't commented on it. It showed his mother, himself and his stepfather. The man whose name he could barely utter. The same man who was, in a roundabout way, responsible for the very career Kit now enjoyed. Go figure.

Kit replaced the photo and cleaned up his sander debris before heading to the shower. He had a sex schedule to create and that meant some serious planning ahead.

He loved a good plan.

Chapter 15

Work was busy the following week and Molly relished it. The audit was over but her pile of accounts seemed to be growing by the second. Declan had handed her several new ones and although she hadn't got to them yet, the prospect was actually appealing.

Her off-work time was also proving to be busy. She'd had two dates with Kit. Two. And it was only Wednesday. When he'd texted to ask her to meet him at Dún Laoghaire pier on Sunday afternoon, she'd freaked out – there might have been a screech or three. Had he changed his mind? Was he reneging on their deal? *Argh!!!* She couldn't even text her sisters to ask for advice as they had no clue what she was up to.

She'd arrived a little early, trying to gauge the walk from the flat to coincide with his arrival. He was sure to be early, he was that kind of guy. But no sign of him. She was perched on a bollard, gazing out to sea when she heard him call to her. Turning, her face broke into a grin. Even if he was breaking their deal, he was doing it in style. Two huge Teddy's ice-cream cones were in his hands and he was walking pretty speedily.

"Hey," he said, "can you grab this? It's starting to melt all over my hand!"

Grab it she could. Who didn't love a Teddy's cone? It was an institution in South County Dublin and it was an unwritten rule that you got one from the hole-in-the-wall kiosk a few hundred metres from the pier before or after the walk. Preferably before. As Kit had.

"Oh thanks," Molly said. "Perfect. And a flake? Excellent. Someone taught you well."

The piece of flake chocolate was pulled out and duly gobbled down.

Kit stared at her in horror. "You don't leave it in?"

Molly chuckled around her chocolate. "I've tried that, believe me. But inevitably I make a huge mess and end up spilling either the flake or the ice cream – often both. I will be very impressed with your skill if you don't come a cropper."

"Prepare to be impressed," he said smugly.

And they'd walked. Meandered, really. On the upper path going down, the lower on the return. They chatted about nothing in particular as they ate their cones but once they were finished, Kit, chocolate and ice-cream free, reached for her hand. She stopped and looked at him quizzically.

"My plan," he said with a lopsided smile, "includes dates. I am absolutely not taking you to bed without a modicum of wooing."

"But," she sputtered, "we're not, you know . . . real." God, she was mortified and tried to pull her hand away. She didn't want to let go. Not one bit. His hand was warm, firm and felt strong wrapped around hers. But this wouldn't do. She didn't want relationship expectations. She just wanted to finally have some bloody sex.

"My way or no way," Kit said firmly. "No, this isn't dating in the traditional sense of the word. I get you don't want a relationship. But I'm not so crass as to discuss accounts with you during the day and expect you to feel comfortable enough to get naked with me later. So, we are going to be social. Or more social then we were."

Get naked with him. Yeah, she hadn't really thought this through.

"How many of these not-real dates do you need?" she asked with serious trepidation.

"As many as it takes for you to feel comfortable with me."

"I *am* comfortable with you. I wouldn't have agreed otherwise."

Kit gave her a look. He stopped walking and pulled her into his arms, his going around her body. He bent his head and nuzzled her neck, kissing his way up towards her ear where he whispered all manner of suggestions. She heard words like breasts and sucking and hard nipples and biting and heat and wet and come ... *Good Lord!*

Molly gasped and pulled back from him, knowing, *feeling* her face on fire. "*Oh.* Oh goodness," she gasped, "I–I guess I'm not as ready as I thought."

Mortified, she tried to move away but he simply changed the angle of his body and urged her forward, one arm lying casually across her shoulders.

"Molly, while I know this is a practical thing for you, something you just want to get out of the way, there is no need for it to be mechanical. Instructional, yes. Sure. But I want it to be memorable in the best of ways. You have recruited a planner, or maybe I recruited myself. Either way, we're doing it slow and steady. Until we don't."

The bastard winked at that titbit and Molly could feel her face flame again. What had she been thinking? She would die of all forms of embarrassment before the deed was done. She should have hired a complete stranger – one with up-to-date medical records, of course. God, would she have to ask Kit if he was 'clean'? This was a disaster. An absolute bloody disaster of an idea.

174

They reached the bandstand on their return stroll and Kit laughed as he reminded her of the gala night and her bathroom conversations. Molly was grateful as they discussed work for the remaining of the walk, though Kit's arm remained in place. She liked it. The weight of it. His hand resting against her upper arm, his fingers stroking lightly. But not lightly enough. Her nerves had sat up and taken noticed and the tingling went all the way down her arm, causing her to feel warm from the inside out. Because of fingers, for God's sake. At this rate, she'd melt in a puddle if he kissed her again.

He didn't. Or at least not on the mouth. Instead her hugged her, like a friend hug, and kissed her cheek as he said a cheery goodbye and that he'd see her on the following morning at the office.

But that wasn't all.

Oh no. Mr Planner sent her a memo to meet him at the office main door after work on Tuesday. No reason. No explanation. Did she touch up her lipstick in the bathroom room and untie her hair from its bun? She might have – it seemed prudent – she decided to loosen up a bit after work, that was all. Not because he had commented on her curls and what they might feel like. Not that reason.

He took her for an early-bird meal at a local Thai restaurant and then a play at the Gate. They talked all the way through the meal and all the way back to the DART station after the play. He held her hand. She felt every inch of his skin against hers and told herself not to be ridiculous. They argued amicably about the play's themes as they walked along O'Connell Street to the train and Molly really, really tried to not hope for a kiss. A Stoneybatter kiss not a Dún Laoghaire pier one.

When Kit brushed his mouth to hers it wasn't like either of them. He held her face cupped in his palms and pressed his lips to hers. And then, *God*, then he tasted her. It was like he had learned her mouth before, but now he was savouring it. Relishing her softness and fullness. Her flavour. It was delicious. And toe-curling. He broke the kiss and pressed his lips to her cheeks and her forehead.

"Thank you for a lovely evening. See you tomorrow."

And with one last smile he was gone and she went up the station escalator, wondering what the hell had she let herself in for.

Chapter 16

Easter was late that year and the entire Fitzgerald crew gathered in Dalkey for the Sunday feast. Caro, Toby and Nick were home and that in itself caused great excitement. They all still got such a kick out of hearing Toby, soon to be fifteen, speaking with Nick in fluent Italian. They went back and forth between English and Italian and it was ridiculously charming.

Caro looked so happy. So content. So at ease with this new family unit. It had been Toby and her for so long they had all secretly worried any man would ever get a look in. Nick was that man. He spoke with Toby man to man. He wasn't his father. Never would be. But he was a father *figure*. But then Toby was no normal teen, either. Caro was mature enough to let them have their own relationship. She did admit, privately, that it had been hard to share parenting. Very hard to ask for suggestions or include Nick in decision-making. There'd been a learning curve but the fact that Nick and Toby had been forming a bond before Caro and Nick's relationship was solid had helped.

There was a leg of lamb resting on the sideboard, the roasted potatoes still in the oven getting as crispy as they could, a casserole of cauliflower-and-broccoli cheese grilling the crust to almost burnt and Jo grinding black pepper over a dish of julienned carrots. Home. It smelled like home on a holiday.

Ali walked into the kitchen carrying a tart of some kind, no doubt a new invention of hers, and Gabe followed on her heels.

"The rest of your family are parking their car," he said in that quiet way of his. He studied Molly seriously for a moment. "*Hmm*," he said and gave her that precious, rare smile. "Things are changing for you. I'm glad." And he went about his business.

Gabe was funny like that. If Molly felt she could read people, Gabe knew he could. And did. It was kind of scary but freakishly awesome too.

Devlin bounced into the kitchen, with a massive bouquet of lilies for his mum. He kissed her soundly and twirled her around. "For the best mum in the world!" he said, laughing. "Happy Easter!"

"Who are you and what have you done with my hothead of a son?" she teased back, burrowing her face in the glorious scent. She was referring to his wild days. Days before he found out that the love of his life actually loved him back. He was, truthfully, still a bit of a hothead but way less frequently, to everyone's relief.

Molly helped with the finishing touches to the table. The Easter Bunny had already left a chocolate egg at each place setting, so Molly had to do cutlery and napkins. She took her time, precious peaceful moments to take a breath. She loved Easter: its ceremonies the few days before, especially Good Friday and Easter Saturday night. Easter felt like a renewal, a promise and a hope. She loved the candles and the incense, the Stations of the Cross and all the kneeling and standing during the long Friday vigil. She used often read at the Easter services, sometimes the narrator part, which she loved because it was telling the story, one that didn't change from century to century. The rhythm and consistency of it had soothed her, every time. But she'd not done it for years now. She had gone this time on the Saturday night, doing the readings like when she was younger, in the local church in Dalkey and strolled home with her parents to overnight at the family home.

They were using the dining room today. It got used frequently but the family were equally happy squishing in around the slightly smaller kitchen table. She set twelve places as she'd asked her mum if Kit could join them. The answer had of course been yes, but Kit it turned out was busy. He volunteered at a homeless shelter kitchen and it was his turn on the rota. He'd come for dessert, if that was okay, he'd said. So, a place was set, in case he got here early and could grab a plate.

She'd seen him at work during the few days since the play, but like ships passing in the night. He was always in meetings with Benson Senior or at his desk, with the door closed and blinds down – the universal 'don't disturb unless the building is on fire' sign. They'd shared a coffee in the canteen but others were about and Kit had seemed distracted. Pleased though, to be asked for Easter dinner. She hoped, as she placed his napkin at the setting next to hers, that he could make it. She'd not been surprised he'd be volunteering. It was, it seemed, a thing with him. Made her feel like a selfish, spoiled, privileged Dalkey-ite – but she could live with that. She knew what her strengths were and volunteering, all that people-ing, was not for her. She needed space and time. But God, she admired the shit out of Kit and anyone else who stepped up like that.

He got nothing from the basketball training either, no recognition, no funding, no payment. When she queried that, he simply laughed. "Are you crazy?" he'd said. "I get so much. Every Saturday when I can, and the odd Thursday evening, weather permitting, I come away on a high. Those kids give me their trust, their time, their commitment, their respect and sometimes, if I'm very lucky, their story. I come away richer, every day I spend with them." What made Molly wonder about Kit was the fact that, on any given workday, not one colleague or co-worker would have a clue what the real Kit was like. The non-nerd, non-geek, non-odd-ball Kit. She was only scraping the surface but, damn, that well ran deep.

"Why are you sighing?" Ali asked as she placed her tart on the sideboard. "Man trouble?"

"Not everything is man-related," Molly mumbled.

"So that's a yes, then?"

"Yes. No. I don't want to talk about it."

"Ah, the classic trio!" Caro carried in the carrot dish and placed it on a mat on the table. "We've all been there, love, and you can bend our ears if you wish."

"No, thanks. There's nothing to tell." Molly took the roasted potatoes from Dev and they too went on the table.

The others filed in with warmed plates, the lamb now carved and on a platter, the gravy and the veg gratin.

"Tell about what?" Frankie asked, sitting next to her husband.

"Nothing," Molly repeated and, with a glare at Caro and Ali, she too took a seat.

"Who are we expecting?" Flynn asked, sitting opposite Molly and indicating the spare setting.

"Kit said he might make it in time for dessert." She tried to sound casual but the instant stares from everyone at the table proved her performance to be shabby.

Flynn arched an eyebrow, Flynn-fashion. Cool and collected, he didn't have to say anything to make her feel like she'd blundered.

"What?" she said. "You've all met him. He's nice. We're friends. That's all."

"Protesting too much?" was Dev's helpful interjection as he selected potatoes.

"Oh, leave her alone," Jo said, smiling at Molly. "All of your friends are welcome at this table, and always have been. Now, gravy, anyone?"

Molly silently thanked her mum as they all dug into the food.

The chocolate eggs were opened even as they ate their main course and how Jo remembered who preferred Crunchie over Beano, Flake over After Eight, they would never fathom but that was just one of her million parenting skills.

The doorbell sounded as they were clearing plates and Molly darted down the hall, smoothing the front of her peasant-style blouse. The flowing almost ankle-length skirt had similar embroidery around the hem, and she knew she looked like she'd escaped from a seventies TV show, or a circus. Did she care? Not a jot. These were the clothes that felt weekend-comfortable. She loved her office suits – their business feel, the authority that came with them, the shoes she had to wear. But she still loved the fabrics and the colours she wore at weekends.

She pulled open the door, a smile starting before she even saw him.

"Hey," Kit said, handing her a bunch of divinely scented hyacinths. "Happy Easter!" He then produced a bag from behind his back and presented her with an enormous Easter egg in dark chocolate from an actual Chocolate shop.

She fell a little, right then. Or rather a little farther. Day by bloody day, Kit Elliot had been getting under her skin. Not in the creepy way. In the way that had her thinking about him instead of columns of numbers, instead of rows of data, instead of tax percentages and tax refunds. Instead of pretty much anything. She thought about his kisses, gentle and small though they were. She imagined what it would be like when he kissed her like he meant business. All-night business. And her stomach fluttered now as he leaned in and laid his lips to hers, light as a feather.

"I've got flowers for your mum, too," he said, stepping back and digging into the bag again.

"Thank you," Molly said, inadequate though that sounded.

He followed her down the hall and into the dining room where dessert was being doled out by Ali. Greetings were exchanged and the flowers delighted over by a grateful Jo.

The dessert was everything it should be. Perfect pastry case and a light lemon frothy thing was how Molly described it. With a dollop of freshly whipped cream, it was the exact finish for the lamb and the whole group partook with enthusiasm. Dev got up to carry dishes to the kitchen, helped by Flynn.

Kit was chatting to Toby when there was a tug at Molly's subconscious brain. Something off? No, not off. Different. There was a vibe coming from the room, not normally there. She glanced about the room, her eyes landing unerringly on Frankie. Ah. There was news to be shared, Molly knew, good news. Happy, welcome news.

Flynn sat as Dev strolled back into the room, a bottle of champagne under one arm, a tray of flutes balanced precariously in the other. He set everything on the table as the family began to wonder what the fuss was for. Dev pulled a small bottle of fizzy juice from his back pocket and handed it to Frankie, a big sloppy grin spread across his face.

"*We*," he reached for Frankie's hand and pulled her knuckles up for a kiss, "*are going to have a baby!*"

The shrieks and shouts of congratulations could be heard far and wide, Molly imagined as she got in line, bouncing with excitement, to hug her brother and sister-in-law. Jo was instantly teary and, as Dev disentangled himself from his mum to pop the cork and pour champagne for all except Frankie, Molly saw her dad blow his nose with extra enthusiasm. It was good news, indeed. Great news. Seeing her brother glow from the inside out was a sight to behold. If possible, he looked happier than on his wedding day and *that* was seriously happy.

Once again as the chatter babbled around her, Molly felt a mood change. *Oh, now that's not good.* And then she sensed it. From Flynn of all people. A wave of such sorrow and heartbreak that Molly gasped as if a knife had twisted in her gut. Across the room she saw Gabe stiffen as if he too felt the uneasy, uncomfortable feeling. She turned her head slightly and saw Flynn, champagne flute held tightly in one hand and the other gripping the back of his chair, knuckles white. The twitch in his clenched jaw had Molly move towards him as casually as she could.

"Hey," she touched his hand lightly, "are you okay?"

He whipped it away, jerking slightly at her touch. "*Yes*," he growled. "Of course." He cleared his throat and continued. "It's excellent news. I'm, *ah*, delighted for them."

But it didn't sound like Flynn at all. This was a bark, a response to a *situation*. Not a brother thrilled and happy for his sibling and the girl they all loved so much. Straightening his shoulders as if bracing himself, he moved towards the happy couple and Molly watched as he hugged them both. If it was strained, to her eyes, she was alone in that. Until she saw Gabe, a worried look on his face too and knew she was right.

183

Flynn was suffering.

Before she could do or say anything that might be useful, Kit handed her a glass of bubbly. She clinked her glass to his and sipped it automatically. When she searched for her oldest brother again, he was gone.

"Your family is a lot, you know that, right?" Kit asked as they strolled back along Coleimore Road to the Dalkey DART station. He had secured her hand as they left the front gateway and, since she didn't pull away, he figured his campaign of not-dating-dating was going along splendidly. He rubbed his thumb across her fingers, liking the feel of her flesh beneath his. He tried to halt the image of other flesh beneath his and failed, failed miserably.

"Yeah, I know," Molly answered. "They scare off a lot of people because they are loud and find themselves hilariously funny."

"You speak as if you're not part of them," he said ponderingly.

"Mostly I feel like a bit of a misfit. I don't have the same sense of humour, I don't get the same jokes, haven't displayed any artistic prowess since leaving college and I often feel like one massive disappointment."

Kit couldn't believe what he was hearing. "Are you listening to yourself? Were you just sharing the same room with me? You're a pivot for them. They ask your opinion on everything and pay attention when you speak. I was an only child and my own mother didn't do that." *God, that was stupid*, he thought. *Shouldn't have mentioned my relationship with my mother. Molly will want to follow that avenue rather than discuss herself.*

Molly turned to look at him, angling her head. "Didn't you get on with your mum?"

See? Trying to turn things around. Not happening. She

needed to let out her own family frustration but he needed her to see how necessary she was to them. He could see it clear as day. They needed her. Her balance to their artistry. Her reason to their rhyme.

"What I saw this afternoon," Kit said, smoothly ignoring her question, swinging their clasped hands gently as they continued to the station, "was a family united." He paused for a moment to gather his thoughts but could *feel* her waiting. "No, you're not the same as the others. You're probably most like your eldest brother in that you are self-contained while the others are a bit more, let's say, flamboyant. But you have a wonderful no-nonsense attitude that they rely on. How many times were you asked questions over the last couple of hours, and not just when I was there?"

He could see her mulling it over and as she did he thought back on the dessert and the chatter. No, it hadn't centred on Molly but every one of them, including her parents, used her as ballast. Not in a bad way, it was obviously done without intention, but she was their touchstone. She gave practical advice. Gave solid, real answers. Asked clever, pointed questions. She was bloody amazing.

As they boarded the train, he began recounting some of what he'd witnessed and she soon laughed at her own silliness, somewhat reluctantly agreeing that he just *might* have a point.

He got off in Dún Laoghaire with her and they began the walk to her flat. He hadn't let go of her hand, except to purchase tickets, and he held it still. Fingers linked, it felt . . . normal. But not in any way dull. Easy, but not complacent.

They reached her house steps and she stopped abruptly. "God, Kit. I'm so sorry. I never thought it through. You should have stayed on the DART to go home." She slapped her hand over her mouth as if she'd done something truly dreadful.

Kit grinned. "Oh, no. You don't get rid of me that easily. I have a new lesson for you. A 'we are not dating but are definitely going to have sex' lesson. And that lesson starts the moment we get inside your flat."

Her instant blush was a delight and, as she sputtered out some kind of denial of his lesson plan, he laughed and, dropping her hand and laying down his bag, held her face in his palms, stroking her rosy cheeks with tenderness.

"This is what you want, isn't it?"

"Um, yes, I think so?" She squeaked out an answer that sounded suspiciously like a question.

"Molly," Kit said, his voice low and steady, "we do absolutely nothing you aren't ready for. Nothing you don't want. And all I ask of you, is that you *say* what you want. Okay? I'll need the words. The consent, as we go along."

"Are we going to have sex tonight? I mean now?" There was abject terror in her voice.

"No. We are not. But we are most definitely going to fool around. Are you up for that?"

"Sure. I mean, yes, I consent. Oh, that sounds stupid. Sorry." She fumbled in her bag for the keys and Kit took them from her.

He climbed the steps, pulling her behind him and opened the front door. She was adorably flustered and probably anxious and unnerved by what he'd said. But Kit knew this much, she needed him to take charge. And that suited him more than fine.

He was a 'take charge' kind of guy.

Chapter 17

Oh God, oh God, it was happening. Okay, slow down, you lunatic, it wasn't happening but some things were! Sex things. Was she ready? Would she ever be ready? *Oh, for fuck sake, take a chill pill.*

Molly's head buzzed as she and Kit entered her hallway. It wasn't like she hadn't done things before. Some good exploratory things. Nice, feel-good things. But with Kit? Everything felt different. His light kisses already felt bigger than any of the other more intense kisses she'd shared with previous boyfriends.

How could that be? He was just Kit. The nerdy numbers guy who mostly dressed appallingly and always looked like he needed managing. Sure, he could talk the talk – really well, actually. And he could schmooze with the bigwigs in the firm but he was still . . . Kit. Her friend.

She could do this. Oh, wait. She was *doing* this.

While she had been cataloguing her crazy notions, Kit had been busy. He'd walked her through to the living room and without her even being aware of it, she was seated in the middle of her couch and he was next to her. Leaning towards her. And this was it.

"Wait, Kit. Stop."

He did. Instantly. "Talk to me, Molly," he said quietly, sincerely.

"I'm scared," she mumbled.

He smiled. "What's your biggest fear right now," he asked as he ran his hand down her arm, from shoulder to wrist and back. Smooth even strokes. Relaxing yet . . . edgy.

"You'll think I'm stupid, but what if I don't turn you on? We're friends, right? You're doing this as a favour. There was no fancying involved. And I'm afraid I'm not experienced enough to be a good kisser." There. She'd said it.

Cold hard facts. And she couldn't look at him.

He was having none of it. Resting his finger under her chin, he tilted her head to his.

"Look at me," he said.

It wasn't a suggestion. It was a command.

She raised her eyes to his and blinked into his steady gaze.

"You," he said softly, the knuckles of his hand on her cheek stroking lightly, "are beautiful." He shifted on the couch, still facing her. "You are truly beautiful. You are so damn fanciable I can barely keep my hands off you. How I've managed to stop from taking you in my arms over the last few weeks completely baffles me. Every curve of your cheek, turn of your wrist," he took her hand and kissed the inner side of her wrist as he spoke, "every smile you bestow on me makes me want to kiss you senseless. This, tonight? This isn't about experience. It's about exploring. About feeling. Enjoying, I hope. It's about this."

His lips landed on hers, not tentatively, not gently. He kissed her mouth like he meant it. Like he needed it. And, God, she needed it too. Didn't know just how much until it began to change. Shift. Deepen. Develop into so much more. He angled her back against the cushions, his mouth never leaving or lifting from hers. He grazed those knuckles along the swell of her breasts now, over the loose neckline of her blouse, tugging the red ribbon holding it all together. She was never so glad to have worn her newest lace balconette bra because nothing was more of a turn-off than her sports contraption that held everything in one solid place. The delicate nude fabric was way more tantalising, she knew.

Dragging his mouth from hers with a gasp, he kissed his way along her jaw, down her neck and across the creamy swells encased in filigree. "Gorgeous," he whisper-moaned. "Your skin is like alabaster."

Well, now. Alabaster. The man knew his sculpting materials. But then Molly forgot about hard smooth surfaces and the fancy names they were called because Kit shoved down the cups of her bra and let his mouth follow where his fingers had been. He found her nipple and made fast work of taking it into his mouth and sucking deeply. He groaned and licked and gasped and swirled his tongue all around, peppering her skin with kisses and sweeps of hot, needy strokes. "Jesus, Molly, your breasts are so . . ." Words seemed to fail him, but she got the gist. All the attention they were getting was starting to pay dividends down below. She'd heard, read and watched on screen how some women gloried in this touch. How they were turned on by breast stimulation and she used to think how bloody unfair it was. There she was, large full breasts at the ready and they'd never done a damn thing for her. Guys had squeezed and fondled them in the past and there had been zilch. No pleasurable reaction from her. At all. Till now. She squirmed. She could feel herself tingle and tremble. Feel herself getting wet and throbby, her belly starting to coil in secret anticipation.

Holy smoke, this felt good. Kit was doing amazing things to her body and she was still almost fully dressed. A fleeting worry about flab and belly-fat and roundy bits tried to edge through her bliss but, for once, she told it to feck off. It was one thing for a man to kiss her breasts and use his hands and fingers on her as had happened but, before, she'd always been an onlooker in her own attempt at pleasure. This was different.

She was participating. She felt it. She believed him as he moaned pleasure words against her skin. Most importantly, her body believed him. She didn't have to endure anything. There was no fumbling, no squeezing, or groping. He was confident and sure. Definite in what he was doing. It was sexy. A total turn-on. She wanted Kit Elliot to keep going. To do more. Explore *her* more. And she knew *he* knew it was her, Molly Fitzgerald, he was kissing, touching. Knowing. She used to feel the few men she'd let have this access to her in the past hadn't really cared whose body they were fondling – it was just a body.

Not with Kit. Not remotely with Kit.

She began to get busy. It was her turn to touch him. She reached up and spread her hands along his shoulders, feeling every sinew, every muscle. Down his upper arms where those muscles bunched and moved beneath her fingers, trembling to her touch. She'd seen him in his basketball T-shirt and had, naturally, checked him out. He was so fit and toned it'd made her mouth water. Now, even under the fabric of his shirt the feel of his hard, heated skin was a delicious tug to her core. She threaded her fingers through his hair, holding him steady to her breast, and breathed him in, let all the feelings of giddy need and want and desire flood her being.

This. This was the *more* she'd always looked for. The *more, please* she'd never felt. And it was hot. *So. Damn. Hot.*

Reaching behind her, Kit unclasped her bra through her blouse and let the silky fabric fall free from her skin. Suddenly embarrassed, Molly reached to pull her blouse together and he grasped her hands. "No," he growled, "these are too beautiful to hide. Jesus, you're fucking gorgeous!" He bent his head again, holding her breasts in his hands as he swept his mouth from one to the other, his tongue caressing and leaving a trail of pebbled skin in its wake.

Pulling her upright, he hauled the blouse over her head and tossed it aside. Without hesitation he bent to her again, kissing her mouth like a man denied water for eternity. Oh, *yes*, she was totally on board with this – who cared that her breasts were on view, that her stomach was exposed to the air let alone Kit's eyes when he eventually dragged his mouth from hers. Maybe if she kept kissing him back, the way he was kissing her, he'd be so drunk on pheromones he'd go slightly blind, just enough to blur the vista below him. Chance would be a fine thing.

But then a funny thing happened. As Kit continued to kiss her, whisper to her, taste her and feel her body, she realised it didn't matter. He wasn't judging so why should she? She also realised she absolutely, right now had to see his body, feel his chest, taste his nipples and if she didn't she'd explode.

"*Off!*" she said, as bossy as she could muster with all the desire flooding her. "I need this *off!*" She tugged his shirt from the waistband of his trousers and began clumsily unbuttoning it.

"God, yes," he agreed, doing that man thing, reaching around to his neck and hauling the whole thing off in one go, buttons still intact. "I need to feel your skin against mine." He lowered his body back to hers and the groan of pleasure that came from both of them was so loud they both laughed – when they caught their breath.

"I imagined you'd feel like this," Kit said. "Soft, hot, smooth." He ran his hand down her body, reverently, over

191

the curves, into the dips, pressing harder in some places, skimming her skin in others.

She watched his hand, letting herself really feel all the touches, enjoy all the nuances of his exploration. She raised hers to his chest, echoing his trail and letting her fingers graze and smooth, press and hold, wherever they landed. His chest was sculpted, maybe not alabaster because he definitely had the sun kiss his golden skin. But as smooth, hard, chiselled. The running and the basketball alone hadn't done this, she thought, as her hand glided down over his ribs, those abs shifting beneath her touch. He hauled in a breath.

"That feels so good," he said, watching her hand, the way she'd watched his.

She brushed a thumb over his nipple and the sucking in of air told her how much that simple touch pleased him. She tried it again and then circled it, feeling all the textures. With daring, she raised herself up and let her tongue do what her fingers had done seconds before.

"*Jesus*," he hissed.

But she knew it wasn't a bad hiss. A stop-right-now hiss. Oh, no. This she could interpret very well indeed. She took his nipple into her mouth, sucked and used her teeth and the response from him was everything. He loved this. It turned him on as much as his attentions had for her.

"You like?" She couldn't help the mischievous smile that tugged her mouth as her eyes met his across the expanse of his chest.

"Hell, yeah, I like. Feel this." He took her hand from where it lay against his pecs and guided it down to the bulge in his trousers. "I like it a lot."

"*Huh*," she said. "I didn't know that was a thing. That guys liked their nipples sucked too. I like this lesson plan of yours."

192

"We do. We are simple creatures and pretty much like every single thing you do. Everywhere you touch. Every feel of your skin against ours."

She knew as soon as he'd begun talking, his eyes never leaving hers, that he wasn't talking about men in general. He was telling *her* how much he liked her touch. She grasped his length beneath the fabric and could swear she felt it swell. It felt hot, hard, long and thick. A little bit scary, if one was being totally honest, and Molly had learned that honesty was good. Kit had showed her that so she knew she could be totally honest with him.

"You're extra-large, aren't you?" she grumbled. "Just my bloody luck."

Kit choked out a laugh. "Try not to sound too enthusiastic! Believe it or not, that's usually something a woman wants. And is always what a man wants to hear." He grinned at her, easing her worry, as she knew he would.

"Yeah, but I bet they're young and stupid when they first encounter a jumbo penis. *And* they don't know the damage it can do." She sighed theatrically. "You'll probably be brilliant at all this sex stuff and ruin me for any other man but don't forget," she added in case he was getting big-headed – the *other* big head – "I'm not young or stupid so I know this can hurt. I know this mightn't fit. I'm not going into this in the throes of first love, gasping for it. I'm a sane responsible adult. And don't you forget it."

Kit's grin widened. "God, you're priceless. If I was less confident in my own abilities, I would have shrunk to nothing by now. But I'm not and I haven't." He put his own hand over hers as it gripped him.

The feel of that, the way he used his own hand to slide hers up and down, along his own cock, was strangely erotic. Molly could feel all hidden parts of her body heat up rather dramatically. Even her damn nipples remained at attention

193

and she couldn't blame a chilly room for that.

"Does this feel good to you?" she ventured. "Cos it's making me squirmy."

"Good squirmy?" He trailed his other hand up her thigh and she definitely squirmed.

"Yeah, good squirmy."

He gathered her skirt, pushing it up over her hip and let his hand trail back down to her thigh.

Her inner thigh. All shivery and sexy and, *hmmm*, *that* felt good.

He used his fingers to trace from the top of her panties to the juncture at the top of her legs. Back and forth, light as a feather. It didn't feel light – it felt scorching. She felt it like her skin was bare to him and he was pressing against her. God, it was so achy-making! Yes, good achy. Time for more honesty.

"You said we wouldn't, you know, do it, tonight. Right? I'm just checking. Don't want to get all bent out of shape and anxious unless I have to."

Kit groaned at that. His hand stilled, but only for a second. As his fingers moved again, slightly firmer, slightly faster, he kissed her mouth and pulled at her lower lip gently.

"No home run tonight," he promised. "Just a slide into third."

As she struggled not to gasp aloud at how his hand movements were making her feel, she said, "See, I have no clue what that means. I watched those teen American movies with all that baseball terminology and just let it run over me. Now I want to google, *oh God that feels good*, what the hell third base is. I can kind of guess the old home run but, oh, oh, is this sliding . . . to . . . third? *Kit!*"

His fingers were certainly sliding. She was wet and slick and Kit had pushed her underwear aside and traced his fingers along her folds, slowly going further with the back-and-forth scenario, grazing the top with his middle finger, circling, then sliding all the way back down. Now his finger was inside. *Inside.* Inside her. But not still. God, he was inserting and retreating and, Jesus, managing to use his thumb on her most sensitive spot at the same time. *Holy shit-balls!* Squirmy and achy. Gorgeous squirms and aches. And wants and needs. And so much of the *more, please.* If this was third base, she was totally googling the whole history of baseball.

"*Kit!*" she mumbled, her mouth dry, probably from panting, or gasping, as her breath just wouldn't catch.

"Talk to me," Kit said, his mouth licking her collarbone and wandering lower. "Tell me how it feels."

Tell him how it feels? Christ no. That would be way too much out of her comfort zone. Was he mad? "It feels amazing. Hot and spicy and tingly." *Huh.* She could, in fact, tell him how it felt. "Shouldn't I be doing something to you? Touching you? Making you feel?"

He raised his head, eyes dark and intense. "Molly Fitzgerald, I *am* feeling all of this, right along with you. This is for you though, just you. I want you to let go. I want you to come. I want you to fall apart in my arms right here, right now. I want you to know that the heat of you, your tightness, your wet sexy scent is driving me crazy. *You* are driving me crazy. Crazy with need. You are the sexiest woman I've ever seen."

He'd been busy while he whispered those words to her. Kissing along her breasts, under them, around them. Down to her navel, kissing there, between those heated words. And all the while his hand had been just as busy and driving her just as crazy. Her body began that lovely humming tense journey it made right before release hit. God, it was so much better when he was the one driving it. So much more than when she fumbled alone in the dark by herself, never really knowing if she was doing it right. If what she felt was all she was ever going to feel. She pushed against his hand, her body straining now, her hands gripping his shoulders as her head fell back and she used him. Used his strength and his steady fast rhythm just like he wanted her to and, oh *yes*. There was so much more to this than she'd thought.

Molly came apart, in his arms, just as he had requested. Maybe he should have been a teacher because his lesson plan sure went according to the rules. She had done exactly that. And it felt *gooood*. *So good*. But it couldn't be just about her. She needed to do her part. Give back. Hell, she needed to learn some sex stuff and she was not going to let him weasel out of it. Although something told her he could be persuaded.

"Now, you show me what you want, what I can do for you," she said, catching her breath and reaching for his waistband. His hand slapped over hers.

"That's not necessary," he said, his voice hoarse.

"Yeah, it is. I need it, even if you don't. Now, either I unzip you or you do it. Wait, never mind. I'm doing it." This time she slapped his hand away and drew down the metal fly. The sound seemed loud, intimate and daring all at once. She'd helped a man out before, used her hand, but it had always been a fumble. In the dark. In a car. Against a wall. This time, she was taking time. And her very own sexpert was going to tell her, instruct her, direct her, in all the ways that made him feel what she'd felt.

They turned so Kit was lying back against the cushions and Molly perched on the side of the couch. He obligingly lifted his hips as she tugged his trousers down. His boxers were the snug, jersey-fabric kind and left feck all to the imagination. She swallowed, her throat dry, and with an inhale, went to work, lowering those to his thighs.

Well, now. Gosh. She lifted her eyes to his, sheer panic in hers, she knew, because that was what she felt. He was all those attributes she'd mentioned earlier only with a plus. He was staring right back at her, his body held rigid, his face grim. But he saw her look and a corner of his mouth managed a quirk.

"Not that bad, surely?"

"*Ummm . . .*" the smart accountant replied.

"I'll help," Kit said. "Would that work?"

"I want to do this right," Molly said, her tone breathy but now eager too. "I want to know what to do and what makes you feel the best. Show me. I mean it. I want you to teach me." She wrapped her hand around him, firm, yet not squeezing, and waited. She looked at him expectantly. "Please, Kit, I need you to show me."

He reached down, and like before, only so much better, he enclosed her small hand with his. Letting out a breath he guided her . . . how much pressure, how much pull, how much glide. He encouraged her to use his own pre-cum to slick over him and she shivered as they began the assault together. Quicker and firmer now, his hand moved hers and like a fledgling on its first flight, he let go when he knew she was off and running. There wasn't much chatter. Conversation seemed to be off the table but Molly knew. She could read him now, feel him grow tighter. Feel him shift his hips beneath her, pushing into her hand faster and faster, chasing his release.

She, ever the student, was fascinated. Riveted. His body grew taut and his thighs trembled. He was close.

"Let me," he grunted.

She let go, feeling the absence of hot strong flesh, and within a couple of firm strokes he came, strong and pulsing across his stomach. He groaned and fell backwards, hauling Molly along with him. He kissed the side of her head, softly, and again, brushing her curls aside.

"Thank you, Molly," he panted. "That was . . . it was unexpectedly excellent."

Christ on a bike, she thought, *could that have been the hottest thing I've ever seen?*

Her experience, limited though it was, had never encountered that. The other couple of boys she'd done this with had let her figure it out as they grunted through. Kit had done some grunting – it must be de rigueur, but with him she felt he was with her, they were together, every step of the way. And that was a one-eighty, for sure.

"Am I supposed to enjoy that too?" she asked. "Because it was, *hah*, I was going to say the coolest thing, but I think I mean the opposite."

Kit snuggled her closer, stroking her arm with long gentle fingers. "If you mean you found it hot, then definitely a ten out of ten for both of us. I, *ah*, don't normally come with my lady friend watching but it was, indeed, the very opposite of cool, in the temperature department, anyway."

That made Molly smile. "See," she poked him in the belly and he let out a laugh. "We can do this, you and me. You can show me all the ways to make a man happy and I can get seriously deflowered by a good man."

She rested her head against his chest, the sprinkling of dark hair soft under her skin. She used her position to trace her fingers over his abs and stomach, thread them through the happy trail from his waist downwards. He was still undressed, boxers about his thighs, but she realised he might not be quite done. Stirrings were happening and she gave herself an inward high five. It was her body, her presence that was the making of these moves. Her. Good old Molly, with her roundy bits and her belly and her ample hips and her crazy hair. With her weird sensitivities and overzealous brain. She was making him feel hot. Turned on. Granted, he was a guy, and ergo, but still. It felt good.

She peeped up at him from beneath her lashes and raised a brow. "Again?"

Kit chuckled and shifted. Much to her dismay, having wiped himself clean with the back of his shirt, he pulled up his clothes, sat up and pulled her close. "No," he said. "I'm flattered you even want to, but let's be sensible and take it one step at a time." He got them comfortable together and, with his arm around her shoulders, the fingers of one hand trailing through her curls he began telling her a funny story about one of his basketball crew.

Hint taken, Molly thought. She felt deflated, suddenly, but just as she was about to pull away, Kit, in between sentences, leaned down and kissed her forehead. Maybe a tad older-brotherish but as usual with Kit, his touch had her riveted in place, soaking in the gentle pressure and absorbing his feel, his smell. Oh feck, she thought. I can feel shitty about him not wanting to go again later.

For now, it was lie back, settle in and enjoy.

Chapter 18

He bent forward at the waist, hauling in deep, lungful deep, breaths. Blood, sweat and tears, Gran said, that's how you push through. You can keep the blood and tears, Kit thought as he straightened, but no one can say I'm not sweating this out. This, of course, being Molly Fitzgerald, and the horse she rode in on.

He wiped his brow with a towel and tossed it aside. The boys from the team would be along shortly and he needed to get his act together. Look vaguely like he knew what he was doing and give them a good practice. He owed them that, regardless of the fact he was a complete mess. That was not their problem, and no, Gran, he thought, I'm not crying. This dripping down my face? Honest, hard-won sweat.

It was all Kit could do. Work out, run like hell, coach basketball like they were the Celtics themselves, work like there was no tomorrow. And this all only a few days since the 'lesson'. How on God's earth would he survive the next? If there was a next. Maybe Molly would back out of their plan. Maybe he wasn't as good a tutor as he'd thought. He'd certainly learned a thing or two himself, stretched out on her couch. Over her and under her. He had learned how much he needed *her* to feel good. To come at his touch, under his hands. Why he was so invested he couldn't figure out. He was, he knew, choosing not to analyse those pesky reasons.

Guzzling water from his bottle he waited for the lads. They came, in twos and threes, and started their warm-ups without complaint. *Huh*. Go figure. Something was working out right.

The practice and game just about flattened him. Why he'd called this extra session was now a total mystery. Oh, yeah. The competition. Or at least that was the excuse. He needed to yell at people, joke with them and get after them. All accomplished in an hour and a half and he was finally ready to head home.

His living-room floor was now finished. That had been Monday evening's torture. Tuesday, he'd varnished the part that was left. And first thing this morning, before work, he'd touched up the areas that had been used as stepping-stones on the previous run-through. It glowed in the evening light as he threw his house keys on the hall table. He wheeled the bike through to the yard and, hauling a beer from the fridge, proceeded to add back on the calories he'd just worked off. Oh well. Such is life. And, man, he *needed* this beer.

He took himself and his beer bottle to his front door and squatted on the stoop. It was dark now, or almost, and a few other neighbours were trading insults or jokes back and forth. He loved this part of his neighbourhood. The camaraderie, the support, the care. It was what had held his gran together when he and his mum had moved to Boston. He'd only been eight and had been heartbroken. But Shelly Elliot knew what she wanted. And she wanted the bright lights and big city. And the very handsome American she'd been dating for the previous year. Kit couldn't even remember his name now, James or Jamie perhaps, but he'd promised her the world and she'd bought the deal.

It wasn't how his mum had planned it. He knew that. Intellectually. It wasn't all her fault. But James or Jamie had set her up in a one-bed apartment in South Boston, in the Irish community. Paid for six months' rent and disappeared. Shelly, only twenty-six and very pretty, got nightwork in a bar. Yes, she left him home alone with a neighbour to listen out for him. Yes, it was illegal. And yes, it sucked. But she was there when he got home from school, usually bruised and bloodied. Being in Southie meant you had Irish connections, Irish roots, an Irish past. But this didn't really translate to a strong Dublin accent amongst his very tough peers.

Kit ended up loving it. Shelly kept a roof over their heads, food on the table and because she was smart and bolshie, she worked her way up to manager of that bar. She took no shit from anyone and the locals loved her for it. They became part of the neighbourhood. Not unlike right here, right now.

He tilted his beer bottle in acknowledgement of old Mr Feeney, who tugged his cap in return. Feeney tried to put the key in the latch but his hand trembled so badly with Parkinson's that it became more of a challenge every day. This he refused to accept or admit so sometimes a neighbour just stepped in.

Kit rose from his perch and ambled across to Number 38.

"Hey, Mr Feeney, how many cats do you have now? I was telling a co-worker the other day about your lovely tabby and they were hoping she might have kittens. Any chance?"

Feeney let his arm fall and rested his hand on the doorknob instead. Christ, thought Kit, it's as if he needs to prop it up. He angled himself so he was resting against the doorjamb and crossed his arms over his chest, not a care in the world. If Feeney thought you were there to help, he'd lose it. It wasn't pretty. His wife was inside, most likely watching *Mr Pimple Popper* or some other awful reality show, but Feeney refused to get her out of the chair. It was her quiet time, he'd say. She'd enjoy no interruptions, was how he phrased it. Kit smiled innocently at the elderly gentleman and they discussed cats and their attributes for a few minutes, Kit embellishing the desire of a mythical colleague to find a soulmate. This man fed many of the neighbourhood cats, including Scout, when Kit was away, so Kit used that bond as needed. Feeney was animated, delighted to share his love of all things feline. Kit asked for the latest photo. A pro move on his part. The old man could never resist showing off his litter. He patted his pockets for his wallet, no phone images for this man – he was old school all the way – and Kit obligingly took hold of his keys for him. The wallet was opened, photos praised and as the worn leather was returned to the deep pocket Kit casually said, "I'll get the door for you while you button your jacket," and the job was done. No harm no foul.

The sound of the door closing with a click behind Mr Feeney, Mrs Feeney's feeble greeting a mere whisper behind the solid wood, left Kit feeling unaccountably sad. He wandered back to his own door, left wide open of course because, *neighbours*, and with a wave through the lace curtain of Mrs Byrnes, his other side resident, he went in and closed his own front door firmly.

A shower, he thought, sniffing his underarms, and bed.

Why he bothered with bed he knew not. The stack of open tabs on his laptop was enough of a clue that he couldn't settle to anything, let alone the tossed duvet and bunched pillows. He rarely worked in bed but the varnish smell from the floor was still somewhat pungent downstairs and he didn't need the headache sure to follow.

What he also didn't need was Molly Fitzgerald in his head. The last few days at work had been bloody torture. Everywhere he went she was there – not intentionally – but he saw her. Talked to her, even laughed with her. But it was like she had put up a glass wall – it was crystal – he could see her, hear her. Touch her. But, not. It made no sense. When he'd left her flat on Sunday things had been good between them. They'd both been sexually satisfied, he'd thought, but by Monday morning a slight chill had invaded their previously warm space.

He was at a loss. He sent texts, she replied. They had coffee together at the break – that had become their norm, they even ate lunch together – albeit with a bunch of others at the communal table. Kit had suggested they go out for lunch, casual-like, but Molly had become flustered, blushed, and brushed his invite aside with an excuse of too much work to be able to take a whole hour.

Truthfully, she had a lot of work on. Kit had seen to it. He needed her on all Twomey's new accounts – accounts that would merit a second look. Kit had also, in previous weeks, created two more false accounts, not just for her but for Donnelly too, with certain problems and irregularities for them to find – or not. Unsurprisingly, Molly had left no stone unturned and either righted the issues, if that was the correct tack, or brought it to the manager's attention. He'd made sure the new accounts came from a variety of sources, so she wasn't bogged down in Twomey's work specifically. That was to come next. Part of his plan to flush Declan Twomey out – to force his hand, to *show* his hand. Kit was certain he had his man. Everything led to Twomey being involved in stealing from the company. With Kit's ties to some shady characters in the dark web he had found Twomey's offshore accounts and they were very healthy. Which didn't make sense as the guy was living in debt here in Dublin. Something wasn't right – other than the fact that he was stealing. It wasn't lining up to be your bog-standard shaving money off the top of client's accounts. It was too large an amount. And then why would he have debts to pay? No, it didn't make sense, but Kit was determined to figure it out.

He'd had another chat with Benson Senior. Told him some of his theories and that he had a plan – Benson didn't need to know just how vague and uncertain the plan was – that was Kit's deal to sort out. And Flynn Fitzgerald needed to be included too. For many reasons.

Kit sighed heavily as he flipped closed the laptop, edged Scout off the bed after a good petting, and turned out lights. Things got worse before they got better – everyone knew that. But he was starting to feel like a bit of a shit, keeping his real job, hell, his real *life* from Molly. Everything he did was temporary. Everywhere he lived, a mere pit-stop. His expertise ensured he moved from company to company, business to business. That he didn't become known as the guy who rumbled all your nefarious dealings and sent you to prison. He had to stay 'hidden in plain sight' and on the move. It was who he was. Who he *had* to be.

Molly would be hurt. He knew that going into this *extra* relationship they had going. But it was temporary too, so should, in fact, be ideal for him. Teach her some moves, initiate her into the joys of the bedchamber, so to speak, and move on. She'd made it clear she was using him as practice material. That kind of stung, though it shouldn't. She'd given up living a lie. Now he knew her, he could begin to imagine how hard it must have been for her, all those years of hiding her real self to her own family. Living her lie. She must have hated it. She was so straight – arrow-straight – when it came to ethics and behaviour. She must have lived in dread of being found out. And then, it was all almost for nothing. After the first few 'seriously's?' and 'no ways!' they had all just accepted her for her new, or in her case, old self. Her own self. Like family. It blew his mind. It wasn't how it had worked out for him, but then when a third party is involved, someone not blood, things can change direction, loyalties can become divided and bonds tested. Big time.

Fuck, he needed to let the past go and get some damn sleep. He would talk to Molly, really talk to her tomorrow. They'd set a date for Saturday. Do the deed. If she was still willing. Ready. God, he hoped like hell she was. He hadn't felt such a rush of desire for a woman in a long time. He couldn't remember when. College maybe? When he was still a green boy. But since then? No. Molly made his blood heat in a way that was new, different, tempting. He was drawn to so much of her – her beauty, obviously, you'd have to be blind or stupid not to see that – and Kit was neither. Her brains. Her humour. Her honesty. The way that clever mind processed and deliberated was a fascination all its own. And then she'd turn and smile at him and, damn, but he'd feel it all the way to his toes. Or when she laughed, and that bubble of silliness would overflow into the world, an actual gift to the universe, and Kit couldn't help wonder why the rest of the world didn't stop in wonder. As he did. Every time.

This was bad. He could absolutely *not* get feelings – real feelings, for Molly Fitzgerald. That was the worst, stupidest idea ever. And it had been established that Kit was not stupid. What was it Forrest Gump said? 'Stupid is as stupid does' – bloody Forrest Gump. He threw back the covers and paced the upstairs as he let his mind wander and settle, wander and settle. It was his own form of meditation, like when he would recite the periodic table or do calculus problems for fun. His mind could go into a different place, a restful place, and it was then that the real thinking began. When he was on a job, like his position with BB&M, it was his happy place. He also knew that most people thought that was plain old peculiar. He didn't care. Sometimes in his office, wherever that turned out to be, he tossed a baseball or a slinky, back and forth. So restful. Tonight though? The real thinking that invaded his brain was most unwelcome. His past. And its shitty fallout. His present and *its* shitty fallout to come. And his future where there was no possibility of Molly. Not when he did what he knew he must.

But first, Saturday night. He went back to bed and counted sheep. Math was not working for him so needs must. *Ovis aries* it was.

She called in reinforcements. It was a no-brainer, really. Molly knew she had to tell her sisters she was about to lose her virginity, not because she felt they ought to know, precisely, but because she needed advice. Female advice. Sex advice. And her three know-it-all's would come armed with it on Friday night. She sent texts to Ali and Frankie and messaged Caro for a facetime chat over dinner. She ordered takeaway, a variety of Indian, Thai and good old fish and chips, keeping Frankie's delicate stomach in mind. She bought wine and lemonade and extra milk. Seemingly, pregnant women could get cravings at any time and Frankie was inhaling full-fat milk. Would she pile on the pounds and look like a beached whale in a few months? No. No, she wouldn't. Sometimes life was just unfair like that, and the rest of them were just going to have to live with it.

Frankie and Ali arrived together and Ali immediately complained that she could have cooked and that there was no need to buy in food. Frankie brushed right past her and began on the chips, like a woman starved. Within seconds she paused as the other two watched her, mouths agape.

"What? No judging here. I'm eating for two," she proclaimed with a decidedly smug and yet somehow righteous tone.

"Never said a word!" Ali threw her hands up in denial of any crime of judgement and turned to the fridge to pull out a bottle of white wine, not even trying to hide her grin.

"Seriously," Frankie said, "this is so crazy – I'm barely percolating this human and already I'm turning into a hunger monster. *Oooh, Pad Thai! Yum.*" She reached for a plate and began loading her food on with no attention to style. Or presentation.

Ali winced and backed away.

"*Ugh.* I can't look, I need a moment. I'll call Caro or do you want to wait till we've eaten?" she asked Molly.

"Let's get our food, or what's left of it when Frankie is done, and then call. She knows to expect it about seven."

Frankie took no offence and happily chose one of everything though Molly knew there was no way she would actually eat it all. Options were important, Dev had told her when she phoned to ask what her sister-in-law might like. "But," he'd added, "she'll need a doggie bag for what's left over. I've never seen her like this and it's kinda fun."

Fun. Molly winced. Yeah. Easy for him to say. She doubted most men would find it attractive if their wives inhaled all the food in the universe. But then, he was married to one of the most beautiful and *slim* women in the world. Molly shook off her mean thoughts and filled her own plate. She was going to need sustenance for this conversation, that was for damn sure.

When they were settled at the kitchen table, Ali phoned Caro and as they waited for the call to connect, she propped her chin on her hand, watching Molly inquiringly.

"Did you win another award? Is that what this is about? We're getting used to your brainy side, you know, you don't have to hide anything anymore."

An award? If only it was that simple.

Caro's bright voice interrupted her musings. "Hey all, what's up?" She was sipping a glass of something golden, a brandy perhaps as it was after her dinner hour in Rome. They did eat later there, but Caro liked to get herself and Toby fed earlier than the Italians liked and Nick was always happy to eat with them if he was home from the hotel he managed.

"Nick working?" Molly asked. She really didn't want him turning up unexpectedly to happen upon a conversation about sex, or the lack thereof.

"Nah, he and Toby have gone up north this weekend. They are visiting with Mia and Marianna. No, don't ask," she added as the three listeners all stared at her in astonishment.

"Don't ask?" Ali was dumbfounded. "I thought you couldn't bear that woman? I know Mia is a darling and Toby misses her but, for fuck's sake, Caro, Marifuckinganna?"

"I know, I know." Caro sighed and swirled her drink. "But Toby really wanted to go and Nick misses Mia too so I agreed on the condition that he went as a guard dog. It'll be fine. Mia says her mum has really changed. I'll know more on Sunday when they're back. Now," she put her glass down with determination to close that subject, "what's up, Moll? Are you okay?"

Well, that all needed processing and she would get more details later, because Marianna had been a piece of work, meddling in Caro's life, but, Molly supposed, people

209

had to do their own thing. And some people knew how to let go. Caro was so mature that way.

Molly heaved a deep sigh and, arranging the laptop so they could all see each other, announced: "I'm about to lose my virginity and I need help."

There. Out there. Real. Truth. Christ, it felt weird. Like a huge boulder was falling from her shoulders. A weight she hadn't realised, till this moment, she'd been carrying.

The silence was charged and long. Very long. Okay, probably only a few seconds but, man, it felt long and . . . judgey? Shocked? Horrified?

"Someone say something," Molly mumbled, getting really uncomfortable. She should have kept her big virgin mouth shut. She should ha–

"About fucking time!" Ali declared and swallowed a mouthful of wine.

"*Yay!*" Frankie said, clapping her hands in delight. "I'm thrilled for you."

"Who?" Caro asked, ever the big sister. "Who is it? Do we know him? Shit, is it a him? Either way is fine, I mean . . ."

"It's Kit. Kit Elliot. You met him."

Molly topped up her wine and went to the fridge for more milk for Frankie and the white for Ali. Let them stew on that for a minute, she thought. Kit Elliot. Not some randomer, or some one-night hook-up. But a grown-ass man with a career. One her parents had met. A man. Not a boy and, for some reason ridiculously important to Molly, not an artist.

Ali held up her glass. "He's hot as shit. Good choice, little sis. He has those shoulders and the tight-ass thing going on."

Frankie and Molly both turned to look at her in shock and they could hear a snort from Caro.

"Hey! You're supposed to be all loved-up with Gabe!

Stop gawking at other men's physiques!" Caro said and the others laughed.

"Physiques? Christ, you're a hoot, Caro. Still so old-fashioned and teachery. But, yes, Ali, keep your eyes straight and front, please." Frankie smiled at Molly in an inviting way. "Right, Molly, tell us everything."

It took a while. She told them about her quest to lose the damn thing and her very short list of potential partners. Her preferences and her criteria. Her list. Ali snatched that from her and began sniggering and then guffawing as she read the order of importance that Molly had laid out, in, yes, a list.

1. *Clean – body and clothing*
2. *No nose hair*
3. *Trimmed fingernails*
4. *Kind*
5. *Minty breath*
6. *Expertise*
7. *Able to hold a conversation*
8. *Dry lips*
9.

"That's it? You couldn't think of a nine? And seriously, Moll, you would know most of these things about any of the guys on your list. I assume you had a list of likely men?" Ali passed the list on to the others. "Except, I mean, are you going to ask about their level of expertise? Would that not be *hard* for you?" Even as she said it, she chuckled at her own innuendo.

Molly rolled her eyes. "Not sexual expertise, you idiot, cos how the hell would I be able to quantify that? No, expertise in anything. I like a man who knows his thing. Whether it be woodwork, or ice-cream making or conversational French. He needs to be good at what he does."

"Like maths or accounting. Like Kit." Frankie nodded

her head in understanding. "I love that Dev is passionate about his photography. That it drives him. That he is endlessly striving to be better. You're right. It's sexy. Competence porn." She blushed as she said that, embarrassed in front of her husband's sisters, but they just laughed. And agreed.

"I get that," Caro put in. "When I see Nick in his natural milieu of the hotel he is like a bloody god. Lording over all he surveys. But in a non-threatening, very nice kind of way," she added quickly.

Ali chimed in, on board now with the whole expertise in one's trade or profession thing. "Yup. Talent is damn sexy. A guy who knows his way around a woman is also sexy." She laughed, a delightful sound, full of fun and lightness.

Molly felt her heart hitch. God, Ali deserved this. This spark of happy that invaded her now. Was part of her. None of them had known it was missing till she found it. Gabe Mackenzie was one very able man.

"Back to business," Caro said. "We know Kit is smart and an expert in all things numerical. Where does he fit in the other categories and, wait, there is nothing on the list about actual sex, so if you know he's the one for right now, *how* do you know? Have you been indulging in foreplay?" Her voice was full of pretend hauteur and Molly smiled.

"Why, yes. We have been indulging. And I didn't *know* what else to add to the list. The intimate things. And he ticks every box. *Every. Box.* That's what has me scared. Maybe I'll be expecting too much now? Maybe I should have picked someone . . . less?"

"No," said Frankie. "Your gut picked him, as well as your head. He's the one to do the deed. Oh, wait. Does he know? That you are . . . you know . . ." She blushed.

"*A virgin!*" chanted Caro and Ali together and Ali high-fived towards the laptop screen. Molly rolled her eyes again.

"Give me a break and let's get down to the real reason I

have you all here. Do I have to wax and, if I do, does it have to be everything, everywhere? And if so, should I do it now, like tonight or wait till tomorrow morning? Or just before I go to his place tomorrow night? How high is the probability of a rash?"

They all began talking at once and when Molly whipped out her notebook and a pen to take notes, the talk turned to hysterical laughter.

Bloody sisters.

They were the *best*.

Chapter 19

Molly dressed with care. They had decided, she and Kit, that she would bring an overnight bag but she could leave, if she chose, at any time. No obligation. No questions asked. Molly had wanted to have her first time at her own flat but Kit said no. He felt it would be better somewhere neutral, like a hotel, but they both balked at that. His rationale was that if she wasn't happy with the outcome of the 'deed', he didn't want her own home to be a reminder. She would never have thought of that and decided his place would work.

"If I hate sex with you, I'll probably never come to your house again anyway," she'd said. Ever practical.

His house it was.

May was turning out to be a beautiful month and she decided on a flowy dress in an old-fashioned Liberty print. It was feminine and loose. No waist to make her feel bigger than she was, low neckline without revealing too much flesh and, she wasn't sure this was important, but, hey, preparation is key, it buttoned down the front. The flowers of lilac and pale blue suited her colouring and she kept her make-up light with a soft rose for her lips.

She'd shaved, in the end. Her legs, her bikini line and some 'trimming' as her sisters had put it.

"You don't want to go bare your first time," Ali had said. "Then it's all expectations to keep that up. Fucking exhausting. No, be neat, be smooth on the legs, sure, but no raising the bar too early. That way it can be a surprise if and when you change your toilette, so to speak." Ali often made loads of sense when it came to simple practical matters. Molly decided going 'bare' also might come across as 'up for anything' and she really wasn't. Mostly because she'd no idea what 'anything' might include. She was nervous enough without adding 'antics' to the mix. God, she was so bloody nervous. All the questions. All the worries. All the 'what ifs?'. She didn't actually list those in her mind, that would be way too damaging to her already shaky confidence.

So she did some complicated times tables in her head as she got off the Luas and walked slowly to his house. The overnight bag with her few belongings felt like a tonne weight as she shifted it from one shoulder to the other. It wasn't heavy – an extra pair of undies, a sleep shirt (to cover her body and her own potential embarrassment), a tube of lube and a packet of condoms (Ali's insistence). Frankie suggested a negligée, because of course she did. She probably wore silk ones floating around their loft space as she wafted a feather duster. Molly smiled as she thought of the divine aqua-silk robe folded in her bag – her sister-in-law had popped over to Molly's flat that morning with a beautifully wrapped parcel which she handed to her with a smile and a hug. "For the morning after," she'd said.

The doorknocker mocked her, Molly decided, as she stood outside, her stomach doing a churning that would give the Irish Sea a run for its money on a stormy day in November. Just do it, she told herself sternly. Kit's a good guy. He'll do his best not to hurt you. And if I change my mind halfway through – a distinct possibility – he won't make me feel like a failure. She believed that. She wouldn't be here otherwise.

The toll of the brass hitting brass sounded awfully like a death knoll.

He was nervous. And that was just daft. He could do this one thing for his new, really pretty, very sexy, friend. He could. God knows he wanted to. He wanted *her*. Maybe that was the problem. If he didn't wish for her so much, he could just look on this whole evening as sex. Pure and simple. While there might be a certain amount of purity to Molly, in relation to this evening's plan, she was not, in any shape or form, simple. None of this was turning out to be simple.

Hopefully the food would work out simply. He'd planned carefully, leaving nothing to get burnt or ruined if things went according to *his* plan. He plumped the pillows and straightened the clean duvet cover. The bathroom was spotless but not for the first time he regretted that there was no upstairs loo or shower. Nothing he could do about that now, but at least there was fresh soap and clean towels downstairs. He'd bought flowers earlier and they sat in jam jars about the room, a touch of colour in his otherwise shades of grey décor. Although it was early evening and middle-of-May bright, he pulled the gauze curtains closed giving the room a soft glowing feel and, for Molly's sake, a certain amount of dimness. He figured she might prefer that. He would prefer full light, but he wasn't completely insensitive to any possible shyness. He'd considered candles but then thought it was trying too hard. He'd gone with a carafe of water and glasses, wine in a cool bucket and a tray of cheese and crackers. These he'd placed discreetly on a side table.

Since this was his first time deflowering a virgin, he

could only hope he wouldn't screw up royally. He certainly hadn't found a rule book on this one and the internet had been less than useless.

In the end, he decided he'd go with several deep breaths and the confidence in his own desire for a gorgeous woman.

He went downstairs and double-checked the living area. More flowers here and new cushions and throws. Yes, he had gone to the Arnotts sale and to IKEA. The colour looked good here. Fresh and summery. The table was set with new crockery and glasses and all in all he was pleased. Quite the domestic god, if he said so himself.

Kit glanced at the oven clock. She was late. Maybe she'd changed her mind. Got cold feet. Chose a different guy. *Fuck*. His gut clenched at the thought of Molly, his Molly, offering herself to some asshole. Surely she wouldn't have gone to Declan-fucking-Twomey? Not after the way he . . . his rambling brain was halted by the sound of the knocker.

She was here. She hadn't changed her mind. He was going to have sex with Molly Fitzgerald. There was a God and he was smiling on Kit Elliot.

Jesus, she was a vision. All curls and flowing fabric, rosy lips and everything that was soft, soft, soft. That's the word that resonated in his brain as he noticed the rose on her lips mirrored on her cheeks. She was flushed, and whether it was exertion from the walk or anticipation or anxiety, Kit didn't analyse. She was here. For him. For his sex moves. Christ, that sounded so cheesy even in his own mind so he gave himself a virtual ass-kick and welcomed her.

"You're here," he said, using all his expensive education to its fullest extent. "I mean, I'm glad you're here, come in."

He pulled the door wide and she moved past him into

the tiny hall space and suddenly he couldn't breathe. She took up all his air with her scent and her softness and her curls and her dress. And her glowing skin. He was so screwed if he didn't get a grip. Now.

"I brought some fizz," she said brightly, eagerly. Enthusiastically.

Ah, she was nervous. That was her nervous voice. He was definitely going with Plan A.

She headed to the kitchen but paused to take in the newly varnished floors. She spun in a slow circle. "Wow, Kit, these are fabulous. Great job, Handyman of the Year."

He grinned. "Yeah, thanks. I'm stoked they worked out so well. I did some work upstairs too. Come see." Plan A in action.

"Sure. I'll just pop this in your fridge." She deposited the bottle of sparking rosé inside. "I know this place is temporary for you. That you are leaving. I get that. But, crikey, Kit, you are making it so nice, how will you be able to sell it? Your gran's home. *Your* home."

His gut clenched at her words. It was a good question. An excellent comment on his state of play and he had no answer. Zero. Each day he added a new colour or trim or accessory, each day he released a breath when he closed the front door to the outside world and wondered the very same thing. How *was* he going to leave? How could he just walk away?

"It's a good question," he said aloud, bringing himself back to the present. The now. The sex moves, dammit. "But for another day, I think. Come on upstairs. I want to show you my –"

"Etchings?" she interrupted with a laugh.

"A version of," he agreed and chuckled when her mouth fell open. "Just messing with you. I did buy wall art. I'd like your opinion."

Reaching out he took her hand and pulled her along behind him towards the stairs.

"Drop your bag there," he suggested artfully. "We can sort it later."

They climbed the stairs, Kit the gentleman allowing her to pass in front of him and go first. No, not being a gentleman. He wanted to see the sway of her skirts as she moved in that naturally undulating way of hers. He wanted to watch the way her ankles stretched as she arched each foot on the treads. The way her calves tightened and relaxed. The way her elbow dimpled as her arm flexed on the banister. He wanted to kiss all those places. Taste them. He was going to get that chance. Soon.

His office door was open and she stepped in, looking about with what he hoped was interest. His other project over the last couple of weeks, when time allowed, was to get the second bedroom redone as an office space. He had chosen a neutral colour for the walls and added a selection of black-and-white prints to give what he hoped was an air of both professionalism and interest. A new desk and chair, a nod to comfort as he spent hours over his computer, sat in the middle of the room, wires and extensions cords trailing to the wall sockets. His desktop computer took up most of the desk space and several filing cabinets lined one wall. So far, so good.

"Why is your desk in the centre of the room?" she asked as she wandered the small floor area. It too was varnished but had an area rug in bold jewel colours beneath the desk.

"I can't decide where it should go," Kit admitted. "What do you suggest?"

He could practically see her don her artistic hat as she surveyed the options.

"Actually, leave it where it is," she said surprisingly. "Sit here, work here, for a while anyway and your body will tell you what it needs. You might, for example, find yourself craning your neck to see out the window or reaching for the cabinet handles or leaning back in the chair and falling without the wall for support. You'll only know when you know."

"Gee, thanks a bunch. You're not much help. I wanted an answer not more options."

"The walls are lovely," she said, smoothing her hand along the surface. "Such a soft warm taupe and the snowy-white trim really lifts it. Oh, these prints are cool!" She studied them intently. "I love how they represent the city in a muted way. Black-and-white can be so stark but these totally work."

She turned back to smile at him, and he felt his chest tighten. Kit had known she would name the paint colour and have an opinion on his art choices. He hadn't realised until she commented that he'd really wanted her to like it. To approve.

He turned away before his eyes blew out heart shapes and exploded into kisses. "Come see what else I did," he said, his voice edging to unsteady. He led the way into his bedroom, the evening glow doing its magic and making the room look, to his eyes and, God, he hoped to hers, like an invitation.

She stopped in the doorway and he tried to see it from her perspective. The gauze drapes in palest blue stirring gently with a light breeze through the open window. The floor, polished to a shine, giving a richness to the cream walls. He watched as her eyes took in the table set up with the snacks and cool bucket holding wine, the fabric napkins he'd purchased knowing she'd prefer them to paper. And then her eyes moved to the bed. It did look imposing and obvious in the smallness of this row-house room, but the bedlinen was fresh and new, along with the pillows and throw. He'd chosen a pale-blue ticking stripe, old-fashioned and, he thought, both quaint and comforting but not, God forbid, too girly. The blanket draped across the end of the bed was in muted greens and he knew it was more for effect but thought it worked.

Molly edged in, hands buried in hidden pockets of her dress. She made her way to the window and peered out.

"I like your street," she said somewhat innocuously. "It's got a certain feel to it. This house too. It's happy."

Kit tilted his head to one side as he approached the small table and gestured to some crackers and cheese. "Happy? This house?"

"Yes," she said. "Thank you." She reached for the crackers and nibbled daintily.

He poured her a glass of Sauvignon Blanc and handed her that too. Filling his own, he tilted his glass to hers.

"To happy houses and streets!" he said, determined not to toast to a night of sex and deflowering.

They both sipped, gazes meeting over thin rims of fine glass.

"Are these new too?" she asked, indicating her vessel. At his nod she smiled. "You've been on a spending spree. For one so set on leaving, you sure are nesting." She selected cheese, set it on a cracker and ate.

The crumbs lingered on her lips and Kit felt a surge of frustration. He wanted to be tasting her lips. Feeling all that plumpness beneath his mouth.

Plan A.

He put down his glass and took hers, placing it next to his on the cloth. Reaching forward he used his thumb to brush away the stray crumbs on her lips and Molly blushed.

"Sorry," she mumbled. "I'm always such a messy eater."

"Don't be. That crumb was doing all kinds of things to me, you'll be delighted to know." He inched closer and, resting both hands on either side of her face, he looked into her incredible eyes. Eyes that were wide, and right now, startled.

"Things?" she squeaked.

"*Hmm*. Things. Bad, wicked things. Dirty things."

She blinked. And again. "Oh. *Oh*."

The second *Oh* he swallowed with a kiss.

See, that was the problem with crackers, Molly thought. If it wasn't inches on the hips it was crumbs on the lips. For once, Molly didn't regret a single nibble. Kit kissed her like she tasted of the very best of crackers – the ones with all the grains and the cracked black pepper. He kissed her like he couldn't not.

She, the pliant pupil she was, kissed him back. It felt so good to feel like a kiss was doing something. Going somewhere. Leading to a destination. This was usually the kind of kissing she dreaded – the leading-somewhere kind – mostly it was a trip-end she didn't want. An arrival at a place where she said thanks but no thanks. Kit's kisses were so different as to be on another stratosphere. If it was his technique, well, he was getting A+ for all the years of practice he must have put in – but if it was him? And her. Together? She was on board with that. Or she would be, when the time came. Later. She'd be on board later. Now, she just wanted the wonderful feelings of Kit's lips and his tongue and his hands and his hard, strong body doing all the yummy delicious things he was doing.

Wait. What *was* he doing?

Breathing heavily, Kit pulled back but only so he could kiss her jaw and on down her neck and across the neckline of her dress. Swiftly he made use of the buttons and, as the fabric slipped away and the tops of her full breasts came on view, the groan from his throat sent spears of lust right through her body.

"God, you're beautiful," he whispered against her skin. Dragging his mouth back along her neck he returned to her mouth, his arms banding about her as he deepened the kiss, knocking all thought, all rational thought that was, straight out of Molly's brain. Instead she heard her own groan, her own pleading as she melted into him, burrowing into his body, feeling his muscles tense beneath her wandering hands. One of his hands moved to the back of her head where he took a handful of her hair and, tugging slightly, controlled the angle of their mouths and, dear God, her knees began to weaken. It felt so good. Hot. Urgent. Like he really wanted this. It wasn't just a project. Maybe she'd been worrying for nothing?

Before she could think straight, Kit angled her back towards the bed, pushing gently so she sat, and he took her face in his hands once more. He looked down at her, his thumbs stroking her warm cheeks as his eyes roamed her face.

"We're doing this, Molly. Right here, right now. Is that what you still want?"

"*Now? We're doing the sex now?*"

It was almost a shriek and made Kit smile.

"Yes. The sex. Now."

"But," she stuttered, her hands reaching up to hold his forearms, steadying herself, "dinner. I mean, shouldn't we eat first? Or you know, wait a bit?"

His smile wider, Kit bent forward and kissed her lightly. "No. We can eat later. Are you nervous?"

She nodded. No point pretending. A blind person could see she was nervous.

"And do you honestly think you could enjoy food, chat about inconsequential things, relax even, knowing what we were going to do later? Or were you, maybe, thinking of chickening out?"

She dipped her head, trying to hide her own smile. "Maybe. The chickening-out part sounds fair," she admitted.

"Molly, do you want this? Really? Do you want to have sex for the first time? With me?"

He was so serious, so focused on her needs. On what she wanted. She could do this.

"Yes." She nodded firmly. "Yes. I want this. With you."

Kit removed his hands from where they cupped her face and sat next to her on the bed. "Okay then, here are the rules," he said, holding her hands loosely in his, his eyes not leaving hers.

"Rules? There are rules? No one mentioned effing rules."

"For us there are," Kit said. "And the first, and most important, is honesty. The excellent thing about doing this, having sex without a romantic relationship, is that we can be honest and not hurt each other's feelings. You don't have to impress me, you don't have to worry that I might be offended if you say no to something or ask for something different. This is about you. What works for you."

Molly frowned. This was all sounding very technical. Very strategised. "Okay, well, let me be honest first. This doesn't sound remotely appealing to me right now." She huffed out on a weary sigh. "Maybe we should forget it."

To her astonishment Kit chuckled.

"See? Honest. That's perfect. Think of it like this, we, our bodies together, are a math problem to be solved. What do you do when you need to solve, say, an accounting issue or problem?"

Molly thought about it, wondering where on earth any of this fitted into her ditching her virginity. But she would humour him with her honesty, as requested. "I collect all the data I need. I investigate potential and likely prospects for a solution and sometimes even try out a few different angles before I come to a conclusion."

"Before you're satisfied with the result?"

"Yes." She paused to think about it. "Oh. You want me to try things? To see what works for me? Is my body a problem to be solved then?"

"Not necessarily. But knowing what brings you the best pleasure, the best orgasms, the best joy, that might take a little data collection and, I can assure you, I am the man for the job." He wriggled his brows at her in a silly gesture. "I'm all about the data," he said as he unbuttoned a few more notches on her dress. "And may I say, in the interests of honesty and full disclosure, this dress is a real turn-on. And may I also say, in the same theme, re data collection et al, even if your head is querying my tactics and how clinical this might seem, your body knows. I can feel your body respond so perfectly to mine that I know it's ready. Your brain will catch up eventually."

Molly could see the sense in everything he said. She actually couldn't believe how much his practical, no-nonsense approach to figuring her body's needs out appealed to her. But she needed to be sure. Absolutely sure. "So, going with the honesty, you genuinely mean I can say anything to you during this *encounter* and that will be okay? And just to be perfectly clear, I can still say yes or no? More of something or even stop?"

Kit leaned forwards and kissed her neck, right where her shoulder joined and she shivered in delight. "Sweetheart, I am going to be listening to everything you tell me. With your body, with your moves, with your words. Especially your words. Remember, this is the only time you get to do this for the first time. You get to say, left, right, up, down. You tell me harder, faster, slower. You can say more, you can beg, you can scream, you can moan. And you absolutely can say, at any time, *any* time, stop.

And I will. Because I'll be listening." He kissed her some more, along her shoulder as he eased her sleeves down her arm and his mouth followed. "You're in control. But I am in charge. I know what I'm doing. I'm not trying to be a braggy asshole, but I've done this before. I know what to do and how to do it. But since I've never done it with *you*, you get to control the pace. Remember, you can't hurt my feelings in this, you don't have to think I'll be pissed if you ask me to change direction, or pressure or anything. I serve at the pleasure of Mary Margaret Fitzgerald."

Molly giggled. She never giggled, but he sounded so earnest. So professional. "You sound like a gigolo," she blurted out and waited for the offence to set in.

But Kit Elliot never ceased to amaze her. He laughed.

"Excellent way to think of me tonight. I am yours to command."

Her dress was around her waist now and before she could cover her breasts to avoid the mortification of him seeing them squished into her bra, he breathed out a sigh of what sounded like wonder.

"Christ, how did I get so lucky in my job?" His large, sure and steady hands covered her breasts and squeezed lightly. He slid one strap down and then the other, slowly peeling the lace fabric away.

The sound he made, between a groan and a growl, followed by his mouth investigating her soft flesh convinced her he liked what he saw. And they certainly seemed to be enjoying his attention. Her nipples had hardened into tight buds, screaming for attention, for the feel of his lips and tongue as he lavished them with kisses.

He did some clever manoeuvre and she ended up flat on her back as he crawled up her body, kissing her belly and stomach, returning again and again to her breasts and then her neck and always back to her mouth. She could feel him, cradled between her thighs. The weight of him. The length of him. The hardness of him. Her bag! She'd left her bag downstairs.

"Wait," Molly gasped out. "Supplies. I brought supplies. They're downstairs. In my bag."

She began to wriggle out from under Kit's chest and legs that had her pretty much pinned to the bed but he dragged his head from her neck where he'd been nibbling her skin to look directly into her eyes. He looked so serious. Focused and yet dazed. How could that be?

"I've got it covered, Molly. I'd never put you at risk. My bedside table has a drawer full of supplies. Including ones you may never have seen."

Molly gaped. "Like, toys? Sex toys? You have them? In your drawer?" Her voice rose and hitched as she imagined all the versions of *Fifty Shades* and her mind boggled.

"I have condoms, Molly. Lots of condoms. That's all we need to think about for tonight. But, yes, I have toys too. Sex should be fun and playful. It should be an adventure and an enjoyable experience. But for now, for you and me, right here, it's about simple pleasure. The pleasure that my body can give yours."

"But what about you? We have to get to your pleasure too, right?"

He must have heard the anxiety in her voice because, pulling back, he took her chin in his hand and angled her face to look at him.

"Molly, do you trust me?"

She nodded.

"Say it, say the words," he insisted.

"Yes," Molly said quickly, "I trust you."

"Then believe this. Believe me." He pressed against her softness, moved, rotated his hips and she gasped at the feel of him. The press of him against her. "This is what you do

227

to me. Thinking about you, wanting you, hoping for this moment, has made me so fucking hard I can barely stand it. You are wrecking me, woman. I want every inch of you, every morsel of your skin, every ounce of your breath. I want all of it. And I want you to give it to me. Can you do that? Can you trust me with your body?"

She looked dazedly into heavy lidded eyes. Into eyes a darker grey than she'd ever seen them. Eyes filled with something she couldn't name, but it stirred her. Deeply. This was just an exercise, she reminded herself. A practice. A tutoring. It meant nothing. It could only mean nothing. No feelings were involved, Kit had said so. She'd agreed. Hell, it was what she wanted. Wasn't it? To use him because she could. Because she trusted him not to hurt her. But when she'd thought that through, it was her body she hadn't wanted hurt. She hadn't really understood that her heart could get involved. That her heart wouldn't see this as practice.

Yes, was the answer. She could one hundred per cent trust him with her body. She could even trust him with her heart.

She just wasn't sure she could trust herself with her own heart. That ship could, quite possibly, have sailed.

Chapter 20

Sometime during the night Kit must have brought up her bag because it sat on the chair by the window. She twisted, the duvet lifting and letting cool air drift across her lower back. She was naked. Still. Or rather, again.

Good Lord. She let her eyes drift to the figure lying beside her. Kit's hair was tousled and fell across his forehead, his dark lashes casting shadows on his cheeks as his steady breathing moved his chest up and down in a calming, rhythmic fashion.

Molly turned back and edged her way out of the bed, tiptoed to the chair and retrieved the silky robe, her swanky negligee, from the holdall. She reached for her toiletries bag and tucked it under her arm to take downstairs to the bathroom. Scout was having a sleepover with Mr Feeney across the road – she might be jealous, Kit had said with a sheepish grin. Swiftly but quietly Molly headed down to the kitchen to use the loo, deposit her toiletries and make coffee. Much-needed coffee. She needed alone time, thinking time. Going-back-over-everything-that-had-happened time. Oh, she was definitely well and truly de-virgined. She knew that wasn't a word, not a real one, but maybe it should be.

She washed her hands, avoiding looking in the mirror –

she wasn't sure what she might see. She wasn't sure she was ready to find out. The oven clock showed 7.35 AM and Molly was disgusted with herself – she couldn't even have a lie-in. The one day her body really needed it. She scanned herself internally. Yup, there were some aches and areas of minor discomfort where there hadn't been before, but, oddly, that felt good. It felt real. She'd had sex, *they'd* had sex. Not once or twice. Oh no, *they* went for the triple play.

Coffee brewing, she sat, gingerly, at the dining-room table. Ah yes, dinner. It had been delicious when they finally got to it. Cold poached salmon, herbed rice and a green salad. Pear tart for dessert. Not quite as good as Ali's but then, Star Baker alert. And she'd eaten every morsel. So had Kit. They had grinned at each other, chatting as if they hadn't just had practice sex for the first time. As if he hadn't just given her two, count them, *two* orgasms. And that was only their first bout.

The maths talk, the data and problem-solving had done it for her. It had made sense. Of course he needed to learn her body and how it worked. Of course she needed to be part of that, part of the solution and the only way for that to be successful, for an answer to be found, so to speak, was to communicate her needs. Her wishes. Her body's desires. Why hadn't any guy explained it like that before? She could have chucked her virgin status out years ago.

But then, it wouldn't have been Kit Elliot who had brought her safely and thoroughly through her first encounter. And what a pity that would've been.

Molly smiled as she eased from the chair and poured some strong Java into a mug. She inhaled and tasted. Perfect. Sitting again she let her eyes wander the room, remembering.

He'd taken it slow and steady. "We're the tortoise, not the hare," he'd said. "We'll get to the finish line if we take it nice and easy." And it had started that way. He'd helped her out of her clothes and, to ease her vocal embarrassment – "I can't let you see all my rolls," she'd declared – he had let her crawl under the duvet as he tossed his own clothing aside and climbed in beside her.

"I wish it was dark," she'd said.

"I'm so glad it's not," he'd replied.

And as she saw his face, as his eyes roamed her body, her curves, her bumps, her aforementioned rolls, she'd almost believed him. He talked to her the entire time and she had found her voice, her sex-moves voice, as they'd laughingly called it later.

"No, not that, move down a bit."

"Harder there."

"Faster with your thumb."

"Oh, yes, do *that* again."

"To the left, no, *your* left!"

And they'd laughed and whispered and mumbled and groaned and laughed some more. And then the laughing stopped and there were just breaths. Deep and fast. Hungry and needy. Her first orgasm tumbled out of her during the laughing phase but the second snuck through her body as his moved swiftly and surely in hers. Hard, steady. So strong. His arms braced on his elbows by her shoulders as he used his speed and agility to press her against the mattress again and again, his hips using their pressure to push at her in exactly the right way, in exactly the right spot. The chatting and laughing had stopped as they kept their eyes on each other, holding each other in the moment and then she'd shuddered as unexpected waves of pleasure swam through her body for the second time and she felt her eyes fill. Before he could see the effect he was having on her, she closed them, reaching up, her arms about his neck as she held on while he kicked up the pace and groaned his release into her neck.

231

It had been so bloody *everything*. Sure, it had been uncomfortable when he'd entered her body first, but he'd readied her. He had lube, he said, but considering how responsive she was, they probably wouldn't need it. They didn't. She'd had no idea that her body would know exactly what to do when she listened to it. When she let it dictate all the ways that brought her pleasure. She was very, *very* proud of herself. Go, Molly, Sex Whisperer!

And credit where it was due. Kit Elliot was very damn good at sex. He was a gentleman to boot. He'd held her close, praising her, telling her how beautiful and amazing she was. Granted he'd just orgasmed himself and she was pretty sure men said whatever they thought you wanted to hear at that stage. Or no, wait. They said what you wanted to hear, *before*. Right?

But then he'd got out of bed and headed downstairs, leaving her spreadeagled beneath the covers. Moments later he returned with a bowl of warm water and a washcloth and he'd gone to work. Tended to her. Cleaned any stickiness from her upper thighs and around her belly. He'd been gentle and kind. Back to chatty mode, probably to avoid any awkwardness.

He had climbed back in beside and held her close, gathering her in his arms as he told her funny stories about escapades from his college days. Then her stomach had rumbled. Growled, really, and in between laughs they'd dressed, sort of, her dress over her nakedness, his jeans pulled on without a shirt or boxers, and headed downstairs to devour the food. They drank her sparkling rosé, toasting her cherry-popping with a snorting giggle on her part, a smug grin on his. They drank wine with dinner too so were nicely merry by the time round two began. It started in the kitchen, against the fridge door as she was leaning back against it and Kit swooped, kissing her soundly. His hand had reached down, clutching folds of fabric and slowly, oh, so slowly, edging her dress up her thighs and finding her naked and wet. That was all it took seemingly, a deep hungry kiss and she was ready. Raring to go. So, they went. Into the living room, onto the couch. And straight back to sexy times.

It was quicker, more urgent this time. Desperate, in a way. And hot. So effing hot Molly had almost exploded. Fortunately, her overnight bag was right next to the couch, supplies at the ready, so Kit didn't even have to race upstairs for a condom. They didn't laugh this time. Or at least not much. And they moved together, like they'd done it a thousand times, she only need to give him the barest essential of instructions and she was flying.

It seemed she was not the only quick learner.

She poured more coffee as she let her mind linger over the third time. She'd awoken in the depth of night, startled and surprised at her surroundings. Then she remembered. Rather she was *reminded*, by a leg, long and muscular, the hairs soft and smooth against her skin, draped over the lower half of her body. He had stirred at her movement and hauled her close, kissing her temple, her cheek, her neck. Snuggling into her. She snuggling right back. It was no time before the feel of each other's bodies ignited a flame all over again. Slow and steady this time, barely any movement, he slid inside, his reach for the condom his only twist away from her. Gentle and easy, it had triggered other nerve-endings, other sensations. He'd stayed inside her body for a long time, adjusting, easing his length in and out, without a care in the world. She had been surprised when the wave of heat appeared out of nowhere and she realised there were all manner of ways to fall apart in this man's arms.

It was a lovely discovery.

Bacon, she decided. This morning called for bacon. As

she moved around the dining table, she noticed a photograph, face down on the side table. She righted it and was about to move on when she realised it might be a Kit moment, caught forever in a timeless second. She picked it up. Studied it. Recognised him and smiled. What a charmer he was as a teenager. Kind of goofy-looking, not smiling, no glasses, cropped hair. Maybe 14 or 15? Gangly, as teen boys usually are. The woman with her arm about his shoulders could be his mum, she supposed, though their colouring was different, and the man was tall and snappily dressed. Not his dad, she knew. He said he didn't know his father. But this one seemed to be part of the family. His arm was about the woman's waist.

Molly looked closer. The man looked vaguely familiar. She studied it some more, eyes flicking between each of the characters, telling a story from this one frozen image.

Breathing deeply, she let her senses free. Allowed herself to *feel* this picture. To know these people. A wave of anger roared through her so fast she snapped the photo back onto the sideboard. *Woah!* That was intense. Not a lot of good feelings shared, there. But who was angry at whom? She'd ask Kit.

But first, bacon.

He reached for her and found space. That wasn't good. Not good at all. Rearing up, he glanced about the room, rubbing sleep from his eyes. Nothing.

Her bag was open. Where was she? She couldn't have left without her things, surely?

Kit threw back the duvet and yanked on his jeans. There was a chill in the air so he tugged on a T-shirt as he hurried down the stairs to . . . bacon? Oh, thank you, Jesus! She hadn't done a runner. And maybe there was coffee too.

The sight of Molly swaying her hips to some ragtime on

the radio was enough to make his heart falter. The silky fabric clung to her ass and shimmied back and forth below that spectacular curve. She was in his kitchen, cooking bacon. This might just be the best day of his life.

"Good morning, beautiful." He leaned in and kissed her neck as she hip-bumped him playfully.

"How *you* doin'?" she asked in her best Joey from *Friends* voice.

"I," he kissed her cheek as he reached around and snagged a strip of bacon from the paper towel, "am doing brilliantly. Why, you may ask? I'll tell you." He took the spatula from her hand, put it down and turned her to pull her into his chest. He kissed her other cheek and then her nose. Resting his forehead on hers, he looked into her upturned eyes. "I had sexy times with the smartest, most beautiful woman I know and it feels pretty damn awesome to wake up and find her cooking bacon in my kitchen." He kissed her open mouth. Yes, he was sure she was about to protest all he said, but too bad. It was what it was. Easing back, he tilted his head, tucking a wayward curl behind her ear. "Are you okay? Are you sore? Do you need pain pills?"

Molly shoved at hand at his chest, her cheeks flushing. "Jesus, Kit, that's a mortifying thing to ask!"

"Why? God knows you used muscles previously unused and I know from doing new workouts it can be uncomfortable the next day. And maybe I need to apologise for that third time? Too much? I should have let you sleep."

Still pink of face Molly rested a finger over his lips. "Stop. And yeah, I can see you're just being a gentleman and asking, so I appreciate it. I'm fine. A bit achy in unexpected, or no, actually *expected* places, but it's all good." She replaced her finger with her lips in a light kiss. "The third time was as special as the others so I'm glad for that experience too."

Briskly, she backed away and continued tossing sizzling bacon on the pan.

Kit felt a chill move through his chest at her choice of words. 'Experience.' Was that what it was to her? An 'experience'? God, he needed to get a grip. Of course it was. That's what she'd asked for, that's what she'd got. He was the idiot thinking the middle of the night sex was something more. Something extra. Something *special*.

He was a fool.

Spying the coffee pot, he poured some into his mug and topped up hers. They clinked mugs in a friendly fashion and he kept a bright smile on his face.

It was all good.

It was exactly as it was meant to be.

With an inward breath he found eggs and began cracking them into the pan and added some sourdough to the toaster. They would have a nice breakfast, be all adult and cool about last night and she would go on her merry way, a virgin no longer. Job done.

They would see each other at work, he would set his dastardly plan in motion, she would end up hating him – and probably never forgive him – and she would rue the day she ever met him. He placed the food on plates she'd laid out on the dining-room table while he'd been cooking. As Kit thought that through, the fact that she'd eventually loathe him, he figured he might have her for one more day. One more night. Teach her a few more things. In the interest of her education, of course. He could have her in his bed – or hers, indeed, one more time. Then the shit would hit the fan but he'd have been her first. He'd be the one she remembered – in years to come when she had hopefully stopped hating him – as her 'starter man'. Despite the knowing sensation in his belly, he chuckled at his own term.

Molly held her fork still as she watched him. "What's so funny?" she asked.

"I imagined you, years from now referring to me as your 'starter man'," he said, smiling.

"I think you mean my Starter Kit!" She burst out laughing at her own joke and, as Kit joined in, she said, "I wish I could patent that! I could make you the 'go to' practice man. The one all the virgins could use to learn the sexy moves. Oh, wait! That might involve cash transactions and you'd be termed a gigolo. Can't have that, sorry!" She popped the bacon into her mouth and spoke around her food. "You'll just have to remain *my* Starter Kit."

"To that end . . ." Kit decided to take a gamble. Push a little bit. See if he could eke these moments out. "Are you free Tuesday evening? I've stuff lined up till then but I could come to your flat with takeaway after work and we could continue your tutoring."

Molly eyed him over her coffee mug. "There's more?"

"Hell, yeah, there's more! So much more." Kit leaned over and stroked the inside of her wrist, felt a pulse fluttering under his thumb. "I consider it my duty to educate you to the fullest extent of my ability."

She sighed. "Oh well, if I must. In the interests of advancement, you understand. And I better get an A+ on my score card, Professor Elliot. Or I'll complain to the sex school."

He quirked his eyebrow. "A+? *Hmmm.* I'm pretty sure, with your talent and aptitude that will be a given."

She smiled. Satisfied and pleased. She liked to be the best at whatever she did. No question of that.

And as for sex, Kit didn't actually believe it was a learned occupation, it was just something that worked between two people or it didn't. Sure, orgasms could happen if you figured out the logistics, read the books, but the connection? The feeling of closeness, of tenderness mixed with heat and passion? That wasn't something learned.

That was a gift.

Molly buttered her toast and applied apricot jam. "This is an excellent combined-effort breakfast," she said. "Who doesn't love apricot jam as the weather warms up? It's such a summer preserve for me. Reminds me of holidays in Majorca and the south of France. Delish."

"I've never been to the Balearic Islands. Worth a visit?" Kit smothered his own toast with butter and jam.

"It is," Molly said. "The major places are packed with tourists and can be overwhelming but the villages in the mountains and along the coast, the hidden places, they are gorgeous. Beautiful scenery and food. Which reminds me . . ." She twisted in her chair and reached for something behind her. "Where was this taken?"

Shit. Why hadn't he tossed that photo? He reached over and took it from her hand, placing it face down on the table. "Somewhere in Boston. Can't remember."

She stared at him. "That's not true."

"Okay, you're right. It's outside Paul Revere's house. We were on a history tour."

"I'm assuming that is your mum. Who's the man?"

"No one important." Kit poured more coffee, not meeting her eyes.

"That's also not true," she said.

"What are you, the Photo Police?" He knew his tone was curt but, Jesus, this was a can of worms he did *not* want to open.

Molly wasn't the smart accountant for nothing. She could be a frigging investigator, like her big brother, the way she sat there, all quiet and patient, waiting and watching. Letting the silence fill the room. He was no match for her.

"It's a sore subject for me so can we drop it?" He knew that was sneaky. She wouldn't push if she thought he was hurting. He wasn't bad at this manipulating stuff either.

"Sure." Molly stood and began clearing dishes. "I didn't mean to pry. It's just he looks so familiar, and I can't put a name to him. Perhaps you'll tell me when you're ready?"

She carried the plates and mugs to the kitchen and Kit watched her for a moment before gathering the rest of the items on the table.

Tell her?

Yeah, when hell froze over.

"Three times? You had sex three times with Kit? Holy shit, Moll! I'm impressed." Ali took a swig of her brandy as she, Molly and Frankie lounged in the drawing room after Sunday dinner.

"Keep your voice down," Molly hissed. "The others might hear you."

"No, it's perfect. My signal isn't great today and I want to hear you. I want to hear *everything*!" Caro's face came and went, along with the sound, from the small screen of Molly's phone. "More details now! Did he make you come? Every time? Oh, Jesus, is he a sex god?"

"Eh, yes!" Molly's voice was full of laughter.

"Yes to which part?" Frankie demanded, sipping the herb tea that Gabe had made for her.

"All of it?" Molly said but it came out like a question, as if she wasn't one-hundred-per-cent sure herself.

Ali did a little dance and wiggled her hips. "*Whoop, whoop!*" she chanted. "Molly's all grown up!"

Molly rolled her eyes. "Give over, Ali. And lower your voice. I don't need the rest of the family to know about this. None of them. And that includes your men," she glared at Frankie and Ali, "and yours!" she added into her phone screen. "I know it's mad that I'm pushing twenty-five and only just did it for the first time but I'm so glad I waited. I also know Kit and I won't be in a relationship, we're not together. Nor will we be, but I'm so glad it was him." She sighed. "He was great. He made me feel so . . . wanted, I suppose. I wasn't expecting that. And we had fun. We put on our geek hats and made a problem out of it."

The three other women looked at Molly in astonishment.

"Sex was a problem?" Caro asked for all of them.

"Yes. In a good way. We found the solution together. Oh, never mind. You had to be there."

"*Ew*, no. We really didn't. I never want to see my little sister having sex!" Ali did an exaggerated shudder and the others laughed and joined in with her.

"I have to go," Caro's voice emerged from the phone. "I have some prep for tomorrow's class to do."

"Wait," Molly remembered something. "You never told us how Nick and Toby got on with Marianna and Mia. What happened? Was it okay?"

"Oh, yes. I forgot I hadn't told you. It went well. Mia and Toby were nattering all the time, Nick said, and the one thing he noticed was that Mia's birth father seems to be in her life and that's good. But not, it seems, in Marianna's."

"*Huh*. I thought they were all childhood Romeo and Juliet shit?" Ali interjected.

"Right. Me too." Caro agreed. "But, get this. Marianna seems to be *very* friendly with another local farmer. Whose name is *Bernadine*."

There was a short silence.

"She's a woman!" Caro said, when no one spoke.

"*Duh*. Good for her," Molly said. "Maybe that's exactly what's she needs. A female friend is worth her weight in gold."

Ali put an arm across Molly's shoulders. "I think she

means Bernadine is a *special* friend of Marianna's."

Molly blinked. "*Oooh, gotcha!* How do you feel about that, Caro?"

Caro shook her head. "Truthfully? No clue. I'm playing the waiting game. As time goes by, I'm letting a lot of that part of my past go. Certainly the parts that don't relate to Toby. Maybe in time we will hear Marianna's true story but, until then, as long as she is a good and supportive mother to Mia, she can see whomever she likes, whoever makes her happy. Makes no odds to me." She looked away from the screen, said something in Italian and turned back to them. "Gotta go. *Ciao* and congrats, Moll!"

Congrats. As Molly helped clear away the glasses later before heading back to the flat, she pondered on that word. Shouldn't it be Kit who got the congratulations? He did most of the work. He led her through a potentially messy situation with humour, technique, it had to be said, and aplomb. He made it fun and as easy as going from virgin to not, could be. God, she really was glad she'd waited for him. It could have been Declan. She shuddered at the thought. He wouldn't have used maths as a tool to lighten the mood and ease her way. He probably would have only thought of himself. Maybe that was unfair. Maybe she should sleep with him, as a comparison? She shuddered again. God, even the thought of doing the things she did with Kit with anyone else made her stomach clench. And that could be a problem down the road. But at least she would have next time. Tuesday. And maybe later in the week too. She hoped he had lots of lesson plans prepared.

For now, she'd chitchat with her parents, try to see what had Flynn in such a dour mood and head home for a long soak in the bath. A plan. She folded napkins, put them in the wicker basket on the table for next day and took off her apron. If she'd learned one thing from Ali it was to always wear an apron when cooking or baking and when washing up. She went to hang it on the hook at the back of the door as it opened.

"Apologies," Gabe said as he caught her arm to prevent her falling from the force of the door swinging in. He took the apron, hung it and closed the door, leaning back against the wall to study her. He raised an eyebrow, his face remaining serious.

"Are you well, Molly? Does it feel right, safe?"

Typical Gabe. Straight to the point. She knew Ali wouldn't have said anything but Gabe, well, Gabe just knew things. Molly might have a touch of ESP or whatever it was called, but he was on a whole other level. Even though she felt comfortable with him, felt connected to him, Molly could feel herself blush.

"Is it that obvious? How cringeworthy."

Gabe reached out and rested his large steady hand on her head. She felt, as she often did when he touched her, a strange sense of calm flood her body. Of warmth. Of acceptance. He smiled at her, his rare gentle smile. Jeez, Ali really lucked out with this guy.

"Not obvious, no. But you are . . . changed, I think. Do I need to have a chat with Mr Elliot? I realise I would have to get in line behind your brothers, and probably Ali, but I am at your service, should you require it."

See? A gentleman to his toes. "No, you don't need to have a chat with Mr Elliot. But thanks for the offer. And I may not be as mouthy as my next-up sister, but I can speak for myself."

"Indeed, you can. Always. However, we males of the species can be complete asses when it comes to matters of the heart, so keep me in mind."

"Oh, no. No hearts involved here. Just, you know, fun. Practice, you might say." Oh God, she was an idiot. You don't lie to Gabe Mackenzie. He sees right through that shit.

His mouth twitched, just a for a second in an almost smile.

Yep. Saw right through that one.

"Alright, then. If you are sure." He pressed his hand gently on her shoulder and then shoved it back in his pocket.

She grabbed her bag, hollered a goodbye to the rest of her family, and headed down the hall, closing the front door behind her with a solid thud. She was walking the three and a half K to her flat this evening, walking off that strawberry shortcake Ali had made and walking off all the Kit thoughts in her head too. She was walking to let her own thoughts, the non-Kit ones, settle and find their home in this new Molly. This 'I've had sex and am officially an adult' Molly. She was walking and thinking, and walking and feeling.

Hopefully three and a half kilometres would bring some answers.

Chapter 21

By the time Kit showed up at Molly's door on Tuesday evening with takeaway and wine, he had put in motion a plan that could, potentially, ruin her. He had spent Sunday afternoon and every minute since then trying to come up with an alternative. The trouble was, she was the perfect patsy. The perfect scapegoat that he knew Twomey would go for. The perfect fall guy – or in this case, gal. The perfect way to finish his job. He knew the best way to catch a criminal was to make them feel safe. When they let their guard down, they made mistakes. They got careless. Twomey would only feel safe if someone else was in the line of fire.

Unfortunately, that someone was Molly Fitzgerald. Kit wished it wasn't but Twomey had already started her downward spiral. He had, Kit discovered over the last couple of days as he hacked deeper and deeper into Twomey's accounts, put Molly's initials on several bum records and financial statements. They were not Molly's work. Any fool could see that, but Twomey didn't recognise her talent. If she had even glanced at these specific ones, she'd have found the errors on her first scan through.

She was that good. Twomey was not. Kit had to now make it look like Molly actually did the inferior work, rather than Twomey faking it. But this was only the tip of the iceberg of the rot that was seeping through BB&M. Benson Senior was right. There was a very bad apple in this barrel. But it wasn't just Twomey. He was getting his orders from higher up and when the shit hit the fan, and it would, Kit would make sure of that – it was his job after all – Twomey and his house of cards would fall. And Benson Senior would be gutted.

That wasn't Kit's problem. Or not his immediate one. And he'd face it when it was time. Tonight though, tonight his problem was how to hide his sneaky, dishonourable soon-to-be-discovered behaviour from Molly.

He was being selfish. He knew it, acknowledged it and went with it anyway. She was so different. So *herself*. So fresh and new to him and his jaded ways. Sure, he was only thirty, but he was jaded. He'd seen many lives go down the toilet because of greed and avarice. Because some people always wanted more and didn't care who they hurt in the process.

Kit knew Molly was going to be hurt – by him – but he was going to take one more night. One more opportunity to show her how good it could be between them. They couldn't be together, not after things went down later this week. She'd never speak to him again – and rightly so. But goddammit, couldn't he just have this?

Her name *would* get cleared. She *would* be exonerated. Her reputation *would* be restored. But she might have left in disgust by that time. Then getting a new role might, okay, *would* be a challenge. But she could go small. Try a firm that would be able to use her talents and give her a bigger role because of their size. That's what he would do. If it were him accused unjustly of a felony.

Oh shit. This was bad. She was going to be arrested and he was relying on Flynn to make damn sure she wasn't actually charged. There was no way he could live with this plan, this decision, if she got a record. Flynn Fitzgerald better be the expert and the 'go to' guy everyone said he was, because if Molly ended up with an actual record as opposed to the threat of one, Kit Elliot better run where Flynn Fitzgerald would never find him.

Molly opened the door wearing a robe – not the silky sexy one from Saturday night – but a fresh cotton stripy one. She still managed to look adorable.

"*Argh*, I'm not ready. This," she swept her hand up and down her body, "isn't intentional! I'm running late and just got out of the shower. Give me a minute?"

Kit chuckled as he kicked off his shoes upon entering the hall. "There's no schedule, no timeline. Take your time but, hey, come here first." He lowered the brown-paper bags filled with steaming Indian curry and naan bread to the floor, reached for her, and took her face in his hands. "Hi, gorgeous," he said and kissed that sweet sinful mouth.

"Hi," she murmured against his lips.

Shit, he could get used to this. He pulled back and, gathering the bags, headed to her kitchen.

He warmed some plates, opened drawers for cutlery and glasses and set the table. He uncorked the red wine he'd brought and checked her fridge for some white. A delicious light Viognier was already opened so he poured two glasses and went to meet her in the living room as she emerged from the bathroom pulling a T-shirt on over some sweats. How she managed to make the mundane pretty was beyond him.

"Cheers," he said, handing her a glass. "I hope you don't mind I raided your fridge?"

She clinked her glass to his. "My fridge is your fridge," she said with a smile. "Something smells great. I'm starving." They bustled about then, opening bags and cartons, spooning out choices of lamb pasanda and butter chicken, onion bhajis and poppadums. There were samosas and chicken on sticks with peanut dipping sauce. And some vegetarian option that Kit couldn't remember the name of as he set it out.

"Good Lord, Kit. How hungry did you think we were?"

"Leftovers are the best and this way you won't have to cook for another day or so."

"Good thinking."

"And I've an ulterior motive," he announced with a quirk of his lips. "I intend to wear you out later so you need sustenance."

Her blush was the cutest thing he'd seen in a long time. Rosy-cheeked, she ducked her head and picked up a fork. "I'm trying to come across as all sophisticated and failing spectacularly. Not just the clothing – most comfy in my wardrobe – but scorching cheeks at your implications for the dessert! Oh well, nothing has changed in my life and I'm still incapable of acting like an actual grown-up. I thought I might have achieved that status but apparently not."

Kit studied her. She was such a mixture of spontaneity and reserve. Of extravert and introvert. He could see she needed space at times, yet also thrived on family and the surrounding chaos that could bring. She had a core of sensitivity that was unreal. In the true meaning of the word. Yet her drive and ambition, her math-brain and her skills, they were second to none.

"How would you describe yourself to someone who'd never met you? Say you were putting up a profile on a dating app?" he asked, curious to see her reaction. Hear her answer.

"A dating app? Never! I'd never go on one. Yeah, yeah, I know they're popular but everyone lies on those. I hate liars – especially since I was living a lie myself for so long. Nope. Not a thing for me. Anyway, it's notoriously hard to describe oneself. How would you do it? Describe yourself, I mean."

His chest had tightened so much at her declaration about liars that it took a moment for him to breathe through it, to find his balance. She'd made it clear before. He knew that. And yet, here he was lying to her about everything. No, that wasn't true. He wasn't lying when he kissed her or touched her or made pleasure sing through her body. That was all truth. All real. He swallowed some food to take a moment and consider his response. He'd brought up the subject – he should wear the big boy pants and say what he thought.

"Most people would call me a dork or a nerd. You have yourself on occasion, and it's a title I wear with pride. I don't care that I use my brain to advance my career. Isn't that what one is supposed to do? I know I think outside the box, think laterally at times and that can freak people out. But I'm sporty too. I've always played team sports as well as being a runner. Gran had me playing soccer by age four. Being an only child, she wanted me to have pals. To be sociable. I was fine with that. I still am. I have good friends, though not many as I move around a lot. Sport is great for that. Every city I go to, I join a team of something. Baseball, softball, basketball, soccer. I don't care, but it gives me an in with the locals, keeps me fit and stops any hints of loneliness creeping in." *Damn.* He shouldn't have said that. He sounded like a big whinging baby. He took a sip of wine, distracting himself from his thoughts, hopefully distracting her.

"You get lonely sometimes?" she asked, her voice soft, almost sad. "Me too. I know I shouldn't, with my bonkers-wild family, but they don't stop the lonely inside." She shook her head, tossing back her mane of curls. "Ah, we're getting maudlin. Enough. Ice cream?"

She hopped up from the table and busied herself about the small kitchen and Kit felt that they had both revealed some things about themselves, things that were scary and private. Normally, he never revealed anything about himself. It was the fastest way to get found out in his job. To be rumbled. He always kept things on the down-low. This woman had a way, though, of sliding under his guard. Not on purpose, not prying, but her open heart made it very hard to stay behind locked bars. He needed to watch his step or he would lie down before her and pour out all the secrets he'd been carrying for years.

That would not be a good plan.

They cleared dishes, both refrained from ice cream and they curled up on the sofa to watch an episode of the latest Netflix series that had gripped the nation. Kit sat at one end and Molly stretched out at the other, her feet resting on his lap. She had small, neat feet, with toenails painted a bright summer pink. He'd never had the urge to kiss a woman's toes before, but a lot in his world was shifting off its axle. He needed to move things forward. He had this one night, he reminded himself, and he wanted it to be memorable for Molly. He wanted it to be special so that, in time, not all her memories of him would be tainted with disgust.

Truthfully? He wanted tonight as a memory for himself, too.

He'd stayed over. Sometime about five thirty that morning, he had leaned down and kissed her cheek as he whispered goodbye. She had turned to him, stretched her arms around his neck and nuzzled into him. "Thank you," she'd murmured, "that was awesome. I never knew. See you later," and promptly fallen back to sleep. Not very hostess-worthy, she thought, but come on, five thirty? Who the hell gets up and is chipper at that ungodly hour? Kit Sex God Elliot. That's who.

Yup. Sex God. As Molly walked briskly along the corridor to her office, she felt tingles all over just remembering. Did people know? If they looked at her now, would they be able to tell? She felt she had a massive sign on her head announcing her new status. 'ORAL SEX QUEEN' it would read. In big bold letters. Yes, it would be a lie. Or rather an overstatement and just not *completely* true. Because she wasn't the queen of it – she'd a long way to go with her own education and tutorials on how to do it but, *man*, she was the queen in all the receiving ways.

All the ways. *Phew!* She got hot thinking about it. He'd read a book, he'd said, as she'd wondered later at his abilities. Yup, the guy had read up on oral sex. His first girlfriend in college, Eliza, had refused to let him go down on her till he'd read a specific book, *She Comes First*, it was called. Eager and enthusiastic, he'd devoured it. It was both scientific, educational, and instructive. He was grateful to this day. Molly was grateful too. *Very* grateful. Thanks, Eliza.

She sat at her desk, fired up her computer and shifted in her chair. Oh yes, tingles indeed. She opened her first set of recent accounts and scanned for any discrepancies. It was merely a trick, a failsafe she'd taught herself when she began – *always* double-check – not just as you are working – but the next day, before you close accounts and return them to the client. She knew from experience that human error was real. She also knew she was very, *very* good at her work so the double, or she supposed triple-check really, was unnecessary. But it was habit. So, she did it. All well on her first batch. Just three clients here – simple and straightforward and good to go. She closed them, invoiced them, and hit send.

She worked like that for another two hours, only infrequently wondering if Kit was in his office. It wouldn't do to go scampering off down the corridor to check. That would be childish, clingy even. Not the behaviour of a cool adult woman like Molly Fitzgerald. Oh no. She had it sussed. Assured and unflappable, that was the new her.

But break time couldn't come soon enough.

The coffee was already brewing when Molly walked into the canteen area. Declan was there, chatting to one of the new interns. Of course, he was. Eyeing up his next conquest, no doubt. Was that mean? Molly didn't care. She studied him objectively. He really was ruggedly handsome. Like a movie star. Confidence oozed from every pore. His clothes looked to be bespoke and his hair perfectly tousled. The fact that he was in fact an overgrown boy child and a complete ass didn't seem to be of any consequence to the young lady he was enslaving with his charms. Molly reflected briefly on the sisterhood and then figured, nah, this one could fend for herself.

She felt him before she saw him. Kit sauntered into the canteen and, filling his mug, took the seat next to hers. He bumped her shoulder casually and said a low-voiced hello. It struck Molly that he was back in geek mode. A complete and stark contrast to Declan. Now, wasn't that interesting. His hair flopped down on his forehead, his glasses looked extra dorky – how many pairs did he have and she really must ask if he even needed them? – and oh, god, he was wearing slacks again. Not trousers – *slacks,* the old-man slacks. Flat-fronted and brown. *Gah!* Had she taught him nothing?

"What's with the gear?" She poked him in the chest of his knit waistcoat. "The last few weeks you dressed like a normal person. Now you have reverted to, what, type? Is it Wear Your Nerd Clothes to Work Day? Because I didn't get the memo."

"I was losing myself in the regular clothing," Kit said stiltedly. "These suit me. They suit who I am."

"No, they don't," Molly instantly disagreed. Just because they'd had amazing, life-changing sex didn't mean she wouldn't call him on shit. "They look like you're dressed up to play a nerd. Like you are acting a role, 'Enter Stage Left, Geek Number Two'. What's up?"

She had felt him stiffen at her words. Go still. But he didn't respond to her jibe.

Instead, he sipped his drink, pushed his glasses up his nose and said, "I've got to go. I've a meeting." And he stood and left. Without looking back. Without acknowledging anything of what she'd said.

Whoa! That was . . . cruel? Unkind? Kit was never unkind. Something was off with him and she couldn't believe her senses hadn't alerted her to it. The very fact that her senses were switched off, for the most part, around him, other than the recent photograph incident, was enough to give her pause for thought. Was he a really good blocker? Did he wear an invisible shield? Okay, now she was getting silly.

But still. It bore thinking through. She got all kinds of vibes around all kinds of people. With Kit it was – all good. All the time. She trusted him, she *knew* him, so maybe that was why she didn't pick up on him. She didn't have to. He was just Kit. A decent honest kind, and okay, let's be truthful here, exceedingly fine with the sexy moves, guy. That had been empirically proven.

She took her time heading back to her desk, peeping as unobtrusively as possible towards his doorway. It was shut. And his window blinds were down. This office area was well designed that way. All the offices opened on to a corridor that surrounded a plaza-like area with a massive skylight. One half was the admin staff open area, the other a good pretence at a courtyard, with a fountain, and shrubs in big terracotta pots. But the best thing was the unwritten rule – close the blinds if there is a 'do not disturb' scenario happening within your walls. Otherwise, all blinds were open. BB&M liked the notion that they had nothing to hide. Everything was above board. And it was. That was why Molly liked it so much. She could do good work here. Learn her trade, so to speak, and one day, several years from now for sure, but one day, have her own firm.

She wasn't so thrilled with BB&M by the late afternoon. Declan's office admin had sent a ton of contracts her way, to be signed off, all ones she had done before so she was mighty pissed that they needed redoing. He must have screwed up and she was covering for him. Again. She didn't mind the small errors he made – that's why she checked and double-checked. And the data wasn't his strong point. He sold BB&M to the potential clients. He was the ultimate salesperson and he got them some really big names. They liked him for that. He brought major players, famous people to their table and it all garnered news and, ergo, profit. For the company and, she assumed, Declan.

There were a lot to get through. He'd wanted them all notated with her initials before he signed them himself, the instructions said. She began flipping through them as she went, remembering the client, or the account, whichever had struck her the most, but that took so long she ended up just flipping to the last page of the invoice and initialling. Who had time? Not her.

Shoulders stiff and neck beginning to ache, Molly swallowed two painkillers shortly after six. She ordered out for food and when it was delivered by seven, she took a well-earned break.

She was not a happy camper. Whatever her senses were

not telling her about Kit, they were yelling pretty loudly right now. About the accounts. Before she returned the stack to Declan's office – he wasn't there – she had flipped idly though a few of the last in the second stack. Checked the names, noted them on her jotter, frowning as she didn't remember or even recognise them. But Declan had needed them by five and she dutifully dropped off the hard copies. Then she went back to her computer and began searching. And became confused and gradually, concerned. None of what she found made sense.

These weren't regularly invoiced clients at all. They were reports on overseas transactions and offshore accounts. For massive amounts of money. Huge. Millions. And she had initialled them. Her name and employee number were attached to each one on the computer but she had never seen them before. Had never worked on these, never heard of them. Unless she was mistaken, unless she was missing something vitally important, she had stepped into something pretty darn shady. BB&M didn't deal in offshore accounts as they were too specialised. Too open to 'vague' interpretation – read, illegal stuff.

Molly decided to text Kit. He'd been an ass earlier, but he was still the smartest person she knew when it came to all the i-dotting and t-crossing with accounts and financial data. Plus, he knew her. He'd know this wasn't her handiwork and would be able to explain why her name was down as the recorder and, in some of the records, the instigator.

Molly: Kit, can you come to my office? I need to show you something that's bothering me.

A couple of minutes passed and no response.

Then:

Kit: No can do. Sorry. Tied up.

Molly: It's important. Work related, not personal.
Kit: I'll come by in the morning.

Well, shit. Molly groaned and dropped her head to her hands. There was nothing she could do. Declan had left the building. The two Benson bosses had left for the day hours earlier and there was no other person she could ask. Not without throwing herself under the bus. It would have to wait till tomorrow. A niggle, a memory, shivered through her. This couldn't have anything to do with the joke email or text, could it? They were jokes, right? Those bribe attempts. She hated questioning herself but a couple of the names on these accounts rang a bell. Seemed eerily familiar yet definitely not ones she knew.

A wave of sadness washed over her. She was disappointed in Kit. She knew she had no right, no real tie to him but it was how she felt. The train journey home to the flat lasted seven hours. No, it didn't but it felt like that. Trudging wearily along the seafront to make the turn for her road, Molly felt lonelier than she had in a long time. Let's be honest, since she had met Kit. When she passed the ice-cream-cone window her throat tightened as she recalled the day walking on the pier. With Kit. With kind and funny and caring Kit. Not the brush-off version she'd texted earlier.

By the time she was in her own kitchen reaching for the wine and the leftovers, she was in a maudlin state. Reheated Indian is delicious, she knew that. She had experienced that. Now? Not so much. She pushed the plate away and plonked herself on the sofa. Her eyes closed against an unexpected sting, she hauled the blanket to her chin and turned into the soft velvet cushion.

And remembered last night.

How could sex be such a mixture of playful and *not*? Of fun *and* of passion. He managed it. Really well. Molly sighed deeply as she let her body replay the touches, the kisses, the gentle strokes, gripping when things got heated. And that had been her, gripping his hair as he did all manner of amazing things to her lady parts. She could feel herself blush at the memory and her body heat as if he was here, doing it all again.

She'd been so fearful of oral sex. So sure it was not for her. Maybe it was subliminally Ali-related, knowing the terrors that had affected her sister, before she met the delectable Gabe, before she faced her own past and revealed her secrets, but either way, it was not on Molly's 'to do' list. Kit, however, had a different list than hers. She was, it turned out, incredibly thankful for that.

He had been smooth. Sneaky, if you will. Lulling her into a false sense of security. She hadn't been expecting it. Thought that oral was something maybe couples did way down the line. That was an untruth she'd happily sold herself for years. Kit had begun his silent but deadly tactics halfway through their Netflix show. Stroking her arm, teasing her wrist with light brushes of his thumb, rubbing the back of her neck in gentle circles, almost like the softest of massages. She had arched into his touch. Not realising how much her body had craved his hands, his mouth. When the credits rolled his mouth was fused to hers, his hands busy burrowing under her loose-fitting T-shirt and sports bra. His words raspy and husky, eager, encouraging. Hot. His words were hotter than Hades. How beautiful, responsive, soft, sexy, glorious she was. She remembered those words as she huddled now in her blanket.

The real work began when he had tugged her from the couch to her bed, tossed her down, stripped her off her sweats and underwear and began kissing his way up her legs. She wasn't too happy about that and told him outright. There had been a minor battle then. He'd won.

"You have strong legs, shapely like a tennis player.

Probably from all the walking you do. Your calves are firm, your knees the perfect construction and as for these thighs?" He'd been using his tongue along the flesh of her inner thighs as his voice floated up to her. "These thighs are so fucking kissable I'm not sure I'll ever be able to move on."

She'd laughed at that because, well, it was silly. She did not have kissable thighs but she was grateful for the wine speaking. She'd take it.

And then he'd spread those thighs and licked her from her centre right up, one long steady stroke and the whimper that Molly meant to let out turned into something way more feral.

"Wait. Stop. You can't do that. It's . . . it's not time. I mean . . . oh, you can't want to. Not yet . . . oh." She clamped her jaws shut as a sensation she'd never before felt shot through her lower body – shimmering and shiny and shockingly good. "Oh, well, maybe just for a moment. Or two . . . Kit!"

He'd done something else. Over and over. Some tongue and lips magic that weaved a spell around her. That made her body twist and squirm in all the best ways. Never, never had she felt her body respond like this. Because it was Kit, talking through all his ministrations, including her in his repertoire of moves. It was Kit, asking her if this felt good or was that too fast or slow. He stopped at one point and, crawling up her body, licking, tasting, kissing and touching as he went, he kissed her mouth long and deep. And deeper still.

When he finally pulled back, he spoke, his voice rough and sexy, "Stay with me now, feel everything my tongue touches, everything my lips caress. This is all for you. All I want is for you to feel good. To feel the magic. To explode in pleasure. I know you can do it because I can make it happen. Your job is to talk to me, just like before. Think of it like another solution we're searching for together."

Once again, he understood what worked for her mentally, as well as physically. She let herself go. Enjoyed it. Revelled in it. He would accept nothing less. Jesus, she'd been a wrung-out mess when he was done. When she had shattered beneath his mouth, over and over. She had wanted to return the favour, knew she ought to, but he cuddled her instead. Let her body come back from its stratospheric flight. Let her regroup. Let her find her calm.

Then he'd started kissing her all over again, those deep, hungry, ferocious kisses. Her body had responded as if it hadn't ever experienced an orgasm and was, shockingly, rearing to go. Again. It was lovely. Simply, perfectly lovely.

They slept for a few hours and somewhere around the wee hours of the morning Molly woke to his hand stroking her hip. Not suggestively but tenderly, with the utmost of care. Her heart had felt so full, she turned over in the bed, kissed him passionately and worked her way down his body, an urgent need to taste him surprising her. Ever the eager student, she asked for direction, made him promise, laughingly, to talk to her as she had done for him, and he obeyed. The power she felt from the interaction was as surprising as her overwhelming desire to pleasure him.

"Jesus, Molly," he'd groaned, his voice raw with desire, "don't ever stop! You feel fucking amazing."

His gruff tone, his unguarded words, sent a thrill through her body. Set her on fire. Made her want more. Of him, and of herself.

They slept then, worn out and tangled together in a jumble of limbs and duvets. Of soft arms and gentle touches and Molly thought, briefly, as she faded into sleep, that she just might die of happiness.

Not now, though.

Now she felt like a discarded piece of wastepaper. It

was stupid to be so upset and truthfully she wasn't sure if she was more upset with Kit avoiding her and acting all weird or the scary discovery that she was, in theory, responsible for sending a gigantic amount of some unknown client's money to a most likely illegal offshore account.

On behalf of her employer.

She was in trouble, with only herself to rely on to locate the elusive 'get out of jail' card. It was times like this that her family called in the reinforcements. Which in Fitzgerald lingo meant only one man.

Flynn.

It was family instinct, born of years of big brother fixing things that had her reaching for her phone. But it was *her* instinct, *her* awareness, that had her pause and let her hand drop. Something was up with Flynn. They all knew it yet no one dared ask. He wasn't a man to share and if he wanted you to know something, he'd tell you. Confiding was not in his nature. But Molly knew – as much as she knew anything and granted that was definitely suspect right now – she knew he was hurting. In some way. Somehow. Flynn was *not himself*, as her mother would, no doubt, describe it.

There was no way she was involving him in her own basket of unravelled knitting wool when he obviously needed his own space. She'd texted him a couple of times since Dev and Frankie's big reveal at the Easter lunch. His replies had been as uninformative as ever. He must have been born holding secrets he was so damn good at it.

She was not going to bother him when he needed space. She owed him that.

This? She'd handle clients, overseas accounts, and Kit and his crap behaviour, tomorrow.

For now, sleep.

Chapter 22

Kit felt sick. Physically, in his stomach, the nausea kind of sick. He'd used employees in his strategies before. He'd made sure the innocent were, of course, exonerated. He would do the same again. He would do it now. Molly's case posed an unfortunate problem. *Unfortunate*? He grimaced wryly at his own choice of word. If that was all it was, things would pan out fine. The trouble was, Kit had never been involved with an employee of a company he was investigating. There were rules. And conditions. He'd broken them, on this job, unequivocally. There was no rule to say a forensic accountant, on a mission for the FBI and the Irish CCA, or Corporate Crime Agency, who were in collaboration on this case, shouldn't *use* an employee. For the greater good.

But using and being 'involved with', were two very different scenarios. Kit had found himself very firmly in the second category. He hadn't intended to, he hadn't meant to, yet, here he was. Flynn Fitzgerald was going to roast his balls for breakfast. And then kill him. Kit couldn't blame him. Not having a sister, he really didn't get the bond, the protective part, but he had seen it, plain as a pikestaff, with the Fitzgeralds. You don't mess with family. It might as well be a motto over the front door of their Dalkey home.

260

He checked his latest message from his team in the FBI. The contact they had been chasing on their end, a local CI, had turned up. Unhappily for them, up meant floating in the Charles river, a bullet hole in his head. Kit stayed away from the physical forensics of a case, tracing and testing, and stuck with the numbers side of things. White crime was huge. And if he was able to lock up the bastards that stole money, stole *livelihoods*, from the small guy, then he felt vindicated in his role. He knew, first-hand, what having your normal whipped from beneath you was like. If you knew the perp? If you'd trusted them? Well, that messed a person up. Trust became a fairy tale, not a reality.

The clients that were being screwed by certain persons via BB&M had no notion what was going on. Had no clue they were about to have a saviour protect their lives from financial ruin. Kit didn't mind being the unsung hero. Wear the invisible cape, so to speak. The last thing he needed or wanted was publicity. It was enough to walk away from a job knowing justice had been served. Or it usually was.

But clients being fleeced, however marginally, was only a part of it – this ran deeper.

Walking *away* from this one, soon, was going to hurt like hell.

His phone binged with another message. The CI had been smart enough to leave a coded message at his apartment. They might have just got the lucky break to tie the US string-puller to the Dublin crew. Time would tell. But meanwhile, things had to move forward today. Plans were set in place to urge Twomey to err in his haste to clean house.

Once Molly was taken, that was.

Kit's stomach turned sour again. He rolled his shoulders in an attempt to alleviate the tension that had been building.

Glancing at his watch, he walked to the window and peered down at the street below. There, right on time, was Molly Fitzgerald, moving in her swift purposeful way, through the burgeoning early-morning crowd. It was early – so again her way to be in before almost everyone else. He had to stay out of view. If she saw him, she would most likely confront him. She wasn't afraid to speak her mind, to tell him straight what an asshole he'd been to her yesterday both in person and via text. If she gave him the angry glare, with those stunning aqua-coloured eyes, filled with confusion and hurt, he'd fall at her feet and confess everything.

This job however, demanded more, came first. She would get over it, get over him. But he wondered, as his chest tightened, if he would ever get over her.

Business-like. All business. Yup, that was Molly today. Queen of the business-like behaviour. Polite, formal, respectful. Engaged with all who spoke to her, inclusive of all who needed her. She would be the fucking epitome of business-like.

Perhaps she also needed to rein in her rising temper a tad. Molly rarely swore, so the terms that were currently stacking up in her brain really needed to stay inside and not come blurting out at an inopportune time, Like, when she went to confront Twomey. When she spoke to Benson Senior. She didn't care if she swore up a blue stream when she got hold of Kit, he deserved a tongue-lashing. Aw shit, *bad* choice of words.

Keeping her morning chat with Patty to a minimum, she entered her office, toed off her sneakers, slipped her feet into heels and settled herself at her desk. She fired up her computer and waited as it hummed to life. It hummed alright. But then, nada. *Zilch. Access not permitted.*

That was strange. She pulled her laptop from her bag and began working on that, sending a note to tech to get when they arrived in for their shift. She lost track of time catching up on emails and checking accounts saved on her USB stick. A knock on her doorjamb returned her to the present sometime later.

"*Hmm?*" She looked up expecting to see Declan or another of her colleagues.

It was the tech guy, Marty.

"Oh great! You're here. I think there's an issue with my PC. I can't access my files. Can you check it for me?"

"Sure." He walked into her office and woke up the computer. He tapped away for several moments and turned to her, perplexed. "Looks like you've been denied access, Ms Fitzgerald. You've been locked out. I'm sorry, there's nothing I can do. This came from above." As he spoke, he indicated with a nod of his head to the upstairs.

"Molly Fitzgerald?" A voice came from the doorway.

Confused and bewildered, Molly twisted in her chair to see who was asking. Three people stood at the entrance to her office – one in front, two others partially hidden behind.

Before Molly could nod her head, the man in front walked towards her, holding out a badge of ID. "Molly Fitzgerald, we need you to come down to the station with us to answer some questions." He turned to the technician. "Sir, step away from the computer. That is now the property of the State."

As Molly rose and studied his badge, her blood began to chill. It was then she realised the other two people, now in the room too, were in uniform. Police uniforms.

"Wait, what's this all about? I don't have to go anywhere with you. I haven't done anything wrong." She took an automatic step back, her skin turning clammy. *This is bizarre*, she thought, *I'm probably still asleep and this is a bad dream.* She wasn't worried. She hadn't done anything wrong. They couldn't accuse her of anything – wait, they *hadn't.*

"There must be some mistake," she continued, keeping her voice calm and rational.

"No mistake." Uniformed man strode over and unplugged her PC, picking it up in his arms.

"Stop, you can't take that!" Molly was indignant. "That's BB&M property. I don't own it, they do. Hey, mister, sorry, officer, put that back!"

She got no joy from any of the three interlopers. Marty looked as stunned as she felt. The woman guard stepped forwards. "Ms Fitzgerald, if you don't come with us, quietly and without complaint, we will be forced to arrest and handcuff you. Is that what you want? To walk out of here in restraints? For all your colleagues to see?"

Well, shit.

No, no, she absolutely wouldn't like that. But, still … "Can you tell me what this is about?" She knew though. The gut-churning in her belly knew.

Bloody Declan Twomey set her up. All that initialling? She'd *kill* him.

"I want to talk to my bosses, please. Can I at least do that? This is mortifying. I can't have police here, taking my employer's things and not say something."

Guard Number One spoke – DI Collins, she knew from his badge. "Your bosses already know we're here. They called us."

What the actual hell? No. They must have got this wrong. "Who?" she demanded. "Who called you?"

"A Mr Bryan Benson," Collins informed her.

"No, there is definitely a mistake. He approves my work. He knows I'm doing a good job. Call him!"

But things were moving out of Molly's control. Guard

Number Two walked to the door, PC and associated wires in his arms.

Guard Kelly, the female officer, stood in front of her, non-threateningly true, but her voice was taking no nonsense. "Please collect your bag, ma'am, and we can get going."

Molly looked about her, her mind whirling. Who should she call? What should she do? This was a frigging nightmare. She picked up her bag and decided to leave her runners under the desk. If she was going to a police station, she was not going in with ugly flat trainers on her feet. It was heels all the way for an ounce of dignity.

Kit! She should call Kit. He would put an end to this craziness. "May I call my friend? He works here and should know what's happening."

"No," Collins said. "No calls till we get to the station."

And they began ushering her out the door after the guard carrying the computer.

The hall area was eerily silent. But not empty. God, no. That would be too much to ask for. As they walked her to the lift, past the open-space area, colleagues gathered in twos and threes, watching. Some looked astonished, incredulous. Others watched as if she was a Netflix show that need to be consumed by all. No one spoke. No one asked what the hell was happening. No one tried to stop her leaving.

No one.

Balancing the computer in one arm, Guard Two pressed the down call button and resettled his load. Neither of the other two guards spoke to her and she felt like she was part invisible part lit up like a beacon. Three figures walked towards them just as the lift arrived.

Oh, thank God, Molly thought. Benson Senior, Kit and Declan. They can put these people straight. Explain the mistake.

"Mr Benson!" Molly called to him. "There's been a mistake, these people think I've done something but won't say what. I don't know what's going on. Can you tell them I wouldn't do anything to hurt the company? Kit!" She swung towards him.

Kit looked . . . different. He stood tall and straight, in a suit. A dark-grey suit and pale-blue shirt. And tie. He looked like an accountant might. In a magazine. On TV. His hair was brushed back from his forehead, his broad shoulders without the merest hint of a hunch. But he was still Kit.

"Tell them," she beseeched Kit. "Tell them I'm innocent of whatever they say I did. You know me, I'm a straight shooter. Tell them."

Kit frowned, not meeting her eyes, and tipped his head in the direction of Collins. "Yes, Detective Inspector Collins, that's her. She's the one responsible for the mismanagement of funds. She signed them all, in the full knowledge of what she was doing. She worked alone, as far as I can tell."

The doors behind them whooshed open, but Molly barely heard them. A roaring was in her ears. A thunderous roar of a thousand waterfalls. Of engines revving for a drag race. Of bellowing elephants as their young are taken away. She couldn't actually hear Collins' reply. Her mouth fell open as she stared at the man she'd been so intimate with, who had tasted her *everywhere*.

"What the hell, Kit? What are you saying? Why are you lying? What the *fuck* is going on?"

"Calm down, Ms Fitzgerald," Benson Senior said coolly. "Now is not the time or place. Your lawyer will see to the details. I assume you won't be actually thrown into jail."

Jail? She was going to *jail*? Molly swivelled to look at Kit once more, trying to catch his eyes. "You owe me a bloody explanation, Kit Elliot. What's going on?"

266

But Kit said nothing. His posture remained rigid, his eyes not meeting hers. It was like he didn't know her. Recognise her. Care about her.

And maybe he didn't.

As the doors slid closed and the airless lift space felt like a tomb, Molly realised a couple of things. Twomey had stood there trying to look serious but had, she'd bet her life on it, been gloating. Kit had thrown her to the wolves, had not been wearing his glasses and had looked both hot as hell and cold as a glacier.

She also realised the most important thing.

Now was the time to call Flynn.

It was a whirlwind in the end. Or at least parts of it were. The rest involved a lot of waiting. Sitting in a room by herself, waiting. Molly's mouth was dry and her stomach was flipping between churning with an overload of anxiety and growling with hunger.

She had phoned Flynn, yes, she got one call, and he said he'd take care of her parents and her lawyer. It was the family lawyer, really, not hers. What twenty-something person had their own lawyer? Mary Foster was the one who had supported Ali through all her angst last year. Molly knew her and trusted her so that was something.

Molly was questioned, again and again. She said very little, knowing to wait for Ms Foster to arrive was the smart thing. But it was hard not to recount everything she had noticed, everything she had done. By the time the detectives were finished round two with her she would have believed herself guilty too.

It was clever. Whoever had set her up was extremely smart. It didn't feel like Twomey because, let's face it, smarts were needed and he was merely competent. The request had come from his office. But who else? And why?

She was eventually given a bottle of water and guzzled it with relief. Her throat still hurt and she knew it was because she was swallowing a massive lump, holding back the increasingly urgent need to burst into tears. And she wanted her mum. She wanted a big Jo Fitzgerald hug because they always made you feel better. It was a known fact.

When the door to the airless, windowless room eventually opened to reveal her eldest brother, Molly was so tired and hungry she didn't even run to him. She wasn't handcuffed or tied up in any way but her body felt like it was on shut-down.

"Hey," Flynn said, striding to her and hauling her into his arms. "Everything is going to be okay, Molly. Take a breath, sweetheart, everything is okay now."

She hadn't realised she was gasping for air. Probably about to have a bloody panic attack. And seriously, who could blame her. "What's going on, Flynn? I never stole anything, I never worked on some of those accounts so how could I be held responsible for them?"

"Take a seat, Moll," he said gently. When she was settled, he took out a notepad and pen and flipped to a blank page. "I know you've spoken at length to Collins but I want to hear it from you myself. Tell me what you know."

She did.

"Who else knew about the two attempts at bribery? And why on God's earth didn't you tell me about them? Even if you didn't tell your bosses?"

"I didn't tell anyone because it was stupid. I'd never do that, take money to either look the other way or change some data to suit someone's greed. For all I knew they were a joke, or a test of some kind, so I ignored them."

"But can you see what it looks like?"

"No. I can't. It looks like what it was. Someone wanted me to do something illegal and I refused. Or at least I refused by not answering. Surely that will stand me in good stead? Not go against me?"

"Who else knew?" Flynn repeated.

Damn. She'd been the stupid one, keeping things to herself. "No one," she admitted again, feeling foolish. She had no one to back her up. "But you could probably find them on my phone or computer. Or your tech person could."

Flynn flipped his notebook closed and stood, checking his phone. "I think Mum is outside with some food, so I'll let her come in. You haven't been charged yet, so there is no reason you won't be going home this evening. Mary Foster is sorting things out with Collins. It's a mess but we'll get it sorted."

"Flynn," Molly grabbed his arm, "I swear I didn't do anything wrong, I'd never cheat people out of their money. Never! I don't know why anyone would believe I did. I'm innocent of whatever is being said about me. I *swear*." She spoke urgently, unsure that her steadfast brother was actually getting it. That he believed her.

"I know that, Molly. It's all good." He kissed the top of her head and left the room.

It wasn't all good. though, was it?

When Jo bustled into the room a few moments later, several bags in hand, Molly almost broke. Her mother opened her arms and Molly was hugged long and hard. It was Jo who could barely hold back the tears and somehow that helped Molly regain her centre.

They sat, Jo pulling out wrapped sandwiches and a flask of tea. It was, Molly reflected a little later, the best meal of her life. "I guess jail makes a person hungry," she said to her mum as she crumpled the paper napkin and tossed it in the bag. "Thanks, Mum. This and you, were exactly what I needed. Now I just want to go home. Can I do that?"

"I'll check, darling – you have more tea."

"Mum," Molly said, her voice serious, "you do know I didn't do anything illegal, right? I wouldn't."

Jo looked up from her bag-packing. "Of course you didn't. Why would you even think I'd believe such rubbish? Now, I'll be back in a moment."

Molly slumped back in the chair as her mother left the room. That, that right there. That complete belief in her. That's what she'd expected earlier – from Kit. Her chest tightened as she remembered his stony face. His lack of eye contact. His cold demeanour. It was like she'd never known him at all. It made her unaccountably sad. As well as stone-cold furious.

A little while later Flynn returned. "I have some tough news for you. You may have to stay overnight. In a cell."

He said all this calmly as Molly stood, open-mouthed with shock. Okay, this was the outside of enough.

"*What?* Why? Am I being charged? And if so, with what?" She could feel her blood boil, feel her anger rise and took some deep breaths to counteract the rage forming in her body. Her entire body was angry and she wasn't sure she wouldn't explode.

"You are being 'held over'," he said, keeping his voice even.

Molly realised that he was struggling to do that and wondered what was going on behind the scenes.

"You will have one night here and, if they don't have any more evidence by morning, you'll be let go. No charges."

"Any *more* evidence? What bloody evidence do they have now, other than my initials on a bunch of papers my boss asked me to sign? I was doing my fucking job, Flynn. *I've been set up!*" Molly slammed her hand on the table, frustration and worry spilling over.

"Set up?" Flynn asked. "Do you have proof?"

"No, why would I? I didn't know I'd need a line of

breadcrumbs leading me here. But I bet I could find out who did it if you let me have access to those files. I could trace them, digitally." Or Kit could, if he ever bothered to believe in her again. But she didn't say that.

Flynn gave her a brief hug. "Stay strong, Molly, you know this will be over soon and will be sorted out. You can cope with one night in a cell. I'll make sure you're alone and no one bothers you. Mum left some toiletries in a bag for you and the sergeant in charge will make sure you get what you need."

"How did Mum know I'd need things?" Molly was puzzled.

"I suggested it when I phoned her," Flynn said.

Molly eyed him incredulously. "You knew, you knew this was not going to go my way and you let it happen? I thought you'd help me, Flynn. I thought you'd talk to people and get me out of this mess. Guess you're not the Almighty Flynn Fitzgerald, after all." She turned from him, arms crossed over her chest, pain and betrayal filling her heart.

The silence was telling.

Flynn spoke quietly as he walked to the door. "I'm sorry, Molly. I hope you'll understand soon. And forgive my part." He closed the door quietly behind him.

What the hell did that mean? His part? What was she supposed to understand? Or forgive? The world had gone crazy and she was living in it. Exhausted, she dropped her head into her folded arms on the table and closed her eyes against all the madness that was her life.

As Molly brushed her teeth in the less than spotless sink at six thirty the following morning, she let herself ramble – God knew she deserved a little rambling.

A night in a cell sucks, she thought. Don't let anyone

tell you different. Granted, it was an upper-class kind of cell in that it was just me and my bed and sink and loo. But it was still a cell. In a jail. Okay, not a jail, per say, but a station house with cells. That made it a kind of jail, right?

It had been a damned uncomfortable night.

The blanket that had been folded at the end of the cot-like structure laughingly called a bed, had been scratchy and Molly, who had quite a nose for scent, couldn't bear to have it near her face. So, like when she'd been forced, through circumstances, to sleep in a sleeping bag belonging to a person other than herself, she'd improvised. Her suit jacket became her pillow, her shirt became a mini-sheet, taken off and thrown over her upper body with the collar up to her nose, so she could inhale her own scent and no one else's. She was never so grateful to be a person who wore a camisole every day under her work blouse. She didn't wear it for warmth but for modesty. All too aware of her curves and boobage that could be on display if she, for example, spilled coffee or tea down her front, she was never going to get caught unprepared. Yes. That had happened. Only once, because Molly was that quick learner, the rapt student, and did not let the same mistake occur second time. Now, if only she could employ those practical tactics to her personal life, all would be well. Or at least, bearable

Sleep had eluded her for the most part, and with her shirt and shoes back on, she did her best to make herself presentable. Would she see the lawyer today? Why hadn't they let Ms Foster in to her yesterday? Molly had a list of questions as long as her arm but the underlying emotion bubbling away today was fear. Fear that this would *not* go the way she hoped. Outright panic that all this, whatever this was, was out of control, her control. And what made it seem like a worse nightmare than it already was? Flynn's lack of sorting it for her. He was their guy, he fixed things. He cared for them all like an overprotective mama bear. He *always* fixed things, so why hadn't he fixed this? More than anything, that scared her.

And yet, here she was. In a frigging cell, after a night in frigging jail. Molly Fitzgerald, felon apparent, at your service.

Dressed, hair scrunched up into an unruly bun, shoes and jacket on – God forbid she looked casual – Molly sat on her cot and waited. She hoped her handbag was somewhere safe and that no had scrolled through her phone. Fat chance. They'd probably taken it apart. Maybe that was a good thing, in that they would see she hadn't been texting notorious criminals or selling goods illegally on the dark web or street corners or wherever things of that nature were sold.

Time passed slowly and when a key turned in the lock, finally, her stomach rumbled. She really hoped it was food. Of any description.

It wasn't.

Chapter 23

She looked as one would expect. Tired, rumpled, anxious. And pale. So goddamned pale. Kit's belly clenched and his hands flexed as he walked into the small airless room. The secured light fixture cast a grey pall on her skin and the normal rosy glow, that gorgeous lush skin, was ashen.

She stared at him, like he was a foreign object. Or a piece of dirt on her shoe. To be expected, he reminded himself. *To be expected.* It was still a shock. Other than yesterday, she had always looked at him with a certain amount of curiosity. With interest. And at times, with desire. Those days were over. And he did this to himself.

Molly folded her arms across her chest, standing as if braced for a blow.

God, he was a shit. He did this to her. No one else. He cleared his throat.

"How are you?"

Her mouth fell open. She snapped it shut. "Seriously? You want to know how I *am?* If I wasn't a well-brought-up woman, I'd tell you to go fuck yourself. But, fortunately for you, my mother raised me right. I'll say please leave instead." She spoke through gritted teeth and the sneer in her tone was artfully aimed.

He reckoned she wanted to pace, but the room gave her few options for a walkabout.

"I can explain," Kit began but she threw up her hand in a stop sign.

"*Do. Not. Speak. To me,*" she said. "The only person speaking here until you leave, is me." She walked to the sink and rested against it, facing him, arms still folded.

He noticed her hands were in fists and he didn't blame her. She probably wanted to throw a punch. At him.

She glared at him through narrowed eyes. "I find I actually have nothing to say to you. Go now, before I lose whatever manners I have left."

She did a little toss of the head with that last remark and the fire was back. He could see it. She had plenty to say to him and he really wished she'd let it out. Then they could talk. He could explain. They could move forwards. Good plan, Kit. Now, if only Molly was on board with it.

He could see very well she was not. Her glare intensified.

"Are you still here? Unless you're here telling me I can go home, I don't want you in my space."

Kit shoved his hands deep into his pockets as he leaned back against the closed door.

"I'm here to explain. To tell you what's happening," he said, keeping his voice even.

"Why you? Why not the police detective who brought me in? Why not Flynn? What has any of this got to do with you?"

With a sigh, knowing it was going to get way worse before it even ventured into getting-better territory, Kit closed his eyes briefly to hide her pain, opened them and began.

"I'm the one who should explain what has happened and why, because I'm the one who set it up and put it in motion. I'm responsible for all of it." He paused and waited for his bombshell to sink in.

"What? You're not making any sense. How could you be responsible? The only thing you need to explain is why you ghosted me yesterday. Why you wouldn't speak to me, let alone stand up for me? No, actually *accused* me! Threw me under the fucking *bus*!" She rubbed a weary hand over her face, the effort to raise her arm almost pitiful. "If you can't do that, then hit the highway, Kit Elliot. And what was the whole deal in the suit? Trying to impress the boss? Cheap shot, you jerk."

"Can I sit?" He indicated the cot, its cover all folded neatly on top of the rather grey-looking pillow. God, it looked awful. *His fault.*

"No."

Okay then.

He paced as she remained standing still. Where to start? Easy to say at the beginning but that would take way too long.

"I'm here, BB&M here, as opposed to here in the station, under false pretences," he began but seeing her frown he tried again. God, he was shit at this. "I'm not just an accountant, or even just a forensic accountant. I'm an investigative accountant. I work for the Corporate Crime Agency, here in Ireland. And FBI, amongst others." There, he said it.

Silence.

Molly suddenly sat on the narrow bed as reality set in. He could see her brain work as certain implications raised their heads.

"Who hired you?"

Straight to the point, needing details. She was back.

"Benson Senior. He believed, for some time, that nefarious dealings were happening in his firm. He chose not to bring this to the attention of his brother or Mr Malone, because he wasn't sure who he could trust. He went to the Irish equivalent of the FBI and asked for help. They knew your brother would know someone who might be able to assist. I've worked with Flynn on a few other smaller cases, so he knew he could trust me and –"

"*Hold it!*" Molly reared up from her seat. "Flynn is *in* on this? Whatever *this* is. You and he are buddies? Pals? Workmates? For feck's sake, Kit, why didn't you tell me?" She lowered herself back down as if her legs could no longer be trusted. "You've been lying to me all this time. Working for Benson, but nothing to do with the audit. Who are you investigating? It can't be me, I've done nothing wrong, so who? And why the FBI?"

Kit swallowed hard. This was where he needed to get her on board. He needed her to see the big picture, not the details – not yet.

"BB&M work with several large American corporations. Benson Senior first noticed an issue when one of those company directors got in touch with him privately – they'd golfed together at various resorts which is how one now worked on behalf of the other. The US guys were, let's just say, unhappy with some of the work BB&M did – how much they charged, to be more precise. The reason Benson was the accounting firm of choice was because the US company had branches here in Ireland and they wanted to ensure the codes were all up to scratch and so on." Kit paused to make sure Molly was paying attention.

She was. Her head was tilted to one side as she listened, a sight so normal that he almost forgot the story he was recounting.

He forged on. "Anyway it appeared the person doing this was in some way connected to a financial mishandling of funds in a relatively recent crime in Boston – that's where I came in – so we have been trying to connect the dots between what's happening in BB&M and what

277

previously went down. In Boston." He really was shit at this. Not usually, though. He was used to giving a report fluidly and completely, dotting i's and crossing t's, like a boss. Molly's presence, her involvement, made him stumble over his words, sound like an idiot. One who couldn't string a sentence together. He continued. "I wasn't on the Boston team when that went down, but because I was here in Dublin since last summer working on other cases for Flynn, he called me in on this because I know some of the US players. Or at least how they operate."

"Which players? The criminals or the investigators?" Trust Molly to hone in on what made him most uncomfortable.

"Both." The truth, though he fervently wished it wasn't so.

She studied him then, really looked and took notice. "You look as shit as I do," she commented neutrally.

Oh God, if only she knew how he looked was only the tip of the iceberg. If she only knew the agony he'd been through, seeing this project come to its close. Throwing her to the wolves, as she pretty much said herself. It didn't matter that it was all illusion, she didn't know that. She didn't know that his time with BB&M was almost over, his role-playing at an end. His contract complete.

Except it wasn't. Not quite. He still needed her. He needed her skills to finish it altogether. To do that, she had to believe it was worth it – even if she didn't want to forgive him. What was he thinking – she'd never forgive him. But hopefully she'd work with him.

"Did you break the law? Commit crimes? Is that how you know the people who were involved?" she asked. "Or were you an undercover agent for the FBI? A mole? God, this is like some awful TV drama only I'm not following the plot."

"No. No, it wasn't like that. Look, that part is a long story, and I'll tell you if you want, another time. Now, I need your help."

She stared at him, incredulity apparent on her tired face. She narrowed her eyes and took a breath.

"Let me get this straight. You, the person who got me thrown in jail. The person who left me here *all night in a cell. In. A. Jail.* You, want me, to *help* you?" Her head moved back and forth in disbelief. "Are you delusional? Did that smart brain of yours get zapped sometime between yesterday and today? You do remember what you did, yesterday, right? You haven't lost your memory?"

Kit grimaced at the hard, cold tone and sucked it up. *Your own fault. You did this. You deserve this. Deal with it.* "Would it help if Flynn asked you, not me?"

"Flynn?" she snorted. "He's already done quite enough, by all accounts. I do *not* want to talk to him."

"Too bad," Flynn's voice said as the cell door swung open. Neither Kit nor Molly had heard the key turning as they'd been so focused on each other. "Because I'm going to talk to you. You are free to go, but," he raised his hand to stop her instant surge to the door, "I would really appreciate a moment of your time. To explain. Everything."

Molly halted mid-stride.

Maybe she heard the exhaustion in his voice, saw the strain in his eyes, the tightness to his mouth. Kit wasn't sure, but she shut her mouth, swallowing whatever biting comment she was about to spew. He was her brother and she loved him. Kit got that. She'd forgive Flynn, probably within the hour. And rightly so. That's what family did.

Or what they were supposed to do. God, sometimes the guilt weighed very heavy.

"Okay," Molly said, her voice tight. "But not here, and I want food. And coffee." Turning she glanced around the cell and, straightening her shoulders she marched out, not sparing a look for either of the men.

Fair enough, Kit thought, they had both played their

part in this debacle. They deserved the snub.

Never had a shower felt so good. Molly scrubbed every inch of her skin and hair twice. She used her favourite smellies, an expensive Jo Malone gift, and wallowed in it.

God knew she needed this little bit of luxury. Switching off the shower, she wrapped warm fluffy towels about her body and inhaled all the scents of her home. Her bathroom. Her body lotion as she liberally lathered herself in its delicious creaminess. Her conditioner, as she sniffed the wet curls lying against her skin. Hers. Her place. Her home. The simple pleasures of life cannot be taken for granted, she thought. Molly had always been good at enjoying the moment, but now? After being a jail bird? Every bloody minute of every bloody day was going to be seen and appreciated with fresh eyes. As long as she didn't end up back inside for killing her brother and his compadre.

That was a distinct possibility.

They had both come home with her. Flynn driving and Kit silent in the back. She still wasn't sure how that had happened but, as she flung open her front door, she gave instructions. "Have hot, tasty, bacon-filled food, with strong coffee and a glass of fresh orange juice awaiting me when I get out of the shower, or don't be here. Those are your choices."

She had strode to her bedroom, gathered fresh clothes and slammed the bathroom door behind her. It was time, now. She twisted her towel-damp hair up in a clip, stoked mascara on her lashes for courage – every woman knew that was a thing – and headed to the kitchen.

Her stomach growled as the aromas hit. *Yes*, bacon and coffee. The very best of all the smells. They had listened, stayed and cooked. Excellent. She would get the story, the *full* story from one or other of them, and then decide. They needed her help? Well, let's just see what was in it for her. A hardened crim like herself knew how to negotiate.

Fresh orange juice was downed in seconds. She was so damn thirsty. Bacon-and-egg toasted sandwiches with a hint of relish got devoured next, aided by hot coffee made exactly the way she liked it. She wondered briefly which of them knew that … and then told herself it didn't matter.

The two men acted like overgrown puppies, tripping over themselves to feed her. *Hah!* No, that wasn't true. Other men may have done that, these two worked like a fecking well-oiled machine, gliding around each other, one fixing more toast, the other making fresh coffee as if they were a dual act on a TV show. She wondered had they actually worked together or had Flynn just bossed Kit around? Didn't seem that way, watching them now. Kit was as self-assured as her brother. The whole nerd-geek thing? Gone. He no more looked like the architype techie than she did. His clothing was smart and stylish, his hair was brushed back from his forehead all slick and neat and no glasses, of any kind, adorned his face. There wasn't a hunched shoulder or a stumble in his step – in fact, he appeared several inches taller. She studied him, curious now and came to the conclusion that he was Oscar-worthy.

He had conned everyone. He had conned *her*. No, he'd outright lied to her. She'd thought she'd been the one living the lie? What a fool she'd been! Her small family deception was a splash in the ocean compared to what Kit did. *Was doing.*

Molly held out her mug for a refill and sat back in her chair, replete for the moment. Prison life was tough on the appetite.

"I'm waiting," she said. "Which one of you two stellar gents is going to begin?"

Flynn pulled out a chair and sat down, Kit remained standing, or rather leaning against the doorjamb, his broad shoulders blocking out the light from the living room. His hands were shoved into the pockets of his navy chinos, one long leg crossed casually over the other at the ankle. There wasn't a casual thing about it. Another lie, right there before her. He was good at this.

And so, Flynn began to speak.

"So, you're telling me that in order for Declan Twomey to do something even more stupid, and hopefully get caught, you had to have him believe you thought it was me who was diddling the books? How does that make any sense?" This question she posed to Kit who had barely shifted his position the entire time Flynn had been breaking the plot apart, piece by piece.

"Twomey is an idiot, albeit a sneaky one," he said. "He is also conceited and spoiled. He thinks he is invincible. He is also broke. On paper anyway. His Irish bank account is hugely overdrawn and his credit cards are maxed out. He is living his life like he is expecting a massive payoff. I believe he is correct in that. And it will be soon." Kit rolled his shoulders as if they were stiff and simply shifted to the other side of the doorjamb.

Molly almost offered him a seat, but, hey, liar. God, that hurt so much. It all hurt. Every memory she had with Kit was now a burning pit in her belly. She flipped her eyes to his form again. Damn he was bloody gorgeous, the bastard. If she'd thought he'd the Clark Kent vibe going before, he was Superman all the way now.

Flynn interrupted her thoughts and brought her back to the issue at hand. "Molly, you know all of Twomey's tells, the digital signatures he leaves on documents. You know how he works and can spot his style. If we get you access to what we think are the real accounts he needs to use for the big payoff, would you be able to tell if they've been accessed by him?"

282

She would, actually. Declan was a sloppy accountant at the best of times. Someone unfamiliar with his style of recording wouldn't notice his errors but she would. Hell, she'd begun fixing them within weeks of her job starting at BB&M.

"Why can't he do it?" Molly flipped her thumb in Kit's direction, choosing not to look on his lanky form unless she absolutely had to.

"*He* could," Kit interjected, "but it would take longer."

Flynn threw him a look. "Molly, I know you're angry, okay, furious with us, and you have every right, but please, see this from our perspective. When I asked Kit to go into BB&M undercover, so to speak, as an extra hand for the audit, only Benson Senior knew. He was the one who contacted me, via some people I know. Kit had already done some investigating for me on behalf of the CCA here, so I was comfortable with his style of work."

Molly couldn't help it – her gaze locked on Kit's at that remark. She wondered if her brother knew exactly what kind of work Kit Elliot had been doing. And with whom. The faint hint of colour on Kit's cheeks was inordinately satisfying.

Good. She hoped he squirmed.

"Go on," she urged Flynn.

He did. Molly thought some of it made sense. The way Flynn explained the connections, the similarities to the way some serious white crime that had gone down in Boston, it was either a copycat or the same person pulling the strings. Kit had the Boston connection, i.e. he knew the lay of the land and the people, having worked with that branch of the FBI before, so the link was already made.

"I had no idea, none, that you were working for BB&M when I sent Kit in. When he walked into our kitchen? Well, let's just say I was . . . surprised. But, in fairness, that's on you. You never told us about your other life."

Molly nodded. That much was true. She spoke to Kit

then, needing the answer. "Did you know? Is that why you befriended me? Because of Flynn?"

Kit shoved away from the door, came forward and bending slightly placed his palms on the table. "No. I swear. I had no clue you were related. I admit, after meeting you a few times, you reminded me of someone, the eyes obviously, but I honestly didn't connect the dots."

"Pretty shitty investigators, the pair of you, I'd say. Background checks, people!" Molly rose from the table, needing to stretch her legs and get some space from the testosterone overload in her small kitchen. She wandered to the living room, swinging her arms in her loose T-shirt, and did a few stretches. She had muscle aches from her night of discomfort on the narrow bed, but they would ease. If she had to swallow some anti-inflammatories and a glug of wine this evening, well, she'd take that remedy.

The men trailed in after her and took positions on the two armchairs. Molly plumped some cushions and took the couch. Unfortunately, all she could see was herself and Kit on this couch, playing and laughing and kissing and touching. She tossed a cushion aside and sat upright.

"Right, so tell me again that none of this will affect my CV," she said. "Convince me, because as of right now, I see zero reason to give either of you the time of day, let alone my expert help."

"Benson Senior now knows it's a 'play'," said Kit. "I told him the morning the police arrived to the office that this was all a ruse and that you are entirely innocent of all wrongdoing. But we had to make it look authentic. We had to make Twomey believe that we thought you are guilty. If we didn't do the whole process, the 'perp' walk, the detectives playing their part, Ms Foster being contacted, your mum coming in – all of it needed to play out so anyone watching would believe it too."

"Watching? Is someone watching me? Christ, it's like Ali all over again." Molly shuddered, remembering her sister being attacked.

Flynn stood and approached the couch. He crouched down in front of her, taking her hands in his. "Mary Margaret, nothing bad will happen. These people aren't violent. They never get their hands dirty. All their crimes are on paper or online. They are transactional, not physical. You have nothing to worry about, but the big picture needs to appear authentic, from the outside. Just in case."

He kept his eyes on hers, mirrors of hers really, the exact colour, the same sweep of lashes. And she believed him. She felt his truth, felt his honesty. Felt his pain as she held his hands.

"What's wrong?" she whispered. "Tell me." They both knew she was not referring to the present problem.

Flynn pulled his hands back, releasing her touch, her senses. He shook his head slightly. "Not now, Moll. It's . . . I'm fine. It's . . . complicated. We'll talk another day."

That she did not believe. He would hold those cards, whatever they were, close to his damn chest, as per. But she wouldn't give up. When this was all over, she and Flynn were going to have a serious heart to heart.

Standing, Flynn paced for a moment than turned to Kit. "I have to go. You figure out the details with Molly. The timing has to be perfect. Keep me informed so we can offer back-up if needed. Do not let anything happen to her. And play nice."

Kit stood and they shook hands.

"You have my word," Kit said solemnly.

Molly couldn't hold in the snort. "Whatever that's worth," she muttered.

Flynn headed to the door but had the last word, of course. "Behave, kiddo. I'm counting on you."

Chapter 24

"We're breaking into his *apartment*? Are you out of your ever-loving mind?"

Kit winced as Molly's voice rose several octaves. It was a good plan. Solid. Doable. Sort of. But she had to be on board. He shouldn't have told her over a snack. In a café. With people. Rookie mistake.

"Keep your voice down," he urged. "It's not technically breaking in – I have a warrant. I'd rather he wasn't there, that's all. We'll be able to discover more if we can look without him watching every move."

"Yet maybe his body language would give him away. You know, like in the movies, when the baddie unintentionally looks towards a painting on the wall, where a safe is hidden. That kind of thing." Molly sucked her strawberry milkshake through a straw.

He really wished she'd ordered coffee or tea or some non-straw-drinking beverage. Seeing her lips pucker around the straw, all pink and luscious, well, it did things to his body. His body remembered all too well that sight of those lips and how they felt wrapped around –

"Hey, are you listening?" Molly snapped her fingers in front of his face, bringing him out of his reverie.

"Sorry," Kit apologised hastily. *Mind out of the gutter, pal. Those days are over.* "I see your point, but in this instance I think us going in, minus Twomey, is the way forward."

Pushing her treat away, Molly rested her head in her hands, elbows on the table. "Will you be packing? Or do they call it *carrying*? Whatever, will you have a gun?" She tried but couldn't keep the grin off her face.

Kit didn't for *one second* think this was a truce. Molly was never going to forgive him, but she had an irrepressible capacity for finding the fun in small things. She was good at compartmentalising. She had riled at him, big time, when she'd arrived at the café, called him every name she could think of relating to what an ass he'd been to her. How hurtful. How unbloodyfair, as she'd said, not to have the manners to, oh, you know, *include* her. Now she wanted to know if he was going to bring a weapon? No, this wasn't a truce, not even close. She promised she was not holding a grudge, swore she now understood why he'd behaved as he had, but he didn't believe that either.

"Definitely too much TV-viewing in your life. Now, are you clear? We'll meet at the church gates at eleven. It will only give us about an hour, but I don't want to chance earlier as the evenings are so bright and we need to be as stealthy as possible. You sure you don't want me to collect you?" He hoped his chatter about the meeting time and place would distract her from realising he never answered her original question. But no, he and Flynn had discussed this plan at length. No guns. Too risky. Too dangerous. Kit had the warrant, and that covered him, professionally should they be caught. Could he do this without Molly? Yes. Should he? Also, yes. But the plain hard fact was she knew Twomey's work better than anyone and he would take too much time figuring out what was what if he went solo. He and Flynn had played down the whole potential

287

danger part of the plan. Yes, white-collar crime lords rarely used violence. *Themselves*. They usually hired thugs to do it for them. That information was need-to-know and Molly definitely did not need to know. They had been reluctant, big time, to bring her into their confidence about Twomey's papers but they had to get to the bottom of the financial mystery and Molly could ease that path. Flynn often used private citizens to help him on a case on the strict understanding they knew what they were getting into. With Molly, he'd been honest that it was not necessary, but *would* be helpful. She'd agreed.

"You're not coming to collect me. I'm a grown-up, despite having been recently treated like a child. I still don't get why you didn't read me into the plan. Maybe then I wouldn't hate you so much. Later." With that, she rose from her seat and sauntered from the café.

Kit groaned. He'd played it badly from the outset. Hindsight and its twenty-twenty vision could go fuck itself. He gathered his belongings, paid the bill and headed out to where his bike was chained to a railing. Cycling back to Stoneybatter gave him much-required headspace. This job was nearly over. Flynn had more projects for him locally, in Dublin, but should he stay? His house had still to be finished but that was work of decoration not structure. He could rent it out or Airbnb it. He *should* go back to Boston, to his life there. He had sublet his apartment in Somerville but knew he could bed elsewhere until that was up. He *should* go see his mom. Start acting like a mature adult and apologise. Trouble was, he wasn't sorry for the things he'd done. Is one supposed to apologise if you'd do it all again? His notion of family was warped, he knew that now. But she was his only family left.

Perhaps it was a moot point. She might not forgive *him*. She certainly carried on as if nothing had changed in her personal life. As if her son hadn't been instrumental in getting her husband sent to prison. And if her weekly Wednesday trips to MCI, Concord, were anything to go by, she still cared for the bastard. Kit shook his head as he eased his bike along the narrow hall of his small home. He wouldn't rent it out, he decided. Some idiot could wreck it. So, what would he do? Sell up and go back to Boston, face his mother and deal with all the fallout once and for all? Or stay here. Work here. Have a life here. This house felt like a home. The apartment in Somerville was spacious, bright and had lovely woodwork and trim features. He could keep the sublet going for another six months. Or more. Then decide.

His mind whirring, he sat down at the table, took out his laptop and, finding his happy place, crunched some numbers. He owned this house free and clear and the sublet paid his mortgage on that apartment. Working as a consultant wasn't always stable income so he did several regular accounting jobs on the side – mostly online where he could work remotely. He could keep those up but his bank account was healthy. Consulting, the way he did it, on site, was lucrative.

And there was Molly. Presently, she hated him. Wouldn't forgive him. That was fine. He got that. But if he stayed? Gave her time. Space. She had leapt into his life almost immediately – she was that kind of woman, vital, lively, glorious, smart. The path to his heart had been more gradual but no less real. He had lusted after her from his first glimpse of her, any man with working parts would, but caring for her, wanting her, *needing* her dammit, that was slow and steady and had certainly won the race. Having slept with her, touched and tasted her, she felt like his drug of choice. His preferred addiction.

Kit was patient. Accountants had to be. Forensic consultants lived by it. He would wait her out. He would give her all the alone time she craved, away from him. But he'd be there, ready. He would not let her down again. Next time he'd court her. Properly. Take her on real dates, woo her like in the old days when men didn't act like twats. Nah, never mind. Men always acted like twats when it came to letting their bodies do the leading instead of their brains. But Kit had a stupid-high IQ, was a member of Mensa, had a PhD from Massachusetts Institute of Technology, Sloan, for God's sake. He could figure out a way to get into Molly Fitzgerald's heart. Because she was already firmly planted in his.

She wore all black. Leggings, sneakers, long T-shirt and oversized hoodie. Yup, she was badass. She didn't tell Frankie and Ali what was going down, but she had told them about her experience as a jailbird. She had kudos now. The others had never spent a night behind bars and for once in her life as the baby sister, Molly felt like the *woman.* They had been agog at her descriptions of her night on a hard bed with a horrid blanket her only covering. They'd applauded her use of her clothing to cover smells and keep the bugs at bay. And they had cheered her on when she told them she'd made Flynn and Kit cook breakfast and beg.

No, those two blasted men hadn't begged, but the girls didn't need all the truths.

Ali had wanted to kick Kit's ass to the curb. Frankie, a kinder, gentler sister, wanted to forgive him – eventually, she said, after he had grovelled sufficiently. Molly herself was conflicted. She was furious with Flynn for misleading her at the Garda Station, for letting her think she was in real trouble. But she was more *furious* with Kit because, hey, they had exchanged bodily fluids, and he'd still lied to her. Used her for his own ends. Disgraced her in front of her colleagues. Molly *hated* that she was extremely good at seeing another person's point of view. That she could see, rationally, why Kit had done what he'd done, why it made sense in a warped kind of way – *if* it had happened to someone else, that was. But, he'd done it to her. And there were feelings involved. Molly knew how unbelievably naïve she'd been thinking she could have sex classes with a man like Kit and come away unchanged. Emotionally, that was. If she'd had sex with Declan – God, perish the thought now – at least her heart wouldn't feel so darned bruised. So trampled upon. Was *anything* they'd shared real? The only mitigating factor in the whole sex episode was that *she* had initiated that plan. At least that was on her. She couldn't altogether blame him for taking advantage since she *had* asked him. He should have said no, of course, because he was already well on the way to using her in every other way, but he hadn't. Why?

The girls had been full of advice, full of questions. Was she going to see Kit again? And if so, how exactly would she take him apart? Slowly, limb from limb? And did she need help burying the body? Then of course, being her sisters, and insatiably curious, they also wanted to know how had the second 'lesson' gone? Molly had felt her face heat as she remembered their night at her flat. How thorough he'd been. How he'd tasted every inch of her, over and over. How she'd finally tasted him. She thought about the whispered conversations throughout the night. The quiet laughs, the shared thoughts, the warmth of his body curling into hers, the presence of his hand, gentle on her hip. Stroking, tending, caring. Sexy as hell. God, she'd been a fool.

As she donned her ninja outfit on preparation for a night of B&E, she also recalled how smart Kit was. How funny, in his own peculiar way. How she now knew he wasn't remotely gauche or shy. He was just a damn fine actor. He played his role to perfection.

He had lied.

She kept coming back to that one rather massive hurdle. Her own inability to have seen it, have felt it, was driving her crazy. She was the one with the supposed extra senses and she hadn't seen or felt a thing. All she sensed, when around Kit, was warmth. No hidden agenda, no playacting. What was wrong with her? Yet just the day before, with Flynn, she'd reeled with the waves of unhappiness radiating from him. It had been like that since Easter.

With Kit? *Zero. Nada. Nothing.*

One possibility was, she supposed, that Kit was genuinely fond of her. Meant her no harm. *Yeah.* Not buying it. She felt pretty fecking harmed after being marched out of her workplace, police in tow, and a night in a police station. That was harm.

The other possibility was that he felt no emotion for her at all, which meant there was nothing *for* her to feel. That caused harm in a different way. Neither sat well with her.

Figuring that pulling up her hood would make her look suspect, she picked up a black beret, tucked her curls up inside and grimaced. Now she looked like a French bandit! All she'd need was a scarf over her nose and mouth and she'd be set! But that was a step too far. She needed to look as normal as possible in the taxi ride over and since beret wearing was part of her arty self, it was comfortable and felt normal. She really shouldn't be looking forward to tonight's caper, but a girl needed some diversity, especially after the last few days.

She wasn't looking forward to spending intimate, close-together time with Kit. Absolutely not. No. Not that, just finding some dirt on Declan-bloody-Twomey. That's what had her heart pumping faster and her pulse kicking up. It was the potential for dangerous exploits and nefarious deeds that had her adrenalin kicking in. She was sure of it.

She took a taxi, had it drop her in the village of Blackrock, thanked the driver and walked back to the church. Kit was leaning against the railings, dressed, no shock there, also completely in black. They eyed each other warily as if unsure this is what they should be doing. Together.

"Come on," Kit said, breaking the silence. "Let's get this done. The apartments are just over here."

He led the way and Molly was more than happy to follow along behind. His black jeans fitted his ass and thighs to perfection. He wore a black bomber jacket, for which she was grateful. Those suckers hugged the waist, leaving that well-formed backside for her viewing pleasure. Yes, it was dark and yes, she was furious with him. Didn't mean he wasn't fine to look at. She was neither blind nor stupid.

They walked quickly and quietly through the back entrance of a large modern apartment block. Kit fiddled with the lock and the wooden gate swung open. They moved briskly along a narrow path and stopped at a locked glass side door. Some more fiddling with locks and up they climbed, three flights of stairs. Molly's hands had begun to shake and she wasn't sure if she was terrified or excited. Both, she figured, and kept on going.

Kit opened a fire door and motioned her past him.

They hadn't spoken a word on the way up and Molly crept down the corridor to Number 304 maintaining the silence. This time Kit produced a key and inserted it into the lock smoothly and easily.

"Where did you get that?" she hissed. "Did you steal his key? When? What if he notices it's gone?"

"I made a replica a few days ago. It's fine. He still has his own and is none the wiser."

"Are you sure this is legal?" Molly was tempted to ask despite his claim to have a warrant.

"Depends on your definition," was the quiet response.

Molly thought she saw a flash of his cheeky grin and realised he was enjoying himself. How bloody typical. He was *such* a boy.

"Are you sure he's not home?" she squeaked.

"I guess we'll find out," Kit winked.

He actually bloody winked. He was so getting shit for this. He was having way too much fun. It also seemed to Molly that he was doing all this sneaking around really easily, like he had done it many, many times before. When this night was over, and even though she was still mad at him, she was asking him some tough, detail-oriented questions. She was getting answers, that was a given.

The apartment was sparse yet still managed to be untidy. A bag left open on a leather couch, a box of cereal on the bar counter and dirty cups and plates both on the eating area and in the sink. The area rug was strewn with magazines and there were coffee-cup rings on the small centre table. Declan Twomey needed to do some major housekeeping chores.

Glancing about it was obvious there were no papers of importance here so they eased down the small hallway. Three doors were closed, one to the left two to the right. Kit opened the one on the left. Declan's bedroom. Also a mess. The duvet was tossed down, pillows awry and clothes draped over a chair. The wardrobe was open as were the drawers from his dresser. It was the room of an untidy child. It looked like he'd left in a hurry as shoes were scattered across the carpet. There was a laptop on a side table and Kit made for that.

Molly opened the doors across the hall. A bathroom and a spare bedroom. She entered the second bedroom cautiously. It was almost empty. A desk and chair. A single bed and a wall of built-in wardrobes. She popped one door open. It was empty, as was the rest. So, he lived by himself.

No stay-over girlfriend or she would have used this closet space for emergency supplies.

There was a computer on the desk and a stack of three drawers down one side. She pulled out the chair and sat, powering up the computer. With minimal hacking skills, she still knew her way around some simple bypasses. Not necessary. The idiot hadn't even password-protected this one. He obviously felt secure enough in his own home.

Not working out so well for you now, buddy, she thought as she began trawling through folders. Account after account. All overseas. Ones she had seen before – but not, on closer inspection, exactly the same. These had been tampered with. Updated. These were all accessed regularly, by Declan, according to the file records. And each was labelled with the initials EC. That, she hadn't seen before. She scrolled through more data, more accounts. More records. Financial records of one EC. He, or she, was stashing a lot of money in the Caymans. Millions in fact. There were a lot of zeros. She inserted the blank USB she'd thought to bring along, just in case, and copied everything on to it.

"Kit," she called. "I've found something. Can you come in here?"

"Be right there. I'm going through emails. Give me a sec."

Molly bent down and pulled open the side drawers one after the other. Jesus, Declan was really an idiot, nothing was locked. There was a stack of files, about a half dozen and she placed them on the desk to pore over. Flipping through, she caught a name and she almost felt her brain push a pause button. She knew that name. *Think, think think . . .* Eddie Cochrane, probably the EC of the files. But that wasn't it. She knew the name from somewhere else. It was right at the edge of her memory, almost within reach. What did he look like? Where had she seen him? How did she know him? *Think, dammit.*

Kit burst into the room, took the situation in at a glance,

grabbed the files off the desk, switched off the computer and, hauling her off the chair, murmured, "Someone's coming. We won't get out in time. We have to hide."

"*What?*" Molly's mouth dropped open. They were about to be caught? What the *actual* hell? Heart racing, she yanked out the USB, dragged him to the wardrobe, pulled open the door, shoved him inside and stepped in after him, pulling the door closed behind them.

"Don't even speak," she hissed. "If I end up in jail again, I swear I'll kill you in the slowest most painful way I can manage."

Kit reached around from behind a put his hand over her mouth.

"*Shhh,*" he whispered into her ear. "And hold still."

Fuck. This was not supposed to happen. Kit hadn't asked for back-up and he was cursing his own stupidity. Why was Twomey back? If it was Twomey? Shit. If it was anyone else, they were screwed. If it was people looking for information, they would open this wardrobe, that was for sure. The muffled sounds he could hear came from the living room. He might have just enough time . . .

"Move to the right," he spoke quietly in Molly's ear.

"*Shhh,*" she whispered back.

"Just do it. *Now.*"

He kept his voice low but the urgency was transmitted as Molly began to shift over, very slowly. Every movement sounded like a boom in the tight space. As she edged over, he inched forward, to stand in front of her. He reached his arm behind, tucking her close to his back and mumbled, "Don't speak. If the door opens, drop to the ground. Got it?"

He could feel her nod. He could also feel her heat and her racing heart, hammering into his back. She must be scared shitless. He wasn't exactly relishing this either but he'd been in similar situations over the years. He had hidden in smaller, more cramped spaces. At least he and Molly were upright.

She wrapped her arms about his waist and he jerked at the contact. It reverberated through his body like an echo of a different time and place. He missed her touch and it was only a few days. God, he was a goner. She snuggled closer, he knew it was for space, but *damn* it felt good.

He grasped the hand at his waistband where his pistol would have normally been holstered inside his jeans. *He should have brought the damn thing*, he thought as he listened to the footfall advancing down the hall.

Twomey spoke, his tone agitated.

"Stop hassling me! I told you I'd get the files. I will. They're right here, in my desk. Keep your fucking shorts on and stop waving those guns at me. They're not helping!"

Molly gasped in his ear.

Kit tightened his grip on her hand for a split second before he released it slowly. There was more than one person with Twomey. He'd said *those guns*. Plural. Most henchmen don't aim two at a single person.

Shit just got real.

Sounded like Twomey was pulling open drawers, one after the other, cursing.

"Get the files. Now." Another voice spoke, rough and accented. Not Irish. East European maybe?

"They're not here," growled Twomey amongst the noise of rustling paper, wood and metal scraping. And something being kicked. "They should be here. They're always here."

"We will search," announced the first voice.

Molly stilled behind Kit and every nerve in his body went on full alert. Any second now they would slide open the wardrobe door. He hoped like hell Molly would do as he'd said and drop to the ground.

This was the worst fucking idea he'd ever had.

Bracing himself he reached out with his left arm, creating a barricade of sorts, whatever it took to protect her.

"*Find them!*" snapped the previous voice. "*Now.*"

Kit took a long inhale, breathed out slowly and forced his body to relax. Being tense at a time like this did no one any favours. He needed to be razor-focused when that door opened, see exactly who was where and in a split decision know where to dive out of harm's way first. It would be muscle memory coming out to play.

"They're not here," whined Twomey.

Kit felt the wardrobe door move, as if someone had grabbed the handle.

"In here. We look everywhere."

Kit pushed back slightly forcing Molly against the back of the wardrobe. The guy would not be expecting a man in the wardrobe so Kit would have the element of surprise – he was banking on that as he hauled in another deep inhale.

"Don't be stupid," Twomey said irritably. "I'd know if I hidden them somewhere else. I must've brought them to the office. We'll go there. Now. There'll be no one about."

There was the sound of feet scuffling.

"Get out of my way!" Twomey spat. "Jesus, fucking foreign morons! Can't understand plain English! *Go, go!*"

And several sets of footsteps retreated. A loud door bang and silence.

Merciful, safe silence.

Molly whimpered behind him and turning, in the confined space, Kit wrapped his arms about her as tightly as he could. She was shaking.

"They're gone. It's okay, they're gone. Everything is fine now. *Shhh*, sweetheart, it's okay." He spoke the words gently, repeatedly, as she burrowed into him.

Moments later she pulled back and, reaching behind

them, he slid open the door. He backed out, head swivelling to check the coast was clear. Molly stepped out onto the floor and took a deep breath. Before he could say a thing, she shoved him hard in the chest.

"Safe? You think we're safe? You have those files stuffed in your jacket, you jerk! We are *so* not safe." Then shoved again, and he let her.

She had every right to be angry. Scared. He knew from experience that adrenalin had many ways of escaping when the danger passed. A valve released could go all manner of ways.

"We are for now," he said. "We have evidence to pore over and I can return it here later, by myself. He'll just think he overlooked it, in his panic."

"That's a stupid plan," she countered. "Since we have it, we should keep it. Use it. Give it to the police. To Flynn. I don't know. But coming back here again? That would be daft." She waved her arms about, indicating the room at large. "Can we go now?"

Kit, checked the files were indeed safe inside his jacket and reached for her hand. She snatched it away.

"Don't touch me!" she ground out. "You've been in my space way too much already this evening. Christ, I need air!" She marched to the front door, her fear obviously waning, but paused before it. "You go first, Danger Man, and if there's a guy outside waiting to shoot you, well, tough shit."

Kit stifled a smile. She was pushing herself to her limits and not backing down. God, he was proud of her.

As they made their way down the stairs, still cautious – one never knew and it paid to stay alert – Kit decided it would be best if they both went to his place. If, by any weird chance, Twomey connected the missing files to Molly's recent release, he could lead the henchmen to her flat. His place would be safer. HR at BB&M had a fake address for him on file – Twomey couldn't track him down. It was good to be an excellent actor – people bought what they saw, what appeared as truth. Very few dug deeper. He used that simple knowledge all the time in his work. Smoke and mirrors and hiding in plain sight. The ordinary Joe? Very gullible.

He hailed a taxi back out on the main road and bundled Molly inside. He didn't ask and she didn't question. He figured she might well be going into shock. It wasn't every day you hid in a wardrobe and waited to be shot. She must have been terrified but other than a moment when he held her, she came out swinging. That wouldn't last.

He scooted over to her and wrapped his arms about her rigid figure.

"*Back off*," she grunted into his jacket.

"No," he replied. "You may not need this, but I do."

And, fuck, if it wasn't true.

Chapter 25

Molly was a lot of things. One of them being cold. She shouldn't be. She had a nice warm hoodie on and the night was clement. But by the time they got to Kit's place, paid the taxi and hurried inside, she was shivering.

Kit motioned her to the couch, where she gratefully sat while he lit the gas fire. Instant heat, hard to beat. *Ha*, that rhymed. Oh, good lord, she was losing her marbles. Kit removed his jacket and placed the files under it on the table. He went to the kitchen and she could hear cupboard doors open and close, the clink of glass against glass and then he returned and handed her two fingers of brandy.

She drank. And drank some more. The shivering subsided, marginally.

"Why are we here?" she asked finally as Kit stopped pacing and sat opposite her.

"Twomey now knows that I'm not what I appeared to be. I had to reveal my identity, up to a point, when you were arrested, to give gravitas to the situation with the bosses. He doesn't know where I live but there is no reason for him to connect me to the loss of personal files anyway. But he might connect you, considering what went down a few days ago."

She raised her brow. "Thanks for that. You sure know how to show a girl a good time." She tried for sarcasm but was terribly afraid it sounded pathetic. Like she felt. She had been so flipping scared. They could have been shot. Wounded. *Killed.*

"We could have been killed," she said, her voice way smaller than she liked. But, hey. *They could have been killed.* Her voice could be as small as it damn well pleased.

Kit dropped his head into slightly unsteady hands. Maybe he wasn't as blasé as he let on.

"Jesus, Molly, do you think I don't know that?" He raised his head, grey eyes tortured. "I'm so fucking sorry I got you into this. I'd never forgive myself if anything had happened to you. I was sure the intel on Twomey being absent from his flat was good."

"So, you call breaking and entering, searching a person's private belongings and hiding in a wardrobe from a bunch of thugs just a walk in the park? That happened to me. *That*!" She took another swig of the deliciously burning and soothing brandy. How could it do both, she wondered idly. No. Pay attention. No brandy ramblings. "It may be all in a day's work for you, but I've never had a more terror-filled few days in the whole of my life."

That, in fact, wasn't true. But he didn't need to know about Toby being kidnapped, Frankie being tortured, Caro barely escaping a madwoman with a gun, Ali being terrorised by her past. Those days, waiting to hear, to know, to see if her loved ones were okay. . . those days were the most terror-filled.

Huh. Go figure. She'd been more scared for them than she'd been for herself just a few hours ago. Yes, the few minutes in the wardrobe wondering what was about to go down had been scarifying. But she'd been *in* it. Not waiting at a hospital or by a phone. No one else in her family knew where she was, what she was doing. The girls had an idea but they weren't expecting baddies with guns. Molly hadn't expected that, not even Kit had.

She watched him now through narrowed eyes. He'd sat back in his seat, nursing his own drink. He looked like hell she was most pleased to note. She was pretty sure her face was pale as a waning moon and her mascara smudged. There may have been involuntary tears.

She hated him. He was a liar and a manipulator. He had treated her like a child, used her and thrown her to the wolves. He had taken her virginity – okay, she handed it to him on a plate – details, mere details – taught her all the good stuff, and now he was done. Was it really wrong to wish he would hold her right now? The feel of those powerful arms, those broad shoulders that strong chest, all enveloping her? *Yup*. She was a traitor to herself because that's exactly what she craved.

She shuddered and the damn shakes started again. Delayed reaction probably. She knew these things happened and picked up her brandy for another gulp. Empty. And still not warming up. So not her day. She caught Kit staring at her, a question in his eyes.

"Stop staring. I'm fine. I just feel cold and trembly. And abandoned." She didn't know where that came from, but the second she uttered the words, they made sense. That was how she felt – as if Kit had abandoned her. It was a childish emotion. She knew that but . . .

He rose, plucked a blanket from the back of his chair and hauled her up. They sat back down in her chair, with her on his lap and the blanket draped over her shoulders. Molly allowed it to happen. *Oh, God*, she welcomed the feel of his embrace, *traitor*, his strength, his protection. Unwilling, but unable to resist, Molly curled into him and finally let real tears fall.

Kit mumbled soft words. They made no sense and she didn't care. He was holding her tight and snug to his chest, one hand stroking her head the other making gentle circles on her back. She cried, she wasn't even sure why, deep gulping sobs that came from low in her chest. Kit let her; he didn't tell her to stop, to dry her tears. He didn't tell her to buck up or hold it together. He let her cry. Maybe even wail a bit. But it slowed eventually, that desire to flood a living room with salty tears. Bit by slow bit, the urge to empty her body of all liquid faded away. There was some minor shudders and snorts. Sniffles and nose-wiping. Nose-blowing too, when Kit reached into his pocket to hand her a tissue.

"Gabe would have handed me a real handkerchief," she said accusingly, sniffing inelegantly.

"No doubt," Kit chuckled. "I wasn't raised right, that's my excuse. But I will consider the practice in future, if it would help?"

"Nah. It would be contrived then, wouldn't it? But I'm grateful for this massive man-sized paper one right here, so thanks."

It was said grudgingly but with a measure of relief. She was grateful that he gave her what she needed, without being asked. Was there anything more pathetic than asking to be held? Yeah, there probably was. And in fairness, most men complain that if women *don't* ask how can they know? Point in their favour. But Kit knew what she'd needed and gave it with care and tenderness.

As he bloody should. *He was a liar, remember?* A manipulating, scheming, smart as sin, sexy as . . . oh, he was kissing her! Molly took a breath and inhaled the spicy scent that was Kit Elliot. He was placing small kisses on her temple, down her cheek, over her now red-rimmed eyes, on her equally, she was certain, red nose. Now he whispered more words and these she heard.

304

"Sweetheart, I'm so sorry." *Kiss.* "You were so brave." *Kiss.* "I'm so proud of you." *Kiss.* "I'll never put you in harm's way again, I swear." *Kiss.* "God, you're amazing." *Kiss.* A soft touch to the lips, *kiss.* Then more pressure, his lips on hers, pressure and release, pressure and release.

Something tugged in her belly. She felt it between her legs. That tightening in her core telling her this was *good*.

Both his hands moved to cup her face and he pulled back slightly, serious grey eyes on her blue. "I want you. So badly. I know this is not the time, I know you can't stand me and rightly blame me for all the shit that's happened. But you need to know this, *this*, is real. This is true. *Me, wanting you. Now.*" His voice was a rasp against her skin, the last few words spoken into her arched neck as he began a trail of new kisses.

"*Ohm!*" she gasped, using her vast array of intelligent words. Her hands went up to tangle in his hair. How did that happen? She dragged his mouth back to hers and took what she wanted. It seemed, despite all knowledge to the contrary, that she wanted him, back.

No questions asked, no reasons given. She wanted him, his kisses, his touch, his body devouring hers. She wanted it all. Manipulating liar be damned.

She parted her lips, allowing him access and, dear God, he kissed her like a man possessed. Like a man starved of vital nourishment his whole life. It felt dark and dangerous. It felt passionate and hungry. He groaned into her mouth, shifting beneath her so she could feel every inch of how she affected him. Changing the angle of his head, he kissed her deeper, harder, more urgently. And, by God, Molly got on board and kissed the hell out of him in return.

Hands moved, clothes got tugged away, the blanket fell to the floor. Gasping and grasping they tasted and kissed, touched and grabbed. A hot cauldron of need and speed.

305

Kit pulled her hoodie over her head and tossed it on top of the blanket. Her T-shirt came next and he swore against her skin as her nipples peeked through lace and pebbled beneath his mouth.

Molly got busy too, sliding her hands up his chest, over the hard muscle, loving the way it rippled and moved under her fingers. His belly quivered as she slid over his ribs and lower, searching for the snap in his jeans. This was not the time for rational thought, for recriminations. After, when reality hit she would dissect her contradictory feelings, but not now, not when all the breath was being taken from her body as Kit showed her all the ways to feel good. To forget. To be alive.

The blanket became their resting place though very little resting occurred. Kit was like a Trojan, flipping her, turning her, positioning her, like she was a featherweight. It felt amazing. So empowering that she believed she could make him feel just as good. Or she would when she caught her breath.

He peeled her leggings and underwear down her legs, to be tossed aside like the rest of her clothes. And then he went to work. This man, God, this man knew how to apply skills. All the skills. He used his tongue, his teeth, his lips and when it was necessary to push that little bit more, edge her just a little further, he used his fingers. Inside, all gloriously twisty and sheer perfection. In spite of what seemed like haste, because he was frenzied in his taking of her, he still managed to give her the time she needed – which, it turned out wasn't long at all. Skills, it had to be said, were a great attribute for any man.

"Jesus, Kit . . . I can't even . . . I don't . . . I . . ."

He kissed his way up her body, loving every inch, finding every spot that made her arch or moan. He knew her body now and the unfairness of it being so temporary twisted a knife in Molly's chest. She'd think on that later. As Kit nuzzled into her neck, telling her how beautiful she was, his hands still exploring her softness, she turned, so she lay over him and after one deep kiss, began her own descent down his torso. His muscles bunched and quivered under her touch, his small grunts of pleasure egging her on, giving her the permission she'd allowed him. She returned the favour and yanked down his jeans and boxers, exposing him to her view. He was a feast. Reaching towards his belly in its fullness, his length awaited her touch. She held him, her fingers wrapping the girth, sliding up and down the silken heated steel.

"*Yes*," he hissed. "*God, yes!*"

She studied him from under a sweep of lashes, noticing the flush of his cheeks, his chest rising and falling more rapidly with each of her moves. She lowered her mouth to taste, the tip of her tongue circling and swirling and his hips jerked.

"*Christ,*" he rasped. "*That. Do that.*"

She tried a few more moves, more daring, more brazen and his response sent an answering tingle of awareness straight through her. A mirrored response. This was turning her on as much as it was him. Like the last time.

He tasted musky and sweet, salty and sharp. He tasted like more. So, she gave more, taking him into her mouth, she moved up and down creating a slow sexy rhythm. She was throbbing now, needing to be touched, but she wanted this. She wanted to give *him* this. He'd be gone soon, but he'd remember this. His hands gripped her head, holding her, moving her. His pants and gasps told her she was acquiring skills too. What a good student she turned out to be!

"*Fuck,*" Kit gritted out. "Enough. I can't take anymore. I need to be inside you. I need *you.*"

It was hot. She wouldn't deny it. It was *hot* when a guy

you fancied/hated was desperate for you. The power? An aphrodisiac all its own. Stretching to the side he grabbed his jeans and pulled a condom from his wallet.

She took the condom, ripped it open and began unfurling it over him. She shifted, lifting, and slowly lowered herself, eased him inside her until they both groaned at how good that felt.

He used his hands on her hips guiding her movements, her speed and her direction. She was grateful for the help, grateful for the experience because all it did, everything *he* did, was a direct path to her reaching the peak. She undulated, rotated, pitched forwards, finding her goal. Searching for fulfilment and all the time Kit kept up a steady but increasing hip action that kept them completely on track.

It built, the pressure, slow and steady and then the pace kicked up and, dear God, she was close. Kit reared up, burying his face in her breasts, sucking on her through the lace cups of her bra as his arms banded about her, holding her tight to him, his pelvis rocking into her in the exact right way. She flung her head back, a shout, a moan, a gasp and then fell onto his shoulder as he came apart beneath her.

Hot sweaty sex was excellent for all types of things – it banished fear and focused entirely on the now. Molly lay across Kit's chest, allowing her breath to find its natural balance, to return to some normal. *Focus on the now.*

"We need to go over the papers," she grunt-mumbled. "I wanted to show you stuff before, well, before everything went awry."

Kit choked out a low laugh. "That's one way to put it. Before I screwed up, is what you really mean."

He eased her off his chest and reached for her clothing. Handing them over, he hauled up his jeans and boxers and, standing, helped her to her feet.

"My intel was that Twomey was out for several hours,

supposed to be engaged at a club he often frequents. I was supposed to be alerted if anything changed. That didn't happen, so there will be consequences, but the fault remains mine."

"Oh, stop being so bloody noble, it doesn't suit you," Molly snapped. Another lie. It did suit him. Very well. He might not have a massive S on his chest, but him protecting her in that wardrobe, ensuring she was behind so he'd get the first blast of whatever awaited them? That felt pretty noble to her. Fairly heroic. Maybe not flying through the air in a cape, but still.

She dressed quickly and hunted for her shoes while Kit headed to the kitchen to fill the kettle. Good plan. She needed tea, strong, hot and though not her usual style, sweet. Sweet tea was the cure for shock, right? Granny used say that, if memory served. But maybe she'd hold off on the sugar, considering she'd just experienced a rather different cure for shock – a *much* more enjoyable one. "Can we have toast?" The question was barely out of her mouth when she realised he'd already popped two slices of thick white bread into the toaster. "Never mind, you got this. You obviously know the routine of how to deal after a night of danger. Experience much?"

"Some," he agreed evenly. "But not like this. Not with someone I ca – with . . . someone I know well. So, it's – it's different." The last words stumbled and were quieter.

Molly straightened and collected the files from beneath Kit's jacket. She laid them out on the table and began sorting them into small piles. Each pile represented a specific client, ones she'd known about but with different records.

Kit's laptop sat on the table so she flipped it open.

"Password?"

There was a moment's hesitation, then, "It's harperlee, lowercase, all one word."

Molly chortled, but a warm glow enveloped her. And she hadn't even had the tea yet. She wondered if Kit knew how cute it was that he used his favourite author as a password? I mean, what guy did that? She wondered, too, if Scout was sleeping upstairs, snug in her bed. She inserted the USB from her hoodie pocket and let it load. She hoped she'd had enough time to get all the data copied. When the screen opened and she'd clicked on various windows, she was able to show several views side by side – comparative studies, as she liked to call them when working like this on her own. It was amazing what one could learn when seeing the big picture. Usually a moment's glance at a screen like this, multiple windows of similar information on view, and Molly could spot a pattern shift or a sequence that was off.

This lot was a challenge. But the discrepancies were there – her instincts for this kind of work was never wrong – and she would find them. She took a mug of hot sweet tea from Kit, blew lightly over the golden-brown surface, and drank.

The aroma of melting butter made her stomach growl and she reached absently for a slice of toast. Chewing, with a keen sense of how delicious this snack was, she nodded towards the screen. "What do you see?" she spoke around her mouthful of saviour food.

Kit leaned forward, his palms resting on either side of the laptop. His gaze flew back and forth across the images and she heard a few *huhs* and *hmmms*. He was smart, this one. Maybe not as quick as she was in this type of thing – this was mostly her extra senses telling her things weren't right and then she dug in and did the actual work. The detective investigative work, the leg work, but without the legs.

"Well?" she asked when he remained silent.

Kit took a step back, a grim look on his face. "There is

310

something familiar with the patterns, but I can't put my finger on it." He sounded puzzled.

"Maybe these will help." Molly gestured to the neat piles she'd stacked on the table next to the laptop. She pointed to various lines, some of which had been circled in red. By the author of the documents, she'd assumed. "See how these are almost replicas of what's on screen but these also have other records inserted – not changing the total, so it's not obvious but as a separate item with some of the other numbers changed There are lots of zeros."

She handed him a pile. He flipped one page after another, his face paling as he scanned to the bottom of each one. "Where exactly did you find these? Were they sitting on the desk, out in the open?" His knuckles were white where he gripped the pages.

"In the drawer. It's what I called you to see." She picked up another file. "Look here, the initials EC and then a few pages on, the name *Eddie Cochrane*. Does that ring a bell for you? It sure does for me. I know it from somewhere." Molly tapped the side of her head in the sign for it's in there if only her brain could find it. "Obviously a big name in finance but where? And when?"

"He was accused of insider trading, money-laundering and using all forms of corruption to swindle people, ordinary people, out of their savings. Think Bernie Madoff only more so." Kit's voice had gone cold. Flat. Expressionless.

Molly frowned, thinking. Then snapped her fingers. "Yes, I remember. About five or six years ago in the US. Oh, in Boston, if I remember correctly. Is that how you heard of him?"

"Not exactly." Kit lowered himself to a chair. "What else do you recall?"

Molly sat too and looked at him. Kit was struggling with something and, for the first time since they met,

311

Molly zeroed in on waves of . . . anger? Coming from him. Mixed with . . . regret? Remorse? No. Sadness. Kit was awash in fury and pain. What the hell?

She stretched out her hand and rested it on top of the fist still clutching the sheaf of papers. His hands were like ice. She met his gaze. Yes, pain and anguish. She narrowed her eyes at him.

"What are you not telling me? You look awful. Can I get you something?"

And then she remembered. The photograph: the one of three people, Kit, his mum and a man. The one who'd looked familiar. The photo lay face down now but she could see it, clear as day in her head.

Eddie Cochrane.

It was like newsreel in her brain as she turned slowly and caught Kit watching her intently. The news items that had reached Irish shores. The scandal. The takedown. The families whose lives had been ruined because Eddie Cochrane had stolen their life savings. The court case. It had been relatively brief but flashy and reported on daily. High-flyer prosecutors and defenders getting all the on-air publicity. Molly had been fascinated, mainly due to her curiosity about all things finance and accounting, but also because of the human-interest side. The hurt and disruption to so many. She remembered the interviews and how hopeless and lost the victims sounded, how devastated they were. Pensions, college funds, mortgages – all gone. The sentence, ten to fifteen years in a medium-security prison had been a surprise. White-collar crime usually merited a minimum security but Mr Cochrane had used scare tactics and had, it was alleged, resorted to buying muscle for hire. He didn't actually do the dirty work, but it got done on his command.

Kit kept his eyes on hers as she remembered. Small details clicking into place like she was flipping through an old-fashioned Rolodex and inserting a finger to stop the spin every few turns. Then it clicked. All fell into place. She saw Kit could tell when it happened.

He closed his eyes briefly, his mouth narrowing into a grim, thin line. Eyes open again, he said, "Yes."

She gasped. *Oh. My. God.* Her hand flew to her mouth as the stunning raw truth hit her. "They said it was an inside job," she said. "That someone close to Cochrane ratted him out. That a close family member took him down. Reported him and brought him to justice."

Kit's head fell back briefly, like it was just too darn weighty for his neck. He straightened and held her eyes once more. "Go on," he said.

Molly swallowed. Hard. "*It was you.* You were the FBI mole. You worked for him and saw what he was doing. You told."

"I did. I did all that. I actually worked for the US Treasury Department at the time, and for Cochrane, but undercover. They sent me in, *because* of my connection. Figured I could find out more as a family member. Knowing what it was going to do to me, to my mother, to his company, I did it anyway. I'd do it again." His shoulders straightened even more, the broad span of his chest strong and firm. Pushing back from the table he stood, tall, admitting what he had done in bringing a high-powered criminal to justice. But it wasn't with pride he stood, it was resolve.

"Who is he to you?" she asked quietly, guessing the answer but needing to hear it.

"To me? Nothing. He is less than nothing to me. But he married my mother so, officially, he is my stepfather."

"And you sent him to prison." It wasn't a question.

"I did."

"Getting to be a bit of a habit," she deadpanned, and handed him more toast.

Chapter 26

Could he be more embarrassed to be the stepson of a criminal? No. He couldn't. It was shit, no matter what way you looked at it. He told Molly the whole sorry tale – not because there was an obvious connection between his past life and his present. But because she deserved to know. He owed her that much.

Memory Lane can lay tricks but Kit knew he was telling the truth. Facts and a timeline were what Molly deserved. If an ounce or two of sentiment or care slipped in, he let it. This was his truth. He told her of the night he first met Cochrane, the big flash man about town. It had been mutual instant dislike. And in hindsight, mistrust. On both sides.

His mother had come home flushed and excited to a quiet, studious thirteen-year-old.

"Quick, tidy the room," she'd gushed. "We have a visitor. He'll be here any minute. Hurry!" and she had flitted about the living space straightening cushions, neatening papers and magazines. His mother loved her glossy Hollywood glamour rags and there were many. She had spat on a tissue and scrubbed at his resisting face and then ran a hand across his hair. Trying to make his mop of dark hair do anything resembling a style had defeated them both.

The second he shook Eddie Cochrane's hand, he knew. How? No clue, just pure gut instinct.

Cochrane was not a good man. Not for his mother, not for him and, as it turned out, pretty much everyone else.

He was flash and showy. Paid cash for everything. Treated all around him, peeling out a wad of bills, like the generous chap he was. All for show. All to prove he was able to buy whatever and whomever he liked. He wanted Shelly Elliot. He didn't so much want a scrawny teenager but that was his penance. Kit made sure he stayed out of the big man's way. He was as ready with his fist as he was with his cash.

It wasn't often, but it did happen. Molly looked aghast when Kit mentioned the intermittent wallops he'd get, but he shrugged them off. Many of his pals had dads who lashed out, especially when they lived in Southie. The odd black eye was a badge of courage. Your mates knew you were a badass. That you had a mouth on you. You gave lip to your elders. It earned respect.

Shelly and Cochrane married within six months. She hero-worshiped him and if the young boy felt neglected and excluded, he hid it as well as he could. He became even more studious, graduating early, getting a scholarship to UCD in Dublin. Kit told Molly that he first began suspecting all was not kosher the year before he went to Ireland when he overheard some phone calls, stepped into their back room, used as Cochrane's study, where snappily dressed men discussed things, sotto voce.

The mistrust never dissipated. In fact, it grew. Kit began taking notes of days and times things seemed off. He began following Cochrane to late-night meetings, escaping out his bedroom window from their new Cambridge home. His mum no longer worked at the bar but took to entertaining Eddie's cronies like the proverbial duck to water.

Molly had moved them both to the couch, the tea replenished, more toast made. She sat at one end, feet curled under her and he wondered briefly how he got here. This gorgeous smart woman listening to his story. She might hate him, with good reason, but she was listening and not judging. That was rare, in his limited experience of relating his backstory. For the first time in his life he didn't feel like he was betraying his mother by repeating the whole sorry mess. He didn't feel like he was letting anyone down. He was just talking his truth.

"What happened when you went away to college? You couldn't see what was going down then." Molly extended one leg, her foot resting at his thigh and it was the most natural thing in the world to pick it up and massage the firm flesh of the ball of her foot. He continued.

"Nothing during term time but I came home to Boston every holiday break and took a job bartending in the local so I could slot right back into my amateur sleuthing." Kit let his head fall against the back of the couch, exhaustion starting to creep in. "My break, for want of a better word, came during the summer of my third year. They were both out at some gala and would be for hours. I was supposed to be on bar duty but I switched with a co-worker. I had acquired some advanced hacking knowledge from a brilliant guy in my year and put it to use. I accessed Cochrane's home computer and downloaded as much as I could from his hard drive to an external drive. That way I could peruse at my leisure, not waiting for the front door to open. Just as well – they came home early. I had to scurry from his study to my room and pretend I left work due to a stomach bug. It was my first real taste of espionage." Kit paused, remembering. Letting that adrenalin rush be a good memory.

"You liked it," Molly's low tired voice said in the darkness. "You found your calling."

He smiled. "Yes and no. It was weeks before I understood what the information I had meant. Before I knew it was, in fact, a criminal at work. I didn't know what to do, so I did nothing. It's hard to forgive myself for that. If I'd acted sooner, many more people would have been spared the trauma of bankruptcy."

Molly wriggled her toes at him, easy since he was still using his thumbs to trace circles on her skin. "Cut that out. Regrets do no good. You can't change the decisions you made years ago. I know that much. But you could, if your inscrutable brain would let you, focus on the good you did. How you *prevented* more damage. And I thought you worked for the FBI, so where does the Treasury come into it?"

"One of my friends in UCD knew a guy who went to MIT, you know how that works. MIT knew a guy who was a detective in the white-collar crime division of the FBI. Funnily enough, though I now consult for him, he sent me initially to the Treasury Department, with the name of certain persons to contact. When it's outright money-laundering, *they* need to know. We did a deal. I made sure my mother would be left out if it, but I agreed to go work for Cochrane in one of his many companies. I used a false identity and got hired in the accounting department. I was now in the process of doing my PhD in MIT Sloan so I could work around those hours."

"Jesus, Kit, what age were you?"

"Twenty-two. I'm obnoxiously bright, remember? A great memory helps. And it's in the genes, so, you know, a natural." Kit grinned at her narrowed eyes. She oozed disdain. He liked it. He liked her sass, her cheek, her sarcasm. He liked her humour. He liked her.

"Smart ass." She tossed her curls, now fallen about her shoulders.

He couldn't decide about her hair. All about her in a

cascade of curls and shine it was stunning. Up and tied in a messy bun, it looked sexy, exposing her creamy skin for his kisses.

And that brought him back to reality. They'd had sex. Again. She'd wanted it too, he knew that, but he also knew it was mostly reaction to the danger and didn't mean anything. It was natural to want to connect viscerally with someone after fleeing from danger. Now he needed to man up. He turned his whole body to face her, and still holding her foot lifted his knee to rest on the couch, placed her foot on his thigh, but kept one leg still on the floor.

"About earlier," he began, but she raised a hand.

"Stop. It's over. We're safe and now we know what's what. Or kind of. We can sort out what to do tomorrow. Or today even." She looked at her watch. It was near two. "Damn, I'd better get home."

"You are not going home, and I didn't mean about the information. I meant the sex."

Molly gave him a side eye. "I'm not so innocent that I don't know hate-sex when it happens."

"Hate-sex? What the hell is that?" Kit hadn't heard the term before but wondered was it like post-danger sex.

"You know, in the romance novels, when the two protagonists are fighting and the passion is running high, they have hate-sex. It's supposed to be awesome."

"And was it? This 'hate-sex' we supposedly had?"

She blushed, her skin turning a soft pink. "It might have been," she said grudgingly.

Kit smirked. Yeah, baby, he was the man! Okay, that was stupid. There were two of them performing this version of romance-novel sex. "I was going to call it post-danger sex, because that's a real thing. And I don't hate you. I couldn't. And before you say it. Again." He held up both hands, releasing her foot to the floor. "I'm aware how you feel about me. I don't like it but I do get it. I lied and let you down. The fact that it was my job does not excuse me. I know that. But you're not going anywhere. I'll take the couch and you go upstairs to the bed. Get some sleep. We have a long day ahead and we need to be sharp."

"Don't be an idiot. Unless you think you can't keep it in your pants, we'll share the bed. And thanks, I don't feel like going back to the flat alone at this time of night. Not after, well, everything. I'm completely wrecked and could sleep for Ireland. I imagine you're the same. We can look at all the info again in the morning. Put our heads together. Thank God it's Saturday – if we have to go to the office it will be empty. Come on, teeth and bed." She shoved at his back, propelling him to the bathroom and he let it happen.

Telling his personal history was draining. He'd only ever told the Treasury Department, the FBI and Flynn Fitzgerald. He was surprised at how easy it had been, in the end, to tell Molly. But then she was an extraordinary person. She judged him harshly for his recent behaviour towards her but was on board and supportive of his actions in the past. It was, of course, because she'd been innocent, and Cochrane wasn't. She had a very simple view of right and wrong. But Kit knew those lines could be very blurred on occasions. Accountants lived with black and white, things added up or they didn't – there was no 'it's kinda the right' answer. Real life, investigative life was different. In that capacity, he often lived in a myriad of grey tones, making it hard to decipher a true path.

Kit wished he could convince Molly he had never ever doubted her honesty. He had in fact chosen her because she was so straight in her dealings at work. He would find a way. It was important that she came to understand that though he involved her as a means to an end – a good end – he did so because of who she was. He yawned, rubbed his hand over his raspy chin and followed her swaying form upstairs to bed.

Yes, he'd keep it 'in his pants' but he *would* be wrapping his arm about her to hold her close, once he got Scout off the bed.

And even if he had to wait until she was asleep.

Coffee, coffee and more coffee. There was no two ways about this, Molly inhaled her brew of choice to keep the nagging headache at bay, to wake her up fully and to stay sharp. And she loved the taste. She fed the cat, put her out and made bacon sandwiches for breakfast while Kit was in the shower. He'd run out of eggs, but this would do.

She had slept. Mostly. Dreams of the rather terrifying nature had invaded periodically through the night but each time she woke, heart hammering, Kit was there.

What a splendid idea of hers to sleep in the same bed. Each wakeful moment was soothed with a tightening arm about her waist or a warm hand rubbing her back and his soft voice whispering calming words in the dark. She hadn't even minded that his hand could feel her belly as she lay on her side. It just didn't matter anymore. They had turned over, in unison, at one stage and her arm had enveloped him. She wasn't quite so well behaved. She'd began stroking his abs, his chest, his peaked nipples, till he took her hand and held it in one of his own, against his heart. "*Stop*," he'd warned. "*I'm only human.*" And she fell back to sleep with a smile.

She smiled now as she heard singing in the shower. It was the old Dean Martin number, 'That's Amore'. Her smile turned to a grin as she joined in. Couldn't help it. He had a good tenor voice, the bastard. Okay, enough. This had got to stop. This returning to a happy place that included Kit. Liar, remember? Manipulator? Cold, hard deceiver. Trouble was, now she knew all the things he'd done and why, in his past, his behaviour with BB&M was more . . . palatable maybe? She had some major analysing to do, that was for damn sure, but first, food.

They ate, cleared plates to the dishwasher and spread everything out on the table. She fired up his laptop and loaded up the records she'd copied. In the cold light of day, it was still pretty damning. Eddie Cochrane was tied to the BB&M situation and Benson Junior was involved. Twomey was too, obviously, but he was an idiot. A lacky who thought he was a player. Kit was shocked, but not. He'd known Cochrane was still pulling strings from his prison cell. He just hadn't realised they had stretched across the pond. While Kit made phone calls to his counterpart in Boston to update their findings, Molly thought about strategy. About a plan to prove the tie-in. What more they needed to bring to a court of law.

Not being of legal mind was a hindrance. Maybe they needed help. Or maybe they really just needed to get into Junior's private files and discover what gems were hidden there.

They plotted and planned for a few hours at Kit's table but substance was missing from the growing pack of information. BB&M business premises must hold more. Breaking and entering Benson Junior's home was out – he lived in a bloody fortress, according to Kit. Kit, who'd been at a cocktail party there, if you don't mind. He said it was boring, the house overdecorated with gilt trim on everything that could take a trim and gold paint and finishes on pretty much everything else.

"A bit like Chloe, then?" Molly suggested with a smirk. "All dolled up in the metal of choice. She is a piece of work. I hear on the grapevine that Twomey, if he is her lover, is not the first. I almost feel sorry for Junior – it must be horrible to be cuckolded time and time again. I mean why stay? If you're obviously that unhappy."

"Money. In situations like this, it's usually money. And maybe Junior is not bringing in enough to satisfy his wife so he's scrambling to get more? We will see. Where do you get these terms? Cuckold?"

"Books," she replied. "Lots of reading in my spare time. I don't really have a social life, other than my family, as you know, but books are excellent company."

They chatted on the way to the Luas, the quickest way to BB&M, Molly still wearing her black outfit from the previous night's adventure. Kit had changed to jeans and a grey henley and looked like a movie star. Gone, completely and forever, was nerd Kit. She missed him. She'd connected to him. *They* suited each other. This new version was a bit intimidating, if she was honest. She was a girl of normal looks – not unattractive, she knew, but nothing special. She certainly wasn't in the same league as Superman Kit. Bring back Mr Kent, was her view. Even as they edged their way up the tram car she caught the glances sent his way by both sexes. So not fair. His dark hair now brushed back from a strong forehead his shoulders made his shirt stretch and move with each muscle ripple. Shit, she could barely keep her eyes off him herself.

So, new problem. She was very slowly coming to terms with the 'I was arrested (okay, detained) and mortified in front of my colleagues by a lying deceiving undercover agent who has sex moves', and now this. Now she had this problem of being attracted, all over again, to new improved Kit. Except was he improved? Jury out on that one. For now.

They agreed that Kit would go in the main door, past security, and then let Molly in the back entrance. Her clearance for entry was suspect, at best. Maybe it was sorted, but if it wasn't all sorts of alarms would go off, drawing way too much attention to their project. As she waited around the back, she pondered on what they were about to do. If it was illegal they at least would have the backing of the police, through Flynn. Or at least Kit in his official capacity as forensic consultant, would. Herself? Well, she'd probably end up back in a jail cell.

She heard scratching at the door and her heart leapt. Would she ever hear those kinds of noises again and not want to freak out?

The door opened, cautiously, and Kit grabbed her arm, hauling her into the back stairwell.

"This is just like last night but it bloody better not end up like it. No more wardrobe hiding for me!"

She knew she was gabbling, pure nerves, but she couldn't stop. The whole way up the several stories to the main floor, she muttered dire warnings about the likelihood of jail time, prison food, visiting hours, the lack of decent sanitation, knives being delivered in cakes, and possible escape plans. Over the top? Yes. But calming in its way.

As they rounded one stairwell turn, she caught Kit's grin and, catching up, poked him in the back. "It's not funny," she grumbled. "Now I'm considered a hardened criminal, who knows what kind of treatment I can expect?"

"It's a little bit funny," Kit said, turning to flash his damn dimple. "And trust me, you are not going back to jail. Not on my watch."

"That's what they all say. And considering I went to jail *on your watch*, your reassurance is not helping."

"Touché," Kit said and halted as they reached their destination. "I'll go in first and make sure no one is about. I'll text your phone when I've cleared the space."

And he was gone.

Once again, Molly was left loitering at a closed door,

pondering her fate. Pondering her recent decisions and her choices. No answers worth a jot came to mind. *Just go with it*, she thought, *think of it as an adventure. When Kit is gone, these moments are all I'll have to cherish.*

Her phone buzzed low and with a thumbs-up sign visible, she opened the door.

They went through Twomey's office first, making sure they had all the data they could use against him. They worked quietly, Molly's earlier verbosity now at bay. Kit smiled as he worked, flipping through files, thinking of her grumblings. She was funny, though she didn't realise it. Her humour was a part of her, like her active brain and her curly hair. She didn't let it out with everyone so Kit relished the privilege. He would, he knew, take these moments with him, when this was all over. Molly had become his yardstick, his measure of what communicating should be. How conversations should flow. How it felt to be wrapped up in someone, physically and emotionally. He paused then, as truth hit him like a freight train on speed. She was more than a project, more than a lesson plan, way more than a co-worker or even a friend. She was special. She felt like she belonged, to him.

What the fuck was he going to do about that?

He needed to park this train of thought. Benson Junior and his body of trouble wouldn't show itself, so they needed to find it. Motioning to Molly, he led her out of Twomey's office and headed up stairs to Benson's. It was spacious and bright – a corner, of course. The lock gave Kit no trouble and Molly's raised eyebrow was one of being impressed. He hoped. Jesus, now he was trying to show off – for a girl – could he get more clichéd?

Molly began searching through physical files while Kit accessed the desktop computer. They worked silently, each taking notes, photographs or in his case, data via a USB, and still they came up with nothing that showed a direct link to Cochrane.

They worked on, afternoon fading into evening. There was a lot of material to get through and neither wanted to stop. They had to find *something*.

Molly began rummaging through other drawers in a side table and then opened the door to a bathroom. It was swanky, more gold so definitely the hand of Chloe at work here. Looks like she had to have a part of every aspect of his life – what a poor sod he was. It was also brash and to Molly's mind vulgar. There was a shower, huge, a loo and a bidet – who had them anymore? – a double sink. The tiles had gold patterns and the taps were also gold. Ugly as sin. Overawed, and not in a good way, Molly leaned back against the sink wall, placing her arms wide out to either side over soft fluffy towels. Who needed two sets of everything when you were the only one working in the office? *Hmmm.* Picturing all the spy movies she'd watched in her misspent youth (or to put it another way, friendless teen years), Molly started to feel her way along each silver towel rack, removing the towels and setting them aside. She studied them both, noting the similarities and the differences. They were minute, but there. *Bingo*, she thought, and kneeling down twisted the bar and knobs of the one farthest from the sink. It took several tries but then she heard a clicking sound and a previously hidden panel opened outwards, just like a safe behind a painting or a hidden door in a castle. It was very well done, no seam visible to a glancing eye. Once it opened of course, it was obvious. Clever. She gave Benson credit. Who would think to look behind towels? Her finding it was a complete fluke. A happy accident.

Should she call Kit? It might be nothing, but her heart was kicking up a pace as she reached in and took out several folders. She sat, like a yogi, and began the hunt.

She'd found the mother lode, she realised, as one folder held photographs of Eddie Cochrane and Junior, arms about each other's shoulders, on a golf course. The sign above the club house was only partially visible but someone would know it. Copies of emails, printouts from banks in the Cayman Islands with names attached, and a promissory note to do business together. Oh God, this was it. This was *it*. Why had Junior kept all this? It was clear evidence of their money-laundering scheme and their trial at skimming from clients. Many of the Cayman accounts had Twomey's name, so he was involved for sure, but Kit had said Declan was broke. Was he being used as a name but not a beneficiary? Was he being duped? Did she care? She whipped out her phone and took pictures, lots of pictures of all the documents and photographs. Something, some little nugget of memory, told her to be safe, to have back-up and she quickly emailed everything she'd found to her private email address.

Scrambling up from the floor she gathered the papers, replaced them in their folders and stood, intending to take them out to Kit to show him her bounty.

That's when she heard Brenden Benson's voice, loud, clear and very angry from the main office.

"What the hell are you doing in my office, Elliot? Why are you using my computer? What the fuck's going on?"

Oh shit! She stuffed the folders under the waistband of her leggings, pulled her hoodie down, thanking the universe for her oversized outerwear, and barely breathing, waited.

"Mr Benson, I wasn't expecting to see you here on a Saturday evening. How can I help you?" Kit was cursing inwardly, a string of curses that would make sailors blush. He knew a good tactic, when caught off guard, was to throw a question back at the asker. Stall, make them feel as they have something to answer, not the other way around. It wasn't working too well with Brenden Benson.

"*Help me?*" he sputtered. "You can help me by explaining your presence in my office. And how you got in. That's how you can help me!"

Improvising, Kit surreptitiously pulled out his USB, palming it discreetly and made a show of clicking various windows with the mouse. "Just one second, Mr Benson, I'm almost done." As if he didn't have records to close asap. As if he *should* be there, officially, working. For Benson.

"*Done?* With what?" Junior marched into the room.

It was only then Kit noticed the two henchmen standing outside. *Oh fuck*. Things just got bad. Very bad.

"I was asked by tech to do some upgrading on your desk computer but of course I didn't want to disturb you during the week. I was hoping it would be all done and done seamlessly before you got back into the office and therefore cause you the least amount of upheaval."

He walked as casually as he could around to the front of the desk, a real nothing-to-see-here vibe going on. He shoved his hands into his pockets, hiding the memory stick and leaned back against the desk, all friendly like.

"Is there anything else I can help you with?" he asked, throwing the ball back into Benson's court but also throwing him off the scent as if Benson himself had asked for him.

But how the hell to get Molly out of here?

The bathroom door opened and a smiling Molly sauntered out, all pink and glowy.

"Sorry I took so long to clean up, darling," she cooed, looking straight at Kit, "but if you will play rough, what can you −" She broke off, apparently only seeing Benson then. A hand flew to her mouth. "*Oops!*" she gasped, her

327

voice breathy now, and coy. She was never so glad to know Junior had been out of the office, probably on a golfing trip, for the last couple of days and hadn't been clued in to what had gone down. "Oh, Mr Benson, I'm so sorry. I hope you don't mind that I used the facilities. Oh my gosh, it's the most gorgeous bathroom ever! So beautiful, so on trend. Who's your designer? My sister-in-law, the actress Francesca Jones, is looking for someone to redo their en suite and I *have* to tell her about yours." She whipped out her phone. "I'll call her now, shall I, and you could talk to her yourself? Oh, that is, unless you can't remember the name of the company. Well, never mind!" The phone went back in her pocket. "We can do that another day. Darling, I'm starved, are you nearly done?" She turned from sending a drooling look at Kit to a sly one at Benson. And on she prattled. "I don't know why he felt he had to get this all done for you *this* weekend, Mr Benson. I said it could surely wait till Monday, but you know Kit, always a hard grafter, always putting the job first. I wanted to go sailing today, but oh no! Mr Stick-in-the-Mud here just had to work. Come on, darling, let's leave Mr Benson to his business." She took Kit's arm, leaning up to kiss his cheek and run a hand through his hair. Familiar. Lover-like. Playing the part.

But she wasn't finished. Pulling Kit behind her, she strutted past Benson, as much as anyone can strut in runners and leggings and an oversize hoodie, smiling at him flirtatiously. "Now, don't stay late yourself, Mr Benson. I'm sure your charming wife is waiting for you. I only came with Kit because I thought this would be the only time we'd get together. You and your wife wouldn't have that problem, so I hope you forgive my presence!" She tugged Kit's hand again, all impatience, "Come on, you. We've some catching-up to do," and winking, yes, *winking* at Benson and his bodyguards, she dragged him to the lift.

Chapter 27

They didn't say a word in the lift, didn't catch each other's eye. When the doors slid open on the ground floor they walked, as nonchalantly as possible, past the small security desk. Kit gave a cheery salute and a "Cheers, Bob!" while Molly had whipped out her phone again and was apparently chatting to someone. A lot of "I know" and "I *know*" was heard amidst *tsk*ing and *tutt*ing. The big glass doors swung open, courtesy of Bob, and they exited the building at a steady pace, just as Bob answered the inline phone with a "Yes, Mr Benson?"

Kit reached for Molly's hand and the second they turned the corner they broke into a run. They raced, Kit pulling Molly's hand as they darted and dipped and eventually came to a shuddering halt next to a bench along the river boardwalk.

Gasping, Molly bent forward, hands on her thighs as she gasped in the murky early night air. "Oh, my, freaking *God!* That was awesome!"

This was not what Kit had been expecting and he took a moment to study her face, lit by a streetlamp, pale, but with bright pink spots on her cheeks. "You're okay?" He had to be sure. This could be the dreaded fight or flight response again and she'd had enough of that.

"Are you kidding me? The best fun I've had in ages!" She threw him a grin. "Well, other than *that!*" She shot up her hand for a high five.

"Okay, then." He smacked her hand and dropped to the seat. She joined him, still grinning and definitely on a high.

"Jesus, Kit, when I heard his voice, all angry and accusatory, I was grateful I was in a bathroom! Seriously, I almost wet myself. I stuck my ear to the door to hear how you were playing it and waited for a cue as to when to expose myself. I thought about staying there, hiding, and sneaking out later, but could you imagine if he'd walked in?"

She paused to breathe, a good idea it turned out because when she twisted on the bench to meet his eyes, hers had turned serious. All merriment gone.

"I found the connection. I found his *safe.* I'm not going to show you here, but I will when we get home. And I have several folders stuck in my leggings waistband which are *very* uncomfortable, so can we go?"

Kit was stunned. She'd found a safe, opened it and had the proof? Hidden, stuffed in her leggings under her hoodie? Holy fuck.

"Let's go," he said and hauled her to her feet, heading to O'Connell Street.

She pulled back.

"No. I want to go home. To my flat. I need to change my clothes and I can't keep putting it off. You're coming, right? So we can decide what to do?"

He was absolutely coming. No way was she going to spend the night alone after what just went down.

They took the DART and walked in the direction of her flat. He took the stash of papers, several manilla folders actually, that she handed him for safe keeping and shoved them down his own waistband under his henley. They had gone over the entire drama of 'coy female and lover outwit big boss' scenario as the train rocked from station to station. He'd been blown away by her performance, her quick thinking, the exact right role to play. They could only hope that Junior hadn't got wind of her drama and assume he was his usual swan-in, swan-out self, only interested in the glamour of his role, the pay-outs and bank balance, not the practicalities – he had minions for that.

"And throwing in your famous sister-in-law? That was pure diamond! And gave him no time to question your being in jail or why you were out."

They passed a row of local shops near her street. Kit's stomach rumbled. They needed food.

"Wait here, I'll get some Indian takeaway," he said. "I'm starving."

"Me too. I'll go ahead and heat plates. Choose whatever, but nothing too spicy. I'll see you at home in a few mins."

Kit wanted to say no, to ask her to wait. But he noticed her jigging up and down and knew she wouldn't. She wanted to be home, in *her* home.

He got that. The last several days had been a massive upheaval and the comforts of home were a balm.

"Okay, be careful. I'll be as quick as I can."

And off she went.

Afterwards Molly admitted she didn't notice the scrapings of wood on the ground as she inserted her key. That there was anything amiss as she kicked off her shoes in the hall. It was as she stopped short, outside her living room, that a wave of chills rippled through her body as the first inkling came. Something was very wrong.

She knew she should wait for Kit. She admitted that later too. But this was her home, her responsibility. The hairs on the back of her neck at attention, her heart hammering and a voice inside screaming *run*, she opened the door anyway. Big mistake. Big. Huge! Yes, even in her own head she was quoting *Pretty Woman* as the scene unfolded before her.

A mess. Everything was a mess. Chairs overturned, the coffee table upended, books and CDs strewn across the floor, her precious table lamp in smithereens. She'd been robbed!

Hands to her mouth to stifle the scream, another sense kicked in, but too damn late. Whirling to run, as her own body had begged moments before, she ran smack into a big barrel of a chest that did not belong to Kit. *Stale sweat* was what she thought as a muscled arm came about her upper body, hauling her, dragging her, to the kitchen. She tried to yell, got one good shout of *"Help!"* before a hand clamped over her mouth. She was shoved onto an upright chair and her arms hauled unceremoniously behind her, around the chair back and tied.

He shoved his hand into her hoodie pocket, pulled out her phone and, tossing it to the floor, crushed it with his heel.

"One word out from you, unless we are saying so, and we will silence you," he growled in her ear.

Another man was leaning against her kitchen counter, cool as you please, slapping a carving knife, one Ali had left behind, easily in his palm. *Oh God, this was so not good.* Molly was aware she could barely hear what the two men were saying, her heart was thundering so loudly in her chest. All she could hear was that rapid beat and the sounds of panic rising within her. *Help, help, help!*

Kit! Kit was about to walk into this. She had to warn him! Or get these goons out of here, somehow.

"What do you want?" she spoke/squeaked.

"We ask questions, not you." It was one of the two from Twomey's flat. Not the henchmen from Benson's earlier. Was that good or bad? How many of these bloody guns for hire were there?

The man with the knife was speaking again, his voice rough and guttural. "Papers from Twomey flat. We want them. Now."

Think, think, think, what would a spy do? I mean, I'm living in some alternate universe, so think like a spy. Act like one. Be one! Drawing a deep breath, and going with coy, silly girlfriend that had worked earlier she said, "Oh those! Yeah, those I sent to the office, by post, in a bubble envelope, you know for protection, so they should be there on Monday, if you want to collect them. How did you know I had them? You must be awfully clever." *Yes*, she thought. *Be a simpleton, add information that is of no value and definitely flatter them. They are men, after all. Egos as big as the sky.*

Man One and Man Two exchanged glances. They thought she was nuts. Good. Nuts was better than valuable. Or no, wait. It was the other way around. Shit. Valuable, they wouldn't hurt. Nuts though? Well, all bets would be off. God, she was an idiot.

"How do we know is true?" Knife Wielder asked. "You could lie."

"Yes, I could. But why would I? You're threatening me with a knife. *A knife!*" Those last words she yelled as loud as she could, startling the two men. She'd heard the front door open but thankfully the others hadn't. She'd been listening for it. Waiting for it. She knew Kit wasn't armed but, forewarned is forearmed and all that.

Then all hell broke loose.

Like with the door and the unusual feelings, it was afterwards that Molly really processed what happened next. Kit powered in through the door, swung a bag of hot food straight at the head of the man standing next to Molly's chair. As the gangster staggered, yelling, from the blow and hot food as the bag burst, Kit did some kind of one-two movement with his hands, so fast Molly wouldn't be able to recreate it, and the guy fell to the floor. The knife man leaped into action, charging for Kit who sidestepped and elbowed him in the chin. The knife went flying and then it was punches and grunts, kicks and thumps. Molly was absolutely bloody terrified. Still seated, hands tied behind her, over the chair back, she couldn't do much except try to shove herself and her chair out of the way. The noise was something she'd always remember. Grunting. Groaning. The crack of a fist against a jaw, so damn loud. And the blood. Lots of blood. The big foreign guy grabbed for the knife and sliced through Kit's upper arm before Kit got another crack to his face. The knife crashed to the floor, spinning towards one of the table legs. Molly did her best to shunt over, and with one foot stretched to kick it under and away. Alas, not far enough.

All she could do was yell. And she did. Screaming for help, hoping a neighbour might hear. But also to warn Kit when knife man was aiming a kick or a punch where Kit couldn't see. Kit went down again, his head slamming on the hardwood floor. No. *Nooooo!* Within seconds, the bigger broader man dived, grabbed the knife again and began waving it in a dangerous fashion but at the last second Kit twisted and the thug landed face down. In an instant, bloodied from nose and arm, bruised and bedraggled, Kit was on top of him, grabbing his head by the hair and smashing his face to the ground. It was a horrible sound and Molly cheered for it. Kit fell away to the side, exhausted, breathing short shallow breaths.

The man who had been felled, in part by Indian curry, was stirring and Kit, satisfied that his current opponent was out for the count, crawled over and promptly chopped the other man again on the side of the neck with a cool karate move, knocking him out.

On hands and knees, Kit looked up at Molly, his face a

mess, and croaked, "Are you okay? Did the bastards hurt you?" He reached for some hanging tea towels, wound them tightly longways and tied separate hands from each man to the various table legs. It would hold them, temporarily at least. It would do, for now.

Molly swallowed, her throat dry but her eyes welling. "I'm fine, Kit. Honest. Can you untie me? My shoulders are starting to ache." She groaned the second she said it. Stupid. Aching shoulders? For God's sake, what was that when she looked at the disaster that was Kit Elliot crouched in front of her. The poor man. He must be in agony.

But not a word did he say as he scrambled around behind her and ripped apart the ties. "Wait," he said urgently. "Do it slowly, it will hurt less."

Jesus, she was such a baby. Easing her shoulders, and loosening her arms did hurt, but, Christ, in the grand scheme, only a little – it had been minutes, not hours.

She stood, her legs unsteady as Kit wrapped his arms about her body, moulding it to his, and it was then that she realised it was he who was shaking.

She eased her own arms around him and held on. "I'm fine, Kit. It's okay. I'm fine. We need to get you cleaned up, put stuff on your wounds, ice your eye. We need to call the police. I want these men out of here." All the time she stroked his back, gentle long rubs up and down his strong frame.

She stopped speaking when she understood he wasn't listening. He was mumbling into her neck, his arms growing tighter about her, holding on.

"Jesus, Molly, I'm so sorry. So fucking sorry. I should *never* have let you come home on your own – I know better. I'm sorry."

"Stop, Kit, stop now," she ordered firmly. "I wanted to come on ahead. I also wanted food. So, no, you couldn't have changed my mind. I'm stubborn like that." She thought she heard a muffled, "Hah!" but ignored it and continued, "We're in shock. Both of us. We need to call the police. We're both okay. We're fine." She kept her tone even, knowing he needed soothing as much as she did. They'd had a horrific ordeal that probably was only going to get worse when the police arrived.

She eased back, forcing him to raise his head. Their eyes met, held. And then they smiled, crooked and tremulous, but they were smiles.

"You were incredible," she whispered and stretched up to kiss his split lip. "Incredible." She kissed the side of his mouth and his cheek where a graze was already changing colour. "You're my hero." She'd barely uttered the words when those gorgeous hero lips of his, cracked and split though they were, settled on hers with intent. Their kiss was one of relief mixed with wonder that they were okay. It was a kiss reminding them that *they* were still standing.

"We need to phone Flynn," Kit said, breaking apart and resting his forehead on hers.

"Yeah, we do." Molly sighed, a forlorn sound. "It was almost fun for a while, the last few days, sneaking around, adrenalin rush of the wardrobe scenario, the playacting in Benson's office earlier." She turned to look at the two bodies comatose on her kitchen floor. "It doesn't feel like fun anymore."

"No, sweetheart, it doesn't." And Kit reached into his back pocket and dialled.

As they waited for Flynn and his cronies to arrive, Kit checked the hands of the two baddies, and added extra ties, courtesy of a ball of thick twine from Molly's cupboard, to their feet. They were now being called Baddie One and Baddie Two, Molly had decided, since that was all the acknowledgement she was giving them. Kit tried to smile but his lip and jaw hurt like a bugger.

He knew his ribs were in trouble when Molly looked at the bashed bag of takeaway food, one container split open and its contents spewed about, some on the floor, a considerable amount on Baddie One, and holding up two other cartons, still intact, said, "Do you think this is evidence or could we eat it?"

He'd tried not to laugh – it was damn sore about his chest – but Jesus, she was funny. He was about to say no when his stomach growled, alerting them to the fact that neither had eaten since breakfast.

"Fuck it, grab a couple of forks."

Molly stepped over a stirring body, gave it a small kick, and reached for the cutlery drawer. "Yeah, I know you shouldn't kick a man when he's down, but I see no men here. Only two baddies and one hero."

He could feel the warmth of her smile, feel it flood up his body and reach his heart. He had a feeling she would always be able to do that – fill him with all the good things. How would he survive without her? How would he live?

"Hey, how's your arm? It's bleeding through your shirt? Do you need a bandage?" she asked.

"Nah," he mumbled. "It's just a flesh wound. Nothing to worry about. He just grazed me."

Molly handed him a fork and a plate. "Dig in," she advised. "It's already going cold but I can't be bothered to use the microwave."

They ate. Amidst squirming men on the ground, now gagged because their swearing was putting Molly off her food, they tasted the cooled delights of India. And they waited for Flynn and crew to arrive.

When they heard a knock and the door opening, Kit could feel relief wave over him. He wasn't sure how much longer he could pretend all was okay. He needed a doctor and probably several stitches. He had wrapped himself in a bath towel claiming to be chilly – that was true – but he was also hiding a knife wound to his belly. The upper arm one was surface and would probably heal by itself, once cleaned and dressed. The belly was a different story. And he didn't want her worrying. As they ate, he could feel himself fade, as if everything was going into a sepia tone. He pressed the small hand towel currently tucked under his shirt, hoping it would stem the bleeding.

Flynn strolled in, confident that all would be well. Kit had told him on the phone the culprits were tied up, and the detective had believed him. Trusted him. Molly flung herself in her brother's arms. She began recounting their story but Flynn kissed her on the top of her head and told her to save it for later. He looked at Kit, walked over, bent forwards and looked into Kit's face.

"How far out is the ambulance?" he asked over his shoulder.

"Two minutes, sir," one of the policemen said.

"Good. Get them in here asap. We have an emergency."

"Wait! What?" Molly was confused. "It's just a flesh wound. He said it was a flesh wound." She rested her hand lightly on Kit's upper arm where the blood had oozed but stopped.

"That's not the problem," Flynn said. Tilting his head, he heard the sirens. "About time," he said quietly, eyes on Kit.

Kit felt his head leave his body, felt the world go grey, saw Flynn look down on Baddie One and say, dry as dust, "Ain't Korma a bitch."

And was caught in strong arms before he hit the floor.

"The *folders*!" Molly said, a couple of hours later. "I still can't believe the stack of stolen papers, now bloody worthless, pun intended, saved him. I didn't even know he was stabbed there. He never said. Not even when we ate our Indian and he was obviously feeling like shit. What an idiot!" She sat down, abruptly, on a hard waiting-room chair.

Flynn leaned negligently against the doorjamb, arms folded. At ease. Calm. Being Flynn.

"They did," he said. "When you handed him the wad from the bathroom safe and he stuck them in his waistband, they inadvertently put an extra layer between Kit's organs and the knife. Your gesture, unintended though it was, saved his life."

"So the doc said, but Jesus, Flynn, what bloody idiot suffers in silence like that?" Molly squeaked. "When he fainted and you caught him and I saw all that blood? I figured only then it was way more serious than a fecking flesh wound!"

"He'll be fine," another voice spoke behind her brother who moved with unconscious grace to let the doctor in. "Detective, we have to stop meeting like this."

Flynn grinned.

The doctor turned to Molly and said, "Are you Ms Fitzgerald? Another sister, I see. We get quite the collection of both your family and your brother's colleagues in here," she said dryly. "Try not to make it a habit." All business-like she checked her notes and calmly told them that Kit would be fine. Vital organs had been missed and he'd had stiches. He'd need to stay in at least overnight, preferably at least another day on a drip to ensure no infection set in. Most likely he'd be out by Wednesday.

Molly thanked the doctor and then she and Flynn were allowed back to see him, albeit with orders to be swift.

"He won't stay till Wednesday," Molly said quietly as they made their way to the bed. "He will want to end it, tomorrow, at BB&M."

"No doubt," Flynn said, brevity personified.

Even if she'd never met Kit, Molly would have been

drawn inexplicably to the prone figure in the hospital bed. He was handsome, old-fashioned handsome. His skin paler than usual, shadows under his eyes, dark lashes swept down in repose. A bed with a waffle blanket couldn't hide his muscled arms, now with a bandage on that wound covered inexpertly in a hospital gown. His firm generous mouth, the creases where secret dimples lay, ready to assail the unsuspecting voyeur. All the parts that made up this man – the long legs, so shapely from running, basketball and cycling, lay inert now, Unmoving.

Molly edged to the bed, her hand reaching for Kit's as it lay by his side above the covers. She almost pulled back, hesitant, unsure if she had the right but before she could, Kit's fingers curled around hers. And held.

"I'm fine," he croaked. Cleared his throat. Swallowed visibly. Cracked open his clouded eyes.

Flynn moved to the other side of the bed, poured some water and leaning down placed the glass to Kit's lips. "Drink," he suggested mildly, but with a firmness Molly recognised all too well. Kit struggled to sit up and Flynn eased an arm about his shoulders to help. Kit winced, but managed a few sips.

"Thanks," he said and lay back, turning his head to Molly. "Hey, why are you here? You should go home to your family. Promise me you won't stay in your flat, alone. *Promise.*" His voice became urgent and Molly rushed to reassure.

"It's grand, Kit. Yes, I'll def go home to Dalkey. Won't be alone, I promise. But Baddie One and Two are in jail or maybe hospital – I didn't wait to find out, but I promise not to take any chances." She ran a hand over his head, brushing the hair back from his forehead. Just touching him felt like a gift. Feeling his skin beneath her fingers, knowing he was alive and would be okay. The tightness that had banded her chest since he collapsed in her kitchen began to unwind. Marginally. "Way to ruin a good Indian meal, hotshot," she joked.

"I'll take you to a proper one when I'm well. Deal?"

"Deal." She smiled, her eyes misting. She was not going to be a watering can in front of these two stalwarts so she took a breath and asked, "What's next?"

Flynn pulled up a chair and Molly sat on the side of the bed, still holding Kit's hand. Flynn glanced at their enclosed fingers and, with a mere hint of a raised eyebrow, brought their attention to the situation at hand.

"Strategy is what happens next. The papers you brought from Benson's safe are soaked in blood and, while we are grateful they prevented a more egregious wound, they are now worthless. Time and the lab department could probably make some sense of them, but time is not what we currently have. Thoughts?"

Molly sat up straighter. "I photographed everything on my phone, which is smashed to hell but, and I want major Brownie points for this, I emailed all the photos to myself before leaving the bathroom. Genius, or what?"

There was stunned silence. The two men contemplated her with what she could only describe as incredulous admiration.

"Indeed," Flynn said with his usual loquaciousness.

Kit lifted her hand to his lips and kissed her fingers. "Definitely genius." His smile was crooked and adorable and so full of pride and something else, Molly wasn't sure what, but the look in his eyes burned into her heart in all the best ways. She could feel herself blush and for once simply didn't care.

Kit turned his head to include Flynn. "We'd better get plotting then."

Flynn shook his head. "Not tonight, Mr Elliot. Rest, doctor's orders. We will come back late morning and chat.

We'll bring all the documents and, if you are well enough to be released, we will go to a safe room at the station. If not, I'll ask for some privacy here and we will have a conversation."

Molly rolled her eyes. Only Flynn would call figuring out the downfall of several criminals a conversation. God, she loved her brother. But he was right. Kit needed sleep. And healing time. And probably lots of drugs. They could make sure that happened.

"I'm on board with that," she said. "We'll see you in the morning." She glanced at Flynn, a silent plea in her eyes.

He blinked, stood, rested his hand on Kit's good shoulder. They did some kind of man-nod thing and he turned to leave.

"I'll see to some paperwork. Molly, be at the car in a few." And he was gone.

Molly swung her eyes back to Kit's. She had stuff to say. Stuff that needed to be said but, suddenly shy, she hesitated. She was falling for this man, big time, more and more each minute. She knew all the reasons not to. She was smart. She knew he'd done a whole heap of things that had pissed her off royally. But he'd also saved her, twice. And he taught basketball to young kids. And cared for a cat named Scout. What was not to love? His actions made it very hard to forgive him as equally they made it even harder not to fall headlong in love.

The man was an enigma, but one she desperately wanted to unravel.

"Hey," he said, drawing her back to the present, "you are some woman." He kissed her knuckles, his eyes never leaving hers. "When this is over, we also need to have a *conversation*." He smiled, knowingly slagging off her brother.

"We do," she agreed. "I'd better go, Flynn doesn't like to be kept waiting." Suddenly, opening her heart to him seemed unnecessary. "For now, anyway. See you tomorrow. Sleep." She tried to make her voice bossy, authoritative, but knew if failed spectacularly. She leaned down, her hand still in his and kissed his forehead, his cheek and unable to resist, his lips.

"*Hmmm*," he sighed appreciatively. "Now I'll sleep." And he let his eyes fall even as she slid her hand from his.

She walked out, looking for Flynn, her lips, her fingers for goodness' sake still tingling from his touch.

She had it bad.

Chapter 28

He wasn't well enough to go home, Kit knew that, but he signed himself out anyway. They had one afternoon to wrap things up or at least figure out a plan so they *could* wrap it up. He let Flynn drive him to the police station.

The well-lit windowless room at the station was fine. Molly looked exhausted and there were signs of strain about her usually sarcastic mouth. The fact that she was neither of those things right now was more of a tell than any dark circles beneath her eyes. Kit had taken all the drugs and had a stash in his jacket pocket for later. He only had to get through today and tomorrow and then he could officially collapse and rest. That wouldn't be too hard. Knife wounds hurt like a bitch but, hey, he believed it was for the greater good. Why else put oneself through it?

They laid everything out on a big rectangular table. Or Flynn and Molly did. All the paperwork, photos printed from Molly's email – such smart thinking – and the copious files from his USB. Kit felt a bit useless lounging in a chair but for once he was happy to play the invalid card. There was no way he could stretch or his stitches could pop.

Then the real work began. Molly, great with detail and patterns, got started sorting out dates and a timeline. Kit was good at the big picture. Flynn developed connections they hadn't even thought about. Having contacts in the FBI, other than Kit's own, helped. Flynn had spent several hours the previous night, after taking Molly home, talking with known CIs in Boston, the prison warden where Cochrane was incarcerated, and had been given access to the visitor records. Now they knew names on both sides of the Atlantic and how they segued together, Cochrane and Benson's plan became alarmingly simple. That in and of itself was worrying. It was way too easy to set up their plan, all while one of the perpetrators was in jail.

Money and fear will buy a lot, they knew that, and it was never more evident than right now, on this table. Now they knew how it was executed and by whom, the next step was to present the evidence to Benson, get him to roll on Cochrane himself and make sure Twomey took some of the fall. Benson Senior was not going to be happy, but he would be grateful.

Chloe Benson, on the other hand, was about to find that her glitzy lifestyle and love of all things golden was going down the tubes. Kit found he couldn't bring himself to be remotely sorry for that. She was about to find out that playing away from home, while titillating, could force your partner to bend and break rules in order to keep you in satin and fur. He bet she would discover that straying, repeatedly, pushed Benson Junior to make stupid greedy decisions. All in order to keep his wife. Kit didn't get it. It didn't compute in his brain. Why would you want to keep someone like that in your life? How could you forgive, forget, move on? Maybe you couldn't. It might all be an illusion, or a carrot, keeping hope alive.

Marriage had never been on Kit's radar. Or at least not for years to come. His line of work, moving around regularly, lying, deceiving, acting and the odd knife tussle didn't quite a 'marriage of two minds make'. His gaze landed on Molly. She sat, perched on the edge of her seat, focused and intent on two sets of papers. As he watched, she wrote on Post-its and attached them to specific pages. She was so clever. So attuned to the data. He knew about her 'sixth sense', but this was all brain matter, all intelligence of the IQ kind rather than the emotional kind. It was rare to find a propensity to both in one person. She was pretty unique.

She was also pretty *and* sexy. Unintentionally, but indisputably, gloriously sexy. He adored her gasps and moans. Her sighs. Her hesitant 'directions'. Her raw laugh when he tickled her along her sides, or when she finally got a joke – long after the punch line. Her curves drove him wild, made him hard at the oddest, most inconvenient times. He could live with that. He'd had more happy shower time since meeting Molly then he could ever remember. Even in college.

He was in a quandary. He wanted her, *god*, how he wanted her. But even if she forgave him, even if she could accept his deception as a job requirement, what could he offer her in terms of a future?

A snap of fingers had his attention return to the tabletop and away from the way curls rested tantalisingly on the back of Molly's neck.

"Focus," said Flynn. "Time, essence, et al."

"Sorry." Kit shook his head, shoving all the Molly, sexy, future, career and forgiveness notions into a separate compartment. He could do this. They could, and would, do this. And it, whatever plan they came up with, would be ready to be executed tomorrow.

Failure was not an option.

But one more ball had to drop before their plan was tied up, one Kit could have seriously done without. Halfway through the afternoon a cursory knock sounded and a head appeared around the door.

"Elliot, heard you were banjaxed. Glad it's not too bad." The well-meaning garda stuck his hand out and wincing, for all manner of reasons, Kit went and shook it.

"Thanks," he said, doing his best to block Molly's view.

No such luck. Too late. He turned back to the table as the door closed. Molly was glaring at him through narrowed eyes.

"Who was that? He looked awfully familiar. Wait, wasn't that Dave Larkin? Dave Larkin of Sports Star Services? It was! What's he doing here?"

Kit closed his eyes and took a breath. When he opened them again, the glare was shooting daggers and hissing steam. "I was going to tell you about that, but things have been, well, you know how they've been."

She didn't give an inch. "Explain this second or I walk. I mean it, Kit, I'm in no mood for more secrets. More lies."

He explained, as briefly as possible, knowing he was losing her by the second. Everything he told her, that it was a test, that Donnelly, the other new hire had one too, fell on deaf ears.

"You sneaky son of a bitch! How dare you? How dare you throw that supposed company in my lap, then tease me how to search deeper, and then, *then* create fake managers? You are the lowest of the low." She whipped around, her back to him. "Let's get this finished so we can go home. I need a shower – suddenly I feel dirty."

Yeah, that went well.

Timing was everything. Every good director kept that as a mantra and Kit, in charge of this production, had it timed to the second. Molly's security privileges had been reinstated early on the Monday morning, courtesy of a phone call from Flynn to Benson Senior. But that was only to get her through the door. As far as the rest of the staff knew, she was still under suspicion of fiddling accounts, minor though they were.

Kit's side ached in ways he'd forgotten existed, but he swallowed the pills as directed. Molly arrived early, as was her usual routine and buried herself in her office, blinds down. Kit too behaved as normal, though he walked a little more slowly. Nerd clothes discarded, he wore a navy suit, crisp white shirt and grey tie. Dull, unexciting, but classic. Professional. Competent. The visuals of this plan were important. Just like when Molly was supposedly arrested and he had to appear to be an authority on the matter. No one wanted to believe a geeky-looking guy was able to take down an operation, or demand respect.

When Kit went full-on FBI or CCA forensic investigative consultant, people paid attention. Like a lot of other things in his life, it was an act. He played the part well, but he was beginning to understand being the lead was taking its toll.

Twomey was due in Benson Junior's office for an eleven-thirty meeting. Chloe was supposed to arrive at noon for a lunch date with her husband. Kit and Molly were intending to arrive at eleven forty-five, thereby allowing Mrs B to witness some of the debacle. Flynn and supporting cast of gardaí were due on the premises by ten past twelve.

It was going to be an interesting lunchtime at BB&M.

Kit had picked the noon hour as it would mean Cochrane would be up and breakfasting back in Boston. He had checked the mess times with the warden and had arranged for a surprise video call from Junior. But, of course, it wouldn't be just Brendan . . .

Nerves gathered, before a confrontation, as they often did, but this time they felt more ragged. Molly being involved changed so much. He hated that he hurt her, caused her embarrassment but hoped, when the Guards arrested Benson and Twomey today, in front of everyone, he would make an announcement, totally exonerating Molly. Making it damn clear that she'd been instrumental in bringing down the culprits.

Molly was due in first and, if her script went to plan, he would saunter in with 'just a couple of questions to clear up a few discrepancies'. He avoided her all morning, knowing if he saw her things could go south. If she looked tired or uneasy, he'd be likely to call the whole thing off. Equally, if she saw him she could quite easily turn and leave. Not that he could blame her. The worry was what they *didn't* know. Did Twomey's sidekicks only answer to him or would Benson expect Kit to be wounded? There was no way of knowing. Baddie One had made his phone call, from hospital, before going to jail, and it was traced to Twomey. But did Benson pull all the strings or had Declan gone rogue?

All to play for.

He positioned himself so he could see Molly leave her office. She was right on time. He expected nothing less. Her role was to knock, go in without waiting for an answer, knowing Twomey would be in there, and when the inevitable 'What are you doing here?' happened she would explain straight to Brendan Benson that she'd been framed. She would thus pretend she was unaware he, too, was involved. She knew her lines. Kit just had to trust the others would react as he, Flynn and Molly expected. Defensive, accusatory and back to defensive.

It went like a dream.

Kit also knocked, perfunctorily, aiming a smile at the befuddled PA who, bless her, tried to stop him but then, shrugging her shoulders, returned to her computer. He swung open the door, as if he had a red carpet waiting. Pretending not to see either Molly or Twomey, he stopped in front of Benson's desk, placed his palms shoulder-width apart and leaned in.

"I need you to answer some questions, Mr Benson. I've been going through your accounts at the behest of your brother, and I am here to inform you I am mighty confused."

Benson pushed back his chair and stood. "You can't just waltz in here, Elliot. I'm in a meeting. Go away. Come back later. Or better yet, not at all." He sounded flustered, as well he might.

Kit made a show of turning and noticing the two other occupants. Molly was standing, arms folded, looking mutinous, next to Twomey who was trying, but failing, to look casual and carefree, hands shoved in the pockets of his trousers. A frown deepened, as he studied Kit. His eyes betrayed him, flicking to Kit's waistband, and back to his face. Kit smiled benignly at him. Yup, the bastard knew all about his stitches.

"Did you show him?" Kit asked Molly.

"I did, but he doesn't want to believe me when I tell him that Declan set me up. That Declan is skimming money from his accounts. I have all the evidence, right here." She unfolded her arms, palm up, memory stick sitting right there.

Twomey made a grab for it, snatching it from her grasp.

"Oh, please. Do you seriously think this is the only one? Give me some credit, you jackass."

Benson looked from Twomey to Molly, unsure what to do. Kit decided to be kind and help him out.

"While you look through Molly's data, proving without a doubt what Declan Twomey has done, with or without your knowledge, you might also look at this." He placed his own USB stick on the shiny desk.

Alarmed, but aiming for innocent confusion, Benson said, "Anything Mr Twomey has done of a criminal nature has had no sanction from me, I assure you."

Declan spluttered, "Hey, you're not tossing me down

the toilet, you bastard! Everything I did was on your say-so."

The two men turned, glaring at each other, shoulders back, acting like they were vying for pole position in a race.

"Gentlemen," cooed Kit. "There's no need for you to be each claiming innocence or allocating blame – there is plenty here to go around. Why don't I show you what we have? Proof, if you will, of all the bad dealings going on, right under the noses of the auspicious BB&M firm."

He walked around the back of the desk, vacant now that Benson had approached Twomey. Molly edged to the side, putting space between her and the men. *Good move, Molly.*

Kit inserted the stick, played around with the keyboard till he got what he wanted and then flipped the screen about, to show the dot to dot, line by line, incriminating trail of skimming small amounts, stealing larger amounts and finally, the granddaddy of them all, the money-laundering scheme, initiated by Cochrane, taken on by Benson with Twomey as the dupe.

It was all so easy. Benson, or Twomey on Benson's behalf, set up a fake account with a sister account in the Caymans. Cochrane shovelled money through the Dublin account and Twomey made sure it landed overseas, through various channels. How Cochrane managed it from his prison cell was still being investigated, but he wasn't a criminal mastermind for nothing. If anyone knew people who knew people and used intimidation to get things done, it was Eddie Cochrane. Bribing guards and prison personnel was his bag.

Kit looked at his watch. "Give me your phone," he said to Benson.

"What? No! Of course, I won't give you my ph–"

Without seeming to move, Kit had Benson's jacket flipped open and the phone whipped from inside his jacket pocket. Thanks to his stealthy surveillance over the previous weeks, Kit had discovered all manner of things about each of the players in this scene. Benson always kept his phone in his inside right pocket. As Benson recovered from the shock, Kit skimmed through the contacts, saw EC, rolled his eyes at the stupidity and dialled. He had, it must be said, a moment of trepidation. Did Eddie know his stepson was involved? Or was it pure coincidence? He was about to find out.

"Would you like to speak first, or will I?" Kit waggled the phone in front of a fuming Benson. "Never mind, I can see you may need to collect yourself. Ah, Mrs. Benson, right on time." This as the door opened and Chloe strode in, all purposeful and proprietorial. She might think her husband was a fool but she wore the prestige of being a company director wife like a second skin.

As Kit waited to hear his stepfather's voice, Chloe glared at everyone in the room. "What are you doing here? You're supposed to be locked up!" she snarled at Molly then turned to Declan. "And why are *you* here?" He got a snap as opposed to a snarl. She turned to her long-suffering husband. "And what are you waiting for? I've made reservations, I don't have all day." Her tone this time was of impatience and irritation.

Molly moved quietly to close the door, saying, "No one is going anywhere, or at least, not yet." She stood, like a sentry, back to the glass.

"What the fuck, Benson," a voice that Kit would have known anywhere blasted in his ear. "I told ya not to call me unless *I* said a time. Betta have a damn good reason, asshole!"

Kit's pause was infinitesimal, then he said softly, the phone on loudspeaker, "Oh, I do. I have a very good reason." And he waited. Waited for the recognition. The awareness that shit was about to happen. That his plans were all about to be blown out of the water. Eddie would know that if Kit was involved, his life had just taken a turn for the worse.

It came. Loud and clear. *"The fuck??"* A roar more than a shout. *"Benson, where are you? Put Benson on the phone! What the fuck is going on?"*

Kit couldn't help the frisson of pleasure as he imagined the red blotches appear on Eddie's cheeks, the quickening of breath, of heart. He had seen it before, all before, when Eddie had turned on him in the court room, blazing with fury. It was years ago now, but Kit could feel it all. The intensity of the hate, the bile spewing from Cochrane's mouth as he swore to get even. Kit had never believed he could, didn't believe it now. Cochrane might have power and funds, but he was at the base of it all a greedy bastard just like any other.

"Shut up, Eddie, and listen," he said. "The game is up. We have all the evidence we need. You and Benson here are being arrested for money-laundering and a myriad of other lesser but pertinent charges. Mr Twomey is also being charged."

Kit paused as he let the room, and the man at the other end of the phone, explode in a cacophony of angry, disbelieving and accusatory yelling.

Things unfolded rather quickly after that. Chloe marched over to Declan, shoved him in the chest, knocking him backwards, and said acidly "You fool." Then she strode to her husband and slapped him hard across the face. Kit almost felt sorry for the man – it must have stung.

Everyone, or at least Eddie on the phone, and Benson and Twomey, all began doing exactly what Flynn had surmised. Blaming each other, refuting the accusations and back to blaming.

Molly looked on, fascinated, filming the entire debacle on her phone.

Kit put the phone back on mute from the other voices and said directly to Cochrane, "Right about now, a couple of officers are approaching you, they will arrest you, bring you to a detention area, and even though you are already incarcerated, they will hand you over to a waiting lawyer where you will be charged with further crimes. How that will all pan out for you is anybody's guess. Frankly, I don't care. It will be more prison time for you, you can be assured of that. The extra time will be tagged on to your sentence, so that early parole you wanted? Yeah, not happening." Kit could hear the scuffle in the background. Could see in his head what was happening, could make out the Miranda rights being read and, unfortunately, before he hung up, his stepfather's vitriol being spilled.

"You little shit, Elliot! You think your mother is ever going to talk to you again, after this? Forget it. *She hates you!"*

Wincing briefly against that pain, one he knew he would have to face, and face head on, Kit shook it off and returned his attention to the room.

All was as before. The two Bensons and the marital interloper were all shouting at each other. It was becoming exhausting. Right on cue, however, Flynn tapped on the door, Molly opened it, and the arrival of the law put a sudden halt to everyone's gallop.

More accusations and denials, more finger-pointing, all to no immediate avail.

"We have the evidence, stone cold, gentlemen," Flynn said calmly. "So, it would behove you to come with us quietly, to the station, where charges can be filed officially."

Benson Senior appeared at the door, his face grey and tired. His shoulders slumped. "So, it is true," he said sadly. "I really hoped I was wrong."

"Jesus, Bryan. Do something. You know I'd never do anything to hurt the firm. You *know* it."

"Do I, though?" Senior shook his head sadly. "Mr Elliot is the best at what he does, I knew that when I hired him, when I knew I had to bring in the police and listen to their advice. Framing Molly Fitzgerald was part of the plan, but Twomey, and you by extension, were happy for her to take the fall. It was Elliot who set the trap, who made sure she signed documents not meant for her. You idiots just ran with it, thereby leaving yourselves open to more investigation. Had you stood up for her, supported her, I might have believed you." He sighed. "Idiots. And now criminals."

Kit was aware that Molly was glaring at him. He hadn't gone into detail about why she was accused, had let her believe it was Declan who had created the mess, not he, Kit, who had set it up intentionally. He was definitely going to face more harsh questions from her later. *Shit.*

Junior meanwhile spun around and pointed a shaking finger at Molly. "You're the cause of all this. If you'd just stayed out of our business . . . and, wait, we can't believe anything you say! You're in league with Elliot. You're lovers! You said so on Saturday. Detective," he grasped Flynn by the arm, urgently, "you can't believe this woman. Whatever she says is a lie. She *did* do all the skimming of accounts. And Elliot got her off. See? She should be re-arrested. And charged. Not me!" His whine was pathetic.

Molly walked over to him, hands on her hips, not content to listen to his drivel anymore.

"You, sir, are a liar and a thief. You are also a gullible fool. Kit Elliot means nothing to me. We were *acting*, pulling the wool over your eyes so we could leave. I never stole a damn thing from your company and I never would. Mr Elliot has uncovered your stupid plan, and you are going to jail. End of. You too, Declan." She rounded on him. "How dare you accuse me of wrongdoing when all the time you, in your high and mighty ways, were already robbing them blind. And bonking Mrs Benson. You all deserve each other."

Whether it was her dismissive tone or her sheer disgust with them all, she set off a domino effect of actions. Brendan Benson pushed his brother aside and ran for the door. Flynn stepped in front of him and cuffed him without much difficulty. Twomey charged for Kit, elbowed him in his side, knocking him back. A shout of fury emanated from Molly who surged forward and, as Kit fell against the table, pain searing through his side, he watched as she kicked Declan right between his legs causing him to howl and fall, writhing, to the ground. Chloe, who for the most part had stood mouth agape at the furore, now advanced on Molly, slapped her hard, obviously a go-to method of preference, and turned to kneel over Declan but Molly stuck out her foot and tripped her, sending her flying to the ground, legs flailing. She was not an elegant faller, Kit mused watching legs and arms tangle, while he nursed his wound, feeling the wetness of renewed blood flow. *There goes another shirt,* he thought, and slid to the floor, conscious but thoroughly wrung out.

Molly, palm to her face, glanced down at Kit, then at Flynn who had handed Benson over to one of the garda, stepped into her brother's arms and said, "I want to go home." She'd had more than enough adventuring.

"Soon," he promised. "We're almost done."

"Jesus, it's like one of those Two Act farces that Granny Flynn used to watch on TV. What a shambolic mess. How did you stop yourself from cracking up?" Ali was laying out lemon squares and flapjacks on a plate as Frankie made tea. Caro was with them, virtually, sipping her own beverage, as she listened to Molly's retelling of the entire event.

They had cleaned up her living room, her brother and

sister helping with the lifting, Frankie not being let near anything heavy as Dev clucked over her. Molly selected a pastry as Frankie passed around the milk, and the women continued dissecting her ordeal. Dev had left, a flapjack in his mouth, to go to an appointment. He'd been a tremendous help. Asking the right questions, being supportive, but not, thankfully, losing his cool. Her brother had matured, Molly supposed, but God help their offspring in the future when hot-head Devlin would, without question, reappear. At least half of the child's DNA would be Frankie's. Thankfully.

Caro cut to the chase. "What happened then? Were they arrested? Did Kit collapse? What did you do?"

Molly took a gulp of tea, a bite of lemony goodness, and at last, a breath.

"Calm down, all of you and I'll tell you." She began answering Caro's specifics. "They were arrested. Kit was taken to hospital and restitched, And I gather he's still there. I went to the police station, with Flynn, made a statement and then home to Dalkey. Then yesterday, obviously I took the day off and pretty much slept the day away. Benson Senior phoned and said he has released a statement to all employees exonerating me and even praising my actions. And he told me to take the rest of the week off, with full pay. I still have my job, if I want it, and all is right with the world." She swallowed more tea. Took another bite. Smiled.

Nobody spoke for a moment. Then Frankie, as good as Caro at nitty-gritty said, "You *gather*? You don't *know* if Kit is still in hospital, perhaps dying of septicaemia? Why do you not *know*?"

Ali scarfed a flapjack. "*Yum!* Shit, I'm good. And what she said," she nodded at her sister-in-law.

Molly shifted, uncomfortable with this line of inquiry. "I'm not . . . we're not . . . it's . . ."

"Don't give us the 'it's complicated' shit," Ali interjected, air-quoting. "We are none of us buying that. You two are an item, if ever I saw it."

"But that's just it, we're not. An item. An anything, really. I think, whatever we *were*, is done." Molly reached for a different treat, breaking the sweet oat-filled bar in two. "He set me up, twice, it turns out. I was duped, he took, sorry, 'partnered in' my virginity-losing," now she used air-quotes, "and there is nothing else." She sighed. Couldn't help it. The realisation that there *was* nothing else cracked her pathetic heart in two.

Caro responded with a gentle "I'm sure that's not the case."

And Ali once again played point. "I call bullshit," she said. "You're just being a cry-baby. No one wants a cry-baby. Buckle up. Go see him. *Check on him*, like a decent human. See where things stand. If you don't ask, you won't know."

"I can't believe I'm agreeing with Ali," Caro's voice came from the screen. "But she's right, Moll. You need to know. And if that means going to him rather than wating for him to make the first move, especially after *you* walked out on *him*, then, well, woman up.

Ignoring Ali's whoop about being right, Frankie added her two cents. "Go see him, pet," she said, a hand gentle on Molly's arm. "You owe it to yourself to either properly finish what you shared or take it further. Right now, you're in no-man's land. Not a pleasant or comfortable place to be. Take control of what happens next, you decide if you want to see him again. You can change your mind, you know. That's your prerogative. Don't wait for *things* to happen to you – *make* them happen. If you want them to."

Molly smiled at her but Frankie wasn't finished. "Why don't you tell us what you *do* want, or at least what you'd like, in theory, to roll out. Do you want more with Kit? Do you care about him?"

Now all Molly could do was close her eyes and feel. What did she want? In an ideal, non-lying Kit world she'd absolutely want that man in her life. He was smart, kind, caring, thoughtful. Handsome. *Soooo* handsome. Good with his hands, his mouth, all the body parts. He made her laugh, he made her think. He pushed her to do better, for herself. But he was also a liar, a deceiver, a manipulator. She looked at these women and told them exactly that. How good he was, and how bad.

There was silence as the sisters, by blood and love, digested this.

Finally, Caro said, "It sounds to me like Kit didn't have a choice. That acting a certain way, being a certain type, is part of his job description. He probably wasn't supposed to be involved with you. I know from some stuff Flynn has shared over the years that he has to pretend to be someone else, every so often. Though personally, I can only ever see Flynn as Flynn."

"I hear you, Caro, I do," said Molly. "But maybe I was part of the playacting, that I was just another extra in his drama. I get he may have to deceive some people, but we slept together, for God's sake. Isn't that supposed to, I don't know, mean something? Expectations of honesty perhaps?" She sighed. "And yes, I accept that I inveigled him into having sex with me, so maybe some deception on my part, but I didn't hold a gun to his head. We were both willing. I wasn't supposed to fall for him. I didn't mean to."

"Oh, you naïve little darling!" Ali said from her lofty experience of all things shitty, relationship wise. "No. Sex means fuck all to most men, except fucking. That's what it means. Body parts doing what body parts are meant to do. Nature. Honesty or decency is not on the menu, most of the time. You can get lucky, I did, but it's not a given that offering the goods gets the reward of having an actual adult human who cares."

"It's true," Frankie agreed. "But Kit is decent. You can see that. I bet you can feel that too, on every level. Go with your gut. Go see him. Talk to him. Listen to him. And if he's an asshole, walk away. No harm, no foul."

Molly groaned. "You make it sound so easy. But it's not. I care about him, with everything I know about him, I still care. That's what makes it so hard, to forgive, to take a chance."

Frankie leaned over and hugged her. "I know, but if you feel this cut up about it, perhaps you more than care about him. And if that's true you absolutely owe it to yourself to admit it. To yourself at least. I'm not saying it will be all roses, especially if he doesn't return your feelings, but at least *you'll* know. You'll be able to look yourself in the mirror. Being true to yourself is very, very important."

Caro signed off shortly after, and the other two headed to their various homes.

Molly wandered her flat, aimless and unsure. She didn't feel in any way scared, just . . . sad. She paused by the front window, looking out over a quiet side street, the odd car going past, a jogger, a group of walkers. All normal. Minding their business. All as it should be. She let her eyes fall closed and focused in. Deep within she listened to her heart, her senses, her instincts. They had let her down with Kit, for some reason, never waving the red flag.

Why? Why was that?

Could it be because there was no red flag? Because he was one of the good guys? Doing his job for the good of others? Maybe she did owe him the opportunity to explain. They had shared so much, gone through so much together, in such a short space of time. Was it that intensity that caused her heart to speed up when she thought of him? The first man she'd slept with and then going all 'double act detective', sneaking about, hiding with danger mere inches away, being tied up and witnessing a knife fight – it was a *lot*. But she wasn't the only one who'd lived all that, he had too.

He was just more expert at it.

Chapter 29

He'd taken the extra day. It wasn't like a holiday, lying in a hospital bed, but there was concern regarding infection after Twomey had clocked him in his stitches. Kit took the antibiotic IV for one day and was now on pills. His room was fine, the same décor as any generic hospital room, in any city. But he still felt like shit. Granted some of that was mental rather than physical. He also felt like an idiot. He should have seen Twomey's intent, should have avoided the blow. Should have done a lot of things.

He'd packed a small bag and was waiting for a taxi to take him home. The chair he sat in was a plastic leatherette mix in dull green and most uncomfortable. He'd be better off standing or moving about. He couldn't be arsed. He closed his eyes and remembered.

The look she had thrown his way when Benson Senior said it was his doing, that Kit had *orchestrated* the whole thing. Not just ignored it, or even discovered it, as Molly had thought. And when she'd said it was all playacting had she meant that? *All* of it? Had none of it been real to her? There was only one way to find out but he couldn't do it. He was a damn coward. Facing her rejection right now, before he took a flight to Boston and faced his mother? No. He couldn't.

Flynn would call him a fool, and he'd possibly be correct.

He'd come back though. He'd come back and try again. Like he'd planned. Woo her, date her, if she'd let him. He'd take regular hours in a regular job. He could settle here, live in his own house, have a relationship. This was not something that had appealed before, the settling in one place, but *Jesus*, if it meant he'd have a shot with Molly being right there with him? Hell, yes, he'd settle in one spot.

When a light knock came on his door and Molly poked her head around, his heart skipped and he knew he was going to have to face reality sooner than he'd expected or wanted. He was so not prepared for this conversation. For her dressing down. Maybe he could play the invalid card? *Jesus, grow a pair.*

"Hey," he said. "I didn't expect to see you here." And immediately realised he'd already fucked it up.

"I can go," Molly said, clearly already uncomfortable.

Though she was the one coming to him, so she had something to say. *Shit.*

"No, God, no. Stay. Sit." He eased himself from the chair, offered it to her as he took the bed. "How have you been? Was it rough at the police station? I'm sorry I wasn't there to help. Or at least support."

"It was fine. Better than my last trip." She raised her eyebrow at him.

Ouch! That was a direct hit. Strangely, it made him feel better. She was giving him grief. He deserved it. Bring it on.

Her voice edged with sarcasm, she continued. "It was even a bit of a trip to see how it felt from the other side, you know, actually sending someone to jail." Her mouth quirked, like she was attempting to hide a smile. "Though of course that didn't happen when I was there. I gave my statement and went home. Missed all the action. I heard from Flynn that Twomey had a meltdown and confessed all, even trying to bribe me, and Benson tried to punch him. I was sorry to miss that but, by then I was so done with BB&M, with bloody Chloe whining in my ear, with everything really, that I just wanted to go home. So, I did." She paused then, looked unsure. "Senior gave me the week off, but I still have my job."

"I heard he emailed an explanation of sorts to everyone. I'm glad. You didn't deserve any of this, Molly, and I am truly sorry for my part in making your life hell." He balled his fists to stop from reaching for her. She wore her arty clothes today, bright jewel colours, soft flowing fabrics. Her hair was a halo of curls, with a simple scarf twisted about her head keeping the wayward strands from her tired eyes. She did look tired. Pale. Unhappy. He'd done that, he thought. Him and his play by play. He hadn't intended for any of it to happen. But he hadn't stopped it either. That was on him, and him alone.

"Molly, I know you don't understand why I did what I did, but . . . "

"You do *not* get to tell me what I understand. Or not. I'll tell you." She rose from the chair, paced, returned and stood in front of him, almost close enough to touch.

He felt like he should sit on his hands. Anything to prevent him taking her in his arms. Where she belonged.

"I get that you had a role to play, geek nobody, nerd who fades into the background. I get that – we have Flynn in our lives so as a family, we know how some stuff works. I even understand why I was set up, taking the suspicion off Declan. Do I wish you'd told me? Yes. But we've been over that. I do wish I'd known it was your set-up, not his. That you had a way to extricate me, should the need have arisen. I would have *trusted* you to do just that. You could have trusted me! You didn't give me the opportunity to make my own choices, and that hurts. I'm a grown woman and despite my lack of experience in some areas, I do know my own mind. Mostly." She paused, took a breath. "The testing me with SSS? That was a low blow. I thought I'd handled myself well, professionally. That I'd made a difference for the company. For their company. Knowing it was all you? Completely undermined my confidence. Granted for only a minute, because I know I'm good, but shit, Kit, you should have trusted me enough to tell me it wasn't real. Were you ever going to?"

Kit swallowed. He hated that she doubted his trust. In her. The only reason all his stupid plans had worked was because she was so trustworthy. She hadn't believed anyone would be setting her up. That anyone could be so callous. So nasty.

"I was an idiot. I see that now," Kit confessed. Truth time. "I never expected that we'd become involved the way we did. I shouldn't have let that happen. It goes against everything I learned in training. But I couldn't resist you. And after a while, I stopped trying. That's on me." He reached out now. Took her hands in his. Just touching her made his pulse race. Made his chest tighten and his breathing hitch.

"Do you regret it? Getting involved?" Molly met his eyes, her own clouded with anxiety and uncertainty.

"*No*. Never. Everything we had, all the fun and the excitement, getting to know you, being with you, that's been the best part of my life since I moved here. The best part."

"But it's over now," she said quietly. "We go our separate ways, right? You'll move on to the next job, wherever that takes you, and I'll go back to work. For a while anyway." She pulled her hands from his grasp. Turned to the door. She looked back at him, her eyes serious and solemn. "Thanks for being my first," she said. "I'll always be glad it was you, no matter about everything else. Pet Scout for me.

365

We were only ever meant to be part-time, right? Mates who helped each other out? Granted I helped you out unintentionally, but still. It was never supposed to be long term. You'll most likely be leaving for your next big job so this is it. Time to say goodbye." And she closed the door behind her.

Shitshitshit. Kit eased himself from the bed and before he could get to the door, his phone pinged. His taxi had arrived. Was that a sign? Leave her be? He picked up his bag and walked to the door. He couldn't run after her, even if that was what they both wanted, not with his side paining like the devil. He'd break his stitches all over again. No, he decided. He'd give her time to think and he'd give himself time to heal.

And he'd go see his mother – and face that particular brand of music. Or discord, in this particular instance. In truth, he had no business trying for a real relationship with Molly until he faced the crumbling one in his own family. He couldn't talk to her again before certain things in his life got sorted, once and for all.

It took ten days. A few to rest and heal, at home in Stoneybatter. There was paperwork, lots of paperwork, so not all rest, but Kit found, with Scout on his lap in the evenings, that he relaxed. He went to visit his basketball team, introduced an interim coach and promised he'd be back in ample time for their competition. It felt good to make that promise, and mean it.

He strolled, was forced to by his injury, in the Phoenix Park in the early mornings. It was beautiful. Restful. The dew lifting in swirls of mist, deer appearing as if by magic, pausing and then leaping away. He saw foxes and badgers. He listened, really listened to the dawn chorus. His birdsong knowledge was abysmal, something he would address upon return. Because he *was* returning. He was not giving up on Molly. When she'd said she was glad he was her first, the thought that hit him on the taxi ride home, was of course, that there *would be others.* Other men would taste those lips, hold her soft warmth against their chests, bring her to fulfilment. Would they be caring? Tender? Make her laugh? *Listen* to her? It made him feel like a bit of a jerk to realise that jealousy had made him face the truth. It was pathetic and childish and probably against all the falling-in-love rules, but it was what it was.

The searing pain in his gut, nothing to do with knives and stitches, that had overcome him when he knew he'd never get to be with her again, and that some other fucker would? No. That could not be. She was his. *His.* And God knew, he was hers. Possessive and Neanderthal that might be but, by God, he would try to make himself worthy of her. So that all her smiles were his. All her laughs, and funny ways. He'd get them. Share in them. Live them, with her. Molly Fitzgerald was it, for him.

He just had to convince her they were meant to be.

So he asked Mr Feeney to watch out for Scout, and got on a plane.

Boston was hard. Harder than even he'd expected. The details of his living and work life he tied up easily enough. The FBI were happy to keep him on as a consultant and would offer him jobs which he could accept, or not. He would figure out work in Ireland when the time came. He released his apartment for another year, engaging an agent to be an interim contact. He wouldn't sell yet. The rent was a good income, steady, and the area was improving year on year. In time he might sell, but for now, status quo.

His mother did, indeed, hate him. It was a horrible reality to face. But perhaps one he deserved. She had a different way of looking at things to him. He had betrayed her. Not her asshole of a husband who was in fact the criminal, but her own son. He was the betrayer in her eyes. He'd always been an enigma to her. Gran had been his support system, they'd been so alike, and maybe that was some of the problem. His mum had felt excluded from their little math-brain club. But was that an excuse to never forgive? Then again, he wasn't exactly forgiving her either. Works both ways, boyo.

She railed on him. Hit him. Right across the face. He knew what Molly must have felt – that sharp sting, fast and furious. The aftermath as it tingled and ebbed. "*Get out!*" his mother had cried. "And I never want to see you again. You've ruined my life. *Ruined it!* Go away and leave us alone!" But there was no us, not really, for her. Eddie Cochrane was facing more charges and Kit decided, there and then, that he wasn't even going to follow the case.

He was done. Cochrane and, to some extent his mother, were now his past. He would email her, check on her. He owed her that, and he wished her no harm. If she needed him, he'd be there. But she was most definitely his past. With determination, with perseverance and luck, Molly would be his future.

On the plane-ride home, he worked on strategy. Then discarded all the big gestures, the schemes, the flowers, the gifts. Molly would want the truth. She would see the truth if he explained it right. He thought about the Fitzgeralds and the type of family he would hopefully, one day, join. How Jo and Patrick, despite Molly's misgivings, had embraced their accountant daughter as easily as they had their artist one. How he himself had been welcomed into the fold. Included. He saw how Gabe fit in and God knows, Gabriel Mackenzie was a very unusual man. Or at least different. But he made Ali her happiest self, by all accounts, and that's what won the hearts of the Fitzgeralds. Make their offspring happy? You're in.

Christ, he hoped he was the one Molly wanted in her life, the one who let her be her happiest best self. What an awesome result that would be.

There was only one way to find out.

Molly blinked back tears. Flynn did *not* need that kind of response. It wouldn't help. Nothing would except the old classic: time. She pulled back from the hug she'd given and said simply, "I'm sorry."

She left him alone for a moment and poured a splash of whiskey into a glass.

"I'm not sure which of us needs this more," she said with a smile, and took a sip before handing it over.

He downed it in one and rested the glass on her side table.

"Thank you," he said, his voice unsteady. "I appreciate it." He gave her a ghost of a smile and, picking up his jacket, headed to the door of her flat.

"Are you still pining for Elliot?" he asked, all nonchalant.

"Me? No. Why would you think that?"

He didn't answer, merely raised an eyebrow, and waited. Damn him and his crafty ways. He had seen the original portrait she'd sketched that night, now so long ago. And the several more she done in recent days. Large charcoal images of a certain gent adorned her office walls. She'd tear them down. Soon. Move on. "Oh, all right then. Yes, there's been pining, and missing, and regretting and more pining. I even went by his house two days ago, to see if we could talk, but his neighbour said he was away. In Boston."

"I could have told you that," Flynn said.

"What? Why didn't you?"

"Did you ask me?"

369

"No."

"Well then. I can tell you he was due back today. Maybe try his home again tomorrow?" Flynn walked down the main hall and rested his hand on the doorknob. "Don't give up if he's who you want. Your gut is not wrong. He *is* a good man." He smiled at her, and it almost reached his eyes.

It had taken a lot for him to come here and talk to her. To share. She'd been right to push, to allow him to unburden. Despite their age difference theirs was a tight bond, one built of an understanding of each other's abilities. His secrets, as much as he'd disclosed anyway, were safe in her hands. Always. He knew that.

He pulled open the front door and stopped abruptly. "Speak of the wanderer. Good evening, Atticus," he said. "I presume you are here to speak with my sister? Mess with her, you mess with me, remember? It won't be pretty." He sidestepped and Kit walked into the hall.

Molly's head was spinning. Atticus? Who the heck was that? "Is someone with you?" she asked Kit, even as it hit her.

Kit was here. In her house. *Here*. She could only stare. He was the same. But better – oh God, how could he be better?

"Hey," he said.

Tongue-tied, she gaped. He wore jeans, well worn, a grey T-shirt and, of all that was holy, a leather bomber jacket. *Not fair!* She was fairly certain her mouth had fallen open and she was now, probably, definitely, drooling.

She tugged her X-large T-shirt down over her yoga pants and cursed her inability to ever get it right. Some other girl would be floating about in a summer dress, with thin straps and ribbons and flounces, but not her. *Argh!*

"Come in, come in, can I get you anything? How was Boston? Did you see your mum?" *Shut up,* she ordered her frantic brain. *Give him two seconds to get in the damn door* of her apartment. "Take a seat," she invited, all perfect hostess, as she grabbed a clean glass and poured from the whiskey bottle on the table. She thrust the alcohol into his hand and stood gaping at him as he stood silently in front of her.

He was here. In her living room.

Clearing his throat, Kit said, "Ah, I was away, in Boston, oh sorry, you know that already. Jesus, I'm more nervous than I thought." He took a sip, held the glass, eyes focused on the golden liquid. He inhaled, looked up, met her gaze, held it. "I need to talk to you. To tell you some things, to ask you others. Is that okay?"

Molly gulped. Okay? Hell, yes, it was okay. She nodded, speech having temporarily abandoned the floundering ship.

Kit sat, stood and paced. Sat again.

The glass was revolving in his fingers so Molly leaned over and took it. "Safer this way," she smiled. His uneasiness calmed her, strangely. He needed her calm, her quiet so he could speak. She could give him that. She'd done a lot of soul-searching while he was away. She was ready to listen, to hear his version of what was between them. She knew, inside, that what happened this evening would finish them. Or, possibly, *maybe*, give them a chance.

Kit cleared his throat, lifted his head and held her eyes. "I'm sorry. I was a complete ass. I know I should have included you, trusted you with my plan at BB&M. I see that now. I was both stupid and blind. How could I not have seen you were perfect for the job as my partner in the long game, the takedown? You proved yourself, over and over, even after I had you detained. Shit, I'll never forgive myself for that." He rubbed his hand over a jaw that was slightly scruffy.

Molly's eyes flicked to that stubble and groaned. *Jesus.* Even unshaven, tired and stressed, the man was downright edible.

"Thank you," she said. "I appreciate you realising that

and saying it to me. It means a lot." He was sorry, she could feel it, waves of remorse and guilt emanating from him. *Now* she could sense his feelings? *Way to go, sixth bloody sense! You weren't so on the ball when I could have done with you!*

There was silence for a moment and when she focused on him, she saw he was looking right at her, again. Watching. She could feel her cheeks warm and feared a blush of massive proportions was about to flourish. His eyes were hot, intense, fierce. On her. She shifted, feeling that gaze everywhere. Warming and stirring in places she'd ignored since he'd left. One of Kit's looks and she was all aflutter. If this was the manifestation of what being in love felt like, Molly wasn't that sure she liked it.

Kit rose and, taking her hands, pulled her upright. He cradled her face so gently she felt her eyes well. His thumbs stroked, softly, across her skin and the heat in her cheeks intensified. He kissed her on the forehead, a soft light touch. Then her nose and at last, her mouth. It was a feather touch, light as air, but she trembled.

"Molly, I hope your acceptance of my apology is real, because if it isn't, if you can't forgive me, there's no point in me saying the next part." He paused, eyes searching hers.

"It's real," she whispered. "I forgive you." And she meant it. Three words of absolution, given with her whole heart.

"*Thank fuck*," was the fervent reply. He rested his forehead on hers for a moment and taking a breath looked at her, a slow smile lighting his eyes. "The fact that you haven't pushed me away gives me hope so I'm just going to get to the asking part of tonight's visit."

It seemed that that deep inhale wasn't enough. Molly noticed his pulse beating at his throat. Easing her hands up along the soft fabric of his T-shirt, over the hard muscles and firm chest, she rested her palm over his heart. It thudded, fast, steady, strong. It felt like a promise all its own.

"Ask?" She smoothed her hand over that thumping heart, feeling her own match its beat, measure for measure. "Ask what?"

"Will you go out with me? On a date?"

Molly frowned. This was not what she was expecting. Whatever about her brain, her body had been hoping for *'Can we have sex now?'*

"A date?"

"Yes, dinner and a walk on the pier. Or go to a play and then supper. You know, like dating."

"Don't you think that's going backwards? Aren't we past that?" God, she hoped they were past that.

Kit's mouth kicked up at the side, one of his dimples showing. "Yeah, I know it's a bit backwards. But I feel like I took advantage of you. I want us to have a proper relationship. I want to be your boyfriend. If you want that too."

That last part was a proffered exit, or her time for consent, she supposed. He wasn't going to push, he was asking. He was giving her the space to make her own choices, not make them for her, or assume. That felt surprisingly good.

"Back up the truck," she said, but smiled so he'd know it was okay. "First of all, no advantage was taken, I asked you to do me a favour. You replied, in the very best of ways. *I. Asked. You, Kit.* You didn't coerce or force or take advantage in any way. Or at least not with that side of things. And second, yes, I'd like to go on a date. Try it for real . . ."

She didn't get to finish. His mouth came down on hers and took. Took everything. Kissed her like it was his first, and his last. His only. The mixture of passion, of tenderness, of *care*, in that kiss brought Molly to her knees. Or it would have if Kit's arms hadn't banded about her body in a possessive hold. It was so good, wrapped up in Kit Elliot, that Molly thought she might never want to be unwrapped again.

They kissed and kissed some more. Hands started to wander, his and hers, a strong thigh was inserted between her legs, pressing and making it very clear, as their bodies lay flush to each other that one of them at least was on fire.

Kit pulled back, easing away from her mouth but still raining kisses down the column of her throat, along her collarbone. "God, I've missed you. The sound of you, the taste, the feel of you. Being with you." He buried his head in her neck, breathing her in. "I thought I'd screwed up so badly, you wouldn't want to see me." His mouth pressed to her skin, he whispered, "I couldn't bear it."

Molly disentangled herself from his hold and reached up to touch his face. "You didn't lose me, I'm right here." She saw, in real terms, how much he meant it. The strain that had been apparent on his face wasn't only the result of a knife wound, the Boston trip, his work, it had been his agony over her. His uncertainly whether she would forgive him. Be there for him.

Kit placed one of his hands over hers, turned it and kissed the palm. "I know it's too soon, but in the interest of honesty, of keeping deception and playacting out of this, I feel honour bound to confess I've fallen in love with you. *No*, don't say anything, please don't say anything. The reason I want us to date, to start again, is to offer you the chance to fall in love with me, the real me. I don't expect you to feel what I feel. But I'm hoping you let me show you how good we could be together." He stopped, hesitated, then said, "It's not just that you are so fucking sexy and gorgeous and make me hard every time I touch you, I love you because you're smart and kind, and funny and so damn interesting to be around. I love the quirks, the

374

way your brain runs in so many directions yet always seems to be on a direct line to what it wants. I don't get that, but, God, I love it. Will you take a chance, Molly? Can we start again?"

"No, Kit. We can't." The pain and hurt that flashed in his eyes was instant and she knew she'd taken a misstep. She had to do better. "I don't want to start again," she said but held him as his breath froze. "I want to *continue*. I want us to move forwards, not go back. I don't want to forget or even change anything that's happened between us, the bad or the good. It brought us here. The messy last few months has got us to this place, to this understanding. Knowing you, if we start dating, officially, you'll probably want to do it all correct and in order. I can't wait for that. I want you now. I want *us* now. Yes, we can have movies and walks and dinners, but as we are, not as some start-over. Does that make sense?"

Kit released a huge breath, mumbled, "Thank you, sweet Jesus," and before Molly could articulate any further thoughts, she was swung up in his arms, carried down her short hall and had her bedroom door kicked open. "I assume," he managed between kisses, "that continuing on means this too?"

"Hell, yes," Molly laughed, her body tingling from one end to the other as he laid her on the bed, discarding his clothes at lightning speed. "Definitely this too."

"I can work with that," he growled as he pulled down her yoga pants. "Did I mention I love how your mind works?"

Make-up sex, time away from each other sex, hate sex? It didn't matter. Sex with Molly was why sex was invented, Kit thought as he stroked the silky skin along her upper arm. She lay cuddled into him, her face nestled perfectly in the crook of his arm, her hand making lazy circles on his chest. This time together, after the heat had lowered to a simmer, was *almost* as amazing as the heat itself. In some weird way, it was *as* amazing. The quiet words shared, the laughs, the closeness, was something he had never experienced before. Molly showed him so many firsts, so much of the new in his life, he was overwhelmed.

He was beyond thankful.

When he'd dropped her on the bed they'd had sex, fast, furious, can't-wait-one-more-second sex. It had taken the edge off. Barely. He wanted this woman so much, so deeply, he figured he could have a lifetime enjoying all the ways they wanted each other. Then when recovery mode had kicked in, they'd made love. It was both different and the same. Go figure. There was fire, need, desire, want, craving. But also, soft sighs, low moans, laughs, talk, directions – his and hers, because communication was everything, and when they came, as close to simultaneous as made no difference, and he'd heard her soft, "*Oh, Kit,*" he'd felt his eyes sting and his heart stutter about in his chest like a brand-new foal on spindly legs. He loved this woman with his whole bloody being. If he could be worthy of hers in return? Well. He could only hope.

"Kit?"

"*Hmm?*"

"You say you're in love with me. What does it feel like? How do you know?"

He smiled in the near darkness. Kissed her temple and pulled her closer. Always the analyst. "When I'm with you, if we're just talking or even arguing, I know I don't want to be anywhere else. If I'm not with you, I want to know where you are, and when I can next see you. When I think about you, I have to catch my breath. When I see you, at a distance, talking to someone else, or coming towards me, or even in the coffee shop, my first thought, always, since I met you, was *mine*. I know I shouldn't say that, it's very cave-man like, but it's the truth. You give me butterflies in my stomach, you make my heart race, and when we kiss, I want to devour every inch of your body, bringing you pleasure beyond your imagination. I feel more myself with you than I do with anyone else. For a loner like me, that was my first clue. And then there's that sexy body of yours. How could I not fall in love with that?" He grunted when she poked him.

Molly sighed. He could feel her warm breath across his chest. He'd never known that was one of the best feelings in the entire world, till her.

"I sometimes get a sick stomach when I see you," she said in her 'Molly tells it as it is' way. "Nearly always, actually. But it's the kind of ache that feels really good, you know?"

He did, he absolutely did.

"I miss your glasses," she continued, "but not your revolting nerd attire. Do you think you could maybe burn the slacks but wear the glasses again, just the odd time? To spice things up when we're not feeling sexy."

Kit snorted. "There will never be a day when you're not sexy, that's an impossibility. But I can wear the glasses, purely to keep you happy."

"Good. I remember Frankie saying love involved a lot of stomach-ache, it twisted into knots in a good way when things were getting hot, but it also twisted in a bad way when you worried about someone. That was her idea of love. I thought she was certifiable. She was actually pretty smart. I should apologise to her." Molly turned, moved so she laid her body along his, starting all kinds of fires, all over again. "I love you, Kit," she said and his chest cracked open. "I love you so much I'm not sure what to do with it. I may need some help with that." She laughed then, even as her eyes welled, that aqua colour deepening to an azure blue. "I was going to say, are you up for that, but," she wriggled her lower body over his more than ready one, "but I can *feel* that it's a moot point!"

Kit wrapped his arms about her, and in one move flipped them over so she was beneath him, breathless with laughter and giddiness. He kissed that beautiful, smart mouth, kissed it as one lover to another. With all the gifts that love could give and all the gifts left over. He kissed her, knowing she loved him back, that they were together now. It changed things. It started light, soft. It started with murmurs of his love, of hers. Of how much, of when, of how long. They kissed as they shared all the moments of discovery, the way new lovers do.

Kit smiled into her unblinking gaze. "No more lessons," he said. "From now on we teach each other. Deal?"

"Do I get to be the professor now?" she managed as he nibbled on her ear. "Can I be bossy and give you punishments?" He thought he heard her breath catch as the words popped out and he laughed. This woman. He must have done something really right to deserve her. She was his home. She was his heart.

"Sweetheart," he said against her breast, feeling her heartrate match his. "I am yours to do with as you wish. I'll always be yours. Just as you are mine."

When they woke the following morning, Molly knew life, as she'd known it, was over. No more secrets. No more pretence, no more hiding who she was, who he was. They were official. They were an 'us'.

And then she remembered.

Feeling him wake, attuned now to his breathing pattern, she elbowed him in the ribs.

"*Off*," he grunted sleepily. "What was that for?"

Done with pretence, were they? No more deceptions? No more playacting? She had only one question.

"Who the hell is Atticus?"

Epilogue

"Why do you do it?" Molly asked.

They were sitting on a blanket, the freshly mowed grass offering its delicious summer smell, and watching a bunch of teenagers kick a ball. The tournament was over. Kit's team hadn't won, this wasn't the movies, but they had got way further than anyone had expected. They had reached the quarter finals. Considering none of them had ever played in any kind of real competition before, it was huge. It was *their* win.

This was the after party. Or so Kit said. Pizza and a kickaround, the only way to celebrate, so he'd dragged them all to the park, had a dozen pizzas delivered to their spot, along with enough fizzy drink to ensure all their depleted sugar stores were well and truly replenished. This wasn't the time to play more basketball, or go over techniques, it was the time for fun.

The boys had been great. Some of the parents had even showed up. Molly had seen pride develop, right before her eyes. Had seen relationships deepen, friendships forged and cemented. Basketball and teamwork did that.

And Kit. Kit did that.

"Why do I do what?" he asked, his eyes on the lads as

they played a mishmash game of soccer, some with pizza slices still in their hands.

"This." She waved towards the motley crew. "Why do you coach?"

Kit kept his head averted, but she saw him swallow, take a breath. Knew this ran deep. His hands, loosely wrapped around his bent knees, knotted together then released as if he became aware of some unwelcome tension.

"I never knew my father. As a young kid, I didn't care much. I was a bit different, self-sufficient, liked my own company, liked being with Mum and Gran. I wished I'd had a father those first few years in Southie, though. Someone to stand over me, watch out for me. When I did get a version of one, my esteemed stepfather, well, you know how that worked out. So, I spent some time thinking about dads, what makes one, how do you become a good one? It dawned on me, that before I could ever be a decent dad, I would need to be a decent man. So, I focused on that. On what that meant to me."

He turned his head then, studying her, a slight smile on his face. Molly returned that smile, leaning in to rest her head on his shoulder, side by side, the way she liked.

"It worked," she said. "You are a good man. But why these boys?"

"Most of them don't have a dad, and those who do? For whatever reason, they're not always the best of role models. I'm not trying to replace anyone's father and, in fairness, a few of the fathers are rock solid. But for those who are searching for a male in their lives, I want to be that someone they can rely on. Someone they can come to. Talk to. Vent to. I didn't have that. Not sure I needed it, but I had resources they don't. It's about trust." He laughed even as he said it and Molly rolled her eyes as she knew what was coming next. "I know I wasn't great in that department with you, and that was a big mistake, but these boys, they trust me. I have to be there for them. They need a safe person. Does that make sense?"

"Perfect sense." Molly cleared her throat, something catching, as she blinked quickly. This man. *He* was the role model. The boys, teenagers really, they looked up to him. They gave him grief, challenged him, ribbed at him and he stayed calm and Kit-like through it all. Steady as she goes, she thought. There for them when they had the need.

She *loved* this man. The last several weeks had brought a strength to them she hadn't known existed. Hadn't known she needed. A bond. An ease and a comfort as well as excitement and fun, flirting and desire. All of it strengthened them. Even the heated discussions. The challenges and frustrations. They were forming a life together and it was *good*.

"Who did you model yourself on, then, if the men in your young life were so lacking?"

Kit raised his eyebrow, waiting.

"Oh my God!" she snorted. "Atticus! Atticus Finch!" She roared with laughter, causing some of the boys to turn in their direction. "Of course you did – your own bloody namesake!"

Kit laughed too. "It seemed like the right way to go," he agreed, kissing her to stifle her chortles. "I'm going to leave you to your chuckles and kick a ball. Save me one last slice," he said, indicating the almost depleted boxes.

"I will," she promised. "Go play."

He stole one more kiss, then rising in a smooth move jogged down to join the boys.

Content, Molly rested her chin on her knees. She loved this fun side of Kit. The happy carefree side. She loved watching him interact with the boys. It made her insides do that good kind of hurting.

Atticus Elliot. She'd never known his full name. Always

assumed the Kit was short for Christopher, which was the only way she'd ever heard it. Seemingly, as a toddler, he'd found it hard to say his own name and the *Kit* sound had stuck. There had been clues, she definitely needed to work on her detective skills, but wasn't hindsight wonderful? Scout, the cat, his computer password. His uncanny resemblance to Gregory Peck. Okay, that wasn't a real thing, though he wasn't far off.

She used to call him Clark Kent. Her Superman. She preferred knowing he was more of a modern-day Mr Finch.

"Any left?" Molly swung around at the sound of Flynn's voice. He crouched seamlessly to the blanket and swiped a piece of vegetarian pizza, the only one not devoured by the lads.

"Help yourself," Molly said redundantly. "Did you see them? They were terrific!" She knew Flynn was involved in some background way with how the boys club was run, but true to Flynn form, she got no real details.

"Caught the last quarter. They made a great showing. Elliot did them proud. Or maybe it's the other way around?"

Molly grinned at her brother. "Hard to say, truthfully, which of those guys out there feels like the biggest winner today. They were fantastic, they really pulled out the stops."

"Kit's done really well with them, in all ways. They were a bunch of brats when I first introduced them to each other – now they are almost human." Flynn chewed thoughtfully. An easy silence settled between them until, putting down his scrunched paper napkin, he nudged her shoulder. "Are you doing okay? Anything I should know?

Molly shook her head at him. "Honestly, Flynn, you don't have to always be in charge. But, to answer your question, we're more than okay," she said, reaching over to kiss his cheek. "We're really good."

He studied her and before rising to his full height and taking off his jacket, he said quietly, "Splendid."

He turned his jacket inside out, laid it carefully on the blanket, away from the scattering of pizza boxes. He opened his shirt cuffs and carefully folded them to just below his elbows.

"What are you doing?" Molly asked in astonishment. He seemed more relaxed than he had in months. Time was helping. They didn't discuss it, didn't need to. But he was doing better.

"I'm going to play soccer and kick Atticus Elliot's ass," he said with determination, and strolled across the grass to play football.

THE END